GRINGA

by

Sandra Scofield

ℚP

THE PERMANENT PRESS
Sag Harbor, NY 11963

Credits:

"Tangier," from NOT DANCING
by Stephen Dunn, Carnegie-Mellon, 1984.

"What Are We Playing At," by Andrée Chedid,
from A BOOK OF WOMEN POETS FROM ANTIQUITY TO NOW,
Aliki Barnstone and Willis Barnstone, eds.
Schocken Books, 1980.

Portions of this book appeared with
the title, "The Parachutist," in
THE MISSOURI REVIEW, VIII, 3, 1985;
and as *Accelerado* in TOUCHSTONE,
Vol X, 2, 1985.

Library of Congress Cataloging-in-Publication Data

Scofield, Sandra Jean, 1943-
    Gringa.

    1. Title.
PS3569.C584G7   1989   813'.54   88-92460
ISBN 0-932966-85-3

Library of Congress Number: 88-92460

International Standard Book Number: 0-932966-85-3

Manufactured in the United States of America

THE PERMANENT PRESS
Noyac Road
Sag Harbor, NY 11963

Note to the reader:

In writing about the events of Summer 1968 in Mexico City, I have tried to adhere to their actual sequence, as I have been able to reconstruct them, but I have not tried to write history. The same must be said for other "actual" people, events and places in the novel, such as the Huastecs of eastern Mexico. All characters are invented, details of locale are freely woven from what is known and what is imagined, and therefore all true happenings are made fiction.

I acknowledge the enormous emotional influence that Elena Poniatowski's *Massacre in Mexico* had in my decision to write this book. This Mexican journalist collected oral histories and many photographs, and her documentation of the tragic events of that summer was a best seller in Mexico. For those who would like to know more about how it was, I recommend her deeply moving book.

S.S.

What else can we do
but stop at the horizon
while far away
and nearby—
the real collision.

—Andrée Chedid
"What Are We Playing At?"

There's no salvation in elsewhere;
forget the horizon, the seductive sky.
If nothing's here, nothing's there.

—Stephen Dunn
"Tangier"

PART I

1.

TONIO SAID, "Remember I was going to show you some pictures?" They had been playing gin rummy. Abilene was putting away the cards. Tonio took an envelope out of his dresser and brought it over to the bed.

Out spilled photographs of something like a cave. A great black eye.

"It's the Swallow Pit. You remember we talked about it when the Swiss archeologist was here. I wanted him to go down in it with me, but he said he didn't have time.

"See? There's the cliff on the far side." She could tell he was excited. She leaned closer to see the picture better. She thought the blackness was like a great heart.

"Isn't it something to respect?" Tonio said. "And now they've finally gone into it this past winter. The Sierra Club. You Americans. It's a quarter of a mile deep."

She looked blankly at his pleasure, his excitement over a hole in the earth.

"That's like the Empire State Building upside down! And once you are down there, they say there are thousands of feet more of caves, and the open space is much greater than the mouth. You could see for yourself."

She blinked. "I could see!"

"Sure," he said, gathering up his pictures. When he found something new to explore, or own, he looked younger, with a boy's elation. He came out of the ring like that, after a kill, though in the ring he showed only his courage, and his respect for the bull.

"If you were braver," he said. "We could go down by rope and see it for ourselves. We could go in the fall, after the rains. But I must think how to train you! Maybe with weights." He reached over and squeezed her bicep. "You wouldn't want to dangle on these."

She was a skinny girl, with big feet for ballast. Her face and hands and arms looked washed with diluted freckles. There was a fragile quality about her, and, under that, a stringy hardness. Now he spanned her wrist with his thumb and finger. She couldn't have pulled away easily.

He loved to joke. She thought he might mean to tease her, with talk about a pit of swallows. "Do people fall in?" she asked.

He laughed at that. "I don't think so. Who would be so stupid? And those Indians up there, they're much more likely to hound someone until he jumps in on his own."

There was a bubble of fear in her throat. It was not such a terrible feeling. "I would like to see," she said. "I would like, at least, to look down. I would, if I didn't have to stand too close."

Tonio said, "As long as you are going in for that other thing you might as well have those little scars scraped off too." He was standing with a pile of boots at his feet. He had decided to have several new pairs made by the bootmaker in town, the son of the man who had made the fancy high-heeled boots that gave Tonio a little extra height.

A boot, propelled in a graceful arc by Tonio's toe, landed softly in a pile. "Too bad none of these boots fits you," he said.

Abilene thought he mentioned the boots as a kind of criticism that she was taller than he, though it was barely so. He was going to throw the boots away. They were beautifully tooled, glossy and rich-looking. He said they hadn't suited him. Though he wasn't particularly extravagant about his clothes, at least not at the ranch, Abilene had learned that it is nothing, if you are rich, to take everything out of your closets and start over, just because you feel like it.

"There must be someone around who could use them," she said. She remembered shopping for school clothes in Goodwill stores and church rummage sales.

4

"Not my boots." His look told her she should have known better. He kicked each unwanted boot aside as if the boot were culpable. There was something human and sad in the boots' ungainly sprawl, as if feet were still inside. Tonio's kick, though, was graceful. He was beautiful, and conscious of her watching him, though he was contemptuous of appraisal.

"I will call Reyles tomorrow," he said. "He can set it all up." Eduardo Reyles, brother of Tonio's good friend Felix, was a plastic surgeon in Mexico. Abilene had seen him once, with Felix, in a suburban restaurant where she had gone with Felix for pompano. Reyles was handsome, a smaller man than blocky Felix. He wore a tidy moustache and aviator's glasses. He had come for the fish, too, and for the company of his elegant mistress. After lunch, in the car, Abilene had asked Felix if many of his acquaintances had mistresses. She had not been in Mexico long then. "Most," he replied neutrally. "And do they all wear white?" she wanted to know. That question amused him. "Only in summer," he said.

It was like Tonio to avoid a precise term for something he disliked, despite his impeccable English. He could have found a word for her "other thing" but he did not. He didn't look at her, either, and she supposed he was put out with her for being careless. She was relieved that he did not appear to be angry. It hadn't seriously occurred to her that getting pregnant was not wholly her responsibility. As usual, she had done something at hand without thinking of the consequences. She had not even been sure it was something she had wanted to do.

She sat on Tonio's bed and watched him. He reached out for her. She recognized the gesture as summons and got up at once to go to him. He put his arm up across her shoulder, his hand in her hair, and pulled her close enough to speak quietly into her ear.

"I always thought I was sterile," he said. Her heart danced in her chest. "The only bull that ever gored me badly," he said—he pulled her hair hard enough to hurt—"got me in the balls."

She tried to face him, because there was no intonation, and therefore no clue, in his voice.

"One good thing," he said, putting his other hand down the front of her jeans. "We can't make it any worse."

5

Scraping was not a precise word, either. Scraping made her think of meat with molds.

Reyles showed her a small wire brush like the one he would use on her face. He showed her his Before and After nose photographs. They were pictures of young women in white dresses with black eyes, painted around the lashes, and elegant hair. In the middle of each face was a flat Indian nose. All the wealthy girls thought of themselves as Creoles, descendants of Spaniards. The noses gave some of them away, linked them to poor doomed girls who had their hearts tossed over the sides of pyramids. Reyles tidied the telltale noses so that, like the cones of rockets, they offered less resistance in movement.

He stroked Abilene's cheekbone. It was an important part of his practice to form a closeness with each patient, a bond to breach the pain and chagrin, a pledge of tenderness and discretion. Abilene looked at the brush in his hand. It was a furry steel wheel. There was still the gynecologist to see. "See you in white," she said to Reyles. He blinked at her from behind his aviator glasses.

The gynecologist's office was on the other side of the Zona Rosa, across the big Paseo de Reforma, past the great gold angel toward the governor's mansion, along familiar streets. The chatter of workmen's drills was everywhere; dust rose from broken buildings, old trolley tracks, cracked paving. The city was in a fever; the Olympics were only four months away.

The doctor was polite and gentle. Abilene thought to herself how perfect a profession gynecology is for a Mexican. As good as bullfighting. Whenever there were two men together in her presence, she became a backdrop. Always they talked about women. Round asses, wet cunts, the breasts of one's mother, and always, always, the welcome of women, their eagerness for these men—. It was a joke nobody seemed to get.

Tonio could probably have managed the abortion himself. If they had been alone on a boat in the ocean, or lost in the jungle, or trapped at the ranch by flood waters, and her appendix had burst, he would have been deft in its excision. But there is this about an appendix: Everyone has one. The incisions are neat

6

against the whiteness of the belly. Only women have uteruses, babies, abortions. And all that hair and folded flesh.

"Might as well do the other," he had said.

She thought about her scars. All the times she had stood in front of mirrors brushing her hair, and never noticed them. They were old scars, and she had forgotten them. They were part of the past. It wasn't like her to dwell on old sad things, but that didn't mean they really went away. You could see a history of ugly sores, yellow pus, over and over again, in certain places. Just past the corner of her mouth, on one side, and along the side of her nose. Just beneath the jaws. How could she have forgotten that they were ugly? Tonio must have always seen them, and minded. Yet he had waited for the right moment and then had suggested surgery casually, as a friend picks lint off a coat.

One night, smoking with Tacho, she had got high and had wailed that she was ugly. (Why had she thought he would comfort her? He was one of Tonio's huge entourage, a *banderillero* and a hanger-on. He could never be a woman's friend.) Tacho got very gruff and called her a clod. He pulled up his shirt to show her his scars from the ring. He tapped his gold teeth so loudly it seemed they would dislodge. He waved his arms around. "In Mexico," he said, "everyone has scars." "Not Tonio," she sniffled. There was nothing he could say to that.

When the gynecologist's nurse gave her a packet of pills and an envelope with instructions written out for her, she took them gratefully. "Thank you, oh thank you," she gushed, and when the nurse took her hand, she clasped it for a long moment. The nurse was very kind, especially when you considered how repugnant Abilene must have been to her. Whatever they were calling it in order to make it legal, it was, still, a baby's murder.

Constanzia, the girl from Tonio's office, let them in the apartment. "Pretty snazzy," she said, or something like that, while Abilene walked around the apartment. They spoke in Spanish.

For Abilene, what other people said in that language was still

7

only approximate. She lived in a constant state of estimating. She got along fine shopping, eating in cafes, getting around in taxis. She had a repertoire of retorts for the insults of street boys and drivers, but she had learned the effectiveness of staying silent. Tacho had taught her expletives and jokes and tender sayings. Mickey had taught her more elegant obscenities. The nuances of real conversation eluded her. Sometimes, if she was tired, the language dissolved into a scrambled code. Yet her own Spanish was very clear and exact.

"It's cold," she said with a shiver. She rubbed the gooseflesh of her upper arms like a spelunker in a new cave. Constanzia, whose own burnished shoulders were also bare, found the window cord and pulled it. Light struck Abilene, and then her eyes cleared and she saw that she faced the flat gray side of a building. She could see nothing of the street. The apartment, tucked into a narrow side street off a busy, chic avenue in the Zona Rosa, must have been very expensive. But it was ugly. The main room was entered abruptly through a heavy door with a jailer's lock—double bolts on a metal frame—and it was small and poorly furnished. The carpet, a dull slate color, was expensive and clean, but most of the room was empty. In the alcove by the window there were a few pillows propped against the white wall. In the middle of the room, under a fancy brass swag lamp, was a small round white formica table with three chairs. A radio sat on a shelf.

The kitchen, to the immediate right of the entrance, was a narrow room out of sight from the main room. It was like the galley of a boat. Stacked beside the refrigerator were cases of beer and orange soda.

"I'll want mineral water and Cokes," Abilene said to Constanzia. "And call Tonio's maid and tell her to come over and wipe everything off." She ran her finger along the shelf where the radio sat, to make her point. Constanzia said, "There are maids in the building. One goes with the apartment already." Abilene was embarrassed. "I'd rather it was someone I know!" she snapped, knowing what she said was ridiculous. She disliked the brash Constanzia, who now stood near the table with her purse held up against her chest. Constanzia acted superior because she was at home. It was her city, her language, her job. Abilene thought how rigid the pecking hierarchy was, how much pleasure each layer of authority had in ordering about the lower. She saw it all the time at the ranch. Even the very young maids, the bottom of the heap, hissed at the long-haired tom when it crossed their paths. (They dared not harrass the hounds!) The system of authority was like the system of *mordidas*, bribes—Tonio's friend Felix had explained it to her long ago. Each official took from those below and gave to those above; each made something on the system and therefore had reason to protect it. Only at the bottom was it all give. There, men could take only from one another. Yet everything was negotiable, except authority itself. All the rules, the laws, the greatness of the Revolution: all could be circumvented. It was as though bribery had been invented to make jobs. Only Tonio seemed unimpeachable, as though he were of the highest order, pure *cacique*.

Abilene walked over to the window again to look for sky. There was nothing to see. "I need something better to sit on," she said in a crisp voice she imagined sounded firm.

The girl yawned. Abilene's annoyance made her flush. She didn't want to lose her composure. If she snapped at the girl it would give the girl moral authority. Owners, *patróns*, officials— they could bark and make you heel. But for most everyone in Mexico, everything had to be swathed in monstrous bandages of courtesy. To forget that was to be a fool.

"There are some large pillows at Tonio's apartment," Abilene began. She had no idea how to say what she wanted.

"Oh yes," the girl said, "I know them. *Bean bags*." She said the English phrase smugly. Didn't she work for a man famous not only in Mexico but in Spain and Portugal, too? She wore a hot pink blouse of shiny rayon, a bright green polyester skirt, and stiletto heels. She knew what was in Tonio's apartment.

And why not? It was only a short walk from the office. Abilene had seen him dictating, screaming orders as he lay propped against a dozen pillows on his bed. Dispensing instructions like that, in a quilted silk jacket like a Chinese potentate, he reminded everyone that his authority needed no more

9

formality than his presence. As if anybody needed reminding. He was like the head of a government; wherever he was, he was everywhere.

He didn't have to be there at all.

The bedroom was filled almost to the walls by a king-sized bed covered with a beautiful down comforter of gray cotton and several pillows. At the foot of the bed, on a stand, there was a television, and beside that, ice buckets, glasses, and sterling silver stirrers. So. That was what the apartment was about. A trysting place. Felix's home away from Mama.

Abilene wondered about the women Felix brought here. Stewardesses from Dallas and L.A. Tonio's ex-mistresses. Maybe a high-class Mexican girl, though probably not. Virginity, or at least exquisite discretion, still belonged in the dowry.

Constanzia sat at the table reading a magazine she had brought with her. The fancy lamp gave off a poor light. "I'll need things to read," Abilene said. Constanzia, without looking up, said, "Oh yes."

"Where will you go?" Abilene asked.

"To Sanborn's, for magazines and the little American books. I'll go tomorrow."

"In English," Abilene said.

The girl smiled a quirky smile. "I said I'd get American books," she said. Abilene saw that her makeup was smeared. The dark shadows under her eyes looked like the pouches of an old woman. A Halloween face. A Day of the Dead face.

"Go away," Abilene said. "There's no reason for you to stay here." She wanted to be alone. Reyles said it would take three weeks to heal. She would stay inside, except when she went to see him.

She felt a wave of panic.

"Go on!" she said. "Go back to work!"

"The *señor* says to stay." Constanzia turned a page.

Abilene took her handbag into the bathroom and put her things away noisily. She carried a little paper sack of grass into the bedroom and put it under the mattress. There should have been another bag already here, brought over from Tonio's, with her nightclothes, robe, cardigan, a raincoat and rain hat. Her summer city clothes. And a bottle of brandy.

Without the bag, she had only her jeans and shirt. In the bedroom she found a shirt she supposed belonged to Felix. It was salmon-colored, with shiny silver threads running up and down it. She could sleep in it for the night. She called out to Constanzia, "I want my bag brought from Tonio's!" She wished she had called him *el señor,* or *patrón.* She detested the sense of familiarity she felt with the girl. She wondered if Tonio sometimes took her into his inner office. He would have her on her knees; there was no couch.

She had never considered, not for an instant, having a baby. She had not even thought of being pregnant in that way. It was like a toothache; you went to the dentist. She only minded that other people knew, and that she had been a problem for Tonio. She had lived for so long now in such a delicate state, asking for nothing, being there when he wanted her, staying an American girl, a Texan, but not being silly, not asking stupid questions or getting in the way.

She sat on the bed and ran her hand over the silky Chinese cotton and wondered how much she would bleed.

At seven the girl went out for food. She returned in an hour trailed by a waiter in a formal coat carrying a tray laden with platters. The girl had paid. The waiter, a handsome boy with limp hair and the puffed-out chest of a vain bird, acknowledged Abilene with exaggerated deference. He was Indian, but a light, yellowish color. His hair fell low on his forehead. He bulged against his shiny tight black pants. She wished for a moment she could send Constanzia away, that she could find a night's comfort with this boy whose name she didn't want to know. She knew he could see it: his black eyes gleamed. She had never been with an Indian boy. But he was a waiter in a good restaurant. He risked nothing. He laid out the food and heavy white napkins on the table. There was barely enough room. Once he was satisfied that the platters were settled, he made a sweeping gesture with the tray and tucked it under his arm. At the door he smiled and said to Constanzia, "Till tomorrow, then," playing with the soft /n/'s of *mañana,* his tongue in his teeth, his freshly licked lips shimmering as he spoke. "He will

11

come for the dishes," Constanzia explained casually as she bolted the door. "I will have things to do here. He might as well come then." Abilene would be in the hospital. They would do the abortion in the afternoon, and if there were no complications, the dermabrasion the following morning. Abilene was not amused at Constanzia's plotting.

"I don't want anyone here when I'm not," she said.

"Oh, just to bring your magazines."

Abilene saw that at some time on her outing the girl had put on a vivid scarlet lipstick. It streaked the napkin like blood.

They both gave their attention to the food. "It's really good," Abilene conceded. She hadn't realized how hungry she was. She ate slowly, thinking of Jello and broths in the hospital. Her steak ran bloody on the platter. She felt suddenly that the girl had done her a good turn; she might have brought her something with tortillas, or awful hamburgers from Sanborn's. The girl finished eating quickly and then closed the drapes and began to stack dishes carelessly, so that she made a lot of noise. Abilene's friendly feelings evaporated. A ridge of lard had congealed along the potato. She pushed her plate to the center of the table.

Constanzia put a set of keys down beside Abilene's plate and looked at her watch. "I'll go now," she announced. At the door she paused to say good luck. Abilene said nothing. The heavy door made a thudding sound as it closed. She thought of prisons, crazy houses. She shivered again; this time she knew it was the cold. She found a thermostat, but nothing happened when she jiggled the mechanism. "Shit!" she said aloud. The sound of her voice was startling in the emptiness of the room. She listened to the evening roar of the city, the incessant honking of horns.

She crawled under the bedcovers in her clothes and shook with chill. I'm afraid, she thought. She wasn't afraid that she would die. She was afraid that everything would change.

She lay still and tried to single out the sounds of the city, the cars and jackhammers (even at night!), the cries and laughter of people, instead of the sounds of peacocks and dogs and rustling palms. She missed the Huasteca night. She drifted away from the city, into reverie:

12

The little cow speaks to her. It says, I'm going to hurt you. But why? she asks, though she knows. Because you are there. Because you are weak, says the cow. She sees the hair on the ridge of the cow's back when she passes it. She sees the place where its horns have broken the skin. The cow knows what to do and cannot help itself, nor can Abilene; she lets the cape drop. The cow, the girl: each waits.

She decided to take one of the sleeping pills from the doctor's office. She undressed to her panties and shirt and drank water from her hand, under the tap. If it made her sick—what would they do at the hospital? Can you have an abortion if you are already sick with the *turista?*

The buzzer made her jump. It was Tacho. His voice over the intercom was thinned and peppered with static. She rang the buzzer to let him in from the street and then made him wait in the hall while she dressed. She took her time, pulled on shoes, brushed her hair, while he banged on the door with his fist and cursed her.

When she let him in, he said, "Tonio says to stay." He was burly and disheveled. He had been back from Portugal a year, and in that time he had gotten fleshy, his face jowly and slack. He needed to shave, and his hair had been badly cut. His sour mood was chronic.

"I don't need a babysitter," she said in English. He made an ugly gesture with his hand. "Bird-talk!" he said, angry because, despite all the Americans who had been around him for years, he had learned almost no English. She told him again in Spanish, except that she called him a watchdog. He shrugged. "There's a dinner party at the apartment," he said. "With caterers." So he would stay with Abilene, he said. He was to accompany her to the hospital in the morning.

There was no place for him to sleep. When she said so, he laughed and pulled a bottle of brandy out of her bag. He sat at the table with his legs open wide, one on each side of the chair, and he drank her brandy. She watched him, thinking of the people who would be at Tonio's, high-ranking people from the government, and actors and businessmen and bullfighters.

Suddenly she was flooded with nostalgia for the ranch, the Tecoluca, as if it was a place she had known long ago. She thought of a time when she drove with the archeologist Martin miles out from the airstrip, and she showed him a place where a wildcat had killed a steer, and a little farther on, the pond where she had fished (with Tacho) for flat bony fish of splendid flavor. She thought of herself with Tonio in the arbor between the gate and the house as people came up from the ferry for a holiday. "This is my Abby," he had said of her, over and over, all through that first year.

He had not called her that in a long time.

She thought of him on his bed in late afternoon, the hair on his chest spare and golden, his hips gilded by the sun coming in under bamboo shutters.

"My Tonio." Would any woman ever say that, except in self-mockery?

"I'm going to bed!" she shouted. Tacho grunted and then laughed out loud. His voice was still ringing in her ears as she plummeted into sleep.

Some time in the night he came to her bed. She struggled up from her drugged sleep to the smell of him before she felt his hands on her. She had been dreaming of him, dreaming of a time before he went to Portugal and threw away the golden ring, before he started passing on the kicks he thought the world had given him. Everyone around Tonio wanted to be more than they were, but nothing Tonio gave would be enough to change them. If they could be with Abilene at least they took a little more from the *patrón*. And there was pleasure in risk.

Tonio had sent Tacho to Portugal to fight, and Tacho had run away from it, to go with the gypsies. He had travelled with them across the borders of four countries. He had learned their songs. He had come home bitter, and he had looked at Abilene with loathing. He had never forgiven her for being there when he came skulking home.

"Why do they blame me, when it is Tonio they hate?" she once asked a friend, Isabel Ruiz. Isabel knew. "You are nobody, and a woman. What a perfect victim you are!"

Tacho smelled of brandy and smoke and rutting. She was weakened by the sedative, but she managed to give him a hard shove with her feet that sent him rolling onto the floor. He groaned and she held her breath. If he rose and came at her, she would have no more strength to fight him. He was too big, and he could hurt her.

It comes to this! she thought. But he lay still, his buttocks catching the barest strip of moonlight through the window blinds. She burrowed in the covers like an animal in a nest. Some time in the night Tacho woke her again, crying out. She thought he had said, "I am *torero!*" and then, "I am animal." Such mournful cries. To think she had once giggled against his shoulder; she had ridden the bus sixteen hours to be with him, when she had a plane ticket in her pocket all the time. She could not blame only him that it came to this. She hadn't thought of his heart. She had thought of him as an animal composite: fine-muscled like a horse, a curious sniffer like a boar, a silly threat like a goose, and sadly, dumbly noble, like the brave bulls at play in Tonio's greenest pasture. She had done what tourists do all the time, she had thought of him as a peasant. But she had thought he looked like Marcello Mastroianni. She had called him Marcello and he loved it.

She started to cry. Then, abruptly, she sat up in bed and wiped her cheeks with the sheet. Outside her a city was alive. She wanted nothing of remorse—not Tacho's, not her own. In the Huasteca she could pass days and nights and never think about guilt or pity or shame.

She had dreamed his cries, as once she had dreamed his affection. She had invented lovers, because she could not invent Tonio.

She wanted no more lies. No more dreams. She wanted the blackness of sleep, a night without stars. Tomorrow the life in her would be sucked out, and she could not know what would be left instead.

2

TONIO'S COUSIN Mickey was her first visitor, the week after she was back in the apartment. "You look just like a green lizard," he teased. Abilene was glad to see him. She was half-mad in the solitude of Felix's apartment.

"Every afternron I go to Dr. Reyles' office, and he picks at my scab and clucks and paints it green. He says underneath I am pink and new again, like a baby's butt." Dr. Reyles was gentle and solicitous, and told her jokes too. It would be easy to fall in love with so nice a man, even if it was only bedside manner. "I've been coming and going in cabs. Yesterday a driver asked me if I had cancer. I told him to worry about his mother's lovers."

"A good Mexican answer!" Mickey approved.

"He looked at me in the rearview mirror with his stupid macho grin and said, 'I'll fuck you, lady. I don't fucky the face.'"

"What a limp *chile!*" Mickey said. "Nobody can care that your face is a green scab. Don't you see newsboys with smallpox scars, blind beggars, syphilitics, idiots? Everywhere you look, mutilation? Mexico is sinking into the ground it is built on. What we're counting on is all those woeful *pobres* as landfill. A whole city walking around on its dead, waiting for the earth to open up and swallow them."

Mickey brought news of Tonio. What he really came for was to tell Abilene his worries. She had a good idea what he wanted, but he never got to ask. She dealt hands for gin rummy. "You look glum," she warned Mickey, "and I will beat you if you don't pay attention." She thought: If he wants to set up stakes, something for me against his goal to crawl in my bed, I'll do it just to liven up the game. She had forgotten for a moment how bad she looked with her old face ground away. Mickey didn't mention stakes at all. They played three hands before he began to unravel.

"So nice to have company," she said wryly. He sat at the table too disconsolate to bother looking at her. He wanted someone to take it all in—his bad luck, his decline, his lost opportunities. Anyone would do. That would have been insulting if she hadn't known him so well. He was full of pain because he had lost his new girlfriend, the one he was so proud to have. The one who was to give him reason to begin Life For Real At Last. The girl he had kidded himself about. The one he had lost to Tonio.

Well, she wasn't going to sympathize with him over that! He had been kidding himself all along. He met the girl at a concert in the spring. Of course the first thing he would have told her was that his cousin was the *rejoneador* Antonio Velez. And he hadn't figured that out! "I'll get you invited to Antonio's *tienta*, it's a fabulous bash. Paco Rivera might come, and Rafael Lara. You can come, and bring your mother." What a fool he was! It was just what he had done with her in Austin. "I have a cousin who fights bulls," he had bragged. They had gone down on the bus. Abilene never went back.

Abilene got them beers and drank hers standing up, leaning against the wall. Mickey might have been sleeping for all the signs of life in him. When would he grow up? Two years out of graduate school, shouldn't an American-trained geologist be able to work? Shouldn't he be able to make enough money for a nice apartment and maybe a car? For a girlfriend, even a wife? He lived in a maid's room on the top of a four-story concrete building in an old section of the city. He had a single faucet for water, a brazier for a stove. At least he had a toilet. She had been there and said, "Oh Mickey, this is terrible poverty!" He had told her that poverty was fifty families on a faucet, and shit running down the street. She had felt reprimanded and resentful.

Mexico was to blame for his life, he said. None of his misfor-

17

tunes came from his own doing. Like the matter of a job. Mickey referred to jobs as "positions." The good "positions" were given as favors, controlled by the government. Mickey's father, who worked for a bank, wasn't in the PRI—the official party of the Revolution, of the country. Mickey didn't go to the national university, so he never had a chance to join the student group that was an arm of the national party. (As though going to school in the states was another piece of bad luck!) He swore he wouldn't have joined the bastards anyway. "The fucking PRI!" he often shouted. "It's supposed to be a people's party! A workers' party! It's a giant *piñata* of a party! It's *Pan Bimbo*, white bread." The workers and the bureaucrats connived to stay on top; the capitalists worked below the desk, with vast sums of money changing hands. Besides—and here Mickey's tone shifted, he could not forget his ambition, his avarice—he was no worker. He said these things to stress his lack of connections. (The underlying accusation was understood, that Tonio would not help his own kin.) The real power was in the chambers of business and commerce. Tonio sometimes dined with cabinet members! He had the ear of the President himself, his best protection against seizure of his land. Hadn't he lent Ordaz his own plane in the last campaign? A campaign like every one since the Revolution, a sham. The signs and festivals, the flyers and bands and hoopla were to let the country know who its father would be for six years. Choice had nothing to do with it.

Mickey looked up from his misery long enough to say, "Half my students are missing every class. Even these young kids! It's like a rot, something eating at the floorboards." He had a low-paying part-time job as an instructor in one of the polytechnical schools. "They go to political meetings, they tell me. Politics!"

"Are they wrong?" Abilene asked.

"Are students ever wrong to question? Isn't that what education is supposed to be about?"

What Abilene wanted was for Mickey to engage her for another hour. All day she had only the racket of the streets. Sometimes she got high and sat by the window. She could hear ice in drinks at the cafe a block away. She could hear the conversations of passersby. "Spare me," she said. "I thought university was where girls went to find husbands. What do I know?" She poured more beer into her glass and licked foam with her fingers. She grimaced and felt the scab give across her cheeks.

Mickey amazed her. He went on, as though he were talking to her on the phone. "They quote and misquote Marx and they chant slogans from Cuba. But they haven't read Hegel or Kierkegaard. They know nothing of dialectics."

"You're forgetting I had half a term of college. Talk English." She tried to smile; the effort pushed the cracks of her scab toward her ears.

"I am."

"I'm dumb and you know it. Stop showing off for me."

"You wouldn't say that if you thought it. I've been thinking lately how smart you've become. How sophisticated."

"Never mind the sarcasm."

"Well, these students. They are very poor. Everywhere they look what do they see? Poor and rich. It is difficult to synthesize that contradiction. They sell Chiclets on the streets as Mercedes cruise by."

"But you're speaking of students! If they're smart won't they go to the university?"

"Oh sure. The university. If they're very smart and very very lucky. If there's a way for them to get fed, buy books. It's easier if you are in the party."

"The PRI."

"There are no other parties! The others are mosquitoes! The PRI pays their campaign costs and laughs at them, even the Communists! They can buzz, but they cannot bite. I don't think this crop of kids understands this. They make me nervous with their talk, and if I am nervous, what is the head of the police?"

"So the poor are angry. They seem classic."

"The poor are hungry! It is the young who are angry." Mickey had rolled his right hand into a fist. Now and then he tapped the table with the fist, like a carpenter taking aim. "They have learned words like 'democracy' and 'prosperity,' and they are very ignorant. They are ambitious in a way different from their parents, different even from my generation. Oh I have friends who despise the system and lament the loss

19

of the true revolution. But what do they do about it? They drink rum and talk all night, and go to sleep in one another's beds. Once a year the old radicals dig out their pens and scribble something for the anniversay of the Revolution, or maybe for the anniversary of the Cuban independence. There's even a joke about it, that there is a rhyming dictionary with a hundred words to rhyme with *Che.* One of our circle did something, a year or so ago. He tried to organize his neighborhood to demand electricity and water for the poor who had made shanty houses on vacant lots. He said the Communists would help them get what they needed. They burned effigies. One day he was there, and the next he had disappeared. Now we talk to one another. We say, 'Maybe he went to the country with a lover.' Such talk!"

"But to disappear! In Mexico! Maybe he was robbed and killed by a street gang—"

Mickey sighed. "Oh yes, *maybe,*" he said sarcastically. "But these kids—they have so much spunk, and they have all our arrogance. They think they have invented idealism. They want to be the conscience of the country. They want to wake the rest of us up. They know nothing of history, of fate. I ask them: 'So you throw out the best system in Latin America. Then what? What will you have?' I ask them that, and they smile at me as though it will all have to be explained to me one day. They want too much."

"All the young are greedy." Abilene was surprised to hear herself say that; where had she heard it; from someone else? "I'm surprised at your lack of sympathy, Mickey. You've always talked like a bitter man."

"Bitter? Yes, I'm bitter. Did I say I didn't agree with my friends? I spend many nights with them, fighting new battles for independence, all with words. When none of us has a woman, we talk all night." He winced at this admission. Abilene wondered how he could fail to see how fortunate he was, despite his concrete floor and cold water. He had mobility, access. He had an education, two languages. He even had his son now; his Texas wife had abandoned the child for a hippie commune. Mickey's parents kept the child. Tonio paid school tuition.

"It will blow over," Mickey said, stretching and yawning. "If they talk too much they'll breathe too much dirty air and fall down sick." He made a face. It was nothing to him. He saw the students as Tonio saw him: impertinent.

She asked him an easy question. "Are you hungry?" She knew he could go hungry for days before he would offer to get food. Two long jaunts with him had taught her his strategies. Kindly she considered: he puts away nuts for winter. He's a squirrel, like me. She touched the gold bracelet on her arm like a talisman. It had been a gift from Tonio.

She fried eggs and tortillas. Mickey stood in the doorway and watched her work. As she was turning the eggs, he said, "Tonio is seeing Anne Lise in Mexico."

"I'm not surprised." She handed Mickey his plate and followed him to the table. In truth she was shocked to the bones. It didn't help that she had seen it coming. She remembered how hangdog Mickey had been at the *tienta*, watching Tonio wipe the very cushion on which Anne Lise sat. Mickey had found no comfort in Abilene, who had gone numb, and then to Sage's bed. She remembered it as an old woman looking back on something very long ago. She hadn't expected Sage's ardor, or his contrition.

"She's beautiful," she said coolly, using her fork to burst the yolks of her eggs. She didn't know if she could eat. "Like Tonio," she said.

Mickey ate heartily, despite his proclamations of anguish. "She's not a movie star. Or a stewardess, or an American student on vacation. She's first class."

How like a child Mickey was! He saw only himself, hurt because his plan to show off to Tonio had backfired. He hadn't even considered what it meant to Abilene. And what did it mean? Maybe it was the perfect thing to happen, to take choice out of the game, as always. Like the death of your parents, the loss of a lover was a catapult.

"Tonio is nearly forty years old," she said. "He's tired of movie stars."

"He's never gone with a girl like Anne Lise."

"How is that?" Despite her intention to remain friendly—

21

when Mickey left she would be alone again—she was rising to his insult. In his own way he was as rude as Tacho.

"She doesn't put out," he said.

Her face burned at the edges, a ragged face torn from a picture. "How colloquial your English still is," she said.

"Some do, some don't," he persisted, but he blushed.

"Put the plates in the sink." She pushed her plate across to Mickey. He was astonished. "Go on!" she snapped. He took the dishes but didn't rinse them. He knew a maid would come in the morning. Poor Mickey knew all about maids.

"Every year you get touchier," he said when he sat back down. "I'd think you would treat me better, all things considered."

She leaned under the light to glare at him. "Whatever you had coming to you, you've been paid twice over." She knew what made him mad, what would make him mad forever, was that she had abandoned him twice in Acapulco. The second time she had walked out while he was in the shower. She had reached the bottom of the hill before he figured it out. She had heard him screaming from the walk outside their room, above her, stark naked, disbelieving.

"He's gone to Morelia to a house party," he said casually. Cool, green, colonial Morelia. "Anne Lise and her mother will be in Morelia, too."

"He told me he was going out of town," she lied. "Did Anne Lise tell you her plans?"

"I read it in the paper. She's a diplomat's daughter. It's minor news but good gossip. She isn't Tonio's usual bitch." He glared at her. One of these days, Abilene thought, he and I will have to punch it out with one another.

She stood. He stood, "I saw Isabel. She said she would come by," he said, in a voice to soothe her. She went into the bedroom and slammed the door hard. Mickey jiggled the handle and called to her a few times. Then she heard him let himself out. She leaned against the door, facing the window, and through it, the blackness of a city night. She talked to herself in a small singsong voice. If she spoke aloud, she did not have to think too much.

Why should I care what Tonio does? I wouldn't want him to see me like this. I don't care about Anne Lise. She's one of those girls who grew up without ever hearing a four-letter word, and he thinks it is fun to play games with her. He wants to break her down. Sorority girls take longer. If I let that bother me, where would I ever be? Who would ever have me?

I miss the ranch as much as Tonio. Before I left I saw how dark it is, the dark places I never looked at before. The thicket with its path grown over. The vines in the tennis court. And the birds.

Tonio said that some men went down in the pit of swallows. How would that be, to fall and fall? At the bottom, is it dark and wet? Would you sink and disappear? I know you would die, but would you disappear?

Would you?

"Cheer up," Isabel said. "Soon Reyles will peel your scab and I will take you out. I promised my sister Ceci and her friends we'd go dancing."

"I dreamed I was on a train. I looked up and my mother was on a seat facing me, two or three rows ahead. She was in her waitress uniform, with her legs stuck straight out in front of her like a dead chicken's. She was sleeping. I tried to talk to her, but she wouldn't open her eyes."

"Bah." Isabel would have none of it. "I don't know about dreams. If I wake up feeling bad, I smoke a little, or drink a bit of vodka or rum, and then I go back to sleep. I don't know about the past either. What did I do as a child? Who did what to me? I don't remember, I tell you! My mother remembers everything. She told me just yesterday at dinner. There was a woman who lived in a house on her street when she was a child. The woman grew an avocado plant so tall and strong it went to the ceiling and broke the skylight. My mother tells me this very solemnly; it has meaning for her, you see. But not for me! I collect my money from the vendors, I go to parties and am a good sport so they will all ask me back. I look for Ceci, because my parents can't see to the other side of the windows on the street. Who has time for the past? For dreams?"

The table was strewn with the remains of lunch. Isabel had

brought roast chicken, mangoes and lime, flowery Guerrero grass.

"Michael Sage says he's in love with me." Abilene belched softly.

"So he's the one!"

Abilene nodded.

"Tonio can't have liked that!"

"He doesn't know. Or doesn't say."

Isabel rolled a neat joint and they passed it back and forth. "You can bet he knows," she said. "He knows everything. And Sage! Tonio hates him."

"Tonio leases to him."

"He's a good rancher. But such a big man!" Isabel giggled. "Tonio minds his size, don't you see?"

Suddenly it was terribly funny. Abilene nearly choked telling Isabel about Sage at the *tienta*. "We made love while Tonio was down at the ring."

"He knows."

"I don't think so. Wouldn't he say?"

"Not until he wants to. Then you'll see."

"Oh what, Isabel? Tell me what he'll do!"

Isabel had known Tonio a long time, ten years or so. Felix, too. She met them at a party where all the men wore togas, and wreaths on their heads. "It'll be Sage he'll get," she said. Abilene was shivering. "Tonio can do terrible things," Isabel went on. "Once he hung a trespasser and got away with it."

"I know all those stories. So what? He can't hang Sage!" Abilene felt her stomach rumble. "Anyway I'm too stoned to worry. I'm glad you came."

"If I was you, girl, I'd be thinking what next."

"Don't, Isabel. It's been awful, all these days in Felix's apartment."

"Maybe Tonio forgives you, because you caped that little cow. I thought she was going to gore you, for sure."

"But Tonio stepped in and saved me! He caped the little cow away. So see?"

Isabel was quite merry. "You had one leg propped up on the other, like a stork. What would it have looked like if he'd let you get hurt, in front of all those people? Oh, you'll hear more about your rancher lover, *chiquita*. Tonio will pick his time."

"Don't frighten me!"

"I've got to go."

"No. Oh, but it's time to go to Reyles'."

"I'll drop you. Then you can come and smoke a little more and sleep like a baby." Isabel touched Abilene's face. "Don't you wonder," she said very softly, "what it looks like inside, after what they did?"

Abilene burst into tears.

"What is it you want?" Sage had asked in April. They were lying in her bed while down in the bar and along the trellised walkway, Tonio's *tienta* guests drank rum punch and made jokes about the bulls. Some of the women would be at the ring, watching Tonio ride.

She answered easily, without thinking first. "To change what happened between us."

"You know I'm sorry."

"Not just that. Not that you beat me like a thief." He shifted away from her on the bed. He was sober, almost grim; she was drowsy and happy, in her way. She was glad to have a chance to tell him how much he hurt her, but she knew it was mean. In two years, she had forgotten. Why remember things that make you unhappy?

"I'd change all of it," she said. "I'd pick it up and put it down someplace else. Away from the hotel, away from Tonio's land. I'd put it someplace where you would be serious—"

"If I hadn't been serious I would never have been so angry—"

She sat up and hugged her knees and stared at the funny print on the wall: Christ at the Last Supper, forever gazing down on women coming undone in bed. She didn't know how to make Sage understand that what she really wanted was to start her own life over, to be a teenager again, to understand that she could say yes, she could say no. She could choose her life instead of letting it happen to her.

She didn't see how she could do that anymore. How she could start so late. "I'm going to go out in the morning and cape one of the brave calves," she said. The business of the *tienta* was over; now the guests could have a good time playing *torero*. Every *tienta* someone had his pants torn. It was never very serious; Tonio only let the bad calves in with the amateurs.

"You're crazy. Tonio won't let you."

"You don't know him! He'll love it. He'll think I'm being ballsy. He'll like watching to see if I get hurt, playing around, he'll like waiting to decide when to step in."

"You could get hurt!"

"Don't I know that!"

"What about us, Abby?"

"There's no such thing." Yet an hour ago she had let him sigh and weep over her, and bring his contrition to climax. He thought that was the same as being forgiven.

"I love you. I've thought about it for nearly two years, Abby. We're two of a kind. I don't think we're such great people, but we're of a kind. I'd be better with you. And you don't belong with Tonio. He can't ever know you."

"He doesn't have to." She went into the shower. "He doesn't have to!" she shouted from under the water. "He owns me," she said, but only to herself. "The way he owns everything."

Like Sage's leased land. His leased life. What a fool she would have to be to think it could be that easy! To start over with a man who hated Tonio? And even if Tonio loved someone else, he wouldn't let her go. Not to Sage.

They would have to start over on the moon.

She walked home from Reyles' office soaked to the skin. She liked the awfulness of the rain, the stripping to the skin inside the apartment, her hair clinging to her neck and face. The rain was so hard it washed her fears out of her, they ran down the streets.

The rain had been hard but warm. There was no reason for her to be cold, but her teeth were chattering. She put on layers of clothes and made tea. She cradled the cup in her hands and took it to bed.

Warm again, she told herself that she was only now reacting to what had happened to her. To be sick in a foreign city, not just sick, but stripped, emptied, swollen, marked? She had been foolish not to see how hard it would be to convalesce. But when had she ever looked ahead at anything? When she tried to do that, it was like her dream, she was on that train, and everything outside was speeding by. She could never see anything until it was past. If she tried to look, the past became sharp. She saw the sun like a white ball of heat over the sandhills. Shabby trailers circled like a wagon train. Her brother with rabbits he'd shot, one in each hand, dripping blood.

She got back up and turned on all the lights and sat at the table to write letters. The cold goaded her. First she wrote her sister-in-law in Austin.

> It was great to hear from you and get the picture of the new baby. I suppose you get teased now about having the perfect family, a boy and a girl, but I'm glad about the girl because maybe she'll be someone you can feel really close to. And Kermit finished school! Now he's a pharmacist! I hope that means you can stay home with the baby. Is your mother there? Has my mother come? She hasn't written me in a long time. I don't worry. I know you'd tell me if anything was wrong. I'm sorry I took so long to answer.

She hated what she had written. She wondered if Sherry ever thought of that day they raced around Lubbock, looking for her father's girlfriend. Had Sherry felt like Abilene did about it, like they'd been friends that day? They had been on the edge of discovering something nobody else knew.

She sat for a long time, and smoked a little of the grass Isabel had brought, and tried to think of what to write to Sage. The corners of the room were moving toward her, into the light; she realized it was almost dawn.

> I told you I would write you when I had thought about what you said at the tienta. I've thought about it every day since. But I was sick and I've been in Mexico almost a month. Can you understand how hard it is to think of there when I am here? To think of you at all? I mean, in any real way. I know what you say. You did say that. That we both love the Huasteca. You're right about that, but why is it we never have talked about it? Do we love the same things? Is it the beauty of the land, where it is beautiful, or the dry hard spaces where it isn't? Is it the isolation? Or the cat in the brush? Is it that neither of us could get along someplace else? A long time after Tonio came back from Europe that spring, I realized

that you and I had never gone the quarter mile from your house to the beautiful grotto where the river is born. I went there with tourists from the hotel, but never with you. Where did you take me? To a cave filled with vampire bats!

Do we have enough to give one another? I don't know if there's very much inside me. Maybe Tonio suits me because he wants so little from me. And which of us would tell him? What would he say? What would he do? He could hurt you!

Maybe Tonio will marry the diplomat's daughter and I will come to you because I have no other place to go except the real world. Would you settle for that? Would it be enough? For how long?

I don't know what to do. I feel like I'm outside a cave in the heart of the city. A city built on an ancient lake-bed. Who knows? Maybe the cave will fall in around me. Maybe the city will fall in. All the rich people and the bureaucrats, right along with the desperate peasants from the country, and me.

Something might happen to all of us, and it wouldn't matter who I loved.

She read the letter carefully. The next day she mailed it to Sage, in care of the Arcadia Hotel.

A few days later she received a letter from Claude, the Arcadia manager. When she saw his name at the return address, she was shocked. Had he written because of Sage's letter? *Had he read it?* Oh, he would dare to do something like that, for all his talk about discretion! He had tried to make her read Camus and Rousseau and Sartre; he thought Sage was ignorant, like her. She clutched the letter in a moment of panic, and then she relaxed. There hadn't been enough time for her letter to reach the hotel. The letters had crossed in the mail. Claude had written her at Tonio's office.

He had sent her a key to his apartment in the city. It was out of the tourist zone, across the avenue beyond the angel. "It is sunny and large, and empty now. It will be much better for you while you are getting well. There are stores nearby." It was even near the doctor's, though that wasn't very important anymore.

"I'll be damned," she said when she showed Isabel the letter. "He wants to manage my life from way out there, imagine that." She wondered who had told him she was in the city, and if he knew the reasons.

"Maybe he has a heart," Isabel said. "What are you going to do?"

"Oh, I'll move, alright. I'm sick enough of this place!"

"Maybe you should just go to Tonio's. Then you might see him when he's in town."

"What do you mean? Is he there? Have you seen him!"

"I'm not in his circles anymore, *chiquita*. Only at the ranch, where I round out a party." Isabel could laugh at herself.

"He never asked me to stay there," Abilene said in a moment. "How would I look among his beautiful things?"

Isabel helped her take her things out of Felix's apartment. The sunlight on her face was hot; Reyles said she would be tender for a year. She ducked her head for a moment and let the sun fall on her like a cloak.

The concierge at Claude's building was expecting her. She led Abilene and Isabel up a flight to the apartment and gave Abilene the key. White, airy, splashed with the colors of bright dhurris on the walls, the apartment might have been Morrocan, she remembered that he had once lived there. No, he had lived in Tangier; she couldn't remember what country that was.

Adele was the only friend Abilene had who was in no way tied to Tonio. She had never even met Tonio, since she refused to come to the Tecoluca. "I'm not a country girl," she said when Abilene asked her to visit, more than once. So Abilene saw Adele in the city when she came in, a few times a year. They had once spent part of a winter together.

Adele had lived for years with two gay men who worked in television, and Abilene looked forward to seeing them again, too. One was a very good cook, and the other told funny stories that made Abilene cry with laughter. But Adele said that the cook was killed in a freak accident. He was running across a busy street and he ran up to a car whose aerial was sticking out sideways; he didn't see it, and it went through one eye and into his brain. After that, his lover went to France and from there to Senegal. Adele had stayed on in their apartment, with her daughter Pola, until a few months ago. Then she had married the publisher of a small weekly newspaper. His name was Daniel Moya. Adele said she was very much in love. "I've been alone ten years," she said. "I wouldn't go with a man who didn't have integrity, and who didn't respect me, and my work." She was a photographer.

She scolded Abilene for staying away and for not writing. "Was there nothing to tell me?" Abilene shrugged. "In the country, everything stays the same," she said. She had never talked to Adele about Sage.

Adele showed her the apartment. It was large and airy, in a decent building, but they had spent almost nothing on furnishing it. In a back room Adele had a closet darkroom, and a makeshift drafting table where she was laying out the pages of a *fotonovela*. "You see how it goes," she said, pointing to the photographs that would make up the comic book format of a romantic story. Such books were cheap and popular. "I'm working with some women from several of the districts where conditions are very bad, where everyone is very poor. It was the idea of a Maryknoll nun, a friend of Daniel's. Of course there are a thousand districts, maybe ten thousand. We only have a little money. But we tell the women, 'Pass it on.' How else can anything ever change?"

"What is the book about?" Abilene was peering at the pictures.

"First aid! You see, the young wife Rosa learns it at neighborhood meetings. For going, her husband beats her, and her mother-in-law calls her a whore. But then one day her husband comes home with a bad wound in his arm, from the factory. They did nothing for him at work but give him a sling, and the wound will fester, he will probably lose his arm. All this is taken for granted; it happens all the time. But our little Rosa—she knows what to do, and she cleans and cares for her husband's arm, and saves it."

Abilene sees that in the last photograph Rosa and her husband embrace. "And after that he never beats her again."

"You tease me, Abilene. We do what we can. Come on to the other part of the apartment."

"Don't misunderstand! I think it's fascinating. I didn't know you were doing anything like this."

"Of course you didn't. It is recent, and I never see you. But here you are now! You look very sweet and young with your pink raw face, Abby. It is good to see you! Come, we'll make lunch, and you can meet Daniel then. Pola is at school this morning, and she has plans with a friend through the afternoon. But now you will come every day! Wait until you see how she has grown, my little Pola."

The lunch talk was about the murder of a young American woman in the *colonia*—near where they lived, in fact. She had been found in the street, bludgeoned. The police had no leads. She carried no identification, or at least there was none left in her purse. Daniel was explaining.

"But now I hear from a hotel proprietor that he has an American guest who is missing. His hotel is in the neighborhood. He calls me first, and we go to the police and to the morgue together. Sometimes American girls disappear off the streets of the city and are never heard from again. Where do they go? Young girls, mostly, who've gone out to buy candy while their parents are at *siesta*. A few years ago workers for the government, excavating a site on a ranch not far north of the city, found graves of young girls. There has been a rumor for a long time that if you have enough money and know the right people, there is a place where you can have a *gringa* whore. I wrote about it once. Word got out before the story was printed, and on the day it came out, federal agents bought all the copies of the paper at all the stands. In an hour there wasn't a single copy of *The Voice* on sale."

"What a scandal!" Abilene said, and added, "I've heard about the ranch with young girls, too, from my friend Antonio Velez. He says it is true, though he never saw for himself." Ardently, she hoped he had not lied about that.

Daniel went on. "The hotel owner has a son who talked too much and got into trouble. He was sent to Lecumberri. I helped get the boy out—a little money, a little pressure. I told the father I couldn't help if they didn't already want to let the boy go. But his father is grateful. He tells me what he hears.

"So this morning the two of us go to the morgue and look at the body. My friend says yes, it's the girl from his hotel. He is sure, though her face—" Daniel stopped and drank his broth.

Abilene groped for words. "The newspaper business—you hear so many things—"

Adele pointed toward the main room where shelves were stacked with black notebooks, and the corners of the room were crowded with boxes of papers and folders. "This is Daniel's work, to know these things. To know about crimes that mean nothing to the law, and crimes that the law itself perpetrates."

Abilene didn't know what that meant, and said so. Daniel waved Adele's explanation away with his hand. "I've got to go," he said. "But first I want to tell you what else my old friend said. The police went back with him and searched the room. They found clothes, shampoo, shoes, and nothing else. 'Did you ever see her passport, a visa?' they asked. But such things are not required of Americans. He had already taken the papers out of the room. They went away. What do they care? They have to bury her. They'll take her fingerprints and her photograph and wait for someone to file a missing report. They will probably never know who she is."

"The papers he held—what are they?" Adele asked.

"Won't he get in trouble?" Abilene asked.

Daniel smiled at Abilene. "This is not an important crime, little friend. This is just a dead whore as far as the police are concerned. There's no identification in the papers. She gave the name Sylvia Britton. The police have given that name to the other precincts and to the embassy. They have nothing to learn from a dead girl's notes. But he wants us to look at them. I think he wants us to take them. I told him I would send you, Adele, this afternoon."

"But what does it matter?" Abilene asked. "You don't even know who she is!"

"That's exactly why it matters," Daniel said sadly. "Who will remember her otherwise?"

Adele tried to explain Daniel to Abilene.

"Daniel documents. Besides the paper, I mean. He says it is

his function to record. He reduces grief and terror to lists. The imprisoned. The assassinated. The disappeared. Sometimes he travels to Oaxaca, Chihuahua. You are surprised to see how many? These notebooks, with their lists? This is not a nation of general repression, not Uruguay, Hungary, Nazi Germany—In the country, one village may know nothing of the next. In the city, each block is a nation. It would be so easy, Daniel says, for the numbers to be lost, the impact of the sums. Oh, Daniel must tell you himself! He speaks with such goodness and passion. Didn't I fall in love with him?"

"Tell me about meeting him." Abilene had her doubts.

"The meeting was nothing special. We met at friends of Jay's—he is in Senegal now. We were drawn together, can that be explained? I suppose it was a physical thing, the same as with any man and woman. I had been alone so long. In his bed I told him about Yannis, Pola's father. I told him about the trip we took to Central America in 1955. In Nicaragua they were so poor I saw children scraping with their teeth the banana peels off the streets. We were both taking photographs like mad. I was only nineteen. I didn't know I was pregnant with Pola. In Guatemala we wanted to visit the Indians in the mountains. They are beautiful people, their lives are very simple and very old, and of course I was so romantic then. The women dressed in wonderful bright colors. One day we were having a beer in a cafe, and we heard there had been a killing in the next village. Men had come into the village and had murdered a dozen men. We raced to our jeep and sped to the village to see for our-selves. We arrived to find the dead laid out in the square. Their wounds had stained their white pajamas black. However each had been killed, he had also been shot in the face. My husband was so excited. *'In an hour we would have missed it,'* he said to me.

"He used to hit me, never very hard, and I wasn't afraid of him. But on that day, when I saw the look on his face in front of those corpses, I was terrified. After, when I learned I was pregnant, I was afraid for the baby, too. I knew I didn't want to live with him anymore."

"What an awful story. You hadn't told me." In Zihuatenejo, Adele had told Abilene about her second lover. He had beat her too, and he had been hard to leave. The two stories together told quite a lot more than either alone. Had she told Daniel both?

"This will sound strange, Abilene, but I think until I lay in Daniel's bed that night—I felt so safe, you see—I had forgotten about it, pushed it way down inside me. Daniel spent a lot of time in Guatemala. Since the U.S. helped to overthrow the government fifteen years ago, things have been very bad for the Indians. When he talked about it, I felt his pain and sorrow so much! He learned something very important there. When there were some executions, years ago, there was quite a stir in the country and in the international press. After that, the executions took place in the mountains or by rivers. Though many are murdered in Guatemala, many more disappear, to rot in dumps and rivers. That's what he fears here. He fears it in every poor nation!"

"And because you both were in Guatemala—"

"Oh yes! He was there at the very time I was. And so now we fall in love. It's as crazy as that. Listen, Abby, don't you see it? Here is a man who expects the best of me. That's what we all want, especially women with bad pasts."

"And this poor American girl—" Abilene felt cold and angry, remembering her. "It sounds like no one ever came along like that."

On the street Adele said something in a very intense whisper. "Why is it that, knowing nothing at all about this girl, we know so much?"

The hotel proprietor was very cordial. His wife made coffee while the women looked at the jumbled papers he gave them. They seemed to be notes from a diary, but they had been torn from a common spiral notebook. There were details of dances, days on the beach somewhere, foods eaten. The papers were very dirty and wrinkled. Nothing was dated. There was a list of men's names: Jorge, Arturo, Paco, and half a dozen others, only their first names. There was a code of some sort after each name. "I think she's *grading* them," Abilene said. She felt hot. "This isn't good, Adele."

"I know." Adele's face had gone white.

"I would like to be rid of them," the hotel proprietor said. "I will destroy them, or you may take them. But if there is something the police should have, you must let me 'find' it and take it myself. The rest—what do they need to know?"

Adele looked sadly. "I have found something, Javier. I want my friend to read it, and then I think you should take it to the precinct station. There's an address in the corner, don't you see? She was writing a letter to a friend and she scribbled the address. Maybe she was going to get an envelope while she was out."

Abilene read:

> *So, dear Katherine, you think I grovel and debase myself and ought to come home and go to work again at something 'useful.' You don't understand why I look for the cockiest of the boys. Stop explicating text. I am not a scholarly pursuit. I will explain it to you. Sex is as simple a thing as your name. Say it and it is yours. I am looking for ecstasy. And I think fear is the way to it. The exhilaration! The game—the stakes— One of these days I will sweep through the fear, and past it, free and clear. Ecstasy is freedom. The ultimate is the end.*

They walked back to Adele's slowly. They passed a bench at the edge of a patch of grass, and Adele motioned for them to sit down. "Do you know who I thought it might be?" she asked.

"You thought you knew her?"

"It's mad! But I thought it was the girl from Zihuatenejo, the one Pola was so crazy about. She called herself Lotus, do you remember her?"

"Oh yes. But what reason did you have—?"

"No reason at all. I *wanted* it to be her. Think what she was like. I could never forget her. She was on her way to something terrible, I could see it on her face—" Adele stopped and stared at Abilene a moment. Abilene shifted uneasily on the bench. "I worried about you, too, you know—" Adele said. Abilene looked away. "I wanted it to be Lotus so that there was only one of them. I didn't want there to be another girl who went the same way—"

"Killed?"

"*Looking for it.* Isn't that what they say about women? When I read the letter—well, it isn't that girl, I'm sure of it, it was too

35

great a coincidence—but I thought for a moment, for just a fraction of a moment: *She got what she wanted.*"

"What she deserved. That's what you really mean."

Adele's face was streaked with tears. She wiped her cheeks with the back of her hand. *"Yes."*

"Then why be so upset!"

"Oh Abby, nobody deserves what happens to them, not that. Destruction comes looking for you."

"Adele! That's what the Indians believe! That old fatalism. Aren't you the one who told me—do you remember, in Zihuatenejo, we talked about fate—'You make your own life, from one day to the next. You don't let the past make it for you. You decide to be happy.' You told me that."

"And I do believe it! Only I have to wonder, does everyone have the power to choose? Daniel's lists—did those people choose their deaths? They were like objects in a high wind, tossed here and there. They came back down so hard."

"Who did decide, then?" Abilene thought the answer had something to do with Mexico. You could talk about fate, and about Mexico, and it was the same thing.

They began to walk again. At the door of her apartment, Adele kissed Abilene goodbye. She said, "I don't believe all those things I said. I was upset. I only meant that sometimes things happen to people and it's too painful to think about. We say, 'What was she doing there, anyway? Why were they up to that?' We say, 'Thank goodness that can't happen to me.' And I don't want—it would be so terrible, Abilene—I don't want to blame the victims. So I say it was fate, or bad luck, or the evil of other people falling down on them. And I still want to say— how can you go on if you don't believe this—I want to say, you can decide to be who you are. You can decide who that is."

Abilene wanted to get away. "Then I hope you're right," she said, because she didn't think she had made that decision yet herself.

PART II

3.

I WAS TEN when I realized families weren't all the same. We were living in Hadicol Camp, in the blankest part of West Texas, and there was nothing to do but stare at the landscape and try to imagine cities and oceans and mountains and trees. I watched tumbleweeds come out of nowhere—I'd see them coming when they looked the size of a tennis ball—and I'd watch while they were tossed out of sight, or hung up on a fence until the wind shifted and tore them loose again. I knew to cover my face in a dust flurry, to speak cautiously to my mother and to teachers, not to expect anything out of each day. I didn't know then that what seems true can be all a lie.

My brother Kermit was named for the last real town my parents had lived in, and I for a song. He was three years older and spent his days, when he could, with a boy who had a gun. They went out on the prairie and came back with gutted jack rabbits and ropes of snakes. Sometimes Kermit hitchhiked into town, thirty miles away, just to walk around and spend two quarters on a cheeseburger. Once he came home after dark, stinking of beer and my mother Lenore hit him across the shoulders with a broom. My father Bud took the broom away. When he did that, I felt invisible; he'd never have stood up for me. As for my mother—well it was her we caught hell from in the first place. She had no soft looks for anyone. She looked lost in her own head, with cigarette smoke curling around her chin and up into her hair. She spent hours in bed, or in the bathroom with her shoebox full of cheap toiletries. I knew what she wanted. Paved streets and curbs, a house with proper closets. Our trailer was stacked with cardboard boxes and plastic buckets and chipboard shelves over our heads; she wanted everything in its place.

The trailer had only one bedroom. I slept in a corner of the main room with the kitchen things, the table and chairs, and a vinyl couch with horse-head armrests. Kermit slept on the floor on a wad of quilts, and he could lie down in the midst of any noise and fall right away. I was the last awake, lying with my eyes fixed on a slice of night sky that showed through the window above my head.

My mother had been talking about moving to town all year, while my father talked about the coal fields and ranches up north, in states with mountain ranges and winter snow. Lenore's complaints provoked Bud's; he didn't like it that he got up so early and that his pay was so low, that he often had to swab floors like a green-gilled high school boy. Before Hadicol we had lived in other camps, where women sometimes cried for days or ran away and left their babies, and I had always seen our moves as random events set off by things that happened at the wells and made the work go away, so that my dad was let off when nobody else was. I was beginning to understand that my parents had something to say about these things, that there was a chemistry between them that came of discontent. For Bud it was dry holes. He hid bits of money away and got in on wonderful deals that never worked out. For Lenore, it was Bud, it was life. Nothing bothered me; what would have been the good? I had seen girls at school weep over the placement of their desks. I didn't care about school. I didn't care that Lenore yelled at me when I'd done everything she'd said. I thought growing up would take care of everything; the future floated in front of me. Kermit had a sharper sense of a life to come. He knew, for example, that he would have apricot jam in his house, and not cheap grape, that he'd have a real house with a built-in shower. He didn't say ten words a week to my mother. Lenore took it out on Bud: his drinking and lack of ambition, the way he chewed on toothpicks and cut cheese with a pocket knife, and walked around the trailer in his shorts. Kermit could leave the table with his dishes dirty at his place. He could pee with the bathroom door left open. And Lenore didn't speak. Once, though, he put some of her rouge on, for a joke, and when she saw him, she hit him on the head with a pancake turner to which bits of potato still clung.

There were two families in the camp that year that made me think about my own. One was the Wellers, next door. Mrs. Weller wasn't much more than a girl, and her baby cried all the time, but she was always smiling and moving slow. She sat out in front in the evenings on a folding chair, with the baby in her lap, and her husband sat on the step and smoked, and they talked in low happy voices. My mother said it was downright peculiar to sit out like that and watch bugs. My father said it was because they were young and the baby was new. Lenore said, "When did we ever talk like that?" The Wellers-this, and the Wellers-that: they kept coming up, a stick my parents tossed back and forth. One morning Kermit stepped out of the trailer in time to see the Wellers on their step, kissing and hugging so hard that Mrs. Weller's housecoat had come open all the way up her legs. Kermit let out a hoot, Bud and Lenore rushed to see, and Lenore banged the door shut so hard the little set-in pane of glass popped out. After that it was closed with a piece out of a box. I knew my mother was jealous of Mrs. Weller.

The other family, the Moosters, lived across from us on the other side of the laundry shed. I hung around with Natty, who was in the class ahead of me at school, and already twelve. She had swingy hips and a pouty mouth. She had little breasts, and her periods. Her bangs were cut deep to make a bushy mass of hair in front that bounced on her forehead. Natty's mother did her hair; she'd once been a beautician, and could do nails too. Mrs. Mooster was fat in the belly and hips, and her upper body looked like a cone stuck on a worndown mountain. She had purple veins streaking up and down her legs. She wore safety pins in her clothes. But I never heard her shouting at her kids to find out what they were up to. She and her family were so different, they were like circus people to me, curious, inimitable, brave.

Mr. Mooster worked in the field like my dad, but he spent all his free time inventing things. Natty said they'd all be rich one day. She had her father's optimism and her mother's good spirits. I didn't know what to believe. To me, life was a chancy thing; happiness came up like high cards in a draw. I thought that was why we were an unhappy family; it couldn't be helped. But I'd watched with longing when Natty came in from the prairie in the Mooster pickup, her face streaked muddy with sweat and dust. Her father was teaching her to drive. He taught his kids all the constellations, too, and sometimes he would stand outside the trailer at night and put his arms over Natty's shoulders and down onto the front of her, across her bumps. I never saw him stand like that with his wife, but maybe Mrs. Mooster didn't have time for it. She had so much cooking and laundry to do. She didn't make her kids do anything at all, but she always had them working on projects. They used thread spools and yarn, broken clothespins and socks worn at the heels, popsicle sticks and paper clips. They glued and tied and cut and *wove. The trailer was lined with their drawings. Mobiles dangled from the ceiling. There were piles and piles of things to step over or around: clothes, books, comics and newspapers, toys, board games, empty cartons and cans, and sometimes the kids themselves, playing or fallen asleep.*

None of the kids did very well in school, and Mrs. Mooster was often called to come and collect her scoundrels; she bought them ice cream and used the drive to get to the grocery store. She sang and played harmonica and a plastic recorder, and all the kids could hum with combs in their mouths. Natty memorized poems like "Ballad of the Harpweaver," and read "Talk of the Town" from The New Yorker *out loud while her mother made supper. She rolled her baby sister Plum's hair with rags, and told fearsome stories about a Norse wolf named Loki that ate villagers. When I went over she handed me lemonade in a jelly jar and told me about other countries like it was a geography class. She said that all that really mattered was to get out of Texas when you were old enough. She said her mother said so. She said she would be a famous performer and be on television all over Texas so everyone would know her. She seemed years and years older, as if she had an entirely different, better life.*

One day my brother grabbed me coming back from the Mooster trailer, and pushed me around to the back of our trailer; the heat off the metal made me dizzy. "That little rooster friend of yours is a whoor," he said. I didn't know what he meant. "You dope!" he shouted. "A whoor. *For money. You know that." All I knew Natty could do for money at her age was babysit, and nobody needed a babysitter in Hadicol Camp. Kermit was getting exasperated. "A whoor," he said, "does sex for money. Now do you get it?"*

"Like what?" I asked.

"Like fuck."

"Who says!"

"Well, maybe I don't know for sure she fucks. But probably. Everybody knows at school. In study hall I saw her reach up under her skirt and stick her hand in her pants and she scratched her goldamned ass!"

"For money?" I was being sullen. Natty was my only friend.

"Twerp."

"Do you do it?" I asked him.

"What?"

"Fuck. Do you fuck." It was the first time I'd heard the word.

"You don't have any business saying fuck, twerp. You don't know shit about it."

"But you do. Because you do it."

He twisted in his own trap. "Not exactly."

I did know one word for sex. "You mean humping, don't you?"

Kermit bent over and whispered in my ear. "I'll bet you a dollar I can get her to put her hand on my dick."

"That's the dumbest thing I ever heard." I couldn't imagine anything worse.

"For a quarter," he said. "I can get her to touch it." His was a sly look. "And for another quarter I bet she'll kiss it."

"If she does it'll be because she'll want to know it's not just a worm in your pocket. Dumbutt! Shithead!"

"Betcha!" Kermit said. He was proud of himself for thinking of it, for making me miserable. "For fifty cents. That bitch thinks she's shit on a stick."

In the back of the Mooster trailer there was an old Chevy with no tires. I told Natty what Kermit had said while we were sitting in it. She thought it was hysterical. "You wouldn't, would you?" I asked.

"I've got brothers. I've seen my pop. What do I care about your brother's little stupid peee-nis."

I felt better, until she said, "I'm going to let him pay me fifty cents and see what he gets."

She started coming around our trailer when Kermit was there. She'd see the two boys coming in with their bloody rabbits and come over and act like it was wonderful, what they'd done. I couldn't believe how she was acting. I couldn't believe he fell for it.

Then one day she brought over beer, while my parents were both gone, and the three of us got a little woozy. She stretched and yawned, so that her belly showed, and she said, "Cold beer makes me want to go outside and get hot again so I can drink some more. She looked at Kermit. "Want to?"

There was just a second of silence, and then they were gone. I felt queasy and apprehensive. I sat there, worrying about what Kermit would do to Natty, or what Natty would do to Kermit—I bolted out of the trailer and ran back towards the Chevy. I could hear Natty laughing like the devil and yelling at me, "Abileeeeen!" I got to the car just in time to catch a wad of clothes flying through the window of the car.

43

Kermit's pants. Kermit made a barking sound and started cursing, but Natty was already out of the car. Her blouse was all undone; I could see how her chest smoothed out over those two little bumps, white and soft like the flesh of a spring flower that only lasts a single morning. We ran as fast as we could to her trailer. Natty was laughing so hard she said it was giving her a stitch. We ran past her mother, who looked up and said, "What's going on?" and buried our giggles in towels, sitting on the floor of the bathroom. "It wasn't a worm," Natty said. "It stood up and begged." I was mortified.

Natty saw my misery and loved it. "I told him he could undo his pants if he'd put his hand inside mine. He was shaking like a leaf!"

"Did you touch him?"

"Sure. Silky. Soft."

I had to know. "Did you kiss it?"

She curled her hand into a loose fist, thumb stuck up. She raised her hand up to her face and bent over a little so that she could place her pouting mouth at the tip of her thumb. "Only a little, like this," she said, and her little tongue darted out and touched the top of her thumb. I ached as if I'd fallen off a step. "Where did you learn that!" I asked.

"From my daddy." She put her arms out and put her hands on mine. "Didn't anybody ever touch you there?" she said. I couldn't say anything. "You don't know!" she cried. She ran her hands down my sides and stopped at my waist like I was a dancer ready to leap. "Come closer," she said. "I'll show you."

Kermit never said anything. Ten days later the Moosters were gone. They were going out farther west towards El Paso. I watched them load up. Mrs. Mooster had thrown away a stack of magazines in the trash barrel by the laundry shed; I dug them out and hid them behind the vinyl couch at home. My mother found them and made me take them back. Then it was time for school again, when all the best parts of the day are spent on buses and sitting like a board at school learning nothing new and taking all day at it.

Maybe it was early to learn this about sex, but at least after that I wouldn't be as surprised: it could be fun, it could be funny, and it could be used to put you in your place. I didn't know about concepts like fate, but I did sense that my life was laid out from that summer forward. I couldn't get out of the way if I didn't see it coming.

My dad found a job driving a cement truck for a driller, and we moved to a small city. There were two high schools (not counting the one for colored kids), two pools in parks like oases, a shopping center and a library. We rented a square squat peeling house in a treeless part of town, and my mother found a job as a waitress. Right after that, Bud went to Lubbock. In a few weeks it was as if he'd never been there. Lenore sagged from the shoulders. She worked a split-shift, serving laborers who lived alone, and old people. She stopped cooking or cleaning. We didn't make any effort to pretend we were a family. I thought of my dad like an old movie: there he was, far out on a ribbon of road, chewing on a toothpick and leaving everything behind.

Kermit had a part-time job as a mechanic's apprentice and a girlfriend two years older who worked at a bank. I was a junior in high school. I slept on a cot between the living-room sofa and the wall, my mother slept on the sofa, and my brother in the bedroom of the house. Sometimes when it wasn't too hot or too cold I slept in the old trailer, parked in back. I liked to lie out there and think I was in space, like a pale far-flung planet. The year went by and school remained remote. I had no friends. The only thing I cared about was my Spanish class.

My teacher, Xavier Morales, was a Mexican immigrant. He had gotten his first degree in Mexico City, and then a Master's in Austin. He made jokes: he said he was one of the few Mexicans to enter the U.S. bone-dry. Everybody laughed except me. He should be proud, I thought; he speaks two languages. He ran his class at a brisk pace that once made a student cry out "shit!" when he couldn't keep up. We did drills, read passages in choral practice, struggled with our accents, until we started grinning at ourselves, picking up our heads and wanting to answer. Some kids weren't as fast, but even they liked Morales' class. I felt it was the one safe place in my day. I liked the way the words felt on my tongue, the cadence and timbre of my voice. Spanish took me out of myself. Mr. Morales offered to lend me records to practice at home, and I was embarrassed because I didn't have a record player. I lay in bed that night thinking about him, and I realized he was the only human being in the world whose opinion of me counted. After that I studied even harder.

One day, coming out of class, he said "You know, you're becoming Mexican in your manners."

"Meaning what?" I asked.

"Meaning you're learning to use words to hide your feelings," he answered. It was the first time I realized there was power in language.

Kermit and his girlfriend Sherry invited me to outings to the sand dunes or to the reservoir to swim, or to the beautiful clear springs a hundred miles away where we could swim and drink beer and get burned by the sun. I knew it was Sherry's idea; Kermit would never have thought of me. Sherry had a niceness about her. I thought it probably made her good at the bank.

I was out of place with Kermit's friends, though. I was too young. I thought the boys were vulgar, with their jokes and crumpled beer cans, though their girlfriends tended to be calm and smiling, unless they got drunk and sick or loud. I knew the boys thought I was standoffish, not so much shy as distant, like maybe I thought I was too good for them, boys with their hair cut close to their skulls, and cutoff jeans with nothing underneath except their genitals they went out of the way to expose, always sitting with their legs up and their arms resting on their knees. I did feel distant; I couldn't follow the talk about sports and cars, and I didn't think their jokes were funny. I was bored and embarrassed when they screamed and belly flopped, tugged at the girls' bathing suits in the cold spring pool, nudged and kissed in the car while I hugged a window, looking out, my cheeks on fire. I was so different, and I didn't know why. I would have liked to be more like the girls they liked. I would have liked to have the boys touch me—I was curious and lonely—but I was too young, and an outsider, a queer foreigner of some kind, and I knew that if I pretended to be like the girls, and they touched me, my brother's hearty sunburned friends, I would fall under them like something liquid, and they would take it all, before I knew if I wanted to give it away. They would know I was trying to keep up, and they'd do what they were always saying they'd like to do to some starlet (Sandra Dee, in "A Summer Place," was the sweetest, they said, and she really needed it), which was to fuck her brains out. Besides, there was my brother. When I looked at him I couldn't imagine what he thought of me. Probably nothing. He was looking ahead.

I got a part-time job at Penney's. They put me in the department that sold men's underwear. I amused myself guessing sizes before they asked. Then I thought: if I have to do this all my life I'll kill myself. It wasn't a farfetched idea. The father of a sophomore girl at school had blown his brains out in his bathtub, and then her mother took an overdose and left her orphaned. Another boy lost his mother when his *father followed her to a motel room where she was meeting his law firm's partner. In Texas you could shoot a woman like that. Worse, a girl my same age held a gun in her mouth one night and begged her boyfriend to shoot her. He liked somebody else, and she was always crying. He buried her in a caliche pit. They quoted him in the paper: "I just did what she asked me to do."*

One day I saw a boy in the library, checking out a book. His eyelashes made shadows, he had extraordinary, glossy hair. I realized he was Mexican; his eyes never looked at mine. I started seeing him here and there, in the gym at assembly, in the lunchroom when I forced myself to eat. I thought about going up to him and saying Como estas," *just like that, and the thought made me laugh at myself.*

I bought a bicycle. Kermit said I looked freaky, zipping around with my little basket in front piled with books and my purse. I didn't care. Suddenly I could get around. I rode it to school, and to work on Saturdays. In the evenings I rode around my neighborhood, going a little farther each time. I realized that most of our neighborhood was Mexican. Their houses were like ours, on lots with scruffy patches of grass and weeds—boxy, delapidated rentals where for block after block you never saw a tree. Cars sat up on blocks, and there were motor-cycles, and sometimes a car polished like a gem, trimmed in pink and orange and yellow, with curlicues in front like moustaches, and ten-drils running down the sides. Sometimes I saw the owners shining their prizes with soft rags. They would look up and watch me ride by. After a few weeks they recognized me and their gazes were more open, a little friendlier. Boys of eleven or twelve made chirping noises at me, but I laughed at them and they went off to other things. The men wore white undershirts with baggy pants, green or khaki in color; their hair fell down around their ears, and many of them sported trim moustaches. The women, in cheap dresses, sat on steps and watched their men, and the babies ran around naked.

One day I realized I was looking for the boy from school. Then, not long after, I came out of school and found one tire flat. The boy I'd seen in the library was coming toward me. He wore a tight black knit shirt and jeans, shiny black shoes, and a chain with a medal around his neck. He said he had a pickup, he was on his way to work. "I'll take you there and patch your tire," he offered. "The Texaco on Sixth. I'll put your bike in the back, okay?" His voice was soft.

"I see you around school," he said as he pulled out of the lot. "Are

you a junior? Senior?"

"Junior. What about you?" I couldn't have guessed his age.

"Senior," he said. "Justaboutout," he added, in a slur.

"What then?" I asked, for something to say.

"No more school. Like, you know. I mean, you just go on making it, huh?" He kept glancing back and forth from his driving to me. "What's your name?" he asked. When I told him I'd been named for the song, "Abilene," he didn't react at all. Of course Mexicans are named for Jesus, and saints, heroes, and states of grace.

"I'm Eddie," he volunteered.

"Eddie?"

"Doncha like it?"

I was embarrassed. I saw hostility flash across his face.

"All right. Eduardo. My family calls me Lalo. But my friends, Eddie. Anglo. Better for getting by."

I wondered what I ought to do. Was he being bold? Would he flirt with other Anglo girls? (Was he flirting with me?!) Maybe he thought I was easy! I sat with my legs closed tight until we arrived at the station. He patched my tire while I stood by watching in silence. He checked the bike all over and got a grease gun to work down around the pedals. Then he wheeled it off to the side and propped it up. "Good as new," he said.

I didn't want to leave. I stepped in front of him to take the handlebars, and I could feel the warmth of him coming off like steam. Somebody called out from inside the garage, "Hey Eddie, qu-hubo, mano?" There was nothing to do but ride away.

That night I rode a long time through the streets near home. I looked at people sitting on their steps in the dark, or under the yellow glow of porch lights. I heard televisions blaring, and fast bouncy Mexican songs. I wished there was someone at my house to sit with. When I went into my room, I thought about Mr. Morales with his hair slicked down and his nylon shirt tight across his chest, and I thought again of Eddie. (Lalo, I rolled on my tongue.) I thought how he would sweat in the heat, how his breath would make a pillow damp. I bet he wouldn't tell, I thought.

I saw Natty Mooser coming out of the gym one day. She had lavender hair and a skirt six inches shorter than anybody else's. She was gone before I could call out to her. What would I say? I wondered. "Remember me?"

At Christmas we went in Kermit's new (used) pickup to see Dad. He had rented a trailer in a cheap park, all dust and garbage cans and screaming kids. Once we'd gone to a cafeteria to eat, and Kermit and I had each given what sounded like little speeches about what we were doing (Kermit was going to start night school in January), Bud started drinking beer and turned on the television. We went home the next day. Bud didn't act surprised. He said he was glad to see us, and maybe we'd come another time. That was all. That was the last time I saw my dad.

Early in the new year Kermit started acting funny. He was out almost every night, and I didn't know what to say when Sherry called. One night he took me to a drive-in and bought hamburgers, and while we were eating in the car, I told him what I thought, that he looked like the cat that ate the bird.

He leaned back and closed his eyes. "What you see is a satisfied man."

"Lord, what does that mean?"

He sat up and took a bite of his dripping hamburger. "It means I'm getting laid," he said pleasantly. "But don't get any ideas, because it's a man's world."

"How come I don't see Sherry anymore?"

He backed the car out so fast my Coke spilled on my lap. I sopped it up with napkins and heard Kermit say, "I don't see her anymore, nose-butt."

He wouldn't say who his new girlfriend was. I figured it out one night when she called and I said he was asleep. "Can't you wake him up?" the girl asked. I said he'd been really tired, he'd worked hours overtime. "Well hell," she said, "how much rest does he need?" She laughed. "Tell him he missed a good time."

I told Kermit it was the wierdest thing I ever heard, that he would go out with Natty Mooster. And "go out" wasn't what they did. He told me to stuff it. But with the secret out, Natty started coming over when my mother wasn't home, lying around with Kermit in his filthy room drinking beer and watching the little television he'd bought for himself. (I hated him for that. All my mother had wanted for years was a TV.) She gave me superior smiles and said things like "Aren't you growing right up now?" and "Wonder, do you take after your brother in any important ways?" Once she came up behind me when I was standing at the refrigerator thinking what there was to eat. She put her arms *around me from the back and pulled herself close, and then she put her mouth down on my neck and made a chill run down my back. I yanked away so hard the pickle jar rattled on the top shelf of the refrigerator. I was going to say something really hateful to her, but when I turned around she had a soft look on her face, sweet as the way she'd look at her sister Plum, and tears came up so fast I had to run out of the house to let my feelings go.*

When a creepy second-string basketball player from history class called and asked me out, I said yes without a second thought. I didn't even know for sure which boy it was until he said something to me after class about seeing an Elvis movie. After we did that, he drove to the edge of town to park. His name was Farin. He had beer on the back floor of the car. It was warm, but I drank two. "God I'm full!" I said in a while, in a giddy voice that amazed me and made me laugh. "I've got to pee!" Farin gestured grandly to the horizon. "Pick your spot," he said. He gave me a smirky smile as I slid out of the car and went around behind. Pee splashed on my shoe, and I tried to wipe it against the tire. I knew I'd die if I had to think of anything to say. I wanted desperately to be at home instead, but not because there was anything so bad about Farin. (He wore a nice aftershave, and he'd been sweet and polite at the movie.) It was that I didn't know what was coming or what to do. I didn't want to do too much. I didn't want to make Farin mad.

When I got back in the car, he pulled me toward him and put his wide wet mouth down over my face. What he got was a mouthful of lips. "You can do better than that, can't you?" he said. He said it nicely.

"Whatever you say," I said, regretting instantly the generosity that implied. I opened my mouth and his tongue went in deep and glided around. I thought the beer from his mouth tasted better than the beer in mine. I was having a hard time breathing. He let off from kissing and began fumbling with my blouse. It was a bleeding Madras plaid from Penney's. My straight skirt matched it. In a moment his hand had slipped inside my bra and over my nipple. I felt as if he had stuck a pin in me.

"Whatcha scared of?" he muttered. I was cold and tense, but I moved a hand up on the back of Farin's neck, and slid my fingers back and forth. "Let go!" he hissed. "You're a-ticklin' me!" Now I didn't know what to do with either hand. I extended my arm away from Farin's ticklish neck. My blouse was pulled out of my skirt by now. I felt

twisted as a pretzel. Suddenly Farin moved away from me. He seemed to be staring at a spot on my throat. Then he lunged at me and pulled my blouse down off my shoulders.

"I don't know—" I faltered. I wasn't sure what was expected on a first date. I felt absolutely nothing. Farin was tugging at me like I was a limp doll when I said, "I hardly know you." I wondered if he was disappointed at my small breasts tucked inside my lightly molded bra. Farin ignored me. He expertly undid the bra. It dangled. He slipped it down so that it hung off the sides of my upper arms. It was ludicrous, my clothes dripped off me. I shrugged out of my blouse and bra and they fell into my lap.

"You're sure a sweet little thang," Farin said in a guttural voice. I was sweating heavily. Farin pushed me back against the door and put his mouth over my nipple. He sucked. I felt like a fool. I knew his hand was along a road he knew well and I was about to learn, I wanted it to be there, but I didn't think it ought to be so dumb, so easy. I had heard all about basketball from Farin, last season and this. I knew how much his new seat covers had cost him, and that he planned to go to Tech and study business, maybe even accounting if he could do the work. This didn't seem like a fair trade for my virginity, even if my virginity was something I was ready to be rid of. I squeezed my legs and twisted hard. His hand was caught between my thighs. I released it as I pushed it out from under my skirt.

"Listen!" I cried, my decision made. He seemed to be holding his breath. "I am NOT going to do it!" Farin rallied and sat up again.

"You tellin me—" he started to say. Both hands went down to his crotch, making a little shield over what he had there. "Shit!" he said. "You some goddamned virgin?" Then he said something that sounded like "Nuuuuh!" I was more embarrassed than anything. Weakly, I said I was. Soft, sweet as a chirping bird, he called me over. He hunched over his jeans, undoing them. "Just put your hand on it," he said. I must have looked amazed. "On the outside, then, baby," he said. He put my hand where he wanted it. He was hot and damp and swollen under the shorts. Size thirty, I thought. He groaned again: "Nuuuh!" He grabbed my bra and stuffed it down inside his shorts under our hands. He made his noise one more time and then fell quiet. Gently, I slid my hand away and put my blouse on again without the purloined bra. He wiped his forehead with his left hand, and pulled the bra out with his right and handed it to me. "Put it in your purse, honey," he mur-

51

mured. He got out of the car and pissed right by the door. I watched him shake himself dry.

When he got back in he patted me on the arm and said, "S'aright." He started the car and gunned the motor a couple of times. "I guess I figgered wrong," he said. "You looked to me like—" He turned the car off again. "Damn it, you looked like a girl who'd like it. Do you?" At least he hadn't said, a girl who'd do it. I didn't have an answer. He leaned over and slid a hand up under my skirt very fast. I twisted away a bit and he snapped, "Be still!" I complied. His hand went straight up my legs like a snake until it bumped against my underwear. Briskly, he worked his hand beneath the nylon and thrust a finger inside me. I jumped, astonished, but he held on, not doing anything with his finger, simply being there, a stationary object. I felt myself pulsing, closing wet and slick around his finger, I felt the finger drawing from me, sucking me into his flesh. As abruptly as he had intruded, he pulled out. He made a big show of wiping his finger on his pants. "I thought maybe you were just teasing me," he said. "Playing games with ole Farin. But shit, you want it and don't know what it is! You got my timing all off, I had you figgered wrong. Then it was too late to slack off and go slow. But you ain't lying. If you knew what it felt like, you wouldn't be able to say no." He adjusted his Levis around his crotch. "You got a sticky cunt," he grinned. He burned rubber pulling away. In front of my house, he leaned across me and opened the door on my side. "See you around," he said. As I got out, he slapped at my buttocks. "When you're ready!" he laughed.

After that I knew what to expect, and I knew I wasn't, in Farin's terms, "ready." I went out because I was lonely and because I would take what there was, but I wasn't going to lie down for some ducktailed conceited dumb boy who asked me out because he couldn't think of any other girl. They rolled up the sleeves of their tee-shirts, these boys; they belched their beer and couldn't think of anything at all to ask me about myself. My dates were a joke, slow and boring, but I couldn't say, "Skip the movie, let's go park." They would never have believed me when I drew the line. Once we were in the dark, and I closed my eyes, I forgot who the boy was, and it was hard to stop in time. I loved the sly journey up my leg, a boy's hand moving so slow. I longed for the finger inside me, the spasms it brought on. I remembered Natalie at twelve, with Kermit, and I struck her bargain with these boys: I would touch them and they could touch me. As for the rest of it, I said, "My brother would kill me." Kermit was no big slugger, but he was older, out of

52

school, and it called on some sort of respect when I said that. "Sure, whatever you say," they said. There were three, then four of them, coming back every two or three weeks, seldom overlapping their calls. I thought maybe they got together and made a calendar for me, but this was so terrible a thing to consider I told myself I was being silly.

One of the boys told me I was giving him blue balls, he was going to die. I said I'd made it clear from the beginning, he knew what was coming and what was not. When he didn't push me any further, slumping down in the seat in a pitiable pose, I remembered what Farin had done, and I offered a little more, just that one time, for that one boy, but I was kidding myself.

The others began to ache and complain, saying they didn't have that much self-control, they were horny for sweet chrissake; they made it sound like I was so pretty and sexy, they fell down a dark deep sweet hole and couldn't climb out, and I let myself believe it. I let them lie, and I bought the lie, and it was me who slid down.

There had been Farin, and then there had been Larry, so what was it to lay a cool hand over Karlie, and then Maynard? They gave something in return, whether they meant to think of me or not. They wriggled faraway extensions of themselves inside me; I learned to put my hand on a wrist to quiet it, and to make the feelings happen myself, in my own rhythm. I learned to take pleasure from these shabby hours on the edge of town. And when I saw my dates in the halls at school, they grinned at me, the way Kermit had grinned that time in the car, telling me about Natty. And those grins—there was nothing hateful in them, nothing terribly smug. They said: Don't we know it's fun? They were all so gawky and young! They had big Adam's apples and their ugly hair. And none of the "neat" girls—the ones in expensive dresses, with hair done at beauty parlors and pulled up in tortoise shell barettes—would have anything to do with them in a hundred years. Sometimes, for just a moment, I felt those boys tug at my heart; weren't we all in the same sinking boat? Sometimes now, looking back, I think: I should have let them all. I should have lain in the back seats of a dozen cars and made them feel important, because in the end, don't I know they had little dreams and lost even them? Don't I know I wasn't any better?

IN THE SUMMER I WORKED as often as they needed me, relieving clerks on vacation. My mother asked me, "What are you

*going to do with all that money, Abilene?" I'd bought a few clothes,
and my bicycle. The rest was in a savings account. As soon as she
asked me, though, I knew the answer was that I was saving to go
away—from her, from West Texas, from all the Thursday nights at J.C.
Penney's, the cycle of dates and necking and the lack of hope. My
mother saw it on my face; she never spoke to me again of my money,
never once asked me what I was going to do after high school. She
hardly spoke to me at all. The hard part was going to be getting
through another year.*

*Then one hot summer afternon Natty came by my house looking for
someone to "round out" a car full of boys. She was with Chip somebody, and Hoot Gibson, whose real name was Andrew, and Charlie
Jamison, all of them out of school now, hot shot graduates. Hoot held
up a six-pack and said, "Cold suds for a hot day," and somebody said,
"Hell, two girls will do, let's get the show on the road." Natty sat in the
front between Charlie and Hoot, while I sat in the back with Chip. He
was as quiet as I was. Besides, we couldn't have gotten in a word over
the other three.*

*We went to a place in the sandhills that Charlie knew. That Natty
probably knew. That I'd thought about a hundred times. I knew that
sooner or later a lot of kids went to the sandhills, white and pale and
yellow and gritty and hot in the sun, with sand that ground itself into
your pores, into your ears and nose and mouth, that found its way into
your private parts and made your hair heavy, sand that was soft to lie
on. I'd never been there, but I'd dreamed about the sand, a Texas
Sahara, to be lost in, to lie down in and say* no, please don't, *not
meaning it, and later* stop stop, *when it was too late. Nobody had ever
asked me to go to the sand,* because nobody had ever asked me out
in the daylight. *But I knew the questions girls asked themselves out
there:* If I let him will he love me? *and* If I let him will he think
I'm awful after? *I'd thought about how it would feel, white and
twitching on the sand. I'd thought:* What if it hurts? *and then,* So
what, it's only the first time it hurts. *There were bargains made in
the sand, and babies, and sometimes trouble. Not rich girls. Boys knew
their fathers would be waiting up when the girls got home, knew that if
you made a rich girl pregnant you didn't have to get married, you
could go to jail. But there were lots of girls who didn't have fathers who
cared. (I knew this, but I didn't know any of those girls. I didn't have
any friends at all. What would I have done? Gone up to a girl and said,*
you're no better off than me, let's be friends?)

I knew Natty knew the tricks. I knew she made boys glad to be with her. Kermit had told me a story, not so much to amuse me as warn me. ("You better not get yourself in trouble!") He said, she gives head. *Once some boys had given her a package of banana popsicles, and she'd laughed like crazy and passed them around to everybody standing near. And I knew something they were too dumb to see, even Kermit: she was using them to practice for the real world, when she would get out of here.*

The sun was glaring. We walked over the hills, carrying an ice chest and blankets and a portable radio. ("Come along and be my party doll!") We stumbled, our bare feet sinking in the sand; our breath was coming hard.

"Jesus Piss it's hot," Natty said, and the boys laughed. "We gotta be crazy coming to the goddamned sandhills in the middle of the goddamned day in the middle of the goddamned summer!" she shouted. "Like it is fucking HOT!" and at that the boys screamed with laughter, looking at her and at each other. I straggled behind with Chip, carrying the blankets.

Someone said, "Hey, how about this tree!" (more hysterical laughter), and just like that, we plopped down and began to drink beer. I drank mine too fast and it made me belch, and when I looked around to see who'd heard me, everybody started laughing, and I laughed too. I stretched out and put my head in Chip's lap. Natalie lay on a blanket between Hoot and Charlie. They told dirty jokes and sang with the radio ("My little ruuuunaway!") and kept popping open beers. Charlie said something that made Natty pretend she was mad, and they wrestled and brawled and ended in a hot sandy embrace, the length of them, right in front of all the rest of us. She pulled away and stood up. "Christ, I am H-O-T!" she said. We all said, "Amen," like in a church.

"You know what let's do?" she said. "Let's take off all our clothes." Nobody said anything. In a minute or two Charlie got up and took his jeans and shirt off, standing in his jockey shorts. "Oh no, macho," Natty said. "Aaaall clothes!" she growled, leaping across Hoot and pulling Charlie's shorts down around his ankle. "Off off off!" she cried, and in a flash she was naked, and then Hoot. The three of them began to dance around like Indians in a cowboy movie, their hands back and forth against their mouths, dancing around Chip and me, still lying on the blanket. "No fair! No fair!" Natty poked at us, and Charlie and Hoot joined in. They shouted, "No fair!" a dozen times or more, and then they stopped, still, spaced around the two of us on the ground.

"Come on, Abby, take it off," Natalie said in a soft sweet voice. The beer and the sun had made me dizzy. I saw Charlie and Hoot standing with their hands on their hips, their faces wet with sweat, their penises hanging crazily in the sun. I thought how much it would hurt to have a sunburned penis. "Off," Natty said, quite firmly.

"Come on, Natty, please," I said. I looked at Chip. "You won't let them make me, will you?" I asked.

"Just hold on," Chip said, but his voice was a boy's voice, with no authority. It made the others grin. What was he going to do about it? I felt something knocking inside me, I couldn't tell where the thumping was, I knew it had to be fear, and I thought: I can't die of this. Then, simply, as if it had been rehearsed many times, Natty and Hoot and Charlie were a tableau in motion. Without frenzy, they moved in on us. Charlie and Hoot knelt beside Chip and put a hand, each of them, on his shoulder. Chip as good as disappeared before our eyes. He lifted his hand off of me, and moved away. Natty, making deep noises like cat's purrs in the back of her voice, noises like a lover crooning, knelt in front of me. I couldn't make a sound; my head went slowly back and forth, pleading. Natty moved carefully, the soft noises from her throat rising like froth, her tongue clicking faintly. She put her hands on me just above the knees, and I knew, as if it had been announced from a sky split open for this purpose, that there was nothing I would do to stop her. That, whatever she wanted, I would do. Our little scene had become a ritual. It was no longer a game; it was a force that made a new space in my world. I forgot about the naked boys, the male eyes fastened on me in horrified elation. Natty ran her hands in soothing strokes down the lengths of my legs, again and again, slowly, strength and tenderness mixed, and then she began to stroke harder, kneading my flesh. I remembered how she had touched me, on the floor of her tacky bathroom in Hadicol Camp, and I began to whine. Natty shushed me like a whining baby. "Don't be afraid," she said. "I love you, sweetie. Don't you know I can make you feel good?"

She took my shirt off over my head and undid the bra that sprang up and flapped softly over my breasts and then lay still. She kissed each nipple, and then she stretched out on top of me, her naked groin against my jeans, while she stroked my arms and hair and face, crooning and shushing and purring. I shut my eyes. I might have been dead as she unzipped my jeans and pulled them off and tossed them aside. Even with my eyes closed, the sun was a white fire; the sand, and the boys now kneeling in the sand, floated.

How long did it take? Could any of us have said? When Natty had stroked me everywhere, had kissed me and reassured me, until I rose onto the cloud of heat under the bare white sky, she began to slide away from me. I felt the pressure of her body ease. And from someone—it was me of course, but I did not know how it could be from me—came a tiny moan, and the moan, and the easing of Natty's weight on me, made me move a little, as if something stirred in my thighs. Then Natty was away, and there were so sounds except for breathing, no birds or animals in the sand. I heard Natty's voice as she bent toward my face. "It's going to be okay, honey," she said. On a hot burst of breath she added, "Now, you guys."

One of them spoke, incredulous: "What!" and Natty said again, "Now." She had moved so that she was above me. I felt her hands on my shoulders, pressing me hard. I still had not opened my eyes. "They won't hurt you," she lied. I opened my eyes and screamed. "Give in," Natty said beneath my cry. "Give in!"

"For God's sake!" Chip said nearby. "For holy sweet Christ!" he uttered as Charlie Jamison climbed on top of me. In a moment Charlie slid away, sighing, and Hoot took his place. One of them put a hand on Natty's breast. "Not me, sport," she said in an ugly way. "I'm just directing this show." I felt the heat more than the pain. I thought: I will die, after all, and it was such a sweet relief!

They packed everything up and went back toward the car. Chip helped me dress, and I staggered after them. We took our same places in the car. Chip tried to hold my hand, but I pulled it away. The boys in the front looked shifty-eyed and scared. Charlie said, trying for a casual tone, though his voice cracked in the middle of his words, "Guess nobody is going to tell about this, huh?" Nobody said anything, and Charlie's head swung around so that he could see me, and then he looked forward, like a door on a tight hinge. I knew Natty was disgusted with him for being dumb and vain and chicken-hearted. "Shut up!" she told him. "Just shut up!"

I slid into the corner of the back seat. "Who would I tell?" I said. "Who would believe me?"

Kermit and I went to the Miss West Texas pageant not long after. Natty placed second in the bathing suit competition. She sang a gritty blues song, and the audience loved it, but she didn't impress the judges; she wasn't even a finalist. When it was over, Kermit pulled me along to go and see her. She let him give her a hug, and didn't look at me. "Tough luck, Nat," he said. "You were the sexiest, that's for sure. Don't you think that was the trouble?" She pulled away and went back to picking up her things. "Screw Miss America in the ass," she said.

A few weeks later, we heard she'd run away to Las Vegas with the high school drama teacher. He was married, with kids. I thought, God, he'll hate her, later.

I went over it again and again. I tried to remember how I felt when there was still time to have stopped them. I knew I could have. Even with three of them, and Chip no more help than a rag, I knew they wouldn't have done it if I had tried to stop them. But it was like trying to remember a dream. I had lost all the details. What I remembered was loss washing through me, a dark flood, drowning out all other feelings. That flood took with it the last of my innocence (and who was I kidding? I thought), my pride (and what of that had I had?), my will to possess my own life. The way I stood in front of the mirror in the morning had changed. The way I felt when I lay on my cot at night had changed. The pain, the guilt—they had burned through me into the cavity inside; I ached to have them excised.

Late in the fall Kermit went back to Sherry. She was bland and affectionate, as if the empty place in her history with my brother had been covered over like fill dirt on a dump. With no fuss, they married one weekend. Lenore bought them towels, a coffeepot, some mugs, as if they had been living at the Y. It touched me to see my mother taking love at face value. Kermit moved with Sherry to Lubbock, where her mother, a widow, had a house. He would go to school at last; Sherry would work. No one mentioned Kermit's father.

The boys I had dated the year before were gone; the boys from the sandhills were gone; my brother was gone, my father and Natty were gone. Even Mr. Morales left, halfway through the first semester. He told me after class, the day before he had to go. It was his mother, he said, in Mexico; a son had certain duties.

"Will your family go too?" I asked. He looked confused. "Your wife, I mean," I said awkwardly.

He smiled. "I'm not married," he said, and I felt a wave of pain that brought salt to my eyes, the taste of blood to my lips. "You must go on with your language study," he said, blind to my anguish. "You have the aptitude for it." We were standing by his desk with the door open, in view of anyone passing in the hall. In a day he would be gone. I touched his arm. "Oh no," I said. He moved his arm away. "Remember that a language opens the heart and intellect of another people." How I wanted him to embrace me! I knew if he kissed me he would taste the blood on my lips. I felt wicked and lost.

During Christmas vacation I worked in the evenings at the store downtown. One night Farin came in, and when he saw me, he said, without asking anything, that he would be back at nine to pick me up.

"Where are we going?" I asked in the car. He answered smoothly.

"To my house. I'm gonna show you my tree."

In his driveway, he leaned over and kissed me. Something between us had improved; a pleasant mild flush of sensation rose along my spine. I followed him into the dark and empty house. He flipped on the lights and said, "Folks out of town. Nice, huh?" He made drinks for us—vodka and 7-Up—and put on a Del Shannon record with the arm set aside so it would play over and over. A Christmas tree stood in a corner laden with ornaments and tinsel, below it a mound of gifts. I admired the tree, jiggled the ice in my drink, and sank onto the couch. Farin drained his glass and ran his hands over my shoulders and then under my sweater. He buried his face in my lap and then, kneeling on the floor, kissed my thighs. I watched this as if it were a film starring someone else. We went into his bedroom. Shannon's whine curled around the hall toward us. Farin had an eerie blue bulb in his overhead light. As he undressed me, I looked at the light on my skin.

"Listen," he said, scooting me up to the middle and toward the head of his double bed. "Are you going to participate, or what?" His scolding made my eyes brim with tears and brought me out of my wandering. He was naked and blue, and the tree he had promised me stood like a purple mushroom sprouted after a rain. My heart was pounding; here I was, and I didn't know how I got here. It was a lame excuse and I rejected it. I turned my body and pressed it down the length of Farin's. He slid a leg between mine. "Are you ready?" he murmured gruffly. I was amazed when he touched me and made me aware of my milkiness, about which he exclaimed, "I knew it!" I was amazed that I felt nothing, floating in the blue light, the song, his groans and murmurs. When he moved into me, the vodka rose in the back of my throat, scalding. My hips clutched and cramped. Farin began to heave and grunt. He ordered me, "Hold my ass!" In a moment he fell off me with a monstrous sigh, and reached down to peel something off his penis.

When he saw me looking at it, he said, "A rubber, dingbat, doncha know a rubber?" I fell back against the pillow, awash in remorse. It was so trivial, and I had only myself to blame. I had known where he was taking me. And I had wanted to go. But why?

Farin got up and changed the record. He came back singing with Buddy Holly's song. When he saw me with my arm thrown across my face—I must have looked ridiculous—he howled. "This is for fun!" he said, pulling my arm away. "Fun! S-E-X. You ain't no virgin." His face above me revealed at this new angle a tiny red scab left from shaving, and a pimple about to burst.

"You on the pill?" I said I didn't know anything about one.

"S'aright, I got Trojans. You oughta get on the pill, though, you gonna fuck around."

"I don't!" I cried.

Farin snorted. "My ass."

I thought he would call, that that would be my reward, though he had told me that he had a girlfriend. He'd asked, "When did you do it?" and I'd said, "Last summer," two words for all of that. When I spoke of it, the experience in the sand receded, became smaller. "Like girls say," I had improvised, "he got what he wanted and didn't want it any more." Farin had said, "Poor kid."

A month later, though, someone did call. He said he was Farin's friend, and Farin had given him my number.

"Do I know you?" I asked.

"I graduated Permian in '58," he said. That was the other high school. "Listen, I'm having a little party Thursday night. Thought you could come."

"I go to school, and I work." What kind of party does anybody have on Thursday? I thought.

"It's gotta be Thursday," he insisted. "I'll pick you up at nine. You won't be out late."

"Listen," I said. "I don't know you."

"Richard. I told you, I'm a friend of Farin's."

"What did he tell you?"

"That you're a good kid, haven't been here too long. You know, I thought you'd be friendlier—"

"Okay," I said. Maybe Farin did feel bad that he couldn't call. "I have to be home by eleven."

Richard's answer seemed to slither out of the phone and down my arm. "It doesn't take that long, honey," he said. Before I could reply, he had hung up.

I've stumbled into a bad crowd, I told myself. It was a mistake. It wasn't my fault. I wasn't halfway down a slide; I could get off.

I rode my bike to the Texaco station where Eddie worked. It was cold and sunny, perfect for a hard, fast ride. I asked the attendant if Eddie was around. I wanted to tell Eddie that I would go out with him, that I was one Anglo girl with no hangups. I thought he looked gentle, and manly, too. I thought he would have asked me out already, but he didn't want trouble. It was up to me to let him know it was okay.

"He's gone," the attendant said. He made a gesture across his front. "That girl of his got herself a bambino," he laughed. I felt sick. I couldn't believe how stupid the attendant was.

"Oh that," I said, as if I knew all about it. "I thought he'd be here, though."

"Gone to Del Rio." The attendant was looking me over in a way I didn't like. "Those spics have more relatives down there. Hell, they have relatives all over!" He was staring at me at about crotch level. "I'd be glad to help," he said .

"You're full of shit," I said, and rode away.

In the flesh, Richard was only another arrogant young man, almost handsome in his dark sullen way. I let him in the door and we stood there for several moments, looking at one another. I knew I was going to go with him. I knew I wanted what he wanted, that it was in my nature, that it was who I was. I could thank Farin for making me see that.

"Farin didn't say you had red hair," Richard said. "He didn't say you were so pretty."

I stood dumb as wood. From my head down, a tingle passed along my body. From my feet up came a leaden numbness. The sensations crossed somewhere in my middle and confused me.

"I can't go!" I said. I added, in a murmur, "Sorry."

He moved a step closer and put his hands on my waist. "Your folks here?"

The house was absolutely quiet. "It's my mom and me," I said. "She works at the Rotunda." Richard ran his hands up under my breasts.

61

With one breath I let go. It was all so inevitable. It settled something, letting go.

I said: "She's not home till midnight."

I hated him, at least part of the time, but it was with Richard that I learned to love the night sky. He talked about the sky as a wonderful conjunction of motion and space; he had once hoped to study astronomy. He said the sky and the sea had a very real connection; like breathing, the sea rose and fell beneath the tug of the sky. I said that if you thought of it like that, of our place in a celestial sphere, then all of us fit, had a home, so to speak. Rich and poor, old and young, maybe even dead and alive, we all mattered so little. I didn't know what I was talking about, or care. It was the first time I'd known the delicious balm of talk. I felt myself drawn up, like the sea, toward blackness; and in it, whorls of new light, young planets, dead stars fought for me, sought to suck me in. Richard said he understood. He touched me so gently. Like a lover.

We lay on a blanket in the sand. A bright moon gleamed on the soft slopes. I remembered the other time, under the hot sun, and I started to cry. Richard stroked my hair and asked me what was wrong. I told him, and I saw his jaw clench down. I thought I had disgusted him. What could any man ever think of me?

He never said what he thought, but he didn't make love to me that night, and he was kind, as a friend. Later I lay in my bed and thought how lucky we are to look above and see the night. Richard said that animals don't do this. There is a loftiness in the human aptitude. I fell asleep wondering how I might rise right into the sky, and beyond.

I saw Richard almost every Thursday night. He had a regular girlfriend whom he thought he would marry some time soon, and that other girl took up his weekends. Once, though, she went to Disneyland with her parents, and Richard took me away for the weekend, to Carlsbad Caverns. On the night we arrived, we watched innumerable bats pour out of the mouth of the cave like a long stormy cloud. An owl in a tree caught one of the bats while I was watching; I turned my face into Richard's shoulder. In a motel we drank watered whiskey and talked about our childhoods. Richard's life hadn't been so very different from mine. His mother was a hairdresser. I felt good, hearing that. It wasn't until days later that I realized that it meant that I couldn't

62

blame my status with him on the difference in our lives. It was something in me that made him see me the way he did, something less worthy than his "real" girlfriend.

In the cavern rooms I had put my feet down carefully; one slip, I thought, and I would plunge into the belly of the cave. That, and the damp chill, made me shiver. On the way home I told Richard I was happy for the trip. He pulled onto a side road and taught me, forty miles from nowhere, how my mouth could give everything. I closed my eyes and saw again the deep black pools in the caves. There was no bottom to their depth.

There were others besides Richard. An almost-engaged man has only so much time. The others were, like him, no longer boys. I never understood how they knew to call me, where they came from. Who had spread the word? I knew I had a reputation, that I was getting in deeper and deeper, but it was like good money after bad. I kept thinking my value would rise for one of them. And I didn't know how to refuse. What grounds did I have? These young men had lost the raw freshness of boyhood. They had more to say, though mostly about themselves, and they had learned a few things. They all sold things during the day, or wrote things down at desks, and they weren't tired in the evenings. They smelled willingness on me like the vanilla stench of Shalimar. I took Farin's advice and saw a doctor. I thought of going out with men as walking along a bluff blindfolded; I knew I would fall, I only didn't know when.

I lay with Richard on blankets in the back of his station wagon, the night mild and bright under a half moon and a sky full of stars. I felt suddenly that I could not make love to men who took no pains to please me. Not any more. And Richard—he should have known! I had once opened my heart to him. It was so hard to swallow the lump in my throat, to find the courage to say, "Richard, I'm unhappy, I've had enough of this, being whatever I am, not your girlfriend, it's not enough, it's not right, it has to change." My voice quivered. I knew I was cutting myself off from him. I meant no challenge, no ultimatum, I fully expected never to see him again. What I wanted was for him to understand why that had to be. Why I deserved more.

Richard was, like me, naked below his shirt, sitting half-raised to lean against the side of the car, smoking in a lazy way. He didn't answer me for a long time, though I saw that he was looking at me as if I were a strange animal who had slunk through a crack in the wall. I felt a surge of anger, so much anger it flushed through me and made me hot and agitated, and then, before I could speak of it, regret washed through and made the anger weak. Richard rolled the window down to toss out his cigarette, and then he turned and moved on me roughly, putting his hand over my mouth as he bit at my belly and breasts. I twisted one leg over the other to lock him out, and he used his knee to break this silly barrier. "I don't want to!" I gasped, summoning resources for a fight. We were fifteen miles from town on an unpaved service road. What a ridiculous spot I'd picked to end an affair based on my own weakness. And Richard—Richard was the best of the lot. At least I thought he liked me. I shuddered, and he put his mouth on mine. I clung to his shoulders and drew him in; I stopped thinking. Only like this could I find release, only like this could a man want me.

"You're bored, is that it?" Richard grunted. There was nothing for me to say. Richard poised just above me, speaking harshly. "You think I don't know how much you fuck?" Plunge. "Farin, and me." I twisted, making room for him. "Howard Black, and Bob Slaughter." He dug his hands into my buttocks and came, savagely, short of the crest I sought. He fell on me, and my moan rose higher than his sigh, despairing, toward the sky. His weight on me was monstrous, the smell of him unbearable. If I had had a knife, I would have sunk it into his back, no, into his belly. "Still not enough, is it?" he spit at me. He grabbed my hand and yanked it down on me. "So you do it!" he commanded. He raised up and sat back, his legs arched over me. "Rub it, bitch," he said. I turned my head, and he slapped me. "Rub it!" he said. This was new. I curved slightly into my side, as much I could manage with him straddling me, and, weeping now, I rubbed my finger back and forth until the friction hurt and my hand ached. Richard got out of the car, and I used the blanket to dab at myself. I dressed and moved to the front seat. Richard climbed into the driver's seat and started the car. "What is it, exactly, that you think I owe you?" he said evenly.

"Nothing, nothing," I said miserably. "But all these months we've made love—"

He whooped. "Made love! Listen, cunt, it's called fucking. Fucking. You make love to your lover. You fuck a cunt."

My stomach heaved. "I might be sick."

He stopped the car with a lurch. "Outside."

64

"I'm okay," I said, humiliated. I got out and stood for a moment by the car. And I thought; he's right. If you call things what they are, you are less likely to make them into something else. Words can fool you, but only if you let them.

I got back in and he said, "You're kidding yourself. Some girls are born cunts. That's you. Jesus, that's you."

Shame licked at me like fire. What he said was true.

"We'll try a little experiment," he said. "We'll wait until you want it again. You call me, any weeknight. I won't call you. You have to ask for it, next time."

"Never!" I said. But I was wrong.

PART III

4.

ABILENE got up late one morning, washed a few things, and took them out on the terrace to drape over chairs to dry. Below on the street, Michael Sage was coming toward the building. She dropped a pair of panties to the sidewalk and called his name. There was no one else in sight. What Mexican would want to be seen near him? He was so tall! He looked up and saw her. She pointed to the underwear. He scooped up her fallen laundry and waved it above his head, shouting something she couldn't hear. She ran down the stairs and buried her face in his chest. "I don't believe it," she said half a dozen times. He put his hands in her hair.

They made love, and after, lay watching the sun pool on the floor beside the bed. "Shit!" Sage said. "What is it?" Abilene asked timidly. Her manner made him laugh at her. "In Claude Girard's apartment," he said. "In his goddamned bed!" Abilene laughed with him at that.

They went to the Plaza Garibaldi and made their way through the bustle to a sausage vendor. They ate, drank beer, and talked about what they saw going on around them, as if in naming things they made them matter. "It makes me dizzy after a while," Sage said. "How I hate cities!"

"But what have you done in Mexico?" Abilene asked. She had been wondering how they would pass the day. It was a relief to discover—and a surprise, too—that he had never done anything in the city. He had never been to Chapultapec or Xochimilco; he had been to none of the museums; he had in fact only been to the city to do business with bureaucrats. He said his eyes stung, and the noise was driving him wild.

She took him to the park. "On summer Sundays there are a million people here," she told him. They found a spot in the shade near a pond where children were calling to ducks and the children's parents were laying out a picnic.

Abilene saw that Sage was watching the children.

"Do you see your kids? Do you miss them?" she asked.

"No. Yes, sometimes. They're in Houston. I'm going to go soon for a week and take them over to the gulf, to Padre Island. I wish you could come. White sand, no buildings."

She didn't think it was a real invitation.

"Then I've got to get back to work. Actually I shouldn't go at all, shouldn't leave the ranch. But she thinks I won't come to see them. She thinks I'll just send money and leave them alone. It's what she wants, and if I skip a summer, she'll say I don't want them, and that they're forgetting— Shit."

Abilene didn't understand the feelings Sage was talking about; she didn't think her father had ever missed her. Of course she'd been much older. She'd had her time.

Sage went on with his earlier train of thought. "I've got my foreman staying in the house twenty-four hours a day while I'm gone."

"Is something wrong?"

"Oh sure something's wrong. The whole damned place is turning into a funhouse. The clutch went out on a jeep and it ran right off into the river. Of course the water's only fifteen inches high, and nobody was hurt, but what a nuisance! And then there have been problems with the generator. That's not new, but so often! And more serious things. Tonio's keeping brave bulls at his father's ranch now, adjacent to mine, and some asshole left a gate down. One of my men was gored—"

"That doesn't sound quite right!"

Sage looked at her sharply. "Meaning what?"

She had steered them into a bad place. "I just meant, anything Tonio does is usually taken care of. Gates—"

"Well this one wasn't!"

"Come on, let's go to the museum. Look, it's almost time for the afternoon squall. Everyone is getting out of here."

He wasn't interested in old things. He wanted to talk. They bought beer and went back to Claude's apartment. Abilene dreaded talking. "How long can you stay?" she asked when they were just inside the door. She held her keys in her hand as though she expected to let him out again in a moment. He looked at her so oddly, she was suddenly embarrassed, and went around pushing things into place to cover the embarrassment.

"Today, tomorrow. I'll take the Thursday plane back."

"What do you have to do while you're here?" She assumed he had business.

He looked disgusted. "I came to see you, woman. What did you think I was here for?"

She thought: At least Tonio never asks me questions! Never pushes me to say things!

The truth was Tonio wasn't interested in what she thought about anything, she knew that. He'd never wanted to know about her life, her family. Oh, he'd wanted to know about her sex life. "Tell me about all the boys," he'd put it. "And girls, too, if there were any!" He said it so playfully, relished the good parts, cut her short when he was bored. So was Sage so different? she thought angrily. He'd asked the very same things!

At least he hadn't interrupted. He'd seemed genuinely interested. When she had asked him about his youth, he had told her long anecdotes about girls in high school, his boyhood's easy lays. She'd tried not to show how deeply shocked she was at the careless way he trotted those girls out: gang-bangs after baseball games; once a girl, blindfolded, sorted out the names of five of them. There hadn't even been the gentling effect of ruefulness in his telling; it was palaver without compassion. She'd felt choked on it before he was done.

Remembering gave her a reason to be angry. "Christ!" she said. "How would I know what you came for? Who ever went across town to see me?!" She kicked a pillow across the room and went around turning on all of Claude's stupid little lamps. It had begun to rain hard. The bare windows looked slick with dying light and water.

He was looking at her, trying to figure her out, she knew. When Tonio looked at her, he looked right through her, like there was nothing in there to stop his gaze. Sage gave her more credit; he thought there must be some reason for the way she acted. She couldn't explain herself, though, and that was the end of that.

She went to the kitchen window and put her hand on it. The keys, still hanging off her thumb like a toy or a talisman, rang against the glass. "There's wind," she said.

Sage went to her and made her put everything down on the counter: the beers she had opened for them, the keys. "I want to get things settled between us," he said very quietly. She wondered if that had the ring of ultimatum, if he didn't know you had to start at the beginning, *where she had never ever been.* She waited curiously to hear what he had to say. He looked at her, looked and looked, and he didn't speak. She picked up a beer again and went in and sat on the floor. He drank his beer standing above her, noisily, with defiance. Tension lay on them like the air before the summer monsoon. She didn't know what would come. She had to break the silence.

"Aren't you going to ask what I'm doing here? Aren't you even curious?"

He sat down, shrugged. "Girard said it was female trouble."

She blinked. "Oh he did?" And who told him? Sage had registered no emotion whatsoever, as if he had said the jeep had a flat.

Oh what would you say! she thought. If you knew. If you only knew!

"And my face? Didn't you notice?"

"Yes, but I didn't know what to say. What's it all about? What happened to you?"

"It was for the scars, Sage. Don't you see?" She leaned closer and ran her finger along the line she knew lay beneath her eye, where the scab had stopped. She thought he would put his finger there then, and such a gesture, tender, would pull them together, but he didn't.

"A favor from Velez?"

She pulled away. "Of course. You didn't think I paid for it with green stamps, did you?"

"Shut up." He began to make love to her on the floor. Sounds of protest rose in her throat and she swallowed them again. His roughness worked as she had thought tenderness would; she moved beneath him, though her back hurt against the bare floor.

"Come back with me," he murmered. "Come back now."

She moved her hands.

"I love you, Abby." She felt that he was close to climax. It made her shiver. Now he would move faster, urgently, pushing away all her thoughts. "I love you!" he said again, and this time she heard, and it stopped her cold. Her hands were caught, one on his shoulder, the other low on his back. Her hips would not move. "What's wrong?" he breathed into her hair. He sounded a long way away.

When she didn't answer he moved and lay on his side. "So where did you go, lady?" he asked in a tight low voice. He put his hand along the side of her jaw and pulled her face to make her look at him. "I said, *what's going on?*"

She was thinking: he didn't say that before. Nobody ever has said that. Oh, he'd said he loved her, in April, but it was part of some silly argument he was posing, it wasn't like this, at such a moment—

She didn't believe him.

"I don't know, Sage," she said miserably. She shook her head to clear it.

"No? No you won't come? No I don't love you? No you don't love me? What are you shaking your head for?"

"It's too—hot—" she gulped. "The doctor says I can't go back to the Huasteca until after the rains."

"I don't mean that! What just happened? Talk to me. Damn you, Abby, you talk to me."

There was nothing to say.

She could feel his anger vibrating between them. She knew exactly where it would take them.

"You know what I want to know," he said. Venom was seeping into his voice.

She shook her head again.

"Oh, you do too. Don't be a bitch."

She felt so weary. "If I say I love him, you'll go away. Won't you?"

"What else? What would be the point after that?"

73

"So."

"So is that what you're saying? Is that what I came to fucking Mexico City to hear?"

He had played Judy Collins and Joan Baez records for her. He had made spaghetti for her, and he had made her laugh. He even made her laugh at Claude Girard, pompous as he was.

"I'm not saying that! Don't push me! Listen. If I say I never loved him, I'm the whore everyone says I am. You'll despise me for that."

"I don't think anybody could love him!"

"If I say I *did* love him, even if I don't anymore, you'll make a cancer of it. You'll let it eat you up. How could I love a man like that? That's what you'll think, what you'll say. You're thinking of his vanity, his cruelty." *You're jealous.*

"I'm thinking this is the craziest thing ever. I was making love to you, Abby. I was *fucking* you—"

That was it. "Which were you doing?" she asked him. What she knew was that everyone who knew Tonio wanted to get back at him.

"I wish I had known—" she began, looking away. Sage was pulling on his pants. "I wish I'd known how miserable—" He opened another beer; the sound of the cap coming off was like a gunshot. He sat down beside her and she said, "If I had it all to do again, I'd go to all the boys—the ones with the glasses and plaid shirts, the ones who worked with their dads digging fence holes, or in the fields—they had burned raw faces all year round, they didn't talk to anyone at school, not ever. I'd go to each of them, one by one, and I'd make love to them. I'd hang out with them." She wanted him to know she didn't take any of it back—her past, her mistakes. She was who she was.

She could see by the look on his face that he didn't have any idea what she was talking about.

In the morning he said, "You can come to the ranch whenever you want. When you feel ready. I know how you feel about the Huasteca, that you love it like I do—"

"Sage, I—"

"Shhh. He's not your father, Abilene. He's certainly not your husband. You can do whatever you want to do."

She shook her head yes, to satisfy him. He didn't see that Tonio was both those things, and more, and less.

Sage said he didn't have a house in Tampico anymore, but he often stayed in a hotel there. They kept mail for him. She took the address. She understood that he didn't want her to write him at the Arcadia anymore. She gave him Adele's address. They were like spies setting up drops. It was absurd.

She thought of all the things she hadn't said, hadn't known how to say, and should have said: That his ranch wasn't his ranch at all, but Tonio's. That even if it were, they would still be under Tonio's shadow there. That if she didn't go back to the Tecoluca, she couldn't go back at all.

That she didn't think she knew Sage, and yet he wanted her to hand her life over to him exactly as she had handed it to Tonio.

That she hadn't decided if she wanted to live without Tonio. Oh, that was the heart of it; that was why they couldn't talk about it; that was what Sage knew and hated.

She thought: Maybe if I leave Tonio that will be all that Sage really wanted, and where will I be?

She touched his face, kissed him, felt his arms around her, and he was a stranger.

They went to Xochimilco, the floating gardens. She scooped a flower out of the water and as Sage watched, she plucked away the petals one by one and collected them in her lap.

"Is this a flower?" she asked, gesturing with the stem in one hand, "or is this?" she said, scooping up petals with the other hand.

"I didn't ask for a fucking Zen lesson!" he growled. She knew he was terribly frustrated with her. He had made such a romantic gesture, and she was not taking it up as he had planned.

"Oh you did," she whispered back. "Yes yes yes, you surely did, Michael Sage." She dropped the bits of flower. She was twisting her thin gold bracelet around and around her wrist— the bracelet Tonio had given her. *As if she could really choose!*

"I don't know what to do," she said. There was so much dead space inside her, it crowded her heart. Sage, sullen now,

couldn't help. He had said, "We're so much alike, you and I."
She was afraid he was right. Neither of them was good enough
to bring the other along.

Sage wrote in a few weeks. He had seen his children in
Houston but hadn't taken the time to go camping. He was
nervous about the ranch, and he had come back to problems.

> *I don't like it. I'm a careful man. Things are going wrong that I
> can't control. There's a maverick wildcat that has come down
> several times. He's killed two steers. My two maids had a quarrel,
> over one of the cowboys, and one stuck a paring knife in the other's
> arm. I took the one to the hospital, and sacked them both. Then I
> hired the hurt one's mother because I knew she would be grateful
> and work hard. She is fat and ugly; aren't you glad? Oh, Abilene,
> I'm feeling tired. I'm going to see the kids again and try to have a
> good time. Are you thinking of us?*

Abilene couldn't think how to answer. Other things were
going on. She felt less desperate; maybe it was because of
Adele, and all the people around her. She did start a letter.

> *Things have always happened to me just because they did. I
> never felt like I had that much to say. I feel I'm in the middle of
> something and I can't see past it. I don't think it's Tonio. He seems
> vague right now. Maybe it has to do with my body, with things
> being done to me, with getting well. I need to get a feeling for
> myself. Most days I think it doesn't matter how I feel, as long as I
> stay afloat.*
> *I see Isabel, remember her from the* tienta? *She had the good
> hash. Here she's a businesswoman, very organized.*
> *I hope you have a good time with your children on your white
> island. Does it not have trees, either?*

She didn't know how to close the letter. She didn't know
what to say. She signed her name and sent the letter to Tampico. She stopped thinking about him. She tried to pay attention to what was going on where she was.

Abilene was fond of Isabel, and glad for her company. Isabel's amiability, generosity, and love of a good joke were

endearing. At the ranch she would make a good time when none seemed in the offing. She had a ready zest for cards or fishing, for scary midnight rides in the jeep, for a good loud drunk or a silly high. Tonio scoffed at her behind her back and called her a city tramp, but Abilene had seen Isabel make him laugh. Isabel had known Tonio a long time. She remembered when he was part of a club of silly rich men who outfitted themselves in opulent costumes to ride in parades, and then vacationed in Acapulco, harvesting pretty girls like fruit from a tree. She remembered his crush on a famous American movie star, older than he, who said—in public!—that he was too short and wore his pants too tight. When Isabel told Abilene that, she laughed until the tears ran. She said that when the actress spurned Tonio, he courted her daughter, until the girl went home with him one night. There he cajoled her into his bed ("He had a mink bedspread then! He had mirrors on the ceiling!") where, as the scene grew intense, she suddenly screamed in pain, and had to be taken to the hospital to have her appendix removed!

Isabel always had a story. She said it was forbidden to be a free woman, as she was, in Mexico. She would never make a good marriage. "But someday I will have a little boutique in a quiet zone, selling American jeans and sexy tops. I'll have handsome boys who work for me until they get too smart and I have to get new ones fresh from the country." Isabel winked, talking about that. "I'm in charge of my life, Abby, don't worry."

Abilene went along on Isabel's dizzying round of collections. She watched her get her money from a delinquent vendor, while Abilene carved her nail into a lime, releasing the warm sharp smell into the drenched market air. She went with Isabel into a church where Isabel lit candles. "One for my mother, who is pious, and one for me, if I should die without absolution." Abilene said nothing; she thought Isabel was strangely serious.

Now they rode in Isabel's little yellow Fiat, rattling and bouncing through the streets toward the university. They were going to fetch Isabel's little sister Ceci, who made their mother worry when she did not come home at night.

"I tell my mother it is nothing," Isabel was saying. "Ceci likes to stay near the campus in the Tlatelolco development. It's a long way home by bus. She stays with my mother's cousin Ofelia. Her apartment looks down on the Plaza of Three Cultures. Lots of students live there with their families. Across the way there are government offices.

"My sister likes it out there because it is noisy and smelly and busy, and our house is stuffy and quiet. The other night Ceci and my mother quarreled, and my mother said, 'You girls are not like we were,' and Ceci said, 'I hope not. You sat around in chaperoned rooms teasing and promising, and then you kissed in the corners, on the sly, for deceit, and not for fun.' She made my mother cry. Why are we so cruel when we are young? It's bad enough that Ceci sings songs in English, like 'Fool on the Hill,' and 'Bye-by Love.' Now, my mother thinks, Ceci will ruin herself as I did, and nobody will want her. Ah, my mother knows so little about the modern world."

Along the streets, the buildings shone as sun struck stone like mirrors. Isabel chatted for miles, telling about her mother's cousin, Ofelia, and her daughter and grandson who lived with her, and her son, Jamie, in Lecumberri.

"Lecumberri. What is that?"

"The old prison." A drop of sweat ran a path down the side of Isabel's nose and fell onto her upper lip, where it clung like dew on the dark hairs. She was driving very fast, playing the traffic like a taxi driver. "The *granaderos,* the riot police, picked him up for painting a slogan on a wall. *People, Open Your Eyes.* He was good in math, and a draftsman. He was supposed to be study-ing engineering, but all he could think about was the move-ment. He's very earnest! Now, for eight months, he sits in Lecumberri, and his mother paints his slogans for him, and forgives him the lost opportunity. She says to everyone, "Look around! Open your eyes."

"You talk like he's dead—for painting a sign?"

"It is an article in the penal code. If you disturb the peace with threats of violence, the *granaderos* can take you off the streets. A snap of the fingers, and there goes another foolish student.

"They say the Revolution was a joke, and they're right. But

what will change? Leftists will never win over the country. Antonio Velez' wealth will never be redistributed. Look at me. I dream about a boy's tight bum and my own shop. These children dream about democracy. Bah."

The excursion had seemed jaunty. Now Abilene turned her head toward the window and wished Isabel would stop talking. She had a hard, unfamiliar feeling in her stomach, a kind of fear. It was as though Isabel was driving her somewhere, not for Isabel's purposes, but for hers. Taking her to a place she ought to be, a terrible place where she deserved to be. She realized she was thinking of the murdered girl. Sylvia, if that was her name. Sometimes terrible things happened because you looked for them.

She turned her head sharply, to listen again to Isabel.

"Ceci loves the boys, the excitement. She talks politics and boils coffee. She talks about Puebla and Juarez and Tabasco, to prove that the movement is spreading. Then she rides around in the nice cars of her girlfriends, putting up posters. Afterwards they go to coffeehouses to flirt.

"My mother doesn't believe me when I tell her Ceci is safe, and my mother is right, but for the wrong reasons. Ceci isn't interested in sex. She's in love with the rhetoric about opening up the university and the government. She doesn't understand the consequences of the games they are playing. She doesn't know she's in the middle of it. What will her virginity be worth in jail?"

Abilene rode the rest of the way in silence. The city belched and sputtered. The sky hung close in a sodden fog of bus exhaust, factory smoke, and the wetness of the imminent afternoon squall. Abilene thought, the city has a pulse, a desperate feeling to it. She thought maybe that was all she wanted, to hear the rhythm of the city, and maybe then to dance.

She followed Isabel into the building. Immediately they were assaulted, in the dark hallways, with the rich fetid smells of people, food, and wastes.

All I've ever been is a tourist, she thought.

What did she know about how people lived?

Ofelia's apartment was cramped. They went into a room with

no window, a room crowded with makeshift cooking arrangements, a cot, a table, some benches. A woman scuttled out, pulling her scarf along the side of her face. Isabel embraced her aunt and patted Ceci's cheek with her palm. Ceci introduced a young woman, an American art student, as "Alley," or so it sounded. The girl laughed and said, "I'm Hallie Livaudias, what about you?" *Abilene* was hard for Mexicans, too. Sometimes, she said, they called her Abelita.

Posters lay in neat piles under the cot. FREEDOM FOR PO-LITICAL PRISONERS, one said, and another, PEOPLE UNITE DON'T ABANDON US. And Jaime's message, OPEN YOUR EYES. Ofelia looked at Abilene. "Are you a student, too?" she asked.

Abilene shook her head. "A tourist."

Isabel began to scold Ceci. "You must come home. I promised Mama you would be there for supper. She is making a *molé* for you. You can't disappoint her."

Ceci shrugged. "I'll go, but I'm coming back in the morning. We've got so much to do. Soon it is the anniversary of the Cuban revolution. We're making banners." She stared at her sister boldly. "You must come. You must think more about politics, about your country."

"*You* think about politics," Isabel replied grumpily. "*I* will think about the money we need."

"I don't like *molé*," Ceci grumbled, but with her chin tucked down.

Isabel asked Ofelia, "Has she gone to her classes?"

"Of course! History and philosophy—that is your schedule, yes, Cecita?"

Ceci lifted her head again and stuck her chin out like a defiant child. "I ask questions. I challenge the professors. My philosophy professor said to me today, 'Can't you get a summer cold, *Señorita*, and give me a break?' He was joking. Don't you think it is good to be in a class with a professor who has a sense of humor?"

Isabel was neither amused nor impressed. "If that is what it takes to teach you, let them all be clowns," she said. Abilene sensed that Isabel was tamping down her annoyance only because of her aunt's presence. It was a side of Isabel Abilene did not know. "You have no right to miss classes," Isabel said. "We are not rich people, you cannot be idle."

"I told you I go!" Ceci's impatience colored her cheeks and made her eyes sparkle. She was much prettier than her plump older sister. "I have free time," Ceci said. "I am not a slave to my studies! And it is my business if I spend it here, doing what needs to be done."

Isabel pointed to a pot of paint. "Do you know that this is serious business?"

"Of course!" Ceci pointed to her aunt. "How could we not know, think of Jaime. It is the most important business of all," she said, with the absolutism of the young.

Hallie said quickly, "Can I have a ride back to the Zócalo or the Zona? I'll get my things—?" As soon as she was out of the room Ceci turned to Isabel. "You are not my mother! You have no right to order me around!"

Isabel had regained her composure. "I am your sister, and I pay your expenses, do not forget that. That is enough authority. Now we need to go." Isabel gave Ceci a hard look, and Ceci tossed her head this way and that like a tethered pony. Isabel went over to sit by Ofelia and put her arm around her.

"I brought you fruit and candy, and dried beef," she said, pointing to a bag she had laid on the floor. "And I have a treat for little Jorge, where is he?"

"Downstairs, playing in the plaza."

"We'll see him on our way out," Isabel said. Ofelia seemed enormously pleased. "You are so good to us," she said. At that, Ceci looked away. As they all stood to embrace good-bye, Ofelia said to Abilene, "You must favor us again to come; you can help us. Americans, they have such good health and so much strength. It comes from your good food, no?"

Abilene put her hand out to shake Ofelia's hand. In the hot room, the woman's cool palm was a surprise. Abilene felt alien, as though her green scales had not been peeled away. Hallie returned with a stuffed shoulder bag. Behind Abilene, on the stairs, she spoke quietly. "It's been a hell of a year, hasn't it?" she asked. Abilene said nothing. "Losing Kennedy. That almost did me in," Hallie went on. Abilene didn't say how late she had been to know about the murder. Felix had brought her a magazine with Robert Kennedy on the cover: Second Son Shot.

In the sunlight Hallie touched Abilene on the shoulder. "How long have you been in Mexico? Where are you from?" Abilene recoiled, reminded of all the times she had been interrogated by other Americans on beaches, in shops and lobbies. No one had been interested in her in Texas.

"I've been here a long time. I'm not much in touch with the news." She took a long step and they were on the plaza. "I'm from Texas," she added, trying to be pleasant. She put her hand up to shade her eyes.

"There's Jorge," Ceci said, waving violently. A little boy of seven or eight ran toward them.

"I left something with Grandmother for you," Isabel said. "But you must give her a special kiss before you ask." The boy looked disappointed. Isabel, laughing, reached into her purse and held out her hands, juggling her bag. Fists closed, she asked the child, "Which hand?" It was an old joke with them. He brightened immediately and tapped both fists. The hands opened to reveal bright jewels of sugar. When he smiled, Abilene saw that he had a new tooth coming in. He ran back to his friends, a candy in each cheek.

The three women stood in the sun for a moment, disoriented. There was a dreary, worn-out feeling to the plaza. The trees seemed to have relinquished their color to the drabness of the government buildings. Abilene gazed at the ancient church of Santiago Tlatelolco, and at the doors of a shabby convent nearby. One edge of the plaza was ragged, dropping to ancient stones, the cropping up of antiquity.

Hallie reacted to Abilene's slightly puzzled look. (Abilene was noticing how the plaza was blocked in by buildings, with only alleys out.) "Look," Hallie said. "There we have the sixteenth century, and behind us, the present. Under us, the Aztecs." She was smiling broadly. "Three cultures! Tourists come here all the time and stand, just like us, waiting for the meaning of it to come clear." She was half-laughing, and her voice had a sweet bell-like quality. She seemed very young.

"Great slaughters took place here," Isabel said solemnly. "And feasts of human flesh. No one has ever had quite the taste for blood that the Aztecs had."

"But why!" Abilene asked before she could think that it did not matter.

"Their gods demanded it," Isabel said, and added, "And— *because*." She frowned. "Because it was the way it was. The way it is."

"Oh Isabel!" Ceci cried. "You can't miss a chance to scold. I know what you mean to say. You're warning me about the university, about Cuba Day, about all of it. *The way things are*. Say what you like, that isn't the way it ought to be! And it doesn't have to be that way!"

Hallie walked near the edge and stood looking down on broken temple ruins. In a perky voice she said, "Don't you think the Aztecs are terribly overdrawn? I much prefer the art of the Mayans. It is elegant, where the Aztec is bulky—"

Isabel was near laughter. "Come on, ladies," she said, leading them to her car. Her suppressed laughter gave her voice a percolated quality. "You have been to your lectures, haven't you?"

Hallie was unperturbed. "Oh yes, and to the museums. And—" she gestured back toward the project— "to your real life, or some part of it. But now what I'd really like is to go to Denny's and have a hamburger!"

At that Isabel smiled, kindly.

"My father would crap if he knew what's going on down here," Hallie confided when she had eaten her cheeseburger. Abilene, expected at Adele's at eight for dinner, settled for Hallie's discarded potato chips.

Hallie twirled a straw in her glass. "He's so uptight lately. One night I came upon him reading, and he had tears in his eyes. He looked at me so sadly, and he said, 'Hallie, neo-Marxism is dead.' God! You look up to your father as somebody who has matured into, well, if not wisdom, at least equanimity."

Hallie was in motion as she spoke. She fiddled with the

straw, refolded her napkin and then opened it again, used her fork to move a pickle around on the platter. She fingered the buttons on her blouse.

"My poor dad. He's just out of step," Hallie continued. "All my life we've eaten beans on Friday night, to think about the hungry, and we've sent off our family checks to charities. I grew up on the word liberal. But that's a joke! Liberal is absolutely right of where it's at. I mean, Johnson is a goddamned liberal! And he thinks he can buy off the Vietcong with Texas cows! Well, we've had it! We want a government that doesn't lie to us, doesn't take away other people's right to choose for themselves."

"I'm surprised your father let you come down here. I'd think he wouldn't want you out of his sight."

"He thinks I'm studying Spanish and making ceramic pots. It was his idea. He didn't want me to spend the summer in Berkeley. The movement there is getting very bad press."

"You aren't making pots, though, are you?"

Hallie made a face. "How could I? There's so much going on! I do go to the museums, I'm taking art history. But it's the streets that have the real art. You know, in Berkeley when we had a demonstration they'd always say, oh they're just spoiled brats. It was hard to argue, even if it wasn't true. But these kids, what can anybody say about them except that they're pure and brave and smart. I love them."

She pushed her dish toward the edge of the table. "My friends would barf to see what I just ate. Are you vegetarian?"

Abilene said, "I eat whatever is set in front of me." Hallie seemed befuddled by the answer. Abilene thought only how true a thing she'd just said.

It was six, a time when nobody was out. Shops were closed; clerks sat on folding chairs and napped. In their homes, wealthy women lay on beds with clean sheets, waiting to dress for the evening. Impulsively, Abilene asked Hallie along to Adele's.

They went to Claude's apartment to wash up. As they went out again, Hallie said, "It's been an amazing year. I used to think history was what had gone by. Now I know it's as recent as this morning, and it hauls you with it, scraping you across stones. It's been a shitty year, really." Then she brightened. "But it's only half over. Anything could happen. Wait to see what happens in Chicago, at the convention. God I wish I could be there, but my dad would kill me first." As they walked, Hallie's step lightened, grew almost bouncy. "I feel it, I swear I smell it." She took Abilene's hands and swung her around like a schoolgirl. "Life!" she cried. "Change!" She slipped her arm into the crook of Abilene's and drew her close "It's like a warm wind. This is the best of all places to be."

A thousand street lamps suddenly came on.

"You see!" Hallie exclaimed. "You see!"

Hallie was welcome at Adele's. Dinner was informal: piles of *sopa seca*, ropes of sausages, hard rolls and fruit. The playwright Simon Augusto was there with an actress from the Belles Artes, Elena Ybarros. Soon after the two women arrived, a professor and writer came in within moments of one another. The writer, Arturo Reza, sometimes worked with Daniel; they often referred, in a kind of shorthand, to their shared experiences.

Abilene ate little and fed on talk. The room had the disjointed sound of an orchestra warming up—tension, crescendo, but no melody. The actress Elena tossed her hair when Simon looked her way, and laughed at his sarcastic jibes at God, the Revolution, Art. When they had drunk several bottles of wine and cleared away the food, the talk became more intense. They rambled among topics: the deterioration of the Mexican film industry into cheap, banal mass entertainment. Rumors of a lynching in a northern state. The pervasive "Americanization" of Mexican culture through Televisa. The chaos of sprawling migrants' slums. The price of coffee. Minor but frequent student commotions. In Spanish, so many words of disconsolation had the mournful sound of a gypsy song, and they came easily, like verse.

Pola sat at one end of the high-ceilinged room with her handwork on her lap. She had a sulky, dusky look to her, dark eyes that looked you over and rejected you, thought you too common. Though she smiled at Abilene when Abilene first arrived, she never said anything to her. She didn't speak to anyone until just before she went to bed. She said, "If you change the world, don't wake me until morning. I want to be surprised." Daniel looked unhappy. Adele rose to go to her daughter, but Daniel pulled her back.

The actress, always flirting with Simon, freshened drinks and made a great occasion of each walk across the room. She had a modest bosom and a shapely waist, but her buttocks were very large, and she swayed from side to side so that they moved provocatively under her clingy dress. When she thought she knew something pertinent, she stood perfectly still and recited bits of dialogue, once a speech of several minutes. No one reacted, except for a muffled giggle from Hallie. Abilene did think Simon was especially alert when Elena was near; once when she stood near him he pulled her to him and planted his face into the flesh of her buttocks. Hallie jabbed Abilene in the thigh and stifled a laugh with her hand. Abilene thought ashamedly of how it must have looked to others, all those times Tonio touched her so intimately in front of others, pinching or fondling, and always so casually, not even bothering to look. On a boat in Acapulco, she had seen someone Tonio knew put his hand down into a girl's bikini bottom and hold it there while he ate shrimp with his other hand.

When Elena turned, Abilene saw her eyes were bright, saw how Elena had liked the vulgar affection.

Simon's "kiss" had come at a moment's silence; now everyone sat awkwardly with nothing to say. When Hallie realized this, she seized center stage. She had been interjecting remarks all evening, with more and more aplomb. At first they had all spoken Spanish, but as so often happens when the languages are mixed and everyone is bilingual, they switched to English after a while. Hallie talked on and on. The Berkeley scene. Girls with flowers in their hair and their breasts loose under gauzy blouses, music and theatre in the streets, demonstrations and protests.

"There's such an appetite for revolution there!" she said, as if revolution were a particularly spicy curry. "It's not enough to go around without a bra!" Elena burst out laughing, and Abilene felt herself blush. Hallie went on. "It won't be enough until it means something to peasants in Vietnam, to black mothers in Oakland, to the migrants, the poor—"

"A revolution," Simon began in an arched tone. "It does clean out the intestines."

Hallie quickly challenged him. "Isn't it our business? Isn't it serious business?"

"To do what?" Simon asked lazily.

"To speak for those who have no power."

"It depends. Have you asked them what they want?"

"We're talking about food, shelter, *civil rights!*"

Arturo Reza spoke softly, like a mother to a child. He said they knew something of such things in Mexico. "Though we are bored with our poor. They need so much, and they are so many."

Hallie was undeterred. "You're—intellectuals—aren't you? Educated men? Lucky men? You can't squat on your education, your good fortune—" She paused to breathe noisily.

Simon interrupted before she could speak again. "Arturo here was in prison almost three years, after the railroad strikes. He was a nuisance, worrying about the rights of workers. In the prison the workers told him his hands were soft. What do you think of that?"

Hallie was young, without cynicism. She turned to Arturo with a gaze of admiration and pleading. "So you know what I mean! And now it's our turn. The young. We've got to stand up for the oppressed who can't stand up for themselves." She pointed at Abilene, whose barking laugh expressed her surprise and dissent. "The world is unfair!" Hallie cried. "Your fight—" this was when she pointed— "and my fight, they're part of the same thing, the reshaping of the world."

Abilene raised her eyebrows comically. "Who, me?" she said.

Simon laughed. "Once they thought a play had to have three acts." He had been drinking heavily. "One big stage. Anything goes. A theatre of the absurd."

Elena went into the kitchen. Simon trailed behind her, cupping his hands low, a few feet behind her bottom.

Hallie sat down, put her chin on her hands for a moment's reflection, and then jumped back up. She paced back and forth across the large room. The wood floor resounded sharply under her steps. "It's not absurd! Not what we're trying to do! What's absurd is the *establishment*. We've got to make them all back down. We're responsible for one another. I can't buy the world the way my parents did—the militaristic, capitalistic, chauvinistic world, hanging out there like a rotting fig." Simon, returned, now stood near her. He jiggled the fresh ice in his drink. She glared at him. "And I tell you this, I accept the responsibility, because my country is the worst of all. It stinks with its rotten politics, stinks with the stench of lynched niggers and clubbed workers. Everything is for money and power. I've got to make my own definition for love and work, for family. I want to be a member of the true human race, of a world nation. What's going on, here, in Mexico—I'm concerned. Didn't my nation help your politicians build progress on the backs of workers? Isn't that what I heard you making speeches about a couple of hours ago?"

Daniel spoke quietly. "You're speaking for the underclass, and no one can accuse you of not caring. But sometimes the oppressed have their own spokesmen, and they say nothing will change except through violence. They say people like you have to die, Hallie."

Dismay flickered across Hallie's face, but she recovered. "Nonsense. They need us." Her face was screwed up in great earnestness. "We can choose sides."

There was a general recess while a jug of wine was found and opened. Simon pressed money into Adele's hands. Hallie stood transfixed (by the possibilities of Daniel's suggestions?).

Abilene was relieved that no one was intent on putting Hallie down. Daniel's exception to her rhetoric had been gentle, though Abilene could see it had affected Hallie. She might have been sport for this cynical circle, with her right ideas, her high purpose, her resolve, but it was her beauty they had attended to. She was lovely in a way that never went out of fashion: long legs, high breasts, strong lines, and that healthy hair that moved like cloth. She walked with the long, hearty stride of an athlete, and sat with the grace of a dancer. She was something Abilene had seen from a distance in school: a secure child. She had always had what she needed, had had enough to give some up. Now she was outraged that others had so little.

Abilene thought that Hallie looked down from too far up to see how many layers there were below her. She took too many people in with her, made her class occupy too broad a space, made too many people responsible. Had Abilene been privileged? Hardly! Had her father perpetrated oppression? The idea was ludicrous; even his death had been petty. Abilene found that she liked Hallie, despite the differences in their backgrounds, but she also found that she was edgy with resentment, to be accused in Hallie's silly assessment of Abilene's place in the world. Abilene thought: She should know what my world is like! She should watch who she hangs around with!

Simon consulted with Daniel and put on records. The jazz they chose made Abilene nervous. It too keenly reflected her own emotional tenor. She didn't want to be in the middle of all this disconnected discussion. She wanted to talk to Adele.

Simon pulled Elena to her feet and tried to dance with her. They touched each other lightly, like blind people, and then suddenly clasped and began dancing without moving their feet. It was quite a display. Gilberto, the professor from the University, rose and gathered glasses off the floor. "It's past midnight," he said in Spanish. "I've got classes in the morning."

Hallie whirled toward him. "Oh, God, me too!" she said. "Art History at ten. Do you have a car?"

They consulted. Gilberto lived in an old section not too far from the university. Hallie was boarding with a family in the elegant Pedregal colonia, built on a lava bed, a little beyond. Gilberto said he would take her home.

Hallie wanted to make a date with Abilene for the next day.

"I don't know what I'll feel like," Abilene said weakly. Hallie ignored her. "Museum of Anthro, the fountain, two p.m.," she said. "We'll eat something, and I'll take you to meet some of my friends. It'll be fun." She looked at the others. "It is all very exciting, you know, the consciousness of the students." No one laughed; in fact they looked solemn and approving. Simon said, "Gilberto is an economist." Hallie took Gilberto's arm as they left.

As soon as the door shut after them, Simon said, "Think what she would be like in harness, or in bed." Abilene was a bit shocked. The actress snickered. Adele said, "Really, Simon, even from you." He defended himself ardently. "I only meant her energy! Her youth and vigor! *Really,* Adele. Is it only pain that provokes you? Only tired old Indian eyes?"

Adele, surprisingly, smiled. "Actually it's enthusiasm that wears me down. When I'm not working, I fidget. When I do work, I'm tense. It's all very tedious."

"Certainly you can't suggest that Adele's sensitivity is over-focused, rolled too tight?" Daniel said. He too was annoyed with Simon. Simon put his hands up to stave off more comment, but Daniel said, "How could that be true, when she's an artist? An artist with ties to the real world, as you must surely know?"

Abilene thought someone hateful could say a lot about that. What was real about high fashion?

"Everyone can't use art for political purposes," Simon yawned. "How boring to always think about what's right."

"Theatre has its own rules, nothing to do with politics," Elena said. "It has only to do with truth and art." She looked smugly toward Simon, who laughed.

Daniel laughed too. "And that's how we sound! Like a cocktail party on stage. In one of Simon's plays we would be undressed, or dead by now. Go home, the lot of you—"

What had seemed a coming quarrel dissolved in embraces and promises for a quick reunion. As Abilene reached for her things, Adele caught her elbow. "But not you, please! Wait." She locked the door and leaned against it. Daniel kissed her forehead and said goodnight.

When he was out of the room, Adele asked, "Are you too exhausted to talk? Really talk, I mean?"

"I'm tired. The evening took—a lot of energy, I guess."

"Oh, them. You're not used to it. It doesn't amount to all that much. That's the way Mexican intellectuals are. Blah blah. They're close to Daniel, you see. They're important to him. We see them all several times a week, it's more like family. Listen, if you can stay a while, you can sleep here. There are cushions and quilts in Pola's room."

"It doesn't matter much where I sleep," Abilene said.

They huddled over cups of cocoa Adele had made them in a bowl in the Mexican way, whipping the chocolate to a froth. Adele kept chewing at her thumbnail.

Abilene asked, "What did you think of Hallie? I only just met her today, you know. It's not like she's a friend—"

"Oh, she's okay. She's probably good for you, all that verve. There are lots of girls like her in Mexico. They say the whole Department of English is made up of fluffy rich girls who like to spend time in the U.S. But these girls—they can work very hard. They have to have something to believe in, just like anyone else."

"Is that what you want to talk about?" Abilene knew she couldn't hold up her own end in a conversation about meaning. She'd been long enough away from the Tecoluca, it was like she didn't have a life at all. Like a battery running down. And if she didn't go back to Tonio— Oh, she wished Adele would tell her what she would do instead! Wasn't that why she'd looked up her old friend, and not just to pass time? It was like the time she raced around Lubbock with her sister-in-law, looking for her dead father's mistress: she'd gotten caught up in the rushing, she'd had a reason for the next hour—

"—Daniel thinks what's going on will be very important." Abilene realized she hadn't heard what Adele was saying. "But that's not what I've got on my mind, not right now. I've been thinking of that American girl, Sylvia Britton—the one who was murdered."

"It happened so close to your house. She was American. It seems natural enough to worry."

"Doesn't it bother you?"

"Now that you ask, yes. It does." Maybe there were things she could tell Adele, she thought. Adele would know what to do. Somebody had to know.

"Wouldn't you think someone would be looking for her? Wouldn't you think she would be *missing?*"

Abilene shrugged. Everyone doesn't have someone.

"Pola heard us talking about it, Daniel and me. She said, 'Well, just because you don't know the story doesn't mean there's not a plot.' What kind of thing is that for a thirteen-year-old to say?"

"I don't know anything about kids."

"She thinks everything is a script for a movie."

"She has a filmmaker for a father."

"Oh yes, her father." The way Adele said this, Abilene thought: It has something to do with blood.

"This last film of his." Adele had fallen back into her chair. "It was sordid. Pretentious and violent. The critics let him tell them what it was about: a parable about revolution. Greece, Cuba, Africa. See? Relevant! The film is about betrayal, he had said. You should see it! There's a girl in it, a young girl. She's kidnapped, raped and murdered. This is parable? Who can argue that the world isn't horrible? But why do they let him posture behind that? This was another romp with one of his child stars, violence reduced to teeny-bopper sexuality." She took a long drink of water. "You don't read magazines, do you? You don't know about him. Child stars are his specialty. High school vamps. Child brides. Gangsters' daughters. He exposes them, like the flesh of guavas cut open for inspection. There are plenty of people who don't like it. Feminists. They picket his films and make him more famous. They give him weight. And they don't even get the point. The girls are incidental, thrown to the public to pant over; the movies are about basic human savagery. The girls are vulnerable and yet inaccessible; they get caught in crossfires. They're victims by chance; chance robs them of their meaning. Martyrs to no cause. It's sick."

"You're bothered about the murdered girl because you don't know why it happened? Do I get it, Adele?" It surprised Abilene, how easily she understood Adele's worry, despite all the words. It surprised her more that Adele should care about such a thing, that anybody would care.

Adele nodded her head bitterly. "There has to be a reason."

Abilene thought of bulls on their forelegs in the dust. Of thumb-sized babies in white enamel pans. Of love.

Adele said, "Yannis says there's meaning in violence. He says it counts for something." Rancor was in her voice. "He ought to know. He has explored it in life as well as art. Come here."

They went into the main room. Adele scrabbled in a box and came up with a file folder. "This has nothing to do with Yannis," she said, "but it has everything to do with violence." She threw the folder on the table. Pictures spilled out: photographs of corpses, some of them laid out with flowers on their chests, others contorted in their last gazes. Some were just kids. One was a woman late in pregnancy, her huge belly like a hill above her.

"We don't ask for these things. They come to us. Sometimes they come in the mail, or we find them outside our door. Sometimes they're left for Daniel at the paper. Braver donors wait in the hallway to shove them into Daniel's hands. These are always women. 'Bless you for what you do,' they tell him. What good does it do? Yet they feel better. Is the meaning not in violence but in numbers? Is the meaning in the record itself? Have they given Daniel a share of the grief, or the guilt? I tell you, Abilene, I can't sleep, I lie awake and ask myself these things—"

"What does Daniel say?"

"I don't ask him."

She tapped a photograph, this one of the pregnant woman. She pulled out another picture, of two young boys lying on the ground in front of a building—boys anywhere from twelve to sixteen years old. "They were students, full of enormous foolish confidence, taking part in a lark, while all the while it was—oh your friend Hallie knew the phrase—it was *serious business*. These pictures are from the provinces. Officials have told Daniel, these pictures have to do with drug wars. Are we supposed to believe that? Oh, here are students. You wait. You'll see them like this here, in the city." She coughed hoarsely. "Lined up like tripe in a market stall, you'll see them."

"Adele—why are you so—so depressed?" She had forgotten her own agenda.

"Pola's father makes death beautiful. What happens to its horror when he does that? Who believes in death anymore? Maybe that's what the pictures are good for!" Adele was weeping now. "These damned kids. They don't know who they're dealing with. This isn't California. If things get hot, girls like Hallie fly home. If she gets picked up, her daddy will come and bribe her way out. Even you've got someplace to go. But these damned kids, don't they know what death looks like?" She gathered up the photographs and took them out of the room. When she returned she had wiped her face and composed herself.

Abilene had spent the moment wondering from what sorts of troubles Tonio would rescue her. It would be a very short list.

"I'm so worried about Pola," Adele said. "She's at the lycée in the mornings, but I can't watch her all the rest of the time. She knows things are getting lively in the city, she hears rumors. She accuses me of not wanting her to have any fun!"

"Maybe I could spend some time with her." Abilene hoped this was what Adele was wanting from her. It was easy enough; the girl intrigued her. "We could go to the movies now and then, a museum, that sort of thing."

Adele seemed pleased. "Tomorrow Elena is taking her down to the theatre for a little tour. Another day, the movies with you—yes, that would help. Oh, I'm so glad you are in the city!" She was nodding, over and over.

"Don't worry, Adele. She just needs something to do. She's just a child."

Adele looked sad and tired. "No one is a child like Pola."

She picked up an allotment of money from Tonio the next morning. Constanzia smiled as if to show off her teeth. It was her way of pretending not to think she was superior.

In the elevator Abilene looked down at her feet and saw how old her heavy *huaraches* looked. She went into the first shoe store she came to and bought an expensive pair of Italian sandals. They took almost all her money. The clerk handed her her old shoes in a bright yellow plastic bag. All through the transaction he smiled at her. So too the clerk at the register, a skinny woman in a scarlet shift. Abilene left the store with their faces in her mind. She knew as soon as she was gone their faces turned cold until the next customer came along. She hated the falseness, the fawning, not because it was false, not because it masked contempt—which it surely did—but because she didn't know how to respond to it. Courtesy put her off guard. Most things did. She was twenty-five years old and she didn't know how to get along with anyone.

She and Hallie went from the museum down the street to a

pleasant cafe. They drank *Cinzanos* and talked. Bits of information fell from Hallie like so much lint. She had travelled in Europe, Mexico, and South America. She spent her last year of high school in Argentina, where an aunt worked for the American embassy. She had a cousin trekking in Nepal. She studied art. She was thinking of joining SDS in Berkeley, or of going to Ohio to live with her grandmother. "They really need leadership there," she said, as if Ohio were an undeveloped country.

"Do you have a boyfriend in Berkeley?" Abilene asked. It was the only reasonable question she could think of.

Hallie smiled. She had had lovers, she said, and, remembering them, she laughed at them and herself too. Going away to school had been like tumbling down a long slope of pillows. She loved school, she loved boys, and she loved the movement. Fortunately, she'd found they went together, so far.

She asked about Abilene, who told a little about Tonio: that he was a rancher and a businessman. That he was away for some of the summer. She was vague. "I'm just doing what I want—"

"Well yes! That's what you must do!" Hallie said; she seemed to think they were speaking of important things.

"You know, I'm not a student radical," Abilene said pleasantly. "I'm not even a student!"

Hallie was being earnest again. "What hasn't hit you, Abby, is the anger. It's anger that sweeps you clean. I envy you, to come to the movement so fresh! It's virgin anger, it will wash over you, sudden, instead of seeping up, like it did for me."

"What is the anger for?" Abilene asked, to humor her.

"Why, for the persecuted and the poor."

"What about me? What if it's me I'm angry about? If I've had a bad time of it myself?" She wasn't certain why she was trying to provoke Hallie, but she wasn't going to base their friendship on something so false as shared dedication to good causes!

"Anger sweeps you clean," Hallie said.

Abilene thought maybe Hallie would take her on as a project. People were always doing that.

Hallie asked, "Your Tonio. Is he like other rich men—cold and powerful?"

"He's a sultan and a magician and a shark. He would really love you."

"Oh, I didn't mean that!"

Abilene knew Hallie did mean that. Somehow that helped.

They rode a bus out to University City. On the way Hallie told Abilene about her boyfriend Refugio, son of a baker. She said, "He's sweet and good, and he kisses me with his mouth closed." This made Abilene smile. "Are you hoping for more?" she asked.

"Oh no. Refugio is icing. The cake is what he's part of—the movement here. You'll see. And maybe you will meet some-one—yes, of course, you must meet Gato. He's older, myste-rious. He would challenge you! He would keep you on your toes!"

"Another student radical? What would we have in common?"

"He's the real thing, Abby."

"What's that?"

"I don't know a word for it. He's not a kid. He's not confused about what he believes. He's so sure. He can be ruthless, you can tell. And he has this quality—charisma! The students really listen to him. He tells them to study ideology and strategy, and wait for the right moment." She seemed very pleased with herself to have remembered all that about Gato.

Abilene asked if he was sexy.

Hallie liked this. "Oh yes, he is! And he doesn't have any special girl as far as I know. He's always in groups, like a pied piper. Actually, I don't think he'd be any good at all at sex. He probably couldn't maintain attention. He has his mind on other things." She paused to search for a word. "He is a visionary."

"What does he see?" Abilene knew what the answer would be.

"Revolution, of course."

To Abilene's dismay, the word stirred her.

"Oh damn!" Abilene said as they went into a building. "I've laid my old shoes down somewhere and lost them." Her new sandals were rubbing blisters. They tried to think back to when she had last had the shoes. She was sure she hadn't left them in the cafe; she thought she remembered them bouncing against her leg on the bus.

"Come on, come on," Refugio said to Abilene and Hallie. "We're starting." He led them down a hallway to a classroom where students were crowded in and everyone was talking. In a moment someone whistled and the room quieted down. "Don't speak," Refugio whispered. "And stay near the door." He left them and went into the crowd.

A man spoke in a soft, compelling voice. He was wearing jeans and a corduroy jacket, a tie loosened at his neck. Abilene noticed immediately the lack of intensification, of embellishment, in his speech. It was like he was saying, *this is too important to exaggerate.* He was talking about change and about how he had been waiting for it.

"When I was your age," he said, "I dreamed about a true revolution. Now I see you hope and dream this same dream. That dream is the heart of the movement. It will beat so loud and strong in the plazas and streets, in the hearts of our people."

A young man stood up and asked, "So you are joining us?"

"I don't have to join! I'm from Poli. I'm from a worker's family. I was born into the movement."

"What do we do?" students shouted.

"Meet with your friends, and then meet with your rivals. Forget your petty differences of ideology, and unite in a common purpose. Vallejo is still in prison. Repression lies like a fog over us. Remember the strength is in solidarity. You must learn to talk to workers and peasants. The movement belongs to us all."

"To Puebla and Juarez!"

"To Cuba and Vietnam!"

"Teachers!"

"Students!"

"Workers!"

"Che! Che!"

The teacher had begun to cry. Tears made his long lashes shiny. He put his hands up and pointed his fingers toward his temples like pistols. "They cannot silence me with fear! I will not let my gray hairs make me weak!"

The shouts began. The true revolution is still to come! The government is run by mummies!

The speaker waited for them to die down and then he spoke at last in the full fervor of a Mexican in love with a cause. "I will never stand apart from students. This is my fight and yours, my wife's fight, and my children's. It is the people's fight!"

Cheers went up in the room. A dark boy with Indian features stood and spoke with the piping voice of a child. "It's time to listen to the voices of the peasants," he said loudly. He raised his arm and saluted with his fist.

"He's just a baby!" Abilene whispered to Hallie.

"Death to the government liars!" someone shouted.

A tall young man called out, "We cannot kill the government! We must free it from the bankers' prison, from the barbed fences of imperialist North America, from the false god of capitalism. We are not *granaderos*, to come in the night with pistols and clubs. We are not corrupt or frightened. We are the true patriots!"

A girl jumped onto a chair. "We won't make revolution in this room, talking about it!" she shouted. "We won't make revolution by fearing blood! We will make revolution in the streets, where the people are." Her long black hair hung in two fat braids over her shoulders. "We must organize for battle. We must form brigades."

"Organize!" someone challenged. "Tell us about it! Will we become our own government, another university? Organization is the blood line of lies and bribes."

"Each of us is no better than a rock thrown at a window!" the young woman retorted. "One by one they are taking us off the streets. They can gag us and bind us and rape us. They can lock us away in prison. And, *one by one*, the people will not know! But together—" She paused dramatically. All the others had been silenced by the power of her speech. "Together we are too strong. Together, in brigades, we are soldiers in a fight for liberation!"

Hallie whispered to Abilene. "I see her everywhere. Her name is Carolina. She lives far away, near Teotihuacan. Refugio says she leaves home before dawn, carrying tortillas for her breakfast. She was studying to become an engineer, but now all her work is for the movement."

Carolina stepped off her chair and the other students gathered around her and embraced her.

Refugio called out from the front of the room. "Watch the boards for notices! Talk to your friends!"

Carolina called out: "Be brave and tireless."

"Isn't she—neat!" Hallie said.

Suddenly everyone was talking at once. Hallie nudged Abilene, and together they went outside and leaned against the building. They were breathing deeply, like two runners. Abilene felt blood at her temples. Her heart raced, and lower, she felt a dampness, an impatience. She felt longing.

To Adele, later, she said, "It really is exciting, isn't it? Not that I understand it, of course."

Adele's face was drawn and pale. "Oh no, it's not exciting. It's frightening. Last night Daniel sat up in the middle of the night, sat up in bed like his name had been called. 'What is it?' I asked. I thought he was ill. 'I've got to start a second copy,' he said, and lay back down. I tell you, something is swelling beyond all space. The other day I came around the corner and there were small boys scuffling. One of them was knocked down and I heard him say, 'I'll call the army, you bastard! I'll tell them you are dirty Fish like Paco's father! I'll see you in prison, you black dirty Communist.' I ask you, Abilene, if it is so big and getting bigger—can we stay out of the way?"

ABILENE DREAMED of the murdered Sylvia Britton. She knew how it might have happened: the woman taunting a Mexican youth, to turn his insults back on him; his sudden violent anger; a blow, to stifle the humiliation.

Tacho had warned her: You American girls. You shouldn't play games with us. Not with Mexican men. Don't think we are stupid because we are not your kind.

Abilene woke, drank a little gin and water, and after, slept without dreams.

She went to see Adele in the morning. "You and Daniel are professionals," she argued. "Don't you want to know what happened?"

Adele said they would ask the hotelkeeper, Javier Piñeda, to call if anyone came looking for Sylvia Britton. She acted to help Abilene, but she was philosophical and distant. "All around me I see violence and death. It makes it harder if you give a victim a name."

Adele asked after the hotelkeeper's son Nando, whom Daniel had once befriended. Piñeda said his son had not learned his lesson well enough; Nando had his head in the clouds.

Adele shook Piñeda's hand. "You will call?" she asked again.

Piñeda regarded the two women with exasperation and wonder. "She was killed by the night, *Señora*. She is one of many."

There were more dreams. Abilene told Adele. "A woman comes out of the dark, under a street lamp. A taxi approaches, and she waves for it to stop. The driver gives her the finger and calls out, 'Hey, *gringa* whore!' "

Adele laughed. "There's nothing frightful about that, Abby. When did it ever kill you to be called a *gringa* whore?"

Abilene looked away. "Doesn't it bother you?" she asked softly.

"There has to be a reason to die like that," Adele said. "Otherwise it could be you. I remember the girls in Vegas used to talk about their dreams all the time. They liked to say, your dream is telling you something. They dreamed about boats and trains and planes; everyone wanted to get away.

"What are you afraid of, Abby?"

Abilene began to cry. "I don't know any people on lists. But I know her."

Tsk, tsk, went Adele's tongue. "Don't I know that?" she said. "Isn't that why the lists matter so much?"

"They're Daniel's lists, though, aren't they?" Abilene said. She thought Daniel must think her very trivial.

"Listen to me," Adele said. She had made tea, and she leaned across the little kitchen table to pour it for Abilene in a white mug veined with cracks at the lip. "The names are just words on a page to me. I say that to you, and to nobody else. I can't live any other way."

Abilene thought she understood, a little. Yannis had made violence so vivid. "But when you met Daniel, did you know he was so—"

"Good," Adele said firmly.

"I was going to say obsessed."

"I was afraid at first, alright. I thought, another well of despair and anger. I thought, by God I won't fall in love with a Marxist!" Adele's laugh was rich and happy and full, a truer laugh than Abilene could remember. "I needn't have worried. He was nothing so pat. He is a modest man. He writes down what people cannot write for themselves. A scribe. I suppose he liked me because I'm much the same, only with images."

"Did he like your work?" Abilene asked. She remembered seeing photographs of peasants in their bright clothes, against a dry hillside.

"He saw more than I meant," Adele said. "He thought I put the models next to the *indios* to make a statement. Does it matter where the impulse comes from? I work from intuition."

Abilene asked to see some of Adele's work. "We've spent our time talking about things I don't know," she said. "You took so many photographs of Pola when we were in Zi."

Adele rose happily and led Abilene back to her studio. She drew out dozens of photographs from a box. There was Pola innocent, Pola seductive, Pola hurt, Pola sleepy. She went from small child at ten or eleven to budding woman at twelve and thirteen. She was immensely photogenic, with her lovely bones and eyes, her high brow and widow's peak, the long slender limbs, her patience and affection for the camera's eye.

"You're so lucky," Abilene said in little more than a whisper. She could not imagine the connection of mother and child. She could not even wish for it; it was that remote.

"You see these—" Adele pulled out several pictures of Pola at her sweetest, her most childlike. "These are the photographs I sent Pola's father. I know I've caught only glimpses of Pola in my pictures. I know she holds things back. And Yannis writes back to me. 'She is uncanny. Look how she shuts us out.' I hated him for saying that!"

Abilene helped Adele stack the photographs and put them away and then they sat, backs against the wall, on the floor.

"Maybe I know part of why you're here, in Mexico, I mean," Adele said. "Because I feel it so much myself. I've always been a stranger, without understanding why. I've always loved places where no one bothers to ask if I belong: Las Vegas, L.A. Here most of all."

"I wonder why the American woman came."

"Like any of us, I suppose." Adele said. "Because it isn't home, and you cannot be blamed for its terrors." She turned to look at Abilene directly. "Daniel changes everything for me, though. He asks the best from me, without demanding anything. He talks about repression and cataclysm, provocation and terror, and I could listen all night. I'm lucky. I told him a long old story about visiting Guatemala with Yannis, and we fell in love! It's like I wanted it to be. People can come together because there is good in them."

Abilene saw for the first time the distance opening up between her and this Adele, this Adele-with-Daniel. She said nothing. Something in Adele's eyes warned her to leave some things unspoken. They both understood the part luck plays in love. They both knew the important factor in the stories Adele and Daniel shared about that poor sad country Guatemala wasn't moral fervor at all, but coincidence.

The hotelkeeper's son Nando called a few days later. He was working the night shift and a man was there looking for the Britton woman.

There were people at the apartment. Daniel and Simon were arguing about a Fuentes novel. Arturo and Gilberto and another of Gilberto's Communist friends were producing a litany of complaints against Mexican artists who, they said, had been led around like dogs on ropes for years, putting the Revolution on the sides of buildings.

Abilene was glad to go out on the street. The evening air was fresh and cool, and Adele seemed eager for the meeting. Abilene wondered if Sylvia Britton might not be a diversion from the steady misery of Daniel's work.

The man who had known Sylvia was waiting in the shabby little lobby in the near dark. Adele asked if he would like to go somewhere and have a drink with them. He looked at Adele and Abilene with suspicion, and with what Abilene decided was a certain greediness of expression. Of course he will want something, she thought. "I'll tell you what I know just now," he said in English. "The clerk said you would pay." He was very good-looking.

Adele gave him some money and told him they would rather speak in Spanish. Carefully, he folded the money away into his wallet, and tucked it into his pants.

"I knew her from the dances. I met her in Acapulco, dancing the line in the red light district." He looked pleased with himself. "I go once a year. I am saving my money to go there and live."

"Was she a good dancer?" Abilene asked.

"Oh yes, she could dance. She stood out, among all the whores and boys, and she was drunk. I told her I was going back to Mexico on the morning bus, and she said she was too. She thought it was a coincidence. So that was how I met her. I showed her this hotel. She said she wanted a hotel for Mexicans, in a safe neighborhood."

"Did you get to know her well?" Adele said.

The young man smoothed his hair with his hand. "I only saw her two other times. We went to dance. I took her to a place with the rokyroll. American music."

"Yes," Adele said. "You know where to go, don't you? Did you come back and stay with her here?"

"Oh no, not in her hotel."

"At your place, then?"

He appeared to be making some decision. He stood up abruptly and said, "She was just a *gringa*. She was an old one, too, maybe thirty. I didn't really like her. She laughed too much."

"But you came to look for her, didn't you?" Abilene asked. The man's eyes turned to her for the first time.

"She borrowed money from me!" he said loudly. "I came to get my money."

Adele reached out and touched him. He put his hand on top of hers, lightly, on his arm. "She owed me money."

"I'm surprised," Abilene said.

He pulled his hand away from Adele. "Because I am a hard-working Indian, and she was a *gringa!* I tell you, she took my money. She said she was waiting for a check from home to arrive. Now I think she lied to me. She took my money to make fun of me."

"Thank you for talking to us," Adele said.

Abilene asked, "What's your name?"

He looked around nervously. "I go to work very early. Now I go home. That girl was no good, even if she was your sister!" He hurried away.

"What did you expect?" Nando asked. He wouldn't take the tip Adele offered. "He has to be hard up, to ask you for money. There's nothing he knows, except how to make a little money from American girls. He was furious when I told him the woman was dead. She did owe him. I'm sure that's why he agreed to talk to you. She owed us rent, too."

"Your father didn't tell me," Adele said.

"Why would he?" Nando shrugged. "Who would pay it?"

"I will. You look it up, and I'll bring the money tomorrow night."

It took Nando a few moments to find the file. He wrote the figure down on a scrap of paper. "She didn't pay her rent for the last two weeks."

"Why didn't your father throw her out?"

"She seemed desperate. She said her check was late. She had long explanations that changed with every telling. I said get rid of her, but my father said no, half the rooms were empty, let her stay. He only cut off her maid service." Nando seemed to think that was funny. "I don't think my father will like it if you pay."

"I will give you the money. By the time he knows, it will be figures in a book. And it will make us feel better. Because she was American, and she had a debt."

"She wasn't worth it. She smoked grass. I told her she couldn't do it in her room, if my father found out he would call the police. She said she was running out anyway. She wanted to know if I could get her more. 'No money, no grass, no fucking fun,' she told me." Clearly, he was disgusted.

"This is Abilene Painter," Adele said. "She lives in the country, near Tampico."

Nando looked over his shoulder at the closed door to his

parents' apartment. "*Señora* Adele, if you want to ask so many questions, why don't you ask about something that matters?"

"What do you mean?"

"Right now, in this city, thousands of students are talking about their rights, and the rights of workers and peasants. Their talk is going to burst into the street. Now there is something worth knowing about! Already some students have been harrassed or hurt or arrested. Some will be killed. They will be heroes, but nobody will look hard for their killers. Why don't you listen to what the students are saying? Why doesn't your husband publish their demands?"

"You bring him a list and I know he'll do what's right," Adele said. "He's not afraid, you know that. As for me, I'm a photographer, not a reporter."

"What is she?" Nando asked, glancing at Abilene.

"A tourist," Abilene said quickly.

Nando's cheeks twitched with intensity. "Then you have picked a time to be here. You will see what it is like when young people will not be held back from hope. And you, *Señora* Adele. You don't have to be a writer to listen. Let the young people speak for themselves."

Adele clasped Nando's hands. "Come to the apartment with your papers," she said. Her eyes were bright. "I'll talk to Daniel."

On the street Abilene said, "Whew! I feel like I'm in on a good spy story."

"You mean Nando? He's in this thing up to his ears. His father will kill him if the *granaderos* don't. But I am going to talk to Daniel about it. I could take the stories, with a tape recorder. If anyone will trust me. With Nando in the middle, maybe they will."

"I want to give you some of the money."

"Money?"

"For Sylvia Britton's bill."

Adele waved the thought away with her hand brushing air. "Don't be silly. What do you have for money?"

Abilene's cheeks were hot. "I have a little of my own here in the city." She felt Adele look at her. "Tonio is going to cut me off soon, I know it," she said in a low voice.

"And what of Sylvia Britton? She's dead. You heard how they talked about her. What did you think of her friend, the dancer?"

Abilene felt pushed, and her answer was brittle. "I thought he was sexy. Nice and skinny in the hips."

Adele said, "I thought it was someone just like him who killed her. But not him. Not if she owed him money."

A few days later, Adele said Nando had come by. He was going to introduce Adele to some of the student leaders.

"What does Daniel think?"

"He said to do what I want."

"And this is what you want? To run around the city asking puffed up kids what they think of government business?"

Adele looked at her curiously. "Why does that bother you?"

Abilene realized with a pang that she was jealous. "It doesn't concern me. What do I know about revolution?

"Isn't revolution just change? Isn't it really just something that happens inside you? One thing dies and another is born?"

"That's damned vague to me!" Abilene snapped. "We aren't all so serious, you know. We aren't all so *good*."

"Don't—" Adele said. She reached out and touched Abilene, and Abilene felt her hand, the way the young man in the hotel must have felt it, as pressure to stay, and to give.

"Isn't there anything you want a lot?" Adele asked gently.

Abilene knew the answer so quickly it scared her. "When I'm all alone in a room, I want to know who's there."

"Oh Abby," Adele said, but Abilene fled. Later, she felt terribly sad, as if Adele had gone around a corner, and disappeared.

5.

FELIX came by to scold Abilene for leaving his apartment, but she suspected his was false objection. "I left word with Tonio's office," she said. "I knew I was inconveniencing you." He kissed her cheek and examined her face carefully. "My brother is very fond of you," he said. "He says your nose on another's face would not work, but on you—" She scoffed at that. "No, truly. He says you are very strong, and he asks me—" he let her wonder for a moment—"He asks when you will leave Velez and make your own life."

"That's hardly his business," she bristled.

"Think of it this way, *chica:* My brother wants something better for you."

"As soon as I decide what it is, I'll take care of it myself. None of you need to talk about it further!"

Felix kissed her nose this time. "I came to tell you that Tonio is in town. He's expecting you this afternoon, after siesta."

The news was like a blow; without moving a muscle, she felt herself reeling. He had become a dream.

"You look like you're going to faint," Felix said. "Come on, I'll buy you lunch."

"I don't want to talk about Tonio."

"Fine. I'll tell you about my new girlfriend. She studies anthropology and has a waist like this—" He held his hands together close. Abilene threw her arms around his neck and held on, to keep from trembling. Felix, kind Felix, waited for her to feel better. Then he fed her linguine with clam sauce in the Pink Zone and said she shouldn't worry. Tonio had missed her, too.

The plump maid let Abilene into Tonio's apartment and whispered that he was resting. Then she waddled off to her own room on the roof. Abilene sat down and undid the straps of her sandals. Her cheeks burned; she tried to cool them with her fingertips, but the fingers were hot, too.

She went to Tonio's room. A fan rustled the satin sheet that lay over him. She closed the door and stood, watching him. The room was softly lit, a room of mauves and roses, a boudoir. Small lamps that looked like candle-lamps hung on each side of the bed. An oval portrait of Tonio in a silvery white *rejoneador's* costume hung near a window. The window was shuttered with soft white slats now closed to block out the daylight; the room was illuminated by the light from the bathroom. Money lay in a porcelain dish. Tonio's watch lay near it on a table. Abilene wanted to go and touch each object; she wanted to regain her familiarity with the man on the bed. If she had known how, she would have called on voodoo.

He lay on his side, one hand cupped under his cheek, the other flung out from his body. He was so beautiful he might have been a marble statue. He had been sleeping. The disorder of the bed suggested that he had been restless, had dreamed, or had not been alone.

At the ranch, Tonio slept behind a locked door, after he sent Abilene away at night. Now he seemed so vulnerable, she felt a surge of tenderness. He will never marry Anne Lise! she thought, nor anyone innocent; how would he fit himself to all the ritual? He would marry a Mexican woman after all, a woman who would accept the way he cut up his existence, the little space she would fill. Instead of relief, Abilene felt immense confusion, as if she had been shaken and then dumped on a wobbly bed. She didn't know what she wanted from this man. She had for so long been his mistress, his child, his pet, she had forgotten how to think for herself. The city, and the time away from him, had shaken sleeping faculties. She remembered long ago, when she had learned so readily the ease of acquiescence. That first failure to say no had led straight to this, from those Texas boys to this man, smaller than any of them, and yet as large as a myth, a country, a dream. Where did he get his power? What gene signaled him to grow so strong? It was something more than wealth and privilege. Mickey had told her stories of Tonio's boyhood arrogance, his assertions of fledgling authority. At ten he had scolded his mother for the way she cut her steak!

Tonio opened his eyes and looked at her with the guarded gaze of a lizard. She felt perspiration beading under her arms and on her palms. If he is gentle, she thought, I will love him.

"Come here, I want to see," he told her. She went and knelt beside the bed. He reached out, as if to clear away a speck of dirt. She wondered if he could feel how hot she was. She wondered if he approved.

"Come up here," he said congenially, patting the bed beside him. She kicked off her shoes, the new Italian ones, and she crawled up beside him and lay on her side facing him. It was a sudden, familiar and good sensation to be so close again. She was afraid of him because she had done silly things—she pushed the thought of Sage away—but she had forgotten the pleasure of his presence. His sweetness, in moments, when he allowed it.

"Did it hurt much?" he asked.

"It stung. I had a reaction to the penicillin, and when I woke up after surgery there were straws in my nose so I could breathe! The worse was when Reyles took away the scabs. Now it's only that I'm hot."

She knew, before she had finished, that he had lost interest. "It's going to be fine, fine," he said absently. He unbuttoned the first buttons of her shirt and slid his hand over her breast. "No change here," he whispered. His first touch chilled her; the sensation raced down her spine and down her arms, like the dye before an X ray. She felt the smooth small strokes of his fingers as he plucked at a nipple idly, looking her over.

"I missed you," she ventured in a moment. He smiled and pinched her nipple hard. "Ow!" she yipped. She thought he must have meant something by it, he had pinched too hard to be playful, but she was bewildered, and now cautious. He withdrew his hand, and straightened the sheet over his thighs.

"I hear you've been busy. Made new friends."

"Not really. I've known Adele for years. Of course I've only just met her husband." She had no idea what Tonio meant.

"I don't want you out at the university. The place is going crazy. There is going to be trouble." Just for a moment she was surprised, and then she thought: Of course, he would know.

"Why would I go there?" she demurred. One part of her wanted him to go on, to warn her and threaten. He was so wise; he could see what was coming. He knew everything. But it was like a smile across the cantina floor: You had to go at your own speed. You had to find your own way. The time, the tension, was everything. For dance, or love, or fear.

"Students are babies," he said sharply. "They know nothing of government or politics or economics. They don't understand that Mexico can thrive only if it is stable. They don't understand the function of the political process, of elections."

She smiled, amazed at his ferocity. She tried to imagine him in a room with students.

"I'm not playing word games with you, Abby. I'm telling you that this was once a country under barbaric rule and now it is one of the most rapidly developing countries in the world. You don't understand, anymore than those silly students do, and why should you? What do any of you know about growth rate and inflation and debt ratio? All you need to understand is that if our economy is unstable the world dismisses us. You don't even need to know that, only that this government will not stand for anything that threatens order. Students! What do they want but to take money out of investments, where the promise is, to stuff into the pockets of the poor? What will that give us but a short generation of full bellies, and a carcass of an economy?"

He paused, glaring at her. She didn't know what he was talking about. He knew what she was good for.

"None of that means a thing to me, Tonio. It's gay talk, like bears dancing in Chapultapec. It's all so much noise."

"So stay out of it." He seemed to mean for the conversation to be over. Then he said, "Felix said you moved abruptly."

"I was there for weeks! I was worried he had no place to take his girlfriends." She gave Tonio a sly look, but he was not provoked. With less conviction, she said, "I was uncomfortable."

Tonio used the hem of the sheet to buff a thumbnail. "You know I don't like Claude Girard."

She said nothing, afraid to make it worse. She did not want him to ask about Sage. It was not the time for it.

She knew she would never talk to him about Sage. If she went with Sage, it would have to be away from Mexico; she would simply disappear, without explaining. She could never argue anything with Tonio. It was inconceivable. And to run away with Sage? It was an adolescent's foolish fantasy. Running away from home.

"Come to the ranch soon."

"Reyles says I shouldn't get too hot."

"Stay indoors." He was sparring with her. "You can turn on all the air conditioners. You can sleep all day." He spoke with exaggerated boredom. She thought: That is exactly what there is to do at the ranch! In three sentences he had summed up a lot of the last five years of her life!

"Actually I've been thinking you should learn to ride," he said. "I'm going to assign someone to work with you every day. And my girl at the packing house is trying to learn English. She needs someone to practice with her. You can go over there several times a week. Make yourself useful.

"Also, I was wondering if you would like to invite your new little American friend to the ranch. I was thinking, if she is pretty, that we could have a good time."

Abilene stared, incredulous. She would have got off the bed, but Tonio had grasped her arm, hard.

"I'd like to see the two of you together, like two sweet fillies—"

"You're crazy!"

"I thought about bringing her here today—"

He was frightening her. He was capable of anything. His hand was biting into her arm. His eyes shone like cold blue marbles. "If you like," he said, "we can invite the American rancher, to make it another couple. Four of us—would you like that? Would that be fun for you?"

She looked down at her arm, where his hand was making a red mark on her skin. She looked at the arm as if it did not belong to her. As soon as she did this, he let go. Letting go showed how much in control he was. He bent over and licked the place where he had marked her skin. His tongue darted over her shoulder and neck and then into her mouth. A brief kiss. To tease.

"When you came to Apaculco that first time with Mickey—When I first met you. You thought you were such a bad girl, didn't you? But there are bad girls everywhere! For all the times you had spread your legs, you were innocent, you were a baby. You looked sixteen."

"I'd been raped," she said nastily. Her courage came back in a flood of anger. "I'd made love in the back seats of cars." How disgusting it was to think of it all.

"I know all that! But you never gave anything away, did you? You never tried to please them. But me—" He shifted tones crazily. "You've nothing to give another man now, Abby. I'd never be jealous, because I'd know how stupid he'd be to think—but don't make a fool of yourself. Don't try to make a fool of me, I warn you—"

There was silence, except for their breathing, and then, in an instant, he was suddenly boyish. "Go ahead, Abby," he purred. He lay back on his pillows. "Suck me off. I'm sleepy still." He curled his body, his buttocks slightly away from her, his knees tucked. One shoulder arched. "It's been too long for us, it makes me grumpy," he said sweetly.

How false his seduction was, how it centered on the picture he made in his own mind. She had always known it; she had always done what he wanted. She had been a bad girl, and he had made her the bad woman she was meant to be.

She closed her eyes and pretended that she loved him. She pretended that this was the first time. The last. She longed to be high. Tonio caressed her hair at the nape of her neck. She laid her cheek for a moment along the inside of his thigh.

"After the revolution," he said in his most amused voice, "we won't have the time for this. There'll be sugar harvests and political meetings." He got up, laughing. It had taken so little time.

While he showered she went into the kitchen and washed her face and mouth in the sink. She lay on the couch blank as sky, waiting for him to dress. He came out wearing a pale blue silk shirt and gray pants. There were pleats below the waist; the pants were so tight the pleats lay pulled open. He put his hand over for her to fasten a gold bracelet on his wrist. He had taken the time to dry his hair. She brought her arms up to fasten the catch of his bracelet; they were heavy as rope.

"I meant to take you to supper somewhere, but you had a nice lunch, didn't you? And I'm not hungry now. I have an appointment later, I might as well go to the office now."

He was dismissing her. Her arms lay at her sides. He went into his bedroom and returned with a beautiful soft leather case. She watched him from the couch, marvelling at the weight in her arms and legs; if she were dropped into the sea, she would plunge to the ocean floor. Tonio handed her some bills. "You go and eat without me," he said.

She took the money and laid it on her belly, saying, "I'm not hungry either." She pretended to miss his cue; she knew he was ready for her to go. She thought he had now put all of it out of his mind, his display of arrogance and witchery, his all-knowingness, his cruelty, *he had put her back in place.*

"Close the door behind you," he said. The sound of his voice pricked her like a nettle. She wanted the argument she might have had. She felt sick with suppressed anger. She wanted to scream, to exchange blows and yells, to fall to the floor. Just once she wanted to shout and make a terrible scene! She wanted to accuse him, of caprice, of being everything that is hateful: smug, rich, safe. She wanted anger to bring back the heat. Her breath was already coming harder.

"Don't wait for me to go to the ranch," he was saying coolly. "Do take your friend if you like. But I want you to be there when I'm there next week. I like it when you come out to meet my plane, looking for all the world like a boy; it makes me horny to see you in my jeans." Tonio moved nearer her, his weight forward on his near leg. He was a vacuum sucking her in. Oh why was she like this, lying on her back while he stood over her? Why wasn't she on her feet, clawing his eyes out! "Oh God Tonio!" she bleated. "For God's sake, let me go!" Tears spurted down her cheeks, a wash of humiliation and fury.

She had been glad to see him! She had hoped for tenderness. What she wanted was love; what a fool she was.

Tonio reached down to touch her breasts through her shirt. He touched her belly, and slid his hand toward her thighs, and then off of her, with a show of mild disgust. The money on her belly fell to the floor. He stood above her and spoke in his most neutral voice, as if he were reading a label. "Stay out of trouble."

It made her sick to think how she looked.

"Don't stumble in your new shoes," he said.

She jumped up as he shut the door behind him. She opened the door and shouted to him as he was stepping onto the elevator. "I'll make my own life you sonofabitch! I'll come and go how I want. Nobody would come to your stinking ranch! My friend has her own boyfriend! She's going back to California! She wouldn't like you!" She took a deep breath. "She'd never fuck you in a million years."

He held the elevator door long enough to tell her: "You're red as an apple, *chica*. See you soon."

She wandered for most of an hour along the streets of the neighborhood, looking at meticulously kept houses, at dogs on leather leashes led by well-dressed women. She stopped in front of a large building of apartments. Through the window on the second floor she could see a pink light from under curly curtains. Someone was pacing back and forth, a small figure, gesturing grandly. She tried to think what might be happening. Someone telling a story. A woman arguing. An American had gotten in her way.

She walked around, reciting the names of the streets: Mississippi (where Tonio's apartment was), Danube, Eufrates, Tiber, Tamesis. She supposed Tonio chose his apartment to be close to his Niza Zone office and still be quietly residential. Abilene liked the river names, the suggestion of escape by water. Mickey had told her that there were small houses in the *colonia* owned by wealthy men with families in Lomas or Pedregal or Polanco, homes kept for beloved mistresses, for love children. Abilene saw no signs of such dramas, except for the single woman in the light of the lamp. If you loved me, she imagined the woman saying. If you loved me, you would come more. In Tonio's apartment there was no drama. There was no drama in Tonio's life. Drama came from conflict and uncertainty; like play it demanded tension and a suspension of control. Perhaps there was that between Tonio and the good bull. Perhaps that was why he fought, season after season, and not because the crowds adored him, their blond god. He cared nothing for the adulation of other people.

On the Paseo de la Reforma, Abilene took a taxi to the Zócalo and got out. She sat on a curb and watched people moving around on the huge square. Across the way the National Palace stared down on her. It was a presence, like Tonio, making order, giving warnings, speaking of unity and the common good. She moved to a bench and watched the cars as they turned into streaks of light in the darkening dusk. The streets wre wet, and the light made the water sparkle. It must have rained while she was with Tonio. It rained every day now.

The students were talking of great demonstrations. Hallie said they could fill this square. Abilene's eyes gleamed, thinking of it. She saw the excitement that was ahead: the square teeming with shouting people. Banners rippling above their heads.

Hallie had said, "When the people come out, it is the most wonderful thing in the world to be there. To be where it is happening. Life."

Abilene tried to imagine it.

She thought of the police with their guns drawn, billy clubs swung high and down. She thought of the weak trampled. Women thrown about, touched brutishly.

Tonio was right. It was none of her business. She stuck her neck out as if it yearned for the hanging.

He would not make her leave now.

There was a moment, sharp and vivid and painful, when she saw that for her, connection was always an act of violence. The thought choked her with revulsion; she acknowledged a place in her where everything happened in the dark. She saw men in army clothes; she was on her back. They were coming for her, their clothes undone.

Adele said that revolution is what happens inside you. She

said Daniel was a documentor, that she, Adele, was an eye. She said, "Remember the cave men drew on stones. Someone always writes it down."

Abilene had thought of revolution as something in the hills. Glinty-eyed fanatics in fatigue pants. A real revolution would mean guns and blood, like a movie by Yannis. Even when she had seen the bulls go down, blood spurting, the distance had made the animals' death unreal, a phantasmagoria, a dance. If the avenue were to run with blood, she would float on it like a flower at Xochimilco.

She knew she was tired and depressed. She knew Tonio had taunted her to tease and not to threaten. She knew, but on a bench, in a square, in a city, she was so far from anything! She closed her eyes, she gave in to the longing she felt to shut out what was real.

A child's voice woke her. It was a boy or nine or ten standing in front of her.

"*Señorita, señorita!*" he begged. He was holding a tiny gilded bird cage with a blue plastic bird inside. It dangled on a string from his hand. "A bird sings of love," he said, already learned in his trade. She reached into her bag for the wadded bills Tonio had given her. She gave him the money and took the cage, then got up and walked away, toward the avenue. The boy held the money in front of his face and swore. He could not believe his luck. The crazy lady had given him a handful of paper money, a fortune for a bird.

IT WAS ABILENE'S idea to try an Arab restaurant. She had heard of a place just off the Zócalo, in a neighborhood where cheap yard goods were sold. Isabel's sister Ceci and her voluble student friends went along, knowing that Isabel would pay for everything. The students talked all through the meal, especially some boys majoring in geology. The girls were smarter, Isabel whispered to Abilene, and in better colleges than the boys, but now they posed and mewed. Like Ceci, the other girls dressed as North American as they could. One wore her kinky hair in a wild Afro style. Isabel and Abilene exchanged indulgent looks. They talked about the Olympics. The girls speculated on what they could make working as hostesses; they all spoke English and some spoke French, too. They dipped their fingers in couscous and flirted. Ceci was pouting. She would rather have talked politics, but her friends were less serious. She had asked them out to please Isabel. She knew what Isabel wanted: to divert her attention. It was a waste of time.

It was also Abilene's idea to go some place and dance. The students laughed and shouted and showed the way to a mariachi cantina. Girls in cheap bright clothes stood on the side, bouncing to the loud music, smoothing their rayon skirts and tortured hair, waiting on boys to ask them to dance. The boys, who all seemed very young, walked around like buyers at a livestock show. "Are they whores?" Abilene whispered to Isabel. Isabel whispered back. "Not yet."

One of the geology boys asked Abilene to dance. The student, whose name was Jorge, was lithe. He danced from the crotch, and when he saw Abilene looking at him, he rolled his hips even more. They danced until perspiration ran down Abilene's face and arms. Then the musicians stopped, suddenly, and left the room. Jorge led Abilene back to their table and the boys there said, "Hey! you're a good dancer, man." The girls looked at her with narrow secretive eyes. Business at the bar picked up, and all around the room people yelled for more music. Another band appeared. As soon as it began to play, Abilene looked to Jorge, expecting to be asked to dance again. Jorge asked Ceci instead. He stayed near the table, so Abilene could watch, she thought, but he never looked at her. He kept his undulating hips in her line of vision. The music was Afro-Cuban, great for dancing; it drove its beat hard, and throbbed. So did Jorge. He paid no attention to Ceci, his dance partner. He was just showing off.

Abilene knew the show was for her, and she waited with suppressed eagerness for Jorge to come back to her. A familiar hum had begun in her. When she got up to dance she and Jorge were the center of attention. His teasing had worked; they danced like lovers sparring, a teasing squence of approaches and retreats, and long moments dancing in place, eyes locked. When they went back to the table, Jorge put his arm across Abilene's shoulders. His thumb slid along her back, a thumb that burned. "American girls really know how to dance," he said slinkily. She walked out from under his arm, smarting from his categorical praise. He probably meant what he said, and probably meant to please her, but when he next asked her to dance, she said coldly that her feet were tired. He was confused for a moment, and then he collected himself enough to sneer. "Not mine!" he said.

She moved her hunter's eyes around the room, looking at the preening boys, their pencil moustaches, slick hair and compact bodies. One boy had an attractive Zapata moustache, but his pants hung too low on his hips; when he raised his arm, his shirt rode up and hung sloppily. These weren't poor boys, everything could not be forgiven them, but they weren't the rich ones, either. The ones with money went to clubs with cover charges, to hotel bars. The Mexican boys liked color, and wore their pants like skin. Like peacocks they loved their own looks. They expected the girls to love them too. They didn't often get to strut for *gringas*, not in a place like this. She would be a nice surprise for one of them.

Across the floor she saw a gorgeous Indian, all sinew and bones, with black shaggy hair. He was vain; he was smoothing his hair. He glanced around for approval, and Abilene thought: I know him! She thought for a moment and then, of course! it was the waiter who had brought food to the apartment with Constanzia, wasn't it? He was standing near the toilets. Between songs, she walked across the floor, conscious of her hips, her stride, the slope of her back. At first she angled away from him, and then at the last moment changed her course and walked right by him. She knew her hair was shiny in the light, that her small breasts jutted out. She knew he had watched her dancing with Jorge. At the last possible moment, she looked at him boldly and stopped. He had been watching her all along; when she realized that, a gush of pleasure shot up her body.

And then she saw that he was the young man who had met with Adele at the Piñeda's hotel, not the waiter.

"I see your dance," he said in English.

"What did you think?" She felt a sudden amazement at the ease, the predictability of this encounter. She felt like an expert fisherman. He was a strutter now, his hand in his belt, his chin up. He wasn't begging now. He was beautiful, with dark eyes and a well-formed mouth. "I think a good dancer like you needs to dance with me," he said cockily.

She thought he was right. The dance: she needed it very much.

She danced without shifting her gaze from him except when she turned expertly. They were the same height, and this made her conscious of their hips as they came toward one another, their thighs brushing, their hands touching. The music buoyed her up, she floated out of herself. She knew what her dancing told this Indian boy, and she knew it was not a lie.

He took her arm and moved her to the bar where he bought her beer. She asked his name. He said it was Angel. He was an artisan.

"You don't remember me, do you?" she asked.

He was now guarded, waiting.

"I met you at the hotel," she said. "I was with the friend who asked you about the dead *gringa*."

He looked very young, and skittish. Perhaps he thought she had somehow followed him, looked for him?

"That's not important," she said. She was afraid he was going to take off. "What's important is dancing." She waited a long moment, while he considered this. She was excited. She glanced around and saw Isabel watching her. Isabel knew exactly what was going on. She had talked about what the rules were in Mexico, but she broke them, too. One of these days, she warned, you will find out what *macho* means.

"I'm going to tell my friends I ran into you—that I know you, understand? Then we can get out of here."

He waited for her. He said he knew a better place, the disco with American rockyroll. But it cost more. "I'd like to go," he said, "but I only have the admission." He took his money out of his pocket for her to see.

"I'll buy drinks," she said. She opened her bag and showed him her money. When their eyes met again, they both laughed.

At the disco they danced close together. He pressed his ample genitals against her thigh. She thought: Mexican boys are never embarrassed! When a Rolling Stones record came on, they pulled apart to dance. It was serious now; they were spelling things out for one another. *I know you danced with a girl who's dead,* she was saying. *I know you wonder if I hurt her,* he was saying. His dark eyes did not frighten her; they were curious and greedy, that was all. Yet she was astonished to feel that she was afraid. It was in her neck: a tight feeling, someone's hands, squeezing. She pushed the feeling away with her dancing.

Then she said, "I'll pay for the taxi."

He had two spare decent rooms in an old house that had been divided into apartments in an old quarter not far from the disco. She had stopped being surprised at the way the shabby apartments sat among finer buildings. Deterioration was borne on the air like pollen, landing anywhere. At the end of Angel's street there was a dead end. It was cluttered with cardboard boxes and sheets of metal piled against one another. She saw someone moving among the boxes, and a glow, not quite a light, maybe charcoal in a can. "Who are they?" she whispered. Angel said they were squatters. "They appear, they disappear. Maybe the officials come to run them out, maybe not." He shrugged. "Sometimes hundreds of them appear on vacant lots, or on the street. They live in caves, on the hills below the Lomas neighborhood. They come in the night. You get up in the morning and there they are. They are called parachutists. They fall from the sky to make lost cities." He ushered her up to his rooms.

The bed was narrow and carefully made. On a table were a hot plate and tins of cocoa and evaporated milk. She took his tidiness as a good sign. On a shelf were paperback books in English. "I was wondering how you speak such good English," she said.

"I took lessons. For seven years. I spent all my money except to have a room and to eat, for lessons. I am going to go to live in Acapulco, and get a job with the tourists." He was quite earnest as he said, "I'll be very good with the *gringas*."

Sylvia Britton was forgotten between them.

She laughed at him and put her hands in his hair. He pulled her close, then onto his lap, and kissed her. His mouth was open and wet; he took too much for granted. She wanted to kiss stingily so that there would be more to come. But he wouldn't know anything about lovemaking. He was sure to know only about fucking.

He shoved her off his lap and stood up. He took off his shirt and pants and stood naked. She waited for him to come to her. She sat unmoving, her eyes locked on the fullness of him, wanting suddenly not to do this, not to be like this, like Sylvia Britton, wanting to lie alone under clean sheets in Claude's apartment. She remembered that she didn't have her diaphragm. She imagined her belly swelling like yeasty bread, imagined an Indian baby. *If anything could live inside her.* He was impatient. "What kind of artisan are you?" she asked, ignoring his look. She really did want to know. "Do you work in silver? Leather?" She wanted to know who he was.

"I make cabinets!" he said in a loud angry voice. "For kitchens." He yanked her up to her feet and tugged at her waistband. She shoved his hand away. "I'll do it," she said angrily. She couldn't leave; he would never let her go now. The doors that closed behind her, that had closed behind her for years now—those doors never opened up again. There can only be so many doors. That was what the American girl had learned. That was what Adele feared, for all her talk about goodness and purpose. *We are only allowed so many doors,* she thought.

The decision had been made for hours, back when he had stayed beside her in the dance hall, instead of running away. Back when she had showed him her money. There was no reason to think of it anymore. She slid her skirt down her legs and it lay around her feet. "I don't want to do this, you know," she said quietly, and then she stepped out of her panties. It was important that she tell him that. This one liked to brag about the *gringas.* How they came to him, paying his way.

Her hands hung at her sides. His nipples were brown and tiny, he had smooth tight skin. Touching him would be pleasure; she wished he were brown marble. She stepped toward him and smelled something unpleasant and sharp, like cheese; he wasn't altogether clean. She thought of creamy sludge where his testicles met his abdomen.

"I don't want to," she said. It was his cue.

He shoved her down roughly and lay on top of her, bruising her mouth with his. He was pressing against her, she knew he

121

would want it in now, that it would be over for him quickly. He would think that his pleasure was the measure of everything. He would not dream that to lie beneath him was anything less. Someone would have to tell him about women if he was to go to Acapulco. *He will have to see if he has the talent to go with his looks.*

She asked him to go down on her. He raised his arm and looked at her. Seven years of English, and he didn't understand. "Down there," she said. "Kiss me there." He was horrified.

"Down there," he said, "I put my cock."

"Not yet!" She pushed hard at his chest. He sat up on his heels. She put her finger on her clitoris and moved it cruelly against the numbness; beneath the numbness something stormed. He panted. He held his hand around his penis like a bun. He didn't know what it was she was touching, he almost made her laugh! She wanted to *feel*, to be alive!

He couldn't wait, or didn't want to. He positioned himself and she saw that he would plunge into her, arrogant, urgent, hurting. She felt so tightly closed against him, she was afraid of the pain. She flattened herself against the bed, spread-eagled; she raised her legs high and opened herself with her fingers for him. Then she dropped into a dark chasm between sensation and knowing.

Afterwards he was wonderfully solicitous. He wiped himself with his shirt and handed it to her. He felt fine. Surely she did too? "I make you feel good?" he grinned. He rubbed his hands on his chest and tucked them, crisscrossed, in his armpits. He was the stupidest man she had ever met. Hah. He was a prize.

She knew her life was against the rules. She thought she might have killed her heart, if it ever lived. Angel, observing her silence, perhaps thinking it was satisfaction that made her quiet, was suddenly generous. He caressed her breasts, licked her nipples, then lay back contentedly. He touched her sore, swollen clitoris. "*Gringa* girls," he said lazily. She put her hands across his mouth. "Not *gringas*!" she said. "Me." He didn't understand. "Me! me!" she said, her finger pointing at her chest. "What about me?"

She should have died caping that stupid cow. It would have been silly, just what she deserved.

"You'll be my *novia*," he said, perfectly serious. "I'll take you all around."

"Go downstairs and find me a taxi," she said. "Make him say how much before I go with him." She knew the drivers were greedy and malevolent this time of night. A woman at large was prey. A *gringa* was a beggar. Once a cabdriver showed her his open switchblade, swinging it around like a conductor's baton until she begged to be let out. She had to say it over and over again: *please, oh please.*

And if he hadn't let her out? She saw it so clearly: The driver pulls into a dark alley and jerks her by the hair until she dangles over the front seat. *See!* he says. He has undone his pants; his penis taps the steering wheel. *See!* he says, and pulls her over the seat, his knife at her throat as she does what he says.

Angel wrote his name and address on a piece of paper and she put it in her shoulder bag. He wanted her address, too, but she would only say the street nearest it, that intersected Reforma. "Tell the taxi that street," she said, pretending not to understand what he wanted. He insisted, though. "I see you again," he said. She said he couldn't come to the place she was staying, certain other people were there. He thought he understood; it made him feel sly. "So then I'll meet you," he said. "Yes," she agreed. "Friday, at the same cantina." Now he believed her. While he went ahead of her to get the cab, she laid some money on his bed.

Later she wondered if he just wanted her to want to see him. He might not have let her leave if she had not agreed to meet him again. She had to want to see him again.

He won't show! she thought resentfully, as if she cared.

6.

ABILENE WENT to Dr. Reyles for a checkup. He said her face was healing beautifully. He touched the skin under her eyes with the soft pad of his thumbs. "Maybe, in a year, we do it again, to make it perfect."

Abilene said, "I know it's better now. I know you did a good job and I'll always be glad we did it. But I don't ever want to be under like that again if I don't have to be. I remember them rolling me from the room to the elevator, and then I remember waking up so swollen." She saw that Reyles was listening closely. "I lost part of my life that way. It scared me."

Reyles nodded gravely. She knew he only thought to postpone the suggestion, but she was through with fixing her face. There was one thing, though.

"It's still hot a lot of the time. I'm glad I'm here and not in the country."

Reyles considered the statement a moment and said, "Is Velez wanting you to return, then?"

She nodded. Her eyes started to fill.

"Well," he said, bringing his hands together, not quite a clap. "It's much too soon! The high cool air is better for you. I'll tell him myself."

"You'll call him?"

"Why no, he'll call me, *chica*. He checks on you."

She felt better. Things could stay as they were for the time being.

To leave was too bold an act, but to stay away—perhaps, she thought, she could manage that.

She thought more about boldness, and wrote to Sage in Tampico.

> *If I went back to the Tecoluca, would you come and get me? Would you take me away? Is that what you meant when you were here?*

Sage wrote back the next week.

> *It's not for me to take, it's for you to go. Tonio can't stop you. Why do you want to put it off on me? This isn't the age of chivalry, or duels, Abby. You're free to do what you choose.*
> *Maybe you should decide. My lease is expiring and Tonio won't renew. Well, there's a lot of world outside the Huasteca, and maybe my life will be better out from under that pompous asshole.*
> *I'm enclosing my brother's address in Houston. I don't know how long it will take me to wrap things up. My brother and I are looking at ranches in Costa Rica. Why do you need to come back to the Tecoluca at all? You don't have a lease, now do you?*

She lay on her bed in Claude's apartment all afternoon. She tried to remember Sage's face, and the feel of his hand on her breast, but the room was filled with images of Tonio. He floated around her, softened by the haziness of reverie. She dozed. It was a pleasant sensation, she was dissolving.

She had cross words with Isabel, over the cantina incident. She tried to joke about it, to make it sound like a good time, but Isabel was in no mood for jokes. "One of these nights they'll find you on the street, *chiquita*," she warned. Abilene shivered. Isabel went away, too busy, she said, for chitchat.

Abilene didn't have the energy to look for Hallie. She went to Adele's, but only Pola was home. Adele was busy all the time now.

What did you talk to a thirteen-year-old about?

"Tell me about your father," Abilene said. She struck a chord.

"He's a brilliant man," Pola said. "They use his films in the film schools. He gets prizes."

"I know. But your mother doesn't like his films. She says they're—bloody."

"You should have heard her after she saw the last one! *Light*

125

on the Hills." She giggled. "They didn't call it that in Spanish. They called it, *Dark Revenge.* Because, you see, it was about revenge." The girl's face was animated; she was pleased with the conversation. "I saw it when I visited him, at his house. He said if it bothered me we could turn it off at any time. But I loved it! It was about a girl a little older than me. She is taken out of her village and carried away into the mountains. The revenge is over that."

Abilene wondered if Adele would mind this discussion.

"The blood was beautiful," Pola said. She moved her arm in an arc. "Like this, in slow motion."

"Have you ever seen a bullfight, Pola?"

Pola made a face. "Oh yes, but I didn't like it."

"All that blood."

Pola tossed her head. "Don't trick me just to prove you're grown up."

"Sorry."

"You're the only one of Mommy's friends who isn't full of herself. Like Elena, who wants to be a star and has a long way to go. And Simon. Did you know his wife was an actress who once stabbed him? Her name was Hespera. Isn't that a fantastic name! Simon took Mommy and me to see her play Lady Macbeth last year. Mommy was very prissy about it. She said, 'You might not understand all of it, it's Shakespeare, but there will be wonderful spectacle in the production.' Does my mother think I'm stupid? When Lady Macbeth held up her hand and tried to rub away the blood—who wouldn't understand that? And why is Shakespeare all right with blood and death but Yannis not? What does my mother have against him?"

"Maybe your mother sees a lot of real troubles in the world, and she hasn't any patience for the made-up ones in movies."

"Did Yannis make the world crazy? Is it all his fault?"

Abilene shrugged. She tried to remember what was on her mind at thirteen.

"He's so cool, you know," Pola said.

"Tell me what you mean."

"He watches everything. You can tell he knows a lot. He doesn't get mad, but people know not to cross him."

Abilene wondered if Pola had been reading movie magazines!

"At least Adele lets you visit him."

"He's my father!"

"But you're in another country. She could make it hard."

"Hah. He sends her money!"

"Where does Yannis live?"

"In Malibu, by the ocean. I love to go there. I can lie in bed at night and hear the sea. When I was there last year he took me all over. Into the canyons, and along the beaches. He took me out into the valley—I can't remember the name—and a big wind was blowing in. It's called a Santa Ana. Yannis said we were near the very place where it begins. Did you ever think of that? Of wind being *born?*"

"There's a place near the ranch where a river is born. It comes up out of the earth, out of a cave."

"That's neat!"

"Wind, I don't know. I grew up in West Texas and I guess I had my fill of it."

"Oh, but this was a terrific wind, Abby! I had to hold onto my father. We were gasping, it was so fierce, and holding on to each other. When we got back in the car, he said he thought I had always looked like my mother, but now he could see I looked a lot like him, too."

"Pola. You didn't tell Adele?"

Pola shook her head and then raised her chin. "I'm not a little girl anymore. I don't tell my mother every little thing. I have secrets."

"From everyone, or only from Adele?"

"I'll tell you."

Abilene, surprised, leaned back involuntarily. Then she moved closer again to Pola. She couldn't help herself. "What, Pola? What's such a big secret?"

"My father is going to make a movie next year. He said he had to start looking for a star. He said to me, 'In a year you'll be old enough.' "

"He's going to put you in a movie!"

"He didn't say that. He just meant he wanted a girl my age.

But he doesn't know I'm getting breasts now. He doesn't know I can act."

"Can you?" How could she possibly know?

"When I'm fourteen I can live with either one I choose," Pola said. "That's the secret. That I know it."

"Oh, Pola."

"She can't stop me. When he sees me next time, he'll find out I can do it. He'll put me in a movie."

"All his movies are so—dangerous." So Adele said.

Pola smiled, almost a girl again. "But it's all make-believe. He explained to me. He said people like to feel that danger has just missed them. They like to think: It could have been me."

"I think you should talk to your mother more."

"You won't tell!"

"No, but it's wrong to shut your mother off."

"It's my mother that does the shutting. She lies in bed at night and whispers to Daniel about murder and arrests and all sorts of awful things. She doesn't care what I do—"

"I'm sure that's not true."

"She doesn't care what any of us do, only Daniel."

"She cares a lot! She's going all over the city asking people to tell her their stories, because she cares."

"Oh that. It has to do with politics. All her boring friends ever talk about—except you."

"I don't think any of it concerns me," Abilene said.

"And you've got time to talk!"

"All I have is time," Abilene said. When Pola reached out to hug her, she kissed her cheek. She thought, how different the smell of a girl is. How different from a man.

"Don't tell!" Pola said.

"Cross my heart."

"Then I'll tell you more."

Adele was frantic. Pola was two hours late coming home from school.

"Make us some coffee. Tell me about your work," Abilene said. What else was there to discuss?

"I went to see my friend, the artist Georgia Azuela," Adele said. "I spent the morning in her studio, away from 'my work.'

128

I thought we would talk about her painting, but she was full of talk about the movement too. Her husband owns an pottery factory. The union is talking about coming out with a statement in support of the students. Georgia is working on plans for a mural on a new government building. Little *indios*, waifs with big eyes. She says it's a silly thing to paint in these circumstances."

"If you were involved, it would be hard not to worry."

Adele dropped a spoon to the floor and stood, staring at it, as if it had sprung from her hands to taunt her. "I should go back to my fashion assignments," she said. "I am getting too full of student rhetoric." She finished preparing the coffees and set them on the table. There were dark circles under her eyes. "I'm not paying enough attention to Pola, am I?"

"She thinks—I mean, she knows you are busy."

"She thinks what!"

"That you are preoccupied, that's all. She's a girl. She doesn't look at big pictures. Neither do I."

"Where is she!"

At that moment Pola burst in, happy and full of news. "The most exciting thing!" she shouted when she saw them. "You can take my story!" she said to her mother, apparently sincere. There was color in her cheeks, a brightness to her eyes.

"Pola!" Adele said sharply. Abilene nudged Adele and interrupted.

"I'll make cocoa for you if you want," she said to Pola.

"Soda, please," Pola said. She pulled up another chair.

"I guess you better tell us about it," her mother said.

"I was leaning out of the window of the school room, flirting with some boys passing by. The teacher had gone down the hall. The boys are from the voc ed school nearby. One of my classmates knew them; her brother goes to school there. They had been out begging money to make posters for Cuba Day. 'Come and help us!' they kept yelling. 'We need some artists.' Then the teacher was coming. The last thing we heard them say was, 'We're going to the market at Tacuba!'" Pola had been talking to them both, but now she kept her eyes from her mother and looked at Abilene. "I went to the bathroom with Cleo, and we slipped away."

"Pola!"

"I had to!" Pola defended herself. "Don't you know it's going on all over the city!"

Adele said wryly, "This I know."

"The boys were doing a play in the market. The Tacuba market is right across from the police station. In the play, some of the boys were the army, marching into a village and throwing Indian claims around—they had these little red balls they tossed in the air and then to one another—and some other boys who played the peasants sang, 'We have no water, we have no life.'" Pola was very intense. "Do you realize that the revolution was supposed to give back land to the peasants, and yet there are still huge ranches, big landowners who have all the best land?"

Adele smiled. "I know."

"Some of the boys played guitars and sang about workers in prison. Soon there were lots of people—a hundred! Maybe two hundred. Oh I don't know! They were throwing *pesos* onto the ground in front of the students. Some people yelled out rudely. 'You are spoiled brats who ought to be locked up!' They were awful! But there were only a few, and everyone shoved them and made them go away. Then a man who could really play the guitar came along and began to sing songs that everyone could sing too.

"Then the police came. They shouted at all of us that we were lazy good for nothings. They had clubs."

"Dear God," Adele said. Abilene could see the fear on her face. She reached over to pat Adele's hand. "Look," she said, "here she is."

Pola didn't seem to notice Adele's reaction. She was full of her story. "Now here's the good part, you two. The bystanders picked up whatever they could find and threw it at the police. They pelted the cops with ripe tomatoes, *chiles,* rolls and bananas. And the police got out of there fast!"

Adele jumped up from the table and began pacing around the livingroom. "Don't you ever—" she began, and stopped. She turned to face Pola. "Don't you know I am scared? Don't you know there are dangerous things going on?"

Pola ran to her mother and threw her arms around her. Then,

stepping back, she said, "I thought you would be so pleased. Don't you see? Now I know what you're talking about!"

Over Pola's shoulder Adele looked at Abilene beseechingly. What could she think Abilene could say or do?

"What did you think you were doing!" Adele said again. She began to weep, putting her face into her hands. "It's babies like you who'll get trampled in the rush. Don't you do this ever again. Never never!"

Pola's disappointment was turning sullen. "I thought you would be pleased."

Adele said, "You were very wrong."

"I want to help Cleo."

"With what!"

"Her mother works at the Red Cross station in their *colonia*. Cleo says they need help. They're getting ready."

Adele said nothing. Abilene gathered the dishes from the table and took them to the sink.

"Getting ready!" Adele's voice skidded off into a shriek.

"The Red Cross is always ready, isn't that what they're for?"

"Yes! For earthquakes and volcanoes and fires and floods."

"Cleo's mother says they have to be ready for trouble." Abilene thought Pola had gotten ruder, as she saw her mother's distress.

"You're to come home directly from school, do you hear!"

"I don't see why I have to go at all," Pola said, pouting.

"To embroider. To improve your French."

"It's summer!"

"I want to know where you are." Adele grabbed Pola's arm. "All the time, I want to know."

"How can you?" Pola asked, slowing down her words, gaining the advantage. "How can you know where I am, when you're not here? How can you know where I am, when you don't see me? How? How?"

Adele slapped Pola's face, and then burst into violent tears. Within the moment, she had slipped to the floor, crying. Pola screamed. "I want to go to California! I want to go to Yannis for good! I hate you! And stupid Daniel too!" She turned and fled to her room.

Abilene sat down on the floor beside Adele and put her arm

awkwardly around her shoulder. She wondered at the easy anger of Adele and Pola. It seemed to Abilene to be over so little, an outing without permission. Of course it was over being a child, being a mother, Abilene could see that, too.

"Couldn't you spend more time here?" Adele asked. "Couldn't you do things with her? She likes you, she says so. You could go to the movies, to the museums, like you said. Couldn't you, Abilene? Couldn't you do this for me, for a little while?"

Abilene, surprised, said, "Yes, if Pola will."

And she thought to herself, so I'm good for something, am I? A babysitter. She would have laughed, but Adele wouldn't have understood.

Adele wiped her face with the backs of her hands. "I'm a mess. Daniel will be home soon."

"Go and wash up. I'll take Pola her soda."

Abilene sat on Pola's bed. Pola, at the chair by her table near the bed, drank thirstily. "Do you remember what it's like, having people tell you what to do just because you're thirteen? Do you?"

Abilene said yes, though she could not remember. Her mother had never kept track of her coming and going, but there hadn't really been any, not at thirteen.

"I've never seen your mother so upset."

"She'll get over it. She'll tell Daniel everything, and then they'll feel better. It'll be me in here by myself."

"Pola, they're married! What do you want?"

"I want to go to California. You could go with me!"

"And do what?" Abilene said, making it seem an outlandish idea, making a face to show she didn't take it seriously.

"We could get good tans," Pola said.

"Ahh," Abilene answered. She thought California did sound nice. Far away. Not Texas. A fresh start. Why not California? "But I have to stay out of the sun," she said, touching her face. "For a whole year."

Pola tittered. "I'll buy you sunglasses and a hat with a big brim. Everyone will think you're someone famous and don't want to be seen. We'll have a lot of fun."

PART IV

7.

ONE LONG RAINY afternoon, Pola asked Abilene about the ranch. "Is it terribly exotic, and dangerous, like Mommy says?"

"I never thought of it as dangerous." What a funny thing to have told Pola, Abilene thought. "There are wildcats in the brush, though, and snakes and insects. And bandits on the roads."

"What about the pits?"

So Adele had remembered what Abilene told her. Why had she never come? Was she afraid of Tonio! "Much of the land is limestone and there are places where the earth has fallen in. The Indians call them basement caves."

"Why hasn't Mommy taken me to see it?"

"She says she doesn't like the country."

"You could take me sometime."

Abilene wasn't sure what she should say. "I'll tell you what it's like to wake up there. First I hear the birds. I lie in bed and imagine the peacocks spreading their tails. Outside the walls a monkey shrieks. *Campesinos* in white trousers tied with string come over the river in the back of a cattle truck and swarm over the grounds. Everywhere you look one is digging or picking at the ground or the bushes or the trees. When I pass them, they freeze and wait for me to go by, their faces hidden under their big hats, their bare feet deep in grass. All day the ferry grinds with its loads of workers, calves, trucks full of bottled water, grain, and other supplies."

"What time is it? When do you get up?"

"Let's say it's eight o'clock. Across the hall Tonio is taking a shower while his valet Asuncio brings his breakfast of coffee and toast. Tonio shouts at him from the bath. Asuncio moves on his feet like a boxer. I hear him shouting, 'Si, Matador!'

"I don't want to get up yet. Maybe I read half the night. Maybe it was three o'clock before I went to bed. I go and open the balcony door to look out across the tile, through ivy and vines, past bougainvillea and palm, across avocado and plantain plants."

"Tell me what you see."

"The hacienda walls. A sliver of sky bordered by the balcony roof. I can hear the maids coming down the walk, they're so silly. They're only your age! I hear the secretary Sofia in her high heels, yelling at the maids to get out of the way. Every once in a while the hounds howl. Maybe it isn't really hot yet, but I turn on the air-conditioner, for the noise, close the balcony door again, and crawl back into bed.

"I can hear Tonio stomping hard with his heels in the hall outside my room. Then he goes down the stairs. His head floats along the length of the crocodile on the wall, it's right at its snout that he takes the last step. Under an arch of ivory he passes through the front door. Now that he is outside, the din of birds is incredible. The monkey beats its chest. The dogs lie like sphinxes along the border of the walk. As he approaches, their noses twitch. He nudges them with his sharp boot toe. They yap and tumble around. Just past the gates there's a little wildcat on a chain. It snaps and claws at everyone, but when Tonio comes up to it, it purrs like a house cat. Animals love him!

"I put the pillow over my head so I can go back to sleep. There is nothing I have to do, nothing to get up for. I like sleeping with all those things going on. I like eating lunch for breakfast, with the foreman and the guard, I like listening to the cook Beto tell stories about the Huastecans. Many years ago he was caught stealing on the ranch; he couldn't even speak Spanish! Tonio beat him and then gave him a place to sleep. Later, Beto went and got his twin brother, who now cooks at Tonio's hotel, the Arcadia. Beto is big as a bear with a huge belly where he wipes his hands on the expanse of white apron. One of the maids spends the whole morning making tortillas and orange juice. When she sees me, she slides me a glass of the juice as though she is afraid of me. A *gringa*, who sleeps all morning: maybe I'm sick and it is catching! She keeps her eyes down and won't look at me."

Pola was fascinated. "If I came to visit, I'd want to go all over the ranch! I'd want to see everything—all the animals, the cowboys!"

"Yes, you'd see it, and you still wouldn't believe it is real." It was paradise, or maybe hell. "There's no place like it. It never stops being strange. I think that's why I love it. I think that's why I feel at home there."

The ranch lay hacked out of tangled low jungle along a wide muddy river. Tecoluca, it was called, a word of no particular meaning, or, like the totems of the *indios* there, forgotten over generations. In early summer, the river went down in places to the depth of alley puddles. When August rains fell, it could swell almost overnight, and run roiling brown. Abilene saw *campesinos* bathing in the river and dipping water out of jars. "What do they do when the river is low?" she asked Tonio.

"It's never dry," he said without bothering to look at her. He would talk an hour or more about the Tecoluca, but not about the *indios*. "What do you care?" he said when she asked.

The *indios* lived in tin or grass-roofed huts walled with branches. Trucks, jeeps and taxis passed them thousands of times, yet as each vehicle approached, they stopped to watch. Abilene wondered what they thought.

She tried to ask Tonio: "Don't you think they wonder about the life on this side of the river?" Don't you wonder if they think you are a god?" He was golden, he came and went in a plane like a silver bird. Tonio had no patience for these questions. It was like the time she reached for a brochette of venison and asked him, "*Venada* or *venado*? Is it feminine or masculine?" Tonio blew a hair from his mouth. She was interested in the most trivial things! "Puhhh!" he said, instead of answering.

The region was called la Huasteca. Abilene said it over and over, trying different aspirations on the "h" or none at all. It was a diverse region, hot and humid, appearing rich but actually thin-soiled, a land loamed with marl and riddled with sinkholes. It was bordered by tropical hills on the north, into the arches of the Sierra de Tamaulipas that crisscrossed the Sierra Madre. To the east the flanks of the Sierra Madre Oriental were green with pine forest; where the warm trade winds struck the mountains with rain, the slopes were misty, fecund, anomalous: pale-leafed sweet gum rose from ferns and Spanish mosses, while half a mile away gnarled oaks entwined with orchids.

The ranch nestled in tropical deciduous forest and ran out into scrub and savannah grasses. Along the water border, broad-based cypresses were sometimes awash in river. The land was pocked with swamps here, pits there, rolling out into tangles and thick brush, to lowland jungle, to the sea.

Tonio had grown up a wild boy on the ranch. Outside the hacienda walls there was a bunkhouse that smelled of formaldehyde. Its walls were from shoulder height to ceiling a catalog of slaughter. Like frames of mounted butterflies, whole groups of identical little deer heads lined the walls, interspersed by sections of great heavy-scaled fish resembling garpike or barracuda. In death the animals bore so little resemblance to what they had once been, it was hard to believe they had ever lived at all. Why would any boy have thought to have undone so many? Without scheme, the heads and carcasses of local game hung forlorn: deer and puma, porcupine and squirrel, peccary and bird. The young Tonio had been to darker jungle, too, perhaps Campeche; tapir, turkey, a pitiful ocelet, toucans, snakes and a large white vulture hung agape, and beneath these boyhood trophies you could play pool or Ping-Pong in the poor light and ponder how great a score it takes to be a man.

Across from the bunkhouse was Tonio's aviary, the size of a public building. Made of net and fencing, with an intricate dome mesh, crisscrossed with perches, the aviary was filled with plants and feeding cups, and of course with birds: macaws, parrots and parakeets, orioles and vermilions, green jays and cuckoos, pyrrhuloxia (looking like faded cardinals), and blue-hooded euphonias. Tonio spent time with his birds at dusk, after he had been riding. He mimicked their calls with uncanny precision and spread his arms as roosts.

The house itself, two stories surrounded on all sides by balconies above and verandas below, was a monument to extravagance and bad taste, rooms filled with massive furniture and gilded frames. Walls full of Mexican masks of wood, clay, tin, goat hair and gilding. Mirrors. Paintings and even a huge mosaic of the Velez family: Tonio at eight, at twelve, at sixteen. Only Tonio's room reflected him. It was furnished as a coffee farm in Africa, with straw matting, crossed spears and shields on the wall, and a lovely patio with high-backed rattan chairs and a table. Opposite Tonio's bed, on the wall, was an antelope's head—a blesbok from Africa, with curved horns and a white mask.

Except for his room and his office, in another building across the bricked walkway, Tonio seemed to care only for his stables, done in bright blue Mexican tiles with high domed ceilings. The rest of the estate, with its grottos, empty swimming pool, groves of limes and oranges, guavas, avocados and papayas, had an air of disuse, as if its owners had died and left it to a child who never came.

It wasn't by ornate furnishing that the hacienda revealed the wealth of its owner. It was by the mass of dead beasts (trophies along every hallway, and in his Colorado-styled bar), the fine quality of his livestock, and the numbers of peasants who poured in every day to work. There were men for cattle and others for the horses, droves of Indians for the grounds, seven or eight maids, cook and cook's helpers, secretary, guard and ferryman, an electrician, carpenters, a foreman. For some the ranch was home, or a second home. Tonio's personal secretary Bruni, wealthy in his own right, had nevertheless devoted seven years to looking after Tonio's affairs, and he had his own luxurious apartment downstairs. He walked with a deep dipping limp, the result of an overturned truck on the way to Tampico. (*Bandidos*, he had explained; he had been transporting bees.) Besides Bruni, there was an old Canadian who had lived in the generator shed since just after World War I, and there was Tacho, who had come in his boyhood from somewhere on the West Coast, passionate to fight bulls. Esteban, Tonio's other *banderillero* for many years, lived at the ranch, but was the relative of dozens who lived in San Marta and worked for Tonio in one capacity or another. His brother held a responsible position in the San Marta packing plant. There were in fact so many people on the ranch, Abilene never felt free of the gazes of others except in her own room or Tonio's. Yet on Sundays, when no one came, she spent most of the day out at the guardhouse with Sapo, listening to the radio.

She tried to explain some of these things to Pola.

"Are you lonely there?" the girl asked. "Is there no one to talk to?"

She told Pola about all the workers. "It's like a little town of its own," she said. "And there are often visitors. Tonio likes to show off with big house parties. He has friends who come from Mexico and Acapulco, from Texas and California, to hunt. To have a good time. He feeds them boar and venison, beef from his own slaughterhouse, iguana, ant eggs—"

"Ant eggs!"

"Oh yes, like caviar. And mounds of rice, black beans and *chiles*. After dinner the men play poker in the wine hut, while their wives or girlfriends drink brandy across the way, in Tonio's Wild West bar."

Pola made a face. "That part sounds boring."

"While the guests relax, Tonio has Esteban come in to play his twelve-string guitar, and Tacho to sing. They are his *band-erilleros*, or used to be—the ones who put the darts with crepe paper streamers into the backs of the bulls—"

"Poor bulls!"

"Now Esteban works with the brave bulls, and Tacho drinks and feels sorry for himself. But you should hear him sing! In Portugal he learned *fado*. He heard gypsies in camp and went out to sing with them, and ran away with them! His voice is rough and terribly sad and hoarse, his face is full of pain, really it's beautiful, Pola. A man from Mexico who works in television was there one year and he told Tacho, 'I can get a record made. You can be a big singer!' Tacho was furious! He says actors and singers are *mariposas*, butterflies—"

"Like Paul and Jay."

"Oh how dumb of me, I'm sorry. I don't mean—"

"It doesn't matter. Besides, they are gay. They are—were—

something like butterflies, with bright colors and lightness of heart. I miss them terribly!"

"I'm so sorry."

"They were so funny, and so nice to Mommy and me. Daniel is okay, I know Mommy loves him—but he's boring, and he looks at me—" She faltered.

"How does he look?"

"Like I just stumbled in! Like he doesn't know how I got there!"

"I don't think that's it. I think he looks at you and he thinks; I wish I hadn't missed the first thirteen years with Pola. What odd creatures girls are, and I know nothing about them."

"Really? You think he's like that?"

"I'm sure of it. He's terribly pleased to have you in his life."

Pola plumped a pillow behind her head and picked up her embroidery. "Paul and Jay used to take me to the park to see the jugglers, the kites and clowns. They liked to have fun. I don't think they worried about the world. And they helped Mommy in her work, they introduced her to important people—"

"Didn't Jay introduce her to Daniel?"

Pola was pouting. "I suppose he did. And Jay wanted to go away by then. It all worked out. I just miss the way it was."

"I think I understand, Pola. It's like—well, I miss certain things, too, with Tonio. Like running into him in the middle of the night in the library, and talking for hours. One night we went into the kitchen and made a pineapple cake, and while it was baking we went out on the patio off the kitchen, and he said, 'This is the hour when the wild cat hunts.' I nearly jumped out of my skin!"

"Does he tease you so much?"

She hadn't thought of it like that. "Yes, I suppose he does tease."

"Daniel never does. My mother never does. We never have any fun."

Tonio liked for Abilene to meet him at the practice ring at five, when he rode, and she liked to do so. Tonio and his horse were one as he rode. The peccary that lived in the forest thicket always trotted out to join Tonio on his ride. It went round and

round the ring with him. When Tonio sat on a bench afterwards, the peccary came to rub against his leg like a cat. Tonio
had a monkey that he let run free too. Usually it stayed away
from people and mocked them from up in the trees, or across
the mesh roof of the aviary. Sometimes it went into the guardhouse with Sapo and other men who gathered there. When the
phone rang and Sapo went to answer it, the monkey went
crazy, screeching and banging his ear. When Tonio was around,
though, the monkey pranced and preened in his sight, begging
for his approval. There was a little wild cat, too, caught not long
after Abilene first came to the ranch. It was an *onza*, a *jaguarundi*, caught in the thicket and chained to the front of the
guardhouse. The monkey got just beyond the reach of the leash
and screamed at the cat. Abilene thought Tonio kept these
animals around as a way to say to the natural world: *I am in
charge.* For her there was something wonderful about the presence of animals turned from the wild by his affection.

"Come along, we'll walk in the thicket," Tonio said one afternoon, that first year. He had been riding in a silvery sweat suit,
to lose weight. He stripped to his soaking trousers and took
Abilene by the arm, his riding whip in his other hand. They
walked in leisurely pace around the hacienda wall, medieval
with its gargoyles and iron spires, down the smoothed road
ribbed by palms and jacarandas, leading to the hangar and
airstrip. Along the way, Tonio flicked his whip at a darting
snake, at a fat bug on a leaf, at the ground. By the time he and
Abilene were thirty feet into the thicket they were in another
world. They strolled down an aisle deeply shaded by trees and
shrubs. Their arms were brushed by drooping branches that
shone as if with polish. They went past tall shrubs, sweet of
scent and tangled, with large heavy leaves. Abilene heard cries
and rustles, sounds unlike those of the more open grounds;
she hoped her shudders were unnoticed by Tonio, who walked
with his chest high, a slight smile on his lips, as if he were
going to meet a lover. Abilene stayed close to him. Now and
then he poked through a tangle of brush with his crop.

They walked in silence, and then Tonio abruptly turned
around. He almost caused Abilene to lose her footing, but she

regained her balance and turned back to face the way they had come, as Tonio had done, and she saw light as at the end of a tunnel. They were shrouded in a tomb of foliage. Abilene felt frightened, though she knew it was silly. Nothing could happen with Tonio there. Tonio let his whip fall to the ground and took her against him. He was slick with sweat; he smelled of horses. He kissed Abilene eagerly and long. Abilene responded, but was aware that her senses were played upon by the thicket as much as by Tonio. Tonio unbuttoned her blouse and pressed his flesh against hers; they made a sticky popping sound as they slid apart. He slid her pants down and bent slightly to come up under her. She felt impaled and esctatic, thrown upward by his swift thrusts.

He said, "If I left you now, bears would come from the north, or puma, eh, beasts of the night, at the smell of woman." He was delighted at her bewilderment; she was out of focus, as in a dream. He threw his arm across her shoulders all the while they walked back to the road, and he stopped once to murmer in her ear, "I'd never feed you to them, I'd eat you myself first."

They played Ping-Pong in the bunkhouse. Putting the balls away, Abilene found herself almost into the face of an opposum hanging by its feet. Tonio came behind her and put his arms around her middle. "There is a local folk belief that says the male fucks the female's nose," he said. He pointed at a place, barely discernible in the wasted hide. "What other paired opening exists for his forked penis?" She asked him if he was kidding. "I haven't the time for jokes," he said. But in his room he jabbed at her ears, her nose, her mouth with his erect penis; she was laughing so hard she gagged, and tears sprang to her eyes. Soon after, a neighboring rancher, Michael Sage, came for lunch, and Tonio told him how gullible Abilene was. She was embarrassed and resentful until she saw how surprised Sage seemed to be. The rancher was studying Tonio, truly perplexed. Tonio cut straight across his guest's gaze to look at Abilene with open fondness.

"I'll do anything for you," she gasped that night. She had fallen into a dark thick fairyland, and he was the Prince.

He answered softly. "Wear a collar? Fuck a dog?"

They laughed at this silly notion, but she shivered in her

sleep that night, dreamed of cats on chains, and woke cold and
startled.

"Who else, Abby? Who else came? Only hunters, to kill
things?"

"Oh no. There were spelunkers, exploring caves. The region
is full of them. And there are birders. And a wonderful man, an
archeologist, Martin Dufour, from Switzerland. He spent five
years coming in the winters to excavate just across the river
from the ranch."

"Did you go to see?"

"Yes, I went. To the dig, it's called. But it was awfully dull
stuff. They brush away the dirt, tiny tiny bits of it at a time, in
the hot hot sun. I tried to be interested—I liked Martin, and it
would have been something to do—but it gives me a headache
to go out there. I liked it better when Martin came to dinner
and told us about his travels all over the world. He had been to
India and China, Indonesia and Japan. He and Tonio used to
talk about outfitting a boat to explore the ocean for a year at a
time!"

"Wouldn't that be something? Oh, I want to go everywhere
and see everything, too. You realize, we could live anywhere
we wanted, Mommy and I. We could move every year, but
instead we stay here."

"Your mother has made her life here. Daniel, and her work.
She has to work!"

"Oh no she doesn't. My father sends us money, lots of it. Do
you think Daniel would pay for the lycée?"

"Your mother is a very good photographer. I'm sure she is
paid well."

"My father pays," Pola said stubbornly. "She hates him, but
she takes his money."

"He's your father. He should help support you."

"Oh never mind! Abby, do you remember that winter in
Zihuatenejo?"

"Of course. The people in town called us witches."

"And the bloody turtle—"

"Why yes, I do remember that. And that poor woman who
drowned. What about Lotus? Do you remember her too?"

"She could tell fortunes with cards," Pola said. "And read palms." She seemed suddenly sly. "She said my life line was very short—"

"What a terrible thing to have said! You were only—what?—nine years old?" Hovering on the brink of pubescence, bristling with indignation. She still had a child's poochy stomach, pale nubs of breasts. She could not go by the tin mirror on the door without checking her progress.

"Would it have been better if she lied?" Pola asked.

"That's nonsense to tell a little girl. It's a good thing your mother didn't know about it. Besides, Lotus was hardly more than a girl herself."

"She was my first true friend, and I've never quit wondering what happened to her."

"She probably went home and back to school. Maybe she has her first job, or maybe she's married.

Pola looked at Abilene with outright disgust. "Don't be silly, she'd never be like that."

"She has to *be* and *do* something!"

Pola knew the answer to that. "Not if she's dead."

Abilene hadn't meant to go to Zi, hadn't even known it existed until Mickey mentioned it to her on their way down to Acapulco. She had been so upset when Tonio said he was going to Europe. He had told her the same weekend Isabel came for a visit. Isabel called Tonio a "stick in the dirt," and shaved hash off a gooey ball for them to smoke. The trip to Acapulco was her idea, and Tonio approved, but in the end only Abilene and Mickey went. Isabel had to make a living; she realized it once she was straight again.

On the way to Acapulco their first-class bus caught on fire, and they had to file out onto the side of the road. The baggage was smoldering. They stood off the highway and watched peasants stream down over the hills as though a bugle had been blown. The bus driver threw all the damaged packages and suitcases onto the ground; from somewhere buckets of water were hauled. In half an hour the driver told them to get back on the bus.

"What about our things?" Abilene asked. Mickey pressed her lips with his fingertips. "Look," he said. "Nobody is saying anything. Everyone knows better." It was incomprehensible. Through the window of the bus, Abilene looked back on peasants scrambling in the blackened suitcases. She saw a large fat woman holding up a lady's fancy bra. In Acapulco the bus company gave them each forty dollars.

They stayed in the same little hotel where they had stayed the first time, when they came down from Austin to see Tonio fight. Mickey had friends there. Some days they stayed up in the hills above the strip with them all day and never went out until dark. The boys liked to talk about women. They liked to list their attributes, their eyes and legs, their nice bottoms and breasts, the way they pretended not to want it, or the way they were so hot. Abilene, and sometimes there were other young women, simply turned away to something else, a magazine or a newspaper on the table, or looked at the hot clear sky through a window.

Nights they danced. Abilene danced all the dances, with Mickey and his friends, and sometimes with the local boys, who said they went to college but didn't like it. She wanted them while she was dancing; she imagined going home with each of them. It was quite enough to think about it; she hadn't sunk so low. Still when a young man told her she was a sweet papaya she almost let him know she understood. She liked to dance the line, too, with boys whose shirts were unbuttoned, with music blaring, and outside on the street, a smell of vomit and decaying fruit.

One night in their room Mickey said, "You really don't know what effect you have on me, do you?" They had been fucking once a night, like an old husband and wife. "You dance like the cheapest whore, you know that, Abelita? It's a miracle you aren't carried off and raped in the streets. You don't think I could do anything, do you? But then, it wouldn't really be rape, would it?" She refused to let him bait her. She undressed down to her panties and pulled on a dirty tee-shirt from off the floor while he blabbed on and on. He was running out of energy. He whispered throatily, "You do a hundred things a day to make me crazy. Do you think I didn't see you today at Marcela's,

146

folding the wash? I saw how you handled her brother's shirts, like he was your lover!" Mickey's eyes met hers. "What will you do for me?"

The shirts had been warm, had smelled of limes.

What struck her was his vulnerability, like her own, and his bravado. She disliked him terribly just then. She could forgive the *chavos* at the dance hall, fingering their balls and purring; they were who they were, pure and simple. But Mickey. He had a lot of experience at other things. He had an education. He thought he was something special, badly estimated by the world. He wanted her to love him instead of Tonio, what madness! She wouldn't have touched him to save his life right then. She would have gone with one of his Apaculco friends, he was right about that; she would gladly have floated on their seas of vanity. But Mickey's lust was sordid. It accused her. It was too close to home.

He woke up in the middle of the night. She thought it was to make love, and she was prepared to do so rather than quarrel. But he only wanted to talk!

"You're kidding yourself," he started in. She laughed. Who else was doing that? (Who wasn't?) He went on. "You're not entitled to anything so special." She turned away from him and his nonsense. Jesus, it was the middle of the night! He leaned down and touched her back, she could feel his hot breath on her shoulder. "What I like is watching you undo yourself," he said. It made some impression on her, though she never let him know.

She went to Zi the next day. She left while Mickey was in the shower.

Zihuatenejo was a mere village around a protected bay. She went to the market to ask about rooms, and there met Adele. Adele took her up on the hillside to her white stucco house. On the way she told about a July when she had had her *palapa* poles blown away in a hurricane. When dawn had come, she had seen a village two feet deep in mud. Sloshing through it to the bus, she had seen a baby pig float by, and some cats. Pola said, "I don't remember that, do I?" Adele smiled fondly. There had been a time pre-Pola.

147

They found the winter sublime in Zi. They got up lazy and drank coffee thick with condensed sweet milk. They spent hours on their porch, and more at the beach. They paid fifteen dollars for a burro, from the landlord's son, and another fifty pesos a month for him to feed the animal. He was always looking for a deal for the *gringas*. He trudged up the long rocky path carrying fake artifacts, polished stones, once some duck eggs, oysters, an ancient tin of Bufferin, string, buttons, empty film cases, ballpoint pens, an Italian dictionary, candles. He offered to sell them dope. They ignored the offer of marijuana and bought everything else. Sometimes they paid too much, but usually not. It was a diversion. They set the objects around on windowsills and in the corners of the house, like charms. They woke up every day and waited for something to happen. Sometimes Pola went down into the village to buy sweet cakes or hard rolls for breakfast; after they ate, they fussed with one another's hair and talked. The child's hair was so thick and curly her face was waiflike at its heart. She was moody, often tearful, sometimes giddy. She liked to sit nearby while Abilene and Adele talked about men, photography, gossip from the city, plans for the day, life in general.

Adele told about her own childhood. She had been a French war orphan (Jewish parents), brought to the bright state of California by an officer's family. No one had ever talked to her about the war, the camps. When she was fourteen her adopted mother had a child of her own, quite unexpectedly, and Adele was transformed in function from child to unpaid *au pair*. At seventeen she met Pola's father, an ambitious and dramatic immigrant who was already making his first film. Abilene found it all passionate and fascinating; it shocked her to realize, eventually, that Adele had some self-pity about the course of her life. Still, she seemed stable, perhaps especially because of the rootlessness of her life. She was affectionate to Abilene, got her to talk about herself, to talk, in general, more than she ever had to anyone. But with her daughter, Adele was strangely brittle. Of course Pola was disturbing, with her startling eyes and hair, her old-young look. She looked as if she had seen too much too soon.

There weren't many tourists then in Zi, mostly kids who

slept in tiny rented rooms and spent their days by the water. Age was a natural barrier between them and the two women on the hill. Adele and Abilene and Pola often ate along the beach, where there were cafes set up under thatched roofs with tables set in the sand. They ate grilled snapper, and salt water crayfish. Sometimes they all went to the little hotel at the other end of the beach where they drank watery drinks at its "disco" (a bar with one big blue light) and danced with one another, singing along to the records. The American kids paid them no attention. Sometimes young studs from Acapulco came on holiday and stood around and watched, but there was no apparent way to break in on two women dancing! It was Pola who heard they were witches.

It was Pola, too, who brought some Americans to the house. She met Lotus at the boats where they had gone to buy off the morning catch. Lotus—more likely Sally, Jane, or Joan—looked no older than eighteen, and sick. She was too thin, her color was bad. An older girl said they had driven down from Guadalajara. She was carrying a woven bag from Mykonos, Greece, and in it she had peyote buttons that she offered to share. The boys were long haired, skinny, nut brown. They all hovered and took any food that was offered, but said almost nothing in the women's presence. Abilene noticed that one of the boys had a hard-eyed look; she thought he was older than the others, maybe in his late twenties. When she pointed this out to Adele, Adele became nervous and told Pola not to go off with them. She gave a cautionary speech to the youth, assembled on her porch. "This is Guerrero, and the hills are full of guerillas and dope growers, either of which type can kill you if you are in the wrong place." She pointed out how casual they had been with their dope. "This is a country, with laws and jails, and you kids can get locked up even if you don't believe it."

They bore her lecture with stony patience and said they weren't "into hiding." Pola sat on Abilene's lap while the kids traipsed off downhill and became absolutely swollen with impatience. "You can go down for two hours," Adele said, broken by Pola's silence and pouting. Pola followed the others. In a while she returned, pale and shaken. "They're cutting up a

149

turtle on the path," she said. The three of them rushed down to see. It was the landlord's son and his friend, twelve or so in age, with long sharp knives, hacking at what had once been some creature's living flesh. The thing between the boys was large and bloody and still jerking. Their little local hustler grinned at them and offered them some of the meat for soup; at this they scattered. Pola whined to Adele that if the boy had brought the turtle wrapped in paper they would have bought it. She was angry at her mother for the slaughter, or perhaps for keeping slaughter secret until then.

The older boy was named Paul. He disappeared for a couple of days and no one in his entourage seemed to know where. Privately, Adele said she had seen him in a jeep with a big Mexican. She had seen sun strike something on the seat, a knife or a gun. Many of the locals carried machetes. The import of this mystery soon faded, however, for they all saw a woman drown fifty feet from her breakfast table, in the surf. They were on the porch above the bay and Abilene noticed a commotion below. A big woman in a bathing suit was waving her arms frantically, while people lined up on the beach to watch. "My God I think she's drowning!" Abilene cried, and ran down the path, the others following. It took nearly ten hard minutes to reach the beach. By then the woman was dead. Still, Adele pushed through the men, a tigress slashing at their hovering; she breathed into the poor woman's mouth and pounded on her chest, then rolled her over, sprawled on her side like an abandoned puppet. Pola buried her face in Abilene's chest and wailed.

Abilene screamed, without thinking, "What did any of you do, assholes?" The Mexicans shrugged and looked at one another for an answer none could give. Finally the cafe cook said the woman had eaten an omelet and then had gone in too soon; he seemed to think the eggs had sunk her. None of the Mexicans knew how to swim. Only the American women were mystified that a woman drowned in water to her chest in full view of a crowd. The Mexicans took it as fate, unhappy as it was. The woman's husband materialized from some errand he had been running and howled with grief and rage. He had gone to get tickets back to Acapulco, where boys dove from cliffs and there were places to dance until dawn. They had been bored with Zihuatenejo, old as they were. The cook told the man about the eggs his wife had eaten; his face fell like something melted.

Adele didn't enforce her sanctions against the American kids, but she began to fret about their influence on Pola. She thought Lotus was pumping Pola full of something secretive and maybe malicious. Abilene said she thought Adele had every right to tell her nine-year-old daughter what to do, and Adele said, "Thank you very much!" as though insulted. She told Pola she could not stay in the village past dusk. So one afternoon when Pola did not return in time, Adele went off to find her and brought her back, herded in front like a balky goat. The child looked puffed up with anger. The women skipped supper and sat on the porch drinking beer. Now and then Pola's long cries split the cool evening calm. Adele ignored the piteous wails though she couldn't relax until they stopped. She talked for hours.

"I've always had some reason to worry about Pola. She was born with no opening in her vagina. It's called an imperforate vagina. A couple of years ago it had to be slit open, and last year they excised her hymen."

"How strange!" Abilene said. She observed that it didn't seem to matter to Pola. Abilene thought the strangeness of this nine-year-old girl could be easily attributed to the lifestyle her mother lived. Why wasn't she in school?

"Well, it bothers me! It's like she grew up overnight. They made her a woman, with a sharp knife. I can't stand to have her out of my sight." Adele had a tutor for Pola, the wife of a clerk in the French embassy. Adele rocked forward and back like a person grieving. "I take her everywhere I go. She has a bomb in her, I hear it ticking when she's asleep. It's something she got from her father. Someday I'll have to let her go. How I dread it. It's Pola who's the witch."

"My God, Adele, she isn't ten years old yet!"

"Going on thirty," Adele said. She felt better in the morning. Paul, who had gone off with the man in the jeep, did not come back. The police came at five one morning and seized his van. They let its occupants scatter. Adele pitched in, helping them all make arrangements to get out of Zi. Lotus made frantic calls to Oregon and let the others go off on the bus without her. Adele sorted out the calls, made a reservation for Lotus from Acapulco home. Pola broke out in shingles, an unbelievable misery like nothing Abilene had ever seen. A doctor met them all in Acapulco and gave Pola a shot before they flew on to Mexico. While they waited, Abilene escorted Lotus to another flight where a ticket was waiting. When she rejoined Adele Pola was weeping; she had thought Lotus was coming with them.

On the plane, in a moment's silence, Adele sighed loudly. She said, "I thought a child would give my life a center." Abilene couldn't know what was the right thing to say.

"Don't lose touch," Adele said in Mexico. She took Pola off in a taxicab without asking what Abilene was going to do. Abilene felt abandoned and insulted; she realized she felt like Adele's other child, left for Pola's more urgent needs. She wrote Adele from the ranch when Tonio got back, and invited her and Pola to visit. Adele called to say she was getting some work and putting Pola in school. Later she wrote and said she was spooked by the tropics. "In Mexico, I'm above that labyrinth of muggy malevolent sluggish life. Up here the air is clear. You come sometime."

They met again, in the city, but it was never the same. Abilene realized that Adele had drawn into another space, away from the self she had been in Zihuatenejo. She asked about Abilene's life without any genuine interest. Abilene didn't know why she bothered to see her at all, except where else would she ever get any good advice? Who else did she know who understood how hard it is to get away?

8.

I WAS IN Acapulco the next winter to see Tonio fight. He was spending an evening with people I couldn't stand, and I asked Tacho if he would take me dancing. We went to a fancy club called the Orpheus, where neither of us felt comfortable; there was too much obvious money in the room. We went down to the red light district, to a place called the Cave. On the way I had an idea.

I paid my own way and ignored the scornful doorman's suggestion that I sit along one wall. I stood right beside the dance floor. Tacho went to the bar. The dance hall was a pavilion open on two sides to the night.

A bold young boy approached me and asked me, in good English, to dance. When I saw that Tacho was watching, I said I would, and I danced with the music in my guts, though I held back, too. Part of the pleasure was in holding something back.

The boy offered to get me something to drink, but I walked away from him without answering. Another young man asked me to dance, and I liked him better. I didn't let on that I spoke Spanish, and his English was terrible. He combed his hair before we went out onto the floor. While he danced—he was easy and unaffected in his dancing—he gave me long burning suggestive looks. It was hard not to smile.

Coming off the floor I bumped into Tacho. He grabbed my arm and pulled me back onto the floor. "Now dance with me," he growled. I pretended to want to wrench away. He pushed me over to the open side of the hall. "I can dance when I want," I told him. "With any of the boys."

His hand dug into my arm. "That's too much!" I told him. He mocked me.

"You think this is your game, don't you?" He kissed me roughly. He

was right, I had meant to play a game. To act out a safe fantasy, to use him— Suddenly I knew I had set up something dangerous, and I was thrilled and scared. Tacho had always been around, like the cook or the foreman. Changing that was risky.

"I don't want to dance now," I told him. "Let's go to your hotel." I was seeing him for the first time, a man in his own right, and not Tonio's peon.

"I want to dance! And if you are not a good dancer, I will leave you here!"

I had wanted Tacho to pretend to pick me up, that was all. I hadn't meant to poke at his damned machismo. "I don't want to dance," I said. "I think I should go back to my own hotel—"

He grasped my buttocks and squeezed hard. I danced. When one dance was done, there were only a few seconds before the next one started. The band was playing brassy cantina music, and I didn't think it was fun anymore.

Finally Tacho said gruffly, "Now we'll go." He pushed me into the street and hailed a taxi, pushed me inside, and as soon as he had given the driver his address, began to kiss me and thrust his hand between my legs. I was very excited, but also terrified at the possible consequences of my foolhardiness.

When we got to Tacho's hotel he slammed the door and pushed me against it, whispering my name. "Abelita," he called me. Weakly, I said, "You're forgetting the game. You don't know me. I haven't told you my name." I did want him, but when we were done, I wanted him to forget what had happened.

"I know who you are," he murmered hoarsely. "Whore. Antonio Velez' whore." I didn't care. He said, "Now you're mine." He had never intended a game.

Tonio had had his own evening. When I saw him in the morning he didn't even ask about mine. There was an American girl, he wanted to take her back to the ranch in his plane for a few days. Did I mind to wait a day and go on a commercial flight? He was boyish and silly about it.

That was how I ended up on a bus with Tacho. All the way to San Marta we talked and joked and got to be friends. In the middle of the night we stopped for a snack at a tiny cafe in the mountains. I was stunned to find myself at the top of the world. Stars swirled around me like snow. I had never seen anything so beautiful, and Tacho had given it to me. Back on the bus we argued about whether you could take Hemingway seriously. Tacho said you could. He said all the young bullfighters read Hemingway.

We had to be very very discreet, we knew that. Conspiracy was a large part of the pleasure. I wasn't bored again for months.

Tonio was gone most of the winter. He was building a packing plant in the city and setting up his distribution, negotiating with the unions—becoming a big businessman. Tacho and I spent long days together. He taught me to curse and sing bawdy songs, to play pool, and to cape a cow. He took me to Tampico to see the Huastecan museum, and then to visit a Russian freighter docked there. He made me wear a scarf around my hair and keep my eyes cast down; he told the Russians I was his ignorant wife. We were so giddy and smug, going through that boat. Afterwards we ate fish at a cafe by the pier, piling bones on the tablecloth and fiddling with them, drinking pitchers of beer. We stayed in the city for the night and made love, though we were too drunk to make a good job of it. I woke in the night sweating. It was a cheap hotel, and I thought I had heard something in the walls. I stared at the door in the dark until I realized I was waiting for a vengeful Tonio to pass through it.

Tonio was in Mexico City, playing around with some actress.

Tacho and I became reckless. He kissed me in the bunkhouse by the pool table. "Someone will see!" I said. He said everyone was a spy, he bared his teeth in a grin, a grimace, a dare. Behind his door nobody could see. I lay on his bed with a scratchy blanket twisted beneath my legs, raw as a fresh wound, and it dawned on me that this was some sort of suicide. I was putting my way of life down for a taste of sex with a stranger. Tacho was a coarse, rude man, used to laundry maids and whores, and I knew he had a chavo's view, the woman as chingada. I was a gringa, the ultimate whore. Beneath him, my fantasy evaporated in the heat of lust; I forgot Spanish as if I had had a stroke. I called out in English, "Stop! stop!" He was never tender, though he would sometimes say he loved me, the words bleating, lamenting, lost. One night he fell into a deep sleep and snored. My passion for him, once so quirky, now seemed gone. It was too much risk, for what? A moment's shudder.

I stopped going to him. I avoided looking at him. I clung to Tonio when he was there until he told me he was annoyed by it. Worry went off in me over and over like tiny firecrackers. I had acted out of impulse and perversity, I scolded myself, when what mattered was staying where I was. The idea of Tonio sending me back to Texas was horrifying. I wondered how I could kill myself if it came to that. I didn't want to do something that hurt.

Tacho came to me one more time. A tremendous rain and wind blew in from the gulf. The palms shook violently, and the bamboo lay down on the ground to wait out the wind. The hounds bayed. I lay in my bed in the middle of the night and thought: How odd it is, how odd I am, lying here in a house in a cleared-out jungle, alone with no future. How odd, I thought, because I knew damned well I was pleased with myself. I had to do no more than blink to see the alternatives: me behind a counter selling who-knows-what. My legs sprawled beneath dull ignorant men. The longest life in the world. I had escaped all that, for as long as I had, for as long as I could.

Out of nowhere—off the balcony—a drunk Tacho came in, shouting and sobbing. I couldn't get him out. Tonio was just across the hall, probably reading. Tacho crawled into my bed and then there was a tremendous clap of thunder, a great clatter as doors flew open. Tonio's hounds, a dozen of them, had come through the front doors into the house and were racing everywhere. Tacho jumped naked from the bed and ran through the house screaming at the dogs. The watchman from the little hut at the gate came, and someone from the servants' shed, and above them all I heard Tonio calling his dogs to heel. Frantic, I scooped up Tacho's clothes and threw them under the bed.

The dogs cleared out. Tonio looked in on me but didn't stay. I slept fitfully.

In the morning I took Tacho's clothes out like a rolled up wad of rags and went to look for him. He was gone. All of a sudden I felt safe again. Tonio and I had our routines: his ride in the afternoon while I watched, gin rummy before dinner, long evenings in the library. Sometimes while he read I smoked marijuana and floated around the room. If Tonio gave me dope, he was very indulgent about it. If I asked, though, he was always curt, he always said no.

One afternoon I was dispatched, with Tacho as driver, to a town some thirty miles away, on the other side of the village of San Marta. I had a bladder infection. I dreaded the ride, but I dared not argue with

Tonio's churlish instructions. I slid onto the car seat not looking at Tacho or greeting him. He told me to get in the back seat. I said I wouldn't. He put his arms across his bull's chest and stared straight ahead. I screamed at him that I had an appointment, and he was my driver! He had instructions from the señor. He laughed in his cold barking manner and said something about women being driven—he said this as though it were something nasty—and he said that women belonged in the back, that was the way it was done in this country. Men sat in the front, and women were lucky to get a ride at all.

I saw myself as a cartoon. Gringa or not, I was, by virtue of sex, a secondary person. I might have argued class, but I didn't have the courage or the language for the argument. Who was I but the daughter of an oil-field roustabout? I had been raised in tin houses, and I was a cold man's whore. I felt myself crumple. All the times couples had come to the ranch and the wives would not speak to me. The times Tonio had patted my ass and sent me off to fetch something he wanted. The times I looked in the mirror and wondered my value. I had never felt this cheap! I had been angry and confused before, I had been lonely, but my bad feelings had always been moored in a kind of sublimity, as if I lived in a sauna and everything was heated out of me. But Tacho sucked from the marrow. Reduced me. When I collapsed the distance between us I made myself subject to his code, an amalgam of machismo, paternalism, and violence. I realized it was Tonio's code too; it was the central precept of the culture. The man (lover or father) has authority. Only marriage and children and age give women any weight.

Now Tacho was getting even. He had picked this ridiculous moment—and how I smarted! how I itched and burned!—to face me down as if I were a mad cow and he, capeless, swordless, was prepared to let me hurt him knowing that it would all be reversed, the goring, the revenge. Tonio, embarrassed—the ultimate insult—would throw us both away like dead toads stinking in the sun.

Meekly, with no argument, I complied, and to compound my own indignity and his, I chose not to open the doors and go around, front to back, but to climb over the front seat, head first and rump in the air, and thence to settle in defeated silence for the long dusty bumpy ride to town. I was sure the groundsmen had seen it all. The peacocks had grown still. I slid down in the seat and shut my eyes.

Later, when I came out of the doctor's office, and remembered the strain of riding with Tacho, I thought, to hell with him. Let him play *chauffeur. As I approached the car, though, I saw him at the wheel, his dark eyes shadowed by heavy brows, his glum mouth hanging slightly slack and dry on the lower lip. I recalled the cold condescension of Tonio at my "woman's problem," and the stern coolness of the doctor. I felt, all at once, affection and pity for Tacho. I felt outrage for all the things that were outside and above us both, and I felt longing, gut-deep and burning, though I didn't know for what. I just wanted to have had a different chance at life, and I wanted Tacho to have had it too. And I saw humor in all this. Who did Tacho and I have better to hurt? Tacho turned, and caught me bemused, and I think he understood. We broke into witless laughter, shrieking and hooting and slapping one another on the arms. He bought us sour lime ices; the ice melted faster than we could eat it, so we tossed them into the billowing dust. All the way back to the Tecoluca, now sitting side by side, close together, in the front, we sang cantina songs and sealed not a truce but our conspiracy. Though we would never dare to wonder aloud at how we had betrayed Tonio, we gave ourselves glorious license to be friends, to place ourselves, despite the life that had been allotted us, in a kind of wonderland, where men and women sat where they wanted, at least between town and somebody else's house. I never went to Tacho again, but I liked seeing him. I liked it that he lived at the ranch, and I missed him when he was away.*

Oh Tacho! There was never a chance in the world, but I swear I loved you. I wish you had been my brother. I wish Tonio had sent you away while you were young, so that you could have made your own life and not one in his shadow. I wish life were fair. I wish we had our rightful share of it.

Tonio no longer treated me like a lover. I would wake up to the sound of his plane leaving, and he would not have said a word. If I wondered where he had gone or how long it would be before he came back, I would have to ask Sofia, his hateful secretary, and sometimes, not often, I did. She always called him the señor, but her tone told me it was not out of respect for him, but disrespect for me. It was like she was saying: I am his trusted employee and he knows my worth. What can you say about yourself? Yet I wasn't afraid of being sent away. I knew by now how Tacho had come at fourteen or fifteen years old, hoping to be a bullfighter, and had been taken on by the young matador and trained to be his dart-sticker. I knew that I used up nothing, and that Tonio liked my presence, as he liked the monkey's, the jaguarundi's, the Huastecan cook's.

When he said he was going away again, for a whole season in Europe, and taking Tacho and Esteban with him, my heart sank at the prospect of so much lonely time, but I heard the news and was immediately resigned. The surprise was that he had made some kind of plans for me. He wanted me to spend the time at his hotel, the Arcadia, which was only twenty miles away, where, he said, I would have some company and some occupation. Anything I needed I could have by asking Bruni. He, Tonio, would be gone, doing the things he did in Europe (fighting bulls, visiting ranches, consorting with the beautiful people, who really existed), and I, Abilene, would lie dormant like an insect to await his return. "My manager Girard is a pendajo and won't like it," Tonio warned, "but you can ignore his Chinaman's queerness and make the best of it. After all, it is a resort."

I was totally surprised by the Arcadia, by Claude Girard. The hotel was a world of intrigue and surprises, the guests were old and had their lives to tell, the food was wonderful. Besides, no matter where I was, I managed to find a way to prove myself to myself over and over again. What Adele had called the "muggy sluggish tropics" seemed just right for me. I moved slowly through without caution; every time I poked into the brush or went out at night, there I was.

I know how my life would sound to a stranger. I know I've never accomplished anything. I know that my life in Mexico reads like a litany of non-events, a grocery list of sins. Mickey said I was "undoing" myself. Was I? Was there something to be undone? I think that was taken care of quite effectively a long time ago. There were things I wanted. I wanted not to be bored, not to pass my life trivially. I wanted not to be a waitress, a clerk, a wife, a teacher, or any other kind of servant to the world. I had no ideas about what to do instead. I had no pictures in my head of what might make a good life. I tried to imagine what the girls in cashmere sweater sets would be doing at thirty; I saw them married, with domestic help, golf lessons, shopping, dinners with their husband's associates. (I knew about these things because I'd gone to the movies, of course.) I wondered what smart girls would become, and I simply didn't know. The thought that you could study and become Margaret Mead or Marie Curie—come on, I would have to say. Didn't they have a few advantages I didn't? Besides, I knew I

159

wasn't very smart. I would have to do the best I could. I wanted to be loved, too, I guess. I couldn't pin that down, and I didn't really think about it all that much. I didn't need parents anymore. I didn't know what love was about.

Meeting Tonio was like being catapulted into outer space. Here was a life I'd never have dreamed up in a hundred years! Here was a man who knew everything, could do everything, and he liked me. Five years came out of that. I stopped thinking about whether he loved me; I thought only: there's a place for me here.

I thought: Kermit should see me now.

Mexico was more than Tonio (more than the other men, too). It was a smell in the air, different with seasons, redolent in the worst heat, before the rains. It was the sensation of moisture around you all day, like an invisible sea, so that you pushed your way through a day and knew it was the cost for all the lushness, the colors, the sounds. There was a whole world entirely unlike my own, and I never stopped loving that part of it. The Arcadia was fresh experience. It opened up the Huasteca to me. It opened up my self, too. When I left, I knew the one thing I must have always wanted and never had: intimacy. I had just a taste of it, to let me know what it was, but I was resigned to a life without it. I didn't think it was something you could work for.

Claude Girard let me know that he disapproved of me. He gave me a room near the center hall, so that I awoke too early in the morning. He told me I would have to have a separate bar bill and Bruni would have to pay it every month. He even scolded me for coming in from the pool barefoot! He didn't bother me at all. I moved to the far end of the building, near an exit to the hot pool. I went to the kitchen in the late morning to get a glass of juice and a slab of bread, and smiled at Claude if he saw me on the way. I made myself useful, helping the clerks with long-distance calls, the guests with plane reservations. I learned to pass the time with the old tourists, mostly midwesterners, retired, who stayed two or three months every few years. I learned to play pinochle, bridge, and Parcheesi. I went on endless outings. There were many things to see in the region of the hotel and I had seen almost none of them. Caves and bats, groves, hill villages. We went in caravans to Tamazunchale, a lovely tropical village forty miles into the mountains by the Moctezuma River. We went to see the market and the sixteenth century church. The American guests loved the drive through lush mountain scenery, the increasing sense of the tropics that began east of the hotel, where a finger of Veracruz lay in lowlands along the coast, and then broadened as it went farther south to Guatemala, and southeast to the Yucatan. Coming back from the village we all bought honey from Indians along the roadside. They sold it in any old container, and the honey had a taste almost of brandy; we dipped our fingers in and sucked the sweetness while we stood there.

South of Tamazunchale was an Augustine monastery of Moorish character, and off the road along the same highway, Xilitla, where indios (speaking a language that linked them to ancient Mayans) grew coffee, bananas and oranges among palm and large-leafed bushes in profusion. To the north were the falls at El Salto, and quite near—on the senior Velez' small ranch La Palmita, in fact—was a beautiful grotto called Nacimiento, where a small river began and then flowed into the greater one and out to sea. I went to Nacimiento many times with tourists, and every time I wondered, where does the water come from, so clean and clear and cold? Where, in the belly of the earth, is it so sweet? I mentioned my question to a knowledgeable old gentleman who lectured me all one afternoon on the wonderful anomalies of the region; he said it was a topography of collapsed surfaces, classic karst, as if it were Adriatic terrain. I thought, why it's just like love, with sinkholes all around. I sometimes went with the man, whose name was Riley, into the nearby town, but it wasn't much, a dusty collection of cobbled or dirt streets coming off a drab square and a church gone seedy. On Sunday the square filled with residents, and the young people passed one another going in opposite directions, around and around, as their parents had done too. But these kids sometimes had radios, bright colored shirts and dresses, a longing for television, white bread, a different life.

Birdwatchers, three cars of them, came through and stayed a few days to swim and rest from their camping and hiking. The baths had attracted them. They called themselves "birders"—they were amateurs, not ornithologists—and they said there were hundreds of species of birds along the slopes of the Sierra de Guatemala. They had come up from the Yucatan, which was gaudy with tropical birds and butterflies, and they were going to camp in the cloud forest north of us. They knew of a Canadian hermit and botanist named Harrison who had cleared some of the land and done some building there. He raised flowers— orchids, they thought—and lived alone. A Texas college had a cabin there, and one of the group had a letter from a friend on the faculty.

161

They asked me to join them for dinner. I liked their company, and I thought they admired me in some way, maybe just for my happenchance settlement in so beautiful and extraordinary a place, as though that were my own accomplishment.

I told them some of the stories Beto had told me, about the Indians' bird fetishes, their fear of snakes, the rites of the old brujos, like witchdoctors. I knew something of the history of the region, all from Martin, and I felt good, passing it on in this way. The birders ate crayfish from the river, delicious as lobster and to some extent renowned. They ate voraciously and then sat idle over their salads (which they asked for as a last dish). They had heard there were chachalas in the area, though higher, in the forest. I said I knew them, olive-colored birds the size of bantams. I had seen them in Tonio's aviary. At that, the birders had nothing more to say to me. The conversation shifted to the Christmas bird-count in Florida. They told me I ought to look around at the free birds, their voices punctuated the free; they said it was too bad there was no adequate field guide for the region. One of them said, "So the Huastecans don't cage any birds, you say?" and I said that was what I understood. They all gave me such a look, as if I were guilty of some transgression, and it dawned on me that they were disapproving of Tonio! As if I had anything to say about what he caged! Was it my fault if he wanted to enclose a bit of jungle and wildlife for his amusement? Did my confederacy with him extend to his birds, his big game trophies, slaughterhouse gore, business done with embrazos and then bribes? Just how did I get so large a responsibility in this world! I was suddenly self-conscious, and then quite angry. I shook my shoulders and excused myself. I was sure to avoid the hot pool because I knew they would spend the evening there, talking about birds and flowers.

The mayor of San Marta died, and to my amazement, Claude invited me to go with him to the funeral. It was a long service with both a priest and a brujo present; the old indio fumigated the whole area with a charcoal torch smelling of pine pitch. In the church yard, women had laid out huge quantities of food on long tables. The mood was one of cordial seriousness; the mayor had been a very old man. I ate tiny bites of everything, wondering about the state of the kitchens where it had been prepared. There were huge tamales with wild game shredded inside, wrapped in banana leaves and baked in pits. There

162

were smaller tamales with chicken and pineapple, a strange combination. Indians with violins joined a man with a small harp and a woman with a timbrel (like a tambourine), and they sang mourning songs, beautiful songs, centuries removed from the modern Mexico's ubiquitous cantina music. As we drove home in the hotel jeep, Claude told me that the mayor had been Huastecan, and that it was the custom of these people to wash the feet of the dead and then use the water in the making of tamales for the funeral guests. "They honor you, and you honor the dead," he said. I believed him. When had he ever shown a trace of humor?

I wanted to ask him what else he knew. What sort of magic did the witches practice? What did he know of their animas and totems? But I was peeved; he had set me up, hoping to shock (or gag!) me and I wouldn't give him the satisfaction of my interest. We rode in silence. Then in a little while Claude said to me, "Why do you make love?" I thought I must not have heard him.

"Make love?" I said in a silly voice.

"Yes," he went on, "I wonder about American girls, I haven't known them well, but they are so free with these things, with lovemaking. I wondered why this is." I saw that he was perfectly serious. It was still an intrusive, stupid question. I told him I made love to avoid answering personal questions.

The next day he asked if I would help him with some repairs on the mural in the upstairs hall. It was a picture of the Velez family on horseback; Tonio was about sixteen. It had faded and was badly chipped—bad paint in the first place, Claude said. He was perfectly civil as we worked. He had a scaffold constructed, and he mixed paint himself. I spent hours on end, for most of a week, repairing the leaves, the legs of Tonio's horse, the long skirt of his mother, the blue sky. Behind the family young girls with gardenias in their hair were skipping along; a miniature General Velez, like an elf, peeked out of a bush at them. Toward the top of the mural, flowering orange trees filled the canvas like stars. Doves, parrots and parakeets, hanging like flat ornaments, contrasted with the pheasants and plump round quail that pranced along on the ground. The pose of the family was similar to the one done in tile on the first floor of the hacienda. Guests loved the mural, and they all traipsed by to visit with me and commend me for my work. Little by little I pieced together stories of Tonio's family I had never heard before. His father was an infamous general, one of the last

caciques *of Mexico, dictator of the state. It had taken a virtual*
shutdown of public services to force him out. And he was known to love
young girls. Once I heard this—it was hardly surprising, though I had
never actually seen him myself—I couldn't keep my eyes off his por-
trait. He seemed about to burst his clothing. Behind him, the teenage
Tonio was slim and elegant, a blond, blue-eyed European, a nobleman
in a pagan land. The mother was garish in brilliant blue, her hair an
unnatural red.

Bruni came over to see how I was doing and said the mural looked
great. He said he knew that the General and his wife had asked Claude
to do something about it, and that he would be sure that they under-
stood that it was "Tonio's friend" who had done such a patient job of
repairing it. (Claude had said only that it was "satisfactory.")

I walked Bruni back to the parrot-green Tecoluca pickup. "Tonio's
corridas," *I asked. "How are they going? How is he doing?"*

I was amazed when Bruni said that he talked to Tonio at least once
every week. "He's a hero," he bellowed to me as we stood by the truck.
"You don't know just how good he is, do you?" He stooped down to
hug me. I was wearing jeans and a halter top, and his big hand on my
bare back made me uncomfortable. He made a show of kissing me loudly
on each cheek, and as he did so, he dipped his hand into my pants and
slid along the sweaty skin as far as he could reach. I was so surprised I
didn't say anything; he withdrew his hand and got into the truck. That
sonofabitch, *I thought. He was supposed to be looking after me while*
the matador was gone. In his way, he was. He asked if I needed money
and he cleared the matter of the bar bill. But he knew how my keep was
earned. He was a slimy bastard and he just had to remind me.

I withdrew from the sightseeing, the card playing, the endless story-
telling of the hotel. I stayed to myself in my room, taking a brisk swim
in the early afternoon when the other guests went to lunch and then to
siesta. At night I went out to the hot pool after the hotel was dark and
quiet. Sometimes I saw Claude on his way to see his pet doe, or going
up the walk to the little hut he had built himself above the gardens. He
had a house on the side of the hotel where the orange groves were, but
he seemed to favor his perch. One night I saw, as he was walking by,
that he was wearing a cloth, wrapped like what I guessed was a sarong.
He was wearing sandals, and carried a walking stick. Suddenly I saw
him an entirely new way, not as the nagging, shrill manager who was

*always scolding the help, nor as the cold distant man who obviously
looked down on me and couldn't be bothered to get to know me. I saw
him as a stranger in this land, as much as I was, and he was a whole
history of exotic places. He had been born in Vietnam of a French father
and a Chinese mother—one of the guests had told me that. He had lived
in North Africa, in France, in the South Pacific—I had heard him
telling stories to the guests. How had he ever ended up in so unlikely a
place? What was there here to keep him?*

*I called out his name before I could think why I was doing so. He
padded over by the pool and squatted on the side of it. "So this is where
you are at night," he said, as if he had been looking for me!*

*"Oh yes," I told him. "This is the part of the day I love the most, the
dark. I like to listen to the bamboo clacking, and there are creatures that
make noises in the bushes. I think this must be Shangri-la!" I heard
myself and I thought: Stop being hysterical! Claude looked almost
handsome in the faint light from a yellow bulb some way off, and the
moon.*

*"But Shangri-la would not be in the tropics," he said. I felt embar-
rassed, and wanted him to leave, but he said, "I was working at the
Hilton in Mexico City, and General Velez asked me to come out here
and put his hotel in order. He had had it for some time, and it was
losing money. He knew it was a matter of thievery and bad management, and I said it might take a year. I did what I came out here to do,
but I have been here nearly six years. It is, as you say, the quality of the
place. This is the very place where the tropics begin—a change of
continents, we are a hundred miles below the Tropic of Cancer. It is a
place of wild rich abundance. So I built my little house above the
gardens in a nest of ferns and shrubs. When I am there, I am completely away from the silly Americans. I am king of the tropics."*

*He laid down his stick and sat on the edge of the pool with his feet in
the water. I clung to the ledge, wondering if I were dreaming this
strange encounter. He went on, talking about how he liked high places,
telling me about the red tiled roofs of Moroccan houses, of how the cats
there stretch and sun themselves. I said nothing. I was mesmerized. I
had thought him such an ugly man, puffy and yellow and sly.*

*I asked him to tell me more about North Africa, though it seemed a
silly thing to talk about, considering where we were. I sensed that he
was fond of the memories he had of the region, and that he would be less
friendly if our talk were more personal. He told me he had spent some*

time in Algeria, too, and he talked about the seacoast, and the long spines of mountains, the resorts where the French came to ski. He talked slowly, as if he were translating from French. I wanted him to talk all night; all he said seemed important to me, knowledge I hadn't known I needed. I was struck with the luck of my landing here, to hell with his distinctions, it was *Shangri-la*. For the first time since Tonio left, I felt sensual, my pores were open. I was no longer suspended, waiting for his return, but was launched on a legitimate journey of my own into this tropical heart. I thought of Claude taking me around the gardens, teaching me the names of plants, holding my hand—

He was saying something about Berber music. He stopped mid-sentence, and I thought he must have realized how inattentive I was. How could I tell him how wonderful his voice was! How I loved his stories. He reached over and touched my earlobe, and the tiny gold hoop I was wearing. "In so many villages where I have lived or travelled, when girls are young, their mothers put a hot needle through their ears, and then insert little hoops like these."

I pulled myself up to sit on the ledge. I was wearing only the bottom of my suit. My breasts were so white.

"You're pretty," he said rather matter-of-factly. "It's so seldom that you seen an American who doesn't eat too much."

I took a deep breath. "Claude, I've seen you going up to your little house on many evenings. I've heard you playing music, faintly, from here. I've hoped you would stop and talk to me. You didn't know I was here, did you?" I was lying; I had always held my breath for fear of discovery, I hadn't had the least interest in Claude. Now, though, I thought it cunning to reveal myself. Seduction came from confession. He came into the water, took a few long strokes to the other side, returned, and heaved himself out. His dripping belly was soft and fleshy. I was suddenly mortified. I felt he had tricked me, to prove what I was like. He had said nothing to make me think he wanted me, and I had acted as if any conversation might end in sex. His soft flab repulsed me. I couldn't look at him anymore. I fell back into the water, into the dark. I heard, rather than saw, as he padded away, up to his retreat. Shortly I heard music, something percussive and unmelodic.

I had learned that Huastecans did not like to go out at night except when it was to see the brujo in secret meetings. Maybe it was their fear of snakes, or of el tigre, which might kill them. (Once they had eaten the flesh of cats, and drunk their blood.) There was something to learn *from such people, who stretched back for centuries. It was this simple maxim:* Stay home at night.

I began to look forward to the visits of the American rancher Michael Sage. He had come by one day to say he had heard Velez was gone, that I was at the hotel, and he had brought me some magazines his wife no longer wanted. I got fairly drunk with him, in the bar. He stayed a few times and had supper with me, though he complained that the price was much too high. He was a tall, fair man, as I imagined baseball players to look, and he didn't interest me in any special way, but he was company. After the odd little encounter with Claude I welcomed Sage's visits, tried to be enthusiastic, especially if Claude saw us together.

I told Sage one day, "I've just got to get out of here." I didn't mean forever, I explained. I just thought I ought to go back to Texas, maybe, and see if it was as I recalled. Sage said he flew to San Antonio once or twice a year. The implication was I might go with him some time. "Does your wife like it here?" I asked.

He scowled. "Certainly not the country," he said. "She stays in Tampico most of the time."

"I see," I answered. In a way I probably did. Sage's casual visits were those of a dissatisfied husband. The idea drove me off. "Yes," I said, a little loudly. "I think I'll go home some time soon." I'd have to ask Bruni about some money.

Before I had time to think it through, my brother Kermit called. He was thoroughly annoyed; it had taken him a whole day to get through. He supposed I wouldn't be there for the funeral, he said, but Dad was dead.

I had to collect my father in my mind before I could respond; when was the last time I had even thought of him? "How?" I asked.

The connection was terrible. "Off a rig," I heard Kermit say. He had fallen off a rig.

"I don't believe it," I said. It was so stupid, nobody could do that.

"Well, they've got him in a box," Kermit yelled. "Believe it." Then he hung up.

167

9.

"OH, I HOPE *he really did fall,"* Sherry *said, startling me. Her face was an open plea not to pursue the implication. She had come along to the airport to meet me. My brother did not put himself out too much for anyone. Sherry told me there hadn't really been a funeral, only the interment, a cortege of three. I could imagine my sister-in-law between Kermit and my mother, holding an elbow on each side, the good-woman wife, long-suffering, sturdy and shy. I couldn't imagine how life with Kermit had been for her. Not good would have been my guess. Yet he had come up in the world marrying Sherry, who came with a widowed mother Ann—a pleasant woman—and her house.*

Sherry said there had been a woman at the funeral home; they had seen her against the back wall when they were at the casket. A dark woman with a lot of hair, caught in a loose rope at the neck. "I went back and asked her how she knew Bud. She wouldn't talk to me. She had looked so sad, and in a moment she looked frightened and then very hostile. I touched her and she bolted. God knows who she was." *Sherry seemed uncomfortable. I suspected she had told me the story to get it over with, but what was I supposed to do?*

I soon realized they had not thought I would come. They looked at me as if I had grown horns and a tail, that native-Texan look of suspicion. I sat with them, hunched over the kitchen table, looking for something to say.

"Guess it's going to snow." *That was big brother Kermit's contribution. He was thinner than I remembered, hollow-chested. Something wasn't agreeing with him. Supposedly he wanted to be a doctor. I asked him how it was going, and he just looked at me.* Stupid question.

My mother seemed beyond it all. Her thinness, unlike Kermit's, had a certain elegance to it. Through her silky green shirt the deep clefts above her collarbone lay like craters on a relief map. Her cheekbones were newly prominent, rouged, a fresh asset on a woman who had always gone around with her head tucked down. She even wore a string of pearls, surely fake. I wished for them to be real, plucked from the ocean, one at a time, by naked boys.

Little Tommy, almost exactly the age of my affair with Tonio, leaned on his knees and banged two fists in front of him. Sherry put a bowl of tapioca in front of him and began sliding plates of cold food onto the table. "Isn't anybody hungry?" she entreated.

"Looks like your dad had himself a woman friend," my mother said. I squirmed in my chair. Nobody would be happy to learn there had been a Mexican mistress, but what could they say in front of me?

Kermit took me to the grave. It was almost dark. We stood beside the fresh dirt, uncertain of each other in our new half-orphaned state. (So what's any different, I thought.) I stole glances of him. His skin, like mine, showed the tracks of old acne, but I had never noticed before. His hair was long, it fell across his forehead. I slipped my hand into his. His arm hung slack. For a moment I thought he was refusing me, his hand gimpy like a flap off his sleeve. Then he gently closed his hand around mine.

"There was a young man from Boston, he bought himself an Austin—"

He was grinning.

"There was room for his ass, and a gallon of gas," I added, and together we finished the limerick: "But his balls hung out and he lost 'em."

I knelt and took up a handful of the fresh-turned dirt. I had always thought dirt was warm, raw like this, but it was cold and damp.

He had liked limericks. That was what we remembered of him.

"Tell me about it," I said.

"He died on a Monday night. We had just had him over for dinner— Sherry keeps saying that, over and over, as if I need reminding, as if it mattered, it made something okay. He hadn't eaten six bites. He was white-faced, except for his blotchy nose. Once I saw him clutching the edge of the table. I didn't know what to make of it. Sherry was clearing the plates, Ann was up getting coffee, and I blurted out, 'See a doctor, anybody can see you're in pain.' He said he'd been having trouble

pissing—he apologized to Ann for the slip—and that he was tired. Too many night shifts at the well, he said. He went away, I swear, like a tired old dog." It hadn't been surprising to hear that he was dead. The dispatcher called Kermit from work. Bud had fallen off a rig. Nobody knew what he was doing up there, he wasn't a derrick hand anymore. The hand who had seen it said it looked like Bud was reaching for something, like he had stepped out to take it.

"Everyone said he was sober," Kermit said. "They decided on an autopsy. There had to be a reason, you know? An autopsy can't explain an accident. He was getting old, his judgment was bad, he was weary. But he did have a kidney stone like a fist in his bladder, and get this, he had a perforated bowel. A swallowed toothpick. Hell, he died of pain to save the wait."

"What did he do? For something to do? Kermit, I don't remember!"

Kermit understood what she was asking. "He watched TV. He read Louis L'Amour."

Relief flooded me. "Oh yes."

"I think he played poker once in a while."

"I hadn't written him in so long."

"I gave him the card you sent us from Acapulco last year. He thought it was terrific, like you'd won the lottery."

"What did you think? What do you think of me?"

"Abby, when I'm out of the house, I don't even think about my wife, my kid. Just whatever it is I'm doing."

"Is it so hard, school?"

"It's a lot of work, and I've got such a long way to go. It's not that tough. It's—life. Shit, you know."

"What does Mom say about Bud?"

"Nothing. I think it was a relief. One less thing for her to think about. Which leads me to say I don't think she cares what you're doing. Whatever that is."

"Getting by. Life, you know."

"So what is it with this guy?"

"I live on his ranch."

"Why?"

"It's an easy life. Sometimes it's interesting. I like him a lot." I thought about the jaguarundi on the chain at the guardhouse. Tonio said they were rare, these cats, yet he'd seemed to take it for granted

that one showed up because he wanted it to. The cat clawed anybody who came close, but Tonio could stroke her russet flanks and make her purr.

I wondered if, being young, the cat had forgotten freedom: long jumps, the smell of prey. I missed the ranch already.

"I meant something else, dopehead. Don't take this wrong. Why you?"

"Luck. I knew his cousin, we went to see him fight, he said I could stay."

"No shit. That doesn't explain anything."

"It's all I know."

I wanted Kermit to understand other things, more important. "Once I went to the ranch on the bus. Ten hours from Mexico City. This marvelous thing happened. We stopped high in the Sierras at two or three in the morning. Ten thousand feet above sea level, and I suddenly stared up into the sky so close, so full of stars, they looked like they would rain down on me, and then I looked out on mountains, ridge after ridge like ocean waves—" I stopped for breath, amazed at the words pouring out of me, the vividness of the memory. "Thrown out among the mountains, infinitesimally small, were the twinkles of fires, like fireflies."

Kermit walked back to the car in front of me. When we were inside, I said, "I missed you when you got married and moved away."

"Sherry was pregnant, and then had an abortion. I married her anyway. We got right to work on Tommy, to make that up."

"She's awfully nice, Kermit."

"Oh, she's better than that. She's the best. I don't know how I lucked out."

I knew there were oceans of words unsaid. I didn't care to know anything about it.

The next day Kermit got out of bed at noon, came into the kitchen where I was feeding Tommy and visiting with Ann and my mother. He made himself an egg, ate it out of the skillet, and then went back to bed. When Sherry came home from work she looked around; Lenore, my mother, saw and pointed a thumb in the general direction of the hall. Sherry's face fell for a moment and then she started moving around in double time. She made me nervous. There was the undercurrent of *ritual in all this, something my brother did that set off certain motions. I didn't like it. We heard Kermit going in to take a bath, doors opening and shutting, water running. He came out at 6:30, with his books. He gave us all, in a general sort of way, a smile, and he went off to class. Sherry sat down at the table and crumpled over chicken-fried cutlets.*

"He's just like his dad, secretive and anxious, stuffing everything that bothers him down in his pockets—" We all looked at Lenore, even Tommy, who had finished his milk and had turned his glass upside down on his plate into a pile of mashed potatoes. Lenore was wearing an old familiar face, the family assayer. She started clearing dishes, banging things around. Sherry looked to Ann for advice; Ann raised her mouth in perplexity. Lenore, at the sink, went on muttering for four or five minutes. "Hiding their feelings, taking off when it suits them—" on and on she went, a litany of barbs, she sounded more muddled than angry. Finally she turned around, drying her hands on a towel.

"He doesn't drink?" she said to Sherry. Sherry said no, he never did. "And he doesn't chew toothpicks," Lenore added, breathing deeply, lifting her rib cage, going back to her newer self. "I have a friend coming up in a day or two to get me." She said this to no one of us in particular. "Carl Matthews, Matthews Appliances." We all lurched toward smiles, then held them back, uncertain; she gave us permission with her sudden sunny face. "I went in to buy a television. I said I wanted the best." Suddenly self-conscious, she sat down. She put her hands over mine, a move that surprised me so much I stiffened. "If your daddy had ever got something going —" She trailed away. I understood. "I don't know if I ever could have divorced him," she said softly. "I meant to talk to him about it, but I kept putting it off. He jumped off that rig, you know he did—"

I knew no such thing. Ann went to turn on the television. Sherry took Tommy to the bathroom. Lenore sat with her palms on the table, like a woman waiting for a fortune-teller.

"I can't get her out of my mind," Sherry said to me as we were going through Bud's clothes. We had found his checkbook, with a check written to cash for three hundred dollars, the apparent balance of his account, but the check was still on the pad. He had signed it on the day he died. We found the title to the trailer, also signed.

Sherry's face grew puffy with grief. She had taken it the hardest, I realized guiltily. She had been through this before. "He was doing some sort of accounting, getting ready—" she said.

"Oh Sherry, if he meant to jump, why not finish all this stuff? Don't make too much of it." We sat side by side on the bed. "Let's ask the neighbors what they know. And I'm going to cash this check." I had decided to go back to Mexico by bus. What hurry was there?

The neighbors were cool to us. I had the idea they knew a lot about my father and weren't going to tell any of it to us. Vexed, we packed the last of Bud's things in boxes, for a flophouse downtown. I was emptying a drawer in the cramped little hall when it hit me that there had been empty drawers. "Why didn't I notice it before? It isn't like he ran out of things to put in them, he had these others stuffed. But there are empty drawers here, and there were some in the bedroom. Would you put your stuff away like that?"

"You think somebody else was living here?" Sherry pulled out a drawer to see for herself.

In the bathroom we found a tube of Desitin. That was the only thing that didn't seem to belong in a man's bathroom. The rush I had felt earlier faded. I hadn't known I was so romantic. Then, as we left the trailer, I saw, in the dirt at the corner of the step, a baby's pacifier. I felt exhilarated. What I wanted to find out was that my dad had been something besides a weary old man. Ballsy. God, I'd have loved it. His neighbors were old retired people. It wasn't their pacifier.

We went out with my mother's friend Carl Matthews. I could hardly eat, I wanted so much to lie down somewhere and make up scenarios about my father and the mysterious woman. Carl talked all through dinner about the improvements in color televisions. Lenore was flushed, happy. When he ran down, like a battery, and looked at Lenore, she patted him on the chest.

Sunday morning Sherry and I went back to the trailer to sweep and close it up. I was washing at the sink when someone knocked at the rattly door. It was a young woman we hadn't seen the day before.

"I heard you were asking about Mr. Painter," she said in a Texas twang so pronounced it made me smile. She didn't seem to notice. "There was a woman living with him last year. Real funny name. Ophelia."

"Mexican? Long hair, plump?" Sherry stood on springs.

173

"Yeah. Wore ribbons braided in her hair. Funny." The girl's own hair was teased and anchored into place. She was a thin young thing, in a short skirt, tights, and a pullover. "There was a baby, five, six months old. Getting too big to carry, but not walking yet. I've got a baby that age, and a two-year-old. I came over once to see if she wanted to get the babies together, or trade baby-sitting once in a while. She was real unfriendly."

"And she lived here?" A baby. I felt funny about that.

"Sometimes she went away for a couple days. But she lived here. They had a little playpen they'd set out by the step. Felia sat on a chair right by it, always touching the baby. Mr. Painter sat on the step. And there was another thing. She always played the radio real loud, Meskin music." The girl wiped her hands on her skirt as if she had been scrubbing something. "I gotta go. I know nobody said nothing to you, but I figgered you got a right to know. Felia cleared out in a hurry."

"How? She wasn't here when my brother came over."

"Her brother came and got her. He came real early in the morning. I was awake with one of my kids. My husband came down to see. They was gone in fifteen minutes, boxes, play pen, everything. Listen, you can't find her. Some people—those people—they all look alike."

"What kind of car?" I asked.

The girl screwed up her face, thinking hard. "Yellow. With real fancy black doo dads all over it. Sharp. My husband says he runs a night club."

"Their last name? Do you know that?"

"I gotta go. I told you all I know!" The girl ran the length of two trailers and disappeared around a corner.

"Oh Abby." Sherry looked ready to cry again. "Does it upset you?"

"The woman? No."

"The baby? Could it have been his?"

"Heavens. How would I know. Maybe. Or he could have met her when she was pregnant. Anything could be true."

Sherry sighed. "Let's not talk about this around Kermit yet. I want to find out more first. He would discourage me. That girl was right. It sounds awful, but they do all look alike. There are what, sixty, seventy thousand people in town. A third of them are Mexican. We'll never find her without a name."

"I don't understand why she ran away."

174

"If they weren't married—I don't know. Don't you think he was going to give her the check, the title?"

"So why didn't he!" I sank into silence like a stone.

When we got back to the house we found Carl ready to take Lenore home. Kermit was in bed. It was awkward, pushing Bud aside to recognize this courting. I followed my mother out to Carl's car. The sky had turned to slate, the sun was as dull as a moon in a daytime sky. "It does look like it might snow, or sleet," Lenore said. Carl revved the engine.

"We'll be home before it starts," he said.

The window on Lenore's side went up, zip! when Carl pushed a button. Lenore put her hands in her lap and stared straight ahead.

Inside the house, Kermit was up.

"You bum, not saying good-bye," I said.

Kermit pulled the short curtain aside at the window behind the table. "What'd I tell you?" he said. Huge wet flakes had begun to fall. I took the newspaper to the couch and spread it around me like a moat. So Dad had had mistress. Peculiar word. It was a surprise, with something bittersweet to it.

Ann had a friend whose daughter was married to a Mexican who ran a restaurant. She made some calls and came up with a name for us.

The friend's son-in-law was expecting us. He came out of the kitchen, dressed in an expensive suit, wiping his hands delicately on a clean white towel. He led Sherry and me past cases of Dos Equis, into his office, where chairs were arranged like still life. He said his name was Renaldo—he didn't give us his last name—and a young man in a white shirt and black creased trousers brought in glasses of beer and a plate of tortilla chips. "This isn't necessary!" Sherry exclaimed. I nudged her with my knee.

"This is generous of you, to take your time for us," I said. I leaned toward Renaldo. "We want to find my father's friend. All we know is that her name is Ophelia, that she has a baby, and that her brother has a yellow car and maybe runs a night club. What does that tell you?"

He took his time answering. He leaned forward, putting his elbows on the desk. "We are good citizens in this community."

"Por supuesto," I said, hoping I did not sound condescending. In Mexico, it is always right to attempt Spanish; in Texas, I wasn't so sure. But I wanted him to know I wasn't naive.

"What makes you think there is such a woman? Who gave you her name?"

Sherry told him about the woman at the funeral home, and what the girl in the trailer court had said. Renaldo pulled his arms back and folded his hands calmly.

"I may know this family. I can't yet be certain. I will take your message to them, if you tell me what it is. In this way, they may decide if it is something they wish to know."

"We want to see her ourselves!" I recognized that Renaldo had control of the conversation, and I knew that it came not just from knowing something we did not, but from his sense of superiority. He was the one who condescended. "We have money for her," I said sharply, trying to curb my anger, reaching for the formal courtesy that I knew would work best. "We think my father may have intended to give her his home. We are prepared to do as my father wished, but we have to talk to her, we have to know her name. And the child—it may be my father's child." To my surprise, I was choking up. Sherry took my hand and clasped it tightly. I was grateful.

"I will look into it," Renaldo said. "I will see if I can find her, if the family I am thinking of is the right one. I will tell her what you have told me. That is all I can do for you."

"But you have to tell us her last name!" Sherry exclaimed.

Renaldo smiled. "Hernandez, I believe. There is another club owner with the name Garcia."

I stood up, furious.

"Sir." The bastard had withheld his formal name, leaving me with nothing to use against him. I was hot with indignation. "I have great respect for the memory of my father. You can understand this." How was I to appeal to him? He was so cold! "I've lived away from my father for a long time. I need to go back to Mexico. But it is important that I first see to it that my father's friend has what is hers." I sat back down, now embarrassed. Renaldo had shown not the slightest reaction to my display of temper.

"Is it very much?" he asked.

"It is very little. But it is what my father had, and we are willing to give it away."

"Miss Painter. If, as you say, there is a child, your father's friend has something already."

176

"Perhaps a burden we could ease." I was promising more than I could ever hope to deliver.

"In our families, a child is never a burden. A child is a great gift."

"You see! You see!" Sherry wailed in the car. "I knew they'd shut her off from us. We'll never find her!" She drove round and round, down long blocks where the stores advertised in Spanish, past cheap clubs with neon signs. "Watch for the damned yellow car," she said, biting her lip. She was half-wrapped around the steering wheel in her intensity. It was no use. We didn't know where to look. "Out by the UPS!" Sherry said. "It's all Mexican out there." She shot out onto one of the frightening arteries of the city, sped on for five miles, and then turned into a neighborhood of cheap frame houses. Some yards had been tidied. In others, pickups sat with their front ends up on blocks. It was getting quite cold, snow was starting to stick, making the streets slick. In the cold dusk, everyone was indoors, all the Hernandez Garcia Santos Rodriguez families—

Sherry turned a corner and skidded. The car swerved into a sharp turn and the front wheels jumped the curb. The car died.

"Damn damn damn," Sherry murmered. "That bastard had us on a string." She rearranged herself on the seat, brisk now, and capable. "Maybe I could put a notice in the personals."

"Oh yeah, she'll read that. Think about it."

"I'll think of something!" She drove more cautiously. "He thought we wouldn't accept her. He never even mentioned her to us. He could have brought her to our house. Was it that she was Mexican? That they weren't married? Was it us? What was the damned secrecy all about?"

"Maybe it was just an instinct for privacy." I knew that might be hard for Sherry. She was married to Bud's son.

When we got home Ann looked up from her reading and asked us how it had gone. Sherry burst into tears and ran to her room. I put together some supper and ate it with Tommy and Ann. I was grateful when Ann took the child to bathe, and left me alone.

I was the only one awake when Kermit came home at ten o'clock. I was sitting at the table, working on a list of things I might do other than go back to the ranch. I had written:

1. school
2. find a job.

I'm glad I didn't pay for this advice! I thought. The words didn't *mean anything. I was so weary, I was seeing things, quick scraps of pictures: Tonio scratching one of his hounds behind the ears. My mother on the couch with her feet out. My dad cutting cheese with a pocket knife. Men—men and boys, lines of them.*

Kermit stood at the refrigerator and drank milk from the carton. He cut off a hunk of cheese with his pocket knife and ate it, still standing with the refrigerator door open.

When he had closed it, he said, "You made it out, you runt. You really did, good for you." I took a moment to realize that what I saw in his eyes was awe, simple as that. He had bought the picture I had willed his way, of a good life, some kind of love, tender mercies. Things Bud had wanted, and Lenore, still.

"How does he do it, little sister?"

For a moment I didn't know what he meant. My mind skipped around and landed on Tonio. I saw him in his aviary, a foot-long parakeet on his arm.

"He's brave and smart," I said. It probably didn't answer Kermit's question, but what I said was important, was true.

"Talk to Sherry before you go," Kermit said. I looked at him carefully, trying to guess what he meant. He had an ugly smile now. "I'd appreciate it a lot," he said. "You can teach her what you know."

I had felt such a stranger, coming back. The mystery about the woman had enthralled me; Sherry had taken me in. I had felt like something mattered. Now I saw that Kermit knew me best.

"I can't imagine why they let you stay," I said.

As I left the room, I heard him say. "It's my potential!"

As I fell toward sleep, I saw the line again, blurry at both ends. There were boys from school, and Tonio, and other men. Michael Sage. I got up, went to the bathroom, rearranged my pillow and slept again. In my uneasy sleep I searched for the faces. I woke before dawn, my gown soaked with perspiration. I had seen my father so clearly.

He had been standing on the very top of that cold iron spire, balanced, humbled—as I had been that star-soaked night high in the mountains—to find what he wanted, held out to him, within easy reach.

10.

I KNEW the instant I heard the plane who it was. Sleepy hounds whined as he circled and buzzed the ranch and then landed. I had been lounging on the cold floor of the library, looking at a book of photographs of insects. I went down the walkway to the office and sat on a low bench across from it, in the tangled shade of climbing vines. Hounds were sprawled like throw rugs, too lazy in the hot afternoon to do more than shuffle their haunches.

I heard him at the gate on the other side of the walls, whistling a tune I knew but could not place, a song from childhood. As he closed the gate, an old gray Mexican hairless sprang from a shadow in the grass and bolted for him, barking like a pup. He took the time to squat and greet the ugly dog, scratching him on the belly and head. When he stood up again he looked down the walk and saw me on the bench, my hands folded in my lap like a schoolgirl. He came toward me in long easy strides, grinning.

I had gone to the ranch to stay for a few days after I got back from Texas. I knew if I stayed at the hotel while I was still feeling so strung out from my trip, I'd do whatever Michael Sage asked me to do. Of course I knew I was only postponing things; he had been vivid in my dream. He was next on some damned list I was writing with my life. Now he was here. He had come after me, gone out of his way. I gave him that as credit.

"Fancy seeing you here," he said lightly. He patted his breast pocket. "I have some things to give Sofia, things I have to take care of with Antonio when he returns. I won't be long." I didn't bother to comment on his ruse.

"I haven't had lunch. Would you like to stay?"

"I'm starved. Let me guess. Black beans and dry sopa."

"What else?"

His voice dropped half an octave and came from some place deep inside him. "You know what I want."

I rose and stepped away to put some distance between us. "Not that," I said.

I saw his top lip quiver like a horse's at the gate. "I intend to have what I came for," he said.

"Not here." He glared at me. I knew I would go with him to his plane, to fly to Louisiana, where he had grown up, or south to Costa Rica or El Salvador. Distance would have made a difference. "I'm going back to the hotel after lunch. Whatever you say, after that." I knew he didn't want to come to the hotel. He kidded himself, thinking we were unnoticed at the ranch.

We ate lunch in the kitchen at the counter while a maid washed the pots from the warming table. I saw the maid looking at Sage's back. Square and squat and brown, she must have been awed by his breadth and height. I smiled. The maid saw it and sent me a look full of good wishes. She was a new girl, come since Tonio was away. She turned the deep metal pots upside down along the counter top and hung the rags she had used on the stones of the barbecue pit on the patio just beyond the screen door. I was teasing Sage by then, saying how fascinating he must be to kitchen maids, when the girl stuck her head back inside for one last look. Sage turned to look at her and caught her with her face thrust forward. The maid broke into girlish giggles and ran. We could hear her feet slapping on the outside stairs. I laughed, my hands flat on the counter in front of me. Sage closed his hands over mine and bent toward me for a kiss. After that, he told me what we'd do.

We constructed an affair full of intrigue. I had developed some taste for subterfuge. I suspected that we deceived no one, but Sage insisted on the air of secrecy. It may have been an ethical pose, rather than a strategic one; he would cheat, but he would not do it boldly. He called infrequently. Usually he buzzed the hotel to let me know he was coming. All day then I waited for the night. The guests wouldn't have cared if he had driven straight up to the front door, and Claude couldn't possibly have been fooled, but under cover of darkness, I plunged into the thick perfume of oranges, finding my way down a path among the trees, meeting Sage where the path came to the road a quarter mile or so from the hotel. The dark and the noises spooked me, but they were aphrodisiacs, too. Seeing Sage took all of a day to get ready and all of the next to recover.

At first it was something like I used to think dating ought to be. Sage made meals for me, sometimes quite elaborately, and other times simple omelets or sandwiches. He brought things from Tampico that I wouldn't otherwise have, like pastrami, dill pickles, cans of Texas-style chili. He played records he had brought from the states: Judy Collins, Joan Baez, Peter, Paul and Mary, The Beatles and Bob Dylan. We danced. We told one another the stories of our lives.

He had grown up the son of a postal clerk. His father's brother had a small ranch in south Texas, and there, summers, Sage had learned the work of animals and crops. His wife had been his girlfriend in high school and when he was home from his three years away at college. He had come to the Huasteca a spelunker, with friends. They had explored some immense caves north of here, he had seen vampire bats, and had gotten the idea of living here. His girlfriend's father, well-placed in an oil company, knew people in Tampico. Someone knew the General. One thing led to another, and marriage brought the money to lease the land. His wife hated the country on first glance. She led her own life in Tampico with their small sons and spent part of the winter in Houston, where her parents now lived. Sage loved the ranch. He had had an eight-year lease, and now he was more than halfway through another. He couldn't buy the land, so everything he did was for the good of the Velez family as much as for him. "Someday I'll want to renew the lease and Antonio will say no." I said I thought it was the old man's ranch. "Old is the key word," Sage said. "His son runs everything. One of these days Antonio will see the writing on the wall and sell the Tecoluca, if he can, and then he'll want this land back with his father's La Palmita."

"He would never leave the Tecoluca!"

"He will someday. Why do you think he lent his plane to the campaigning president? With each new administration, his life enters a fresh period of risk. It is as if he has his leases, too, six years at a time."

"But why?" I had never considered such a thing.

"Their revolution wasn't all sham. There are laws about land. They are bent in all ways to help the rich, but each president returns some land to the peasants. Tonio has land registered in the names of cousins and nephews, in his mother's name, and his. He is no fool. He is

181

building an empire out and away from the cattle. The Tecoluca is not his life."

He moved his hands to distract me. "Antonio will grow up some day and move to the city," he said. That dismissed Tonio as a topic. Sage wanted to know about me. He was endlessly curious. Little by little I told him everything. He loved the story about my brother and Natty Mooster. He followed my teenage years like he was reading a cheap novel. He cheered me and booed the boys.

"I love your nose," he said. "Your tiny wrists." He said he was going to count my freckles. He liked to smell and taste and feel. He was truly with me, he gave me all his attention. Going to bed with him was something different. He was a large man, in all ways lean. I liked to stretch out beside him while we talked. I liked to run my hands over his back and legs. I couldn't believe his attention.

He said his wife was cold now that she had his children. He always kept village girls around—one or two to do his laundry, clean the house, sometimes to cook. He kept them a year or two and then traded them in on sisters and cousins. I said that didn't seem Mexican of them, to be so willing. I didn't want to think of him coercing the girls; I remembered the fascination of the kitchen girl at the Tecoluca. Sage said I was naive. "What I pay one of these girls feeds the whole family, maybe is the reason a brother can go on to a few more years of school. They have chicken now and then, because of me. Because she fucks me."

It wouldn't be so bad, I thought. I told Sage that Bruni liked the maids. When I started telling about Bruni, I realized that Sage might be insulted to be linked with him, but I went on anyway. When I had been at the ranch a few weeks ago, Bruni had gotten drunk at dinner, and I had locked my bedroom door, afraid he would want to come to my bed. Instead, I heard fumbling in the hall, and muffled giggles. I had opened my door to see the back of Bruni and the youngest laundry maid, maybe thirteen, disappearing into the bedroom by the library. It surprised me that Bruni would bring a girl upstairs, even with Tonio gone. Sage had no problem with the idea. He said the girls were wide-eyed, dull and willing. He had once told one of them to take off her clothes so he could fuck her. She had complied dutifully and bent over, "like a little red-assed baboon," he said.

Like a dog, I thought.

Sage had a beautiful little parrot, a real loro real, *not a macaw like the ones at the Tecoluca. The* loro *had the run of the house and patios, as well as a perch in the kitchen and another on the patio outside the bedroom door. It loved to screech and laugh, and sometimes sounded like a monkey. Sage had had a monkey too, but the two creatures had quarreled incessantly, and the monkey lost the toss. The parrot had a vocabulary of outrageous English phrases, including,* Fuck a duck, Kiss my ass, Eat my grits, *and* Praise the Lord. *Sage explained that the parrot had originally been in the Tampico house and that both he and his wife had become attached to it. It had been much prized by the city maids who were known to ask its opinion on important matters of style ("Shall I cut my hair?") and love ("Will he marry me?"). Sage wanted to take the bird to the ranch, so he began to teach it vulgar phrases. He won; his wife wanted Birdie out of the house and hearing of their children. Thus it was that I could lie with him in his bed and suddenly hear, "Kiss my ass!" Birdie also whistled. One night as Sage was closing the patio door against its epithets, the bird suddenly began a rousing rendition of "Coming 'round the mountain," which I imme-diately recognized as the song Sage had whistled that day he landed at the Tecoluca to look for me. It became "our song," a cherished joke.*

Sage said he loved the color of my pubic hair. He called it my "strawberry site." He often kissed and touched me for long stretches of time, insisting that I lie still and enjoy it. "Don't you think you deserve it?" he said.

Then he began to ask me to tell him stories about myself over again, with all the details. He wanted lengthy descriptions, which he said aroused him. It seemed perverse to me that his sex should rise at the memory of other men, but when I protested, he cajoled me, saying fantasy was part of the range of it, part of the fun. Once I had told him about Farin and his "Christmas tree," Sage sometimes pretended to behave as crudely, and I tried to laugh. He didn't want to hear anything about Mexico. Tonio was never mentioned. After a while I wanted to know more about him, too. I asked him about his wife. This irritated him. A simple fuck, he said, and besides, she was his wife. Only his wife called him Michael. He said he didn't like the name.

We had exhausted what we had in common, and we began to seek continuance in the novel. I realized that I was more experienced than he, and when he realized it too, he seemed angry. I wished I had told him nothing.

He told me his wife wouldn't let him in her bed if he had not just showered. I took this as a hint of some sort, and stopped coming to him freshly bathed. He began to give me small slaps and pinches, not enough to hurt. Then a bruise appeared on one breast, another on my thigh. He wanted to sit on the couch while I undressed in front of him, and when I was naked he began to slap: on the breasts, lightly, harder on the buttocks, arms and legs; hard again, and startling, on the face, and then the buttocks more, until I whimpered. That was when he was excited.

Claude came to me one morning at breakfast and said he wanted to talk to me. He said, "I know you are a foolish and ignorant girl, but now I think maybe you are out of your mind." I got up and spun on my heels, gave him the table with my cocoa in a china pot. I imagined my waiter at lunch eyed me with rash abandon, and when a guest remarked on the pouches under my eyes, I was offended and acted rudely. Sage was as agitated as I was. He howled one night that his schedule was upside down, his children hadn't been to the ranch in months (hardly my fault!). He stopped cooking for me, stopped his wooing, drove without caution, and hit me until I cried. He picked me up one afternoon, a surprise, an hour before dusk, and took me to see bats swarm out of a cave like a cloud of soot. Away from him, I knew things were getting out of hand. But there were fine lines in sex (and pity, fear, and loss), and I thought we were on the reasonable side. He wasn't really kinky. I had read the whole of Olympia Press from Tonio's library. What Sage and I did was nothing. It passed the time.

He went home for a weekend and didn't reappear until the middle of the week. He called me to set a time. He sounded strange, but I decided he had had a bad time with his wife, and I would set it straight.

I plunged into the blackness of the grove, adrenalin pumping, breath coming short and hard. He wasn't where he said he would be, and I wasn't early. I sat on the edge of the road at a place where gravel spilled toward the trees, able to see nothing, hearing frogs and insects, what I thought was a growl, and far away the lowing of an animal as mournful as a dirge. It was a cool night, and I was underdressed for the wait. I clasped my knees for warmth and leaned my cheek against one's bony rise. If I kept this up, I thought, I would be ruined for Tonio's return. Tonio had become a ghost, never quite out of mind but no longer clear in my mind, either. If Sage asked me to go with him, I knew I would go. With an American, I could understand what was what. I thought. The wife he didn't love could go home again. I could love Sage and the ranch as well. Was that what it was, love? Or

English without pauses? Was it just that he was there and I was lonely? I knew this much: when I left Tonio, if I did, I would always wonder what there might have been. I would miss the comfort of his authority, I would sigh for his beauty and long for what had never come, his praise. But I knew I could never have those things, no matter how long I stayed; there could never be a Tonio attained. Sage, blond and broad and less complex, was more my friend than Tonio had ever been. If there weren't the blasted barriers (the children more than her), he could be truly mine.

In this way I passed the time, waiting for him.

He came too fast and stopped too short. His wheels dug into the gravel and spewed grit all over me. "Come on! Get in!" he called from the cab of the truck. I clambered in and reached for his arm. He moved it away to change gears. He drove a few miles from the hotel and found an off-road, and parked. I turned to him again, expecting his embrace, and he hit me with his fist. I do see stars! I thought. He punched at me viciously, while I screamed for him to stop. His blows caught my ear, my arms, my back, and once I'd turned, my head and neck.

"Oh why oh why?" I cried when he stopped.

He said he had gonorrhea and had given it to his wife. It took me a moment to realize what he was saying. I knew very little about such things, only what I had learned from gossip in school. Then I realized he was blaming me. My hands slid up the door and hung on the open window's pane. I lay slumped away from him, disbelieving. He had fucked maids and whores, yet he blamed me! I said this, now bitter and fully aware. "Not like that, I didn't get it like that," he said. "It was you and your French fag. Something he ground out of some boy's ass. Fag clap. That's what you brought to me." He hit me again and I tried to open the door. He had taken the handle off the inside and I couldn't get out. I crouched toward the floor while he poured blows on my head and shoulders; at least they were now open blows, from palms, not fists. He stopped as suddenly as he had begun, got out and opened the door. With a yank, he pulled me onto the ground. "How could you!" he said.

"I didn't, you idiot!" I shouted. Why hadn't he just asked me? I could have made a joke of it. Me and Claude! Claude a fag. Why hadn't I thought that.

"I know you did," he screamed, "because I asked him."

He backed out and I breathed the dust he made. I had to stumble and *half-crawl the two miles back to the hotel. A car passed and I lay flat beside the road to keep its lights off me. I stumbled around the back of the hotel and up to Claude's hut. His light was on. When he opened the door, it struck me that he showed no surprise. "Please," I begged.*

I knew he was cold and superior, that he would not have bothered to deny Sage's accusations. But he would see what he had done. He would take care of me, though I was an American girl, though he had never liked me.

By the time Tonio returned, there was only a pale bruise on my cheek below the eye. I told him I had slipped coming in from the pool because I didn't take the time to dry. He touched the spot with his fingertips. I knew it would be yellow for a few days, and then gone.

The fault that had opened with his going had closed again. Whatever had dropped in was lost, and lost, was forgotten.

In June, Bruni bought a trailer in Brownsville and married the laundry maid Octavia. He had acquired a virgin ranch and set about clearing it, as Antonio had done, with AID funds. The land was in the state of Veracruz, where savannah ran to lowland forest, and the trailer was as venerated as a pyramid by the Indians there. Four months later, Bruni's daughter was born. They named her Enriqueta, in memory of Octavia's irascible brother, who had hung himself at sixteen after losing a minor altercation with a friend. He was Huastecan, and this had once been their way.

In Portugal, Tacho disappeared. Tonio had left him to train and fight and to take the *alternativa* in Spain when he could. He went away with a band of Romanian gypsies, leaving his suit of lights boxed, his swords safely sheathed, on the ranch of Tonio's friend Don Amparo. He wrote his *patróns* Don Amparo and the matador Antonio Velez identical letters, from France, saying he had fallen into a madness wrought by the minor keys.

Esteban, Tono's other *banderillero*, and no longer young, married in San Marta and began working with the breeding of brave bulls on the Tecoluca. Though Tonio planned to fight many more years, he took on no more *banderilleros*, preferring to hire them without attachment. In a Tijuana *corrida*, Tonio was gored (his seventh injury) and then, for the sake of healing,

186

circumcised. He brought to the ranch a Portuguese novice, Clemente Cortazar, at the request of Don Amparo. Clemente fought on foot and not in the Portuguese way. He had a haughty expression in the ring, which hid quite nicely his bad teeth. He taught Antonio's young *gringa* to make the *verónica*, and he played the bull for her, though it was hard not to laugh. He could have had her in his bed but he was old-fashioned and believed spilled seed was courage lost.

Mr. Mac the Scot-Canadian died a gentle death on his disheveled bed in the corner of the generator shed. At his request the *cacique curandero* crossed the river in the night. The shaman messaged the old man's legs and fumigated his sleeping area with a torch of pine. Mr. Mac was buried on a knoll above the new practice ring, after his feet had been carefully washed.

With Bruni gone, Sofia's job took on new importance. She bought a refrigerator and a bed with a mattress made in a factory. Not long after she was seen in San Luis Potosí by a cousin of Tonio's head carpenter; she was looking at Volkswagens in a used car lot.

While excavating for a new bullring (to test the yearlings and brave cows), workers discovered a mass of artifacts, as thickly clustered as grapes. Federal archeologists came to the ranch for half a year. The site was claimed by the government (as are all prizes underground) and fenced as out of bounds. Construction of a ring was completed a quarter of a mile farther on. Esteban was promoted to foreman when the old one slipped a disc and was pensioned.

Tonio tore down the aviary and had a tennis court built. Three dependable hands went to Monterrey to learn to mind the nets. Sometimes Tonio and Abilene volleyed balls back and forth, but neither had the knack and they lost interest. The second year, vines broke through the surface, and in no time it was ruined.

The hermit botanist Harrison was murdered by Mexican squatters who thought he had found gold beneath his orchids. A small Texas college made his Ranch of the Sky a field station, and birders pressed to include the site in the annual Christmas count.

Mickey, thoroughly desperate, jumped in a second-class bullring with a bright red rag and had his pants ripped off. Not long after, Tacho came home from Portugal and the other countries where he had been.

Calves were bought, grazed, and then transported away to slaughter in San Marta. More than half their meat was bound for export from a country where one man in ten eats beef some of the time.

Tonio fell giddily in love with a Mexican starlet, Pilar Acosta, and took her with him to Kenya and Mozambique. Their safaris were given much play in the actress' publicity, but were in truth the last events of their affair. Tonio brought home to Abilene a bracelet made of elephant hair, though he had already given her one before, made of gold. Later, photographs arrived from Mexico City. There was one of a Kikuyu with a penis fifteen inches long, hung in a loop along his thigh. Then came shields and spears, masks and drums. Later still the trophies came: the hides of wildebeests and zebras, a rhino's head, a lion golden as a field of grain. Tonio said Pilar made him silly; as he said it, his upper lip tucked down as over a smothered grin. Abilene thought he pined. She didn't pay much attention.

Thinking that Tonio must someday marry, Abilene did consider sadly the attributes the woman would have to have: fair hair and beauty, equestrian skill, and languages, a privileged family, and youth. Such girls did not come by by chance. Those men who did come were adventurers, like the spelunkers who talked of the Pit of Swallows and its unmeasured depths; wastrels like the Houston oilman whose girlfriend shot a steer in error, and Mickey with his sighs. A girl did not appear until a festive *tienta*, held one April. She was accompanied by her mother and courted, in his way, by Tonio, in front of sixteen guests.

The American rancher Sage observed Antonio taking the diplomat's daughter by the hand and helping her into the jeep to drive up to the ring. Now divorced, Sage was touched by this affection and it gave him some ideas. He dawdled after breakfast to stay with Abilene, while the other late-risers smoked Acapulco gold. He did not approve of Abilene's getting high, but he knew it would prove advantageous to his suit. Dreamy, lank and moist, Abilene yielded to his plaintive regrets for old mistakes, and granted him a tender try at recompense. So pleased was he (how perfectly life sorts itself out!), he fell asleep, and missed the spectacle of her as *espontánea*, caping a mooing cow.

Now that I look back I see myself a student again, passed from tutor to tutor. Tonio taught me about dope and sex, about patience and emptiness, days and days of emptiness; taught me about the lining inside me, where I am dry. Taught me that there is freedom in yielding. Under his tutelage I learned to be evasive, to use words as masks, to distrust.

Martin, my archeologist friend, taught me about looking back from far away, creating a perspective so vast that I see I am nothing in it; or in another glance, am everything. He taught me about superstition, and about faith, about holding on merely because others have managed before you. He taught me that life is, when immediacy is gone, only an accumulation of tools and vessels, only something to be eaten and drunk and left for the sand to cover, or vines, or stone or water.

Michael Sage taught me that there was a laughter inside me, free of spite or self-derision, undefensive and happy. He taught me to want fiercely, without calculation; and then he taught me there is no vulnerability like that which comes of love. He took the love away, and taught me my place.

Tonio knew me best. Knew who I was all along. When I came to him, I had everything to learn, and he already knew it all.

PART V

11.

TUESDAY, AUGUST 27. *A quarter of a million people march from the Museum of Anthropology to the Zócalo.*

They are a block away when they see the lights. Hallie leads the way, half-fairy in her excitement, jumping and leaping to let the energy out. Behind her Abilene and Pola walk arm in arm. They have walked more than a mile, with Simon and Elena falling behind as the crowd joined the procession. Hallie turns and walks backwards, waving over heads into hundreds of men and women, some with banners they have stopped to unroll.

"I can't see Simon!" Hallie says. She stumbles into someone in front of her. She laughs and apologizes. The woman she bumped says, "Bless you children, you good boys and girls! You children know the truth!"

Everyone is smiling.

There is the festive spirit of a street fair. Girls dance along the walks with sweaters tied at their waists, the arms hanging below the hems of their short skirts. Boys call out to them and run alongside. "You came!" they say, as though it was for them.

The Plaza de la Constitucion is ablaze with lights. Thousands and thousands of candles flicker. Blankets of flowers line the plaza. Banners and flags ripple and slap above the heads of their bearers. Everywhere the faces of the young are radiant. The bells of the cathedral ring once, twice, and yet again, fabulous long peals that are met by deafening applause, a sound like thunder that spreads out into the side streets and then comes back like an echo, back into the Zócalo, the heart of this magnificent city. A chant goes up: "ME XI CO LI BER TAD. ME XI CO LI BER TAD."

Hallie finds the core of the demonstration. She finds Refugio and other mates from Poli, professors and parents and friends. There are so many friends.

A girl cries out, "Oh look! Everyone I love is here!"

Someone speaks from a platform, but Abilene cannot hear. Elsewhere songs are being sung. The candles blur into a cover of light. It is the sky fallen to earth. A night of stars.

Abilene turns to Pola. By a trick of light, one of Pola's eyes is flickering while the other is black. She is laughing. Abilene wonders what Pola thinks of all this, what it is that moves her so. She doesn't care; it's good to see a child laugh from joy. For her, Abilene, the pleasure is in the phenomenon of a great space filled with people, without trouble. It is the effect of ten thousand candles on the night.

Pola reaches for Abilene's hand. "It's so beautiful!" she says, and when Abilene turns, smiling, to speak to her, Pola kisses her on the mouth and throws her arms around her. Abilene can feel Pola's heart. "Beautiful!" Pola says again. Then, "Where do you think Mother is?"

Adele has gone ahead of them, to find a place to photograph. Abilene points to the rows and rows of windows and balconies above them. "Adele could be anywhere," she says. From those windows a thousand bulbs could flash. A thousand guns could fire.

Abilene shivers, to free herself from such a thought. There have been no incidents tonight, though someone said he saw army trucks as they left the Santo Tomas campus earlier in the evening. The windows give nothing away. The buildings appear empty.

They wait in the center of the plaza as the people turn the other way and begin to pour out into the adjoining streets. The boys and girls, some of them still singing, put away their banners and placards and candles, and make plans to eat or dance, make love, or plan another day.

Pola, Abilene and Elena head home together, back to Obregon Street. Simon has already slipped away, and Hallie has gone with Refugio.

Pola cries out suddenly, "Oh look!" as all the street lights go out. They huddle close and pause to get their bearing. They walk along the Reforma in darkness, their way lit by the lights of cars. As they turn a corner and plunge into the black maw of a side street, they can still hear the sounds of hundreds of youngsters yelling: "Did you see! Did you hear!"

The laughter and jokes. The great joy.

Abilene feels cold in the sudden blackness; she has been sucked into a vacuum, the light now far away.

She doesn't know what it is she fears. All her troubles are of her own making. How foolish she feels all of a sudden, to march with these people in this place. To pretend to be a part of something so important.

Pola takes her hand. "What a trip, huh?" she says, smug with her good English.

Neither Daniel nor Adele come home for hours and hours. Abilene stays the night, sleeping in Pola's bed, her back warmed by the child's body. She dreams of the march, the lights, and then the dark. She dreams that in the blackness she runs away, runs for blocks and blocks. She runs, with no place to go, so that she cannot stop.

ABILENE WAS frequently with Hallie. She attended meetings in churches and school buildings, sometimes in cul de sacs off the main streets. In the evenings, though, Hallie and her friends seemed too young. Abilene felt out of place. Now and then she went to a movie with Isabel, or sat with her in Claude's apartment smoking dope or drinking quietly. Isabel had grown sombre as the summer progressed. She told Abilene that she had stopped trying to look after Ceci's welfare. "Or yours," she added. "But I have to say you're looking for trouble, Abelita. This business with the students is getting too big. The government won't let it be. You will get to see Mexico in a new light. You should take care not to be in the middle."

It was easier to go to Daniel and Adele's apartment in the evenings, when Daniel's friends clustered for long hours of talk. They came to diffuse the energy they picked up from the city during the day. They talked in long rambling discourses about the meaning of the Revolution, and the callowness of youth. They cursed by name a hundred bureaucrats, governors, army officers and union leaders. They reviewed the old railroad strike and its imprisoned heroes. They discussed the psychological and philosophical impact of torture on the individual and his society.

They made everything abstract.

Simon drank too much and talked about ramming officials in the ass. He was directing a revival of a Ionesco play, and he ran around the room with his hands at his forehead, acting out the part of a rhinoceros.

Gilberto said sourly that they ought to burn down the National Palace. He had warned his friends, the other fish, he said. It was a pun, *los peces*, a play on the initials of the Communist Central Committee. "And apt!" Simon ranted. "Swimming aimlessly, little guppies, little minnows. Conceited, self-deceived, in their tiny little aquarium—"

"Be careful you don't talk about yourself," Elena said. The others looked at her in surprise. In a while she left with Simon, following after him like one in court traipsing after a king.

"Now my friends are in prison," Gilberto said. Headquarters had been sacked. Gilberto had been meeting classes at the university when the office on Merida was raided. When his friends went in to protest (and were arrested), he was lying down with a cold. "I'm a coward!" he cried.

The others rallied around him. "What good would you do in jail?" they said.

Arturo had the most weight and was forgiving. "I know about prison," he told them. "Will hammered kidneys help the party?" They turned to Daniel, keeper of the data. Was it as bad as it seemed? It was possible to go about your business all day and not know anything was going on except preparations for the Olympics. Bright orange signs for the subway line that had opened. Freshly painted buildings. Olympic symbols everywhere. Then you could go around a corner and see army trucks, with men and carbines in the back. You could see soldiers with bayonets jeering at kids, and herding them into trucks.

Daniel said that Military Camp 1 was swollen with political prisoners, and they were clearing a wing at Lecumberri for more. Gilberto grieved more loudly. "I can't just stand on the side," he said. "The professors have to join their students!" Everyone could see he didn't want to go along.

Adele, who had been busying herself with domestic details—rinsing glasses, putting out bowls of tortilla chips, wiping up a spill—sat down and said quietly, "The students say there will be strength in numbers. At every meeting, hundreds gather, just by word of mouth. There is talk of another demonstration in the Zócalo, this one bigger, bolder. Of course we all have to be with the students. They are speaking for what is right."

Abilene could see that Daniel was surprised at Adele's passionate words. Adele had been spending a lot of time with Nando, the hotel keeper's son; they were often out, meeting with students, or holed up in the hotel, transcribing.

Daniel looked on the edge of a smile. He reached over to squeeze Adele's shoulder, a gesture Abilene took to be affection and praise. Adele looked tired, but pleased with Daniel's attention.

Pola lay on her bed in her room, reading *The Stranger* in French. She was trying to teach Abilene the language, to pass time.

Gilberto said, "We have met to draw up a statement—" He stopped in mid-sentence, as though he had swallowed something in a lump.

"Cat got your tongue?" Simon goaded. He had come back, entering a conversation that had gotten nowhere. He was alone. He glared at Gilberto. "Can't trust us?" he accused. "Afraid it's a nest of spies? Check the chairs for mikes!"

Adele went over and put her arm along Gilberto's back. The poor man was on the edge of a breakdown. "Don't mind Simon," she soothed. "He's trying out lines for a new passion play. 'The Temptation of the Intellectual.'" Simon gave her a dirty look and poured himself a drink.

The tension passed quickly. What these people had among them was stronger than Gilberto's fear or Simon's bitterness. Could it be friendship? Abilene thought. Daniel went back a long way with his friends. Daniel had been there the day

Arturo was released from prison. The first thing Arturo said was, "You shaved your moustache." Daniel had never had a moustache, but he didn't argue. He said Arturo looked okay. Arturo said everything had changed while he was away.

Pola said she hoped when she was grown up there would be something to do besides drink and quarrel and talk philosophy. Abilene said, "You have to pass the time some way." She did not say that Daniel's friends provided a kind of cover for his activities. Nobody took anyone in this crowd seriously. For Daniel and now Adele, there was a reduction of significance by association. One did not look for heroes and villains in a crowd of clowns.

For Abilene, the truth was Pola was better company, but Abilene would have been embarrassed to ignore the gathering and spend her time with a child in her room. She liked Pola for the way she burst out with sudden thoughts, and then spent hours brooding before she said anything more. She liked her curiosity when they were out, the way Pola noticed color and expressions in other people. Pola saw the future as a vast canvas, an appealing thought, coming from her. One minute she was sure she would be a movie star. (Didn't she have a head start, being Yannis' daughter?) Another time she was going to study at the Sorbonne. She had many suggestions for Abilene's future, too, as though Abilene were another girl at the lycée. She thought Abilene could be an archeologist and go on digs in Greece and Egypt. She thought Abilene could learn about movies and work on Yannis' sets. She thought Abilene ought to fall in love and be swept away.

Abilene happened to have brought Hallie to Daniel's the night the army attacked the San Idelfonso Preparatory School in the middle of the night. The group was about to say its farewells, around midnight, when Nando came with news. A skirmish in the streets had the smell of real trouble. He came back later to say the army had splintered the beautiful old door of the school in order to rout out the students hiding there in the patios. The army had lined the students up, and beat them on the legs.

Nando had barely made it away.

They listened to the radio. Daniel went downtown to get press releases, and then to go to the paper. A little after three in the morning they heard the Secretary of the Department of Internal Affairs:

The upward course of the Mexican Revolution which so irritates the naive militants is slowed down when there is unrest and interferences with the rules of law and order.

"Here! Here!" Simon raved. "Let's hear it for law and order! Fuck the naive militants! Fuck their mothers!"

"That does it," Elena wept. Abilene didn't know if she was commenting on the army actions, or on Simon's response.

Hallie started to cry. "This would never happen in the U.S.," she said. Everyone looked at her coldly. "Maybe to Blacks," she amended. "But not to students." She cried harder. "I shouldn't even mention the U.S., should I?"

Adele had purplish bruised shadows under her eyes. She snapped at Hallie. "Don't play these troubles as your song." Hallie left abruptly, pushing away Abilene's offer to go along. Abilene insisted, though. It was far too late, and maybe dangerous, to travel out to Pedregal.

Abilene took Hallie to Claude's apartment. They lay side by side on the bed, too tired for sleepiness. "Don't let Adele bother you," Abilene said. "She is full of these stories she's been taping. She should have stuck to skinny women in expensive clothes. This trip has gotten too real." She didn't try to explain what seemed so obvious, that being young was a lark, that Hallie was young. That Adele and Daniel and the others all knew that in Mexico youth could be punished. That there were young people with no route of escape, no fathers to call.

And then there was Abilene, no longer young, without connection, acting with all the meaning of a dog chasing a car.

She went to sleep thinking of the sounds of birds at the Tecoluca. She wondered if it had begun to rain there.

Abilene read the transcripts Adele showed her. The students had chosen names for themselves, and kept their real ones secret. They were eager to talk. They thought they were making history.

Quecha: A young sweet girl from one of the housing projects, a nursing student. Her father drove a cement truck:

They say we are spoiled. They don't want to take us seriously, they want to make us feel little. But we can feel the people rising up with us. All we want is what the Revolution promised—a chance for all to have a decent life. Those of us who are students, we've had better luck than the peasants. It's up to us to speak up, no matter how hard they try to make us quit. I might end up in prison, and I don't want to, but that isn't enough to make me afraid. Even dying wouldn't be enough. If I die my life will go on in the sky like a star. When there are enough of us, the sky will be lit so bright everyone will see. That's what this is about. It's about our rights, the rights of everyone.

Rosa: a student's mother, a resident of the Tlatelolco housing units, with a son in Lecumberri and a daughter active in the Movement:

All night I boiled water to pour on their shitty army heads. In my apartment we had a mound of stones and jars, all that we could find that would hurt when we threw them from above. There was tear gas and shots fired, but we didn't give up. Even little kids were on the roofs and on the balconies, shouting and throwing stones. Dozens of people were wounded by their bullets, but in the end the granaderos went away with their tails between their legs. They saw who they were dealing with! Not just students, but their families and neighbors. The whole neighborhood!

One day Elena had shown up and said she had something she wanted Adele to have for her records. She was very different without Simon, quieter and more thoughtful, with a softer expression.

The granaderos came to the Belles Artes Institute with police dogs and took away directors, dancers, even scene painters! I hadn't realized—oh, I had been to a public meeting on the esplanade. I might have gone to their big demonstration. But now I'm really with them. Remember when we went on tour, and in Montevideo we heard about the Indian troupes in the hills, where they don't even have radios? That's how they got the news, from actors who showed them what was going on. Now we've formed brigades, like the Indians, to go out and show what's happening. We go to all the markets and the squares. They should have left us to our rehearsals, who did they think we were? But I thank them for waking me up! I thought this all had to do with students, but it's my business too. I'll fight with the students until their petition is granted. I'll fight until wrongs are righted. Otherwise, what good are Lorca and Shakespeare?

Abilene laid the file down and asked Adele if they could go somewhere for lunch. "My treat," Abilene said.

Adele, without looking up, said, "Couldn't you make something for us here? Pola will be home in a while, and I have so much to do."

"I know you're busy, Adele, but I'm at loose ends. The summer is over. Pola's going to be going to school all day. She's a kid, Adele! Tonio is losing patience with me. Claude will want his apartment soon for his own time in the city."

"You mean you aren't going back to the ranch?" Adele said, as though she hadn't tried to talk Abilene out of that very action years before. "I assumed you were waiting out the rainy season."

"Maybe," Abilene said weakly. She didn't think she could feel worse, but in the next moment she did.

"Look, I can't be your mother right now!" Adele said. There was a terrible moment between them, Adele with her mouth still partly open, Abilene unable to move. Then Adele threw her head back and sighed loudly. "I can't even mother Pola."

"I don't know why I'm here," Abilene said in a small voice. She felt such a fool.

"I really am sorry," Adele said. The hurt hung between them. "I could use Yannis right now, to help me sort all this out. Sentiment, truth, danger, hysteria. He always knew what to make of God and large emotions."

Abilene went down onto the street and began walking toward the avenue, where she could get a taxi. As she turned a corner, she saw an army truck coming up the street toward her. She stepped away from the curb. Bits of paper skittered across the walk in a light gust of wind. As the truck passed she saw there were young soldiers in the back, carrying guns. The truck moved so slowly, Abilene met the eyes of a young man leaning out toward her. Their gazes seemed fixed for a moment. He had a full mouth, parted, as though to say something. He might have been asking Abilene along, it was that sweet a look on his face. He didn't belong in a truck with soldiers. He would rather have been with her.

Daniel came with news that the police had found the murderer of the American woman. Her name was Sylvia Barton, not Britton. They had found her passport by chance; that was how the murder was solved.

This is what the murderer said:

> Yes, all right, I killed the American woman. She was a slut, she asked for it. Any man with balls would have done the same thing.
>
> I'm a pre-med student. All I've ever wanted was to be a doctor. I grew up in the slums. I had six baby brothers and sisters die in the years I was growing up. My father has always thrown himself around like he's a big shot, but he's never been able to get what we needed to live. Now I know it's not his fault.
>
> I get up at five in the morning and ride buses into the city to attend classes at the university. Then I go to the hospital where I work in the morgue. I clean off the blood and guts from the dumb jerks who have got themselves knifed in fights out there, sometimes they've shit all over themselves, too. I work until midnight and then I try to get some sleep and start all over again. I catch naps at work, but I never get enough sleep.
>
> I came out from work that night thinking I needed a drink. Usually I don't spend my money that way. What I really wanted was to get high. I was thinking this, coming around a corner, walking the long way to the bus line, looking for a pulqueria open at that hour, and I saw this girl leaning against an abandoned shanty house in a side street. I knew by the way she was standing that she was smoking grass. I went up to her and I said, "I could use a drag of that awfully bad. I work in the hospital morgue and it was a bad night, you see."
>
> She was pretty, but she had this hard mouth, like an old whore. She laughed at me but she gave me a long drag. She said it was the last of her dope. She asked me about my work and let me finish off the joint. I made it sound like maybe I was an intern, I said I was studying to be a doctor and I had a bad turn at the things they make you do. She gave an ugly laugh. "You, a doctor!" she said. She ran her hand down my shirt. All right, I was dressed cheaply, how would you dress to go to work in the morgue? What kind of clothes would you wear if you were feeding your family and going to school? But she made me feel real bad. Ugly, you know. She made me feel I wasn't sexy, like nobody would want me. She was letting me know I wasn't good enough for her gringa taste.

I moved closer to her and put my testicles up against her crotch. She leaned back against the wall of this little shack and the whole thing shuddered. A piece of scrap wood, this big board, fell off right beside us on the ground. She said, "Maybe I'll fuck you, but I won't kiss you. I don't think you brush your teeth, they're all yellow—" I put my hand over her mouth and told her to shut up. Now I wanted to fuck her real bad, I was big and hard and I could tell she wanted me to, but she wanted me to make her. Gringas, you know? Not that I had any experience. I'd never had a gringa, but I'd heard. They come down here because they want us to treat them bad. They want to laugh at us for doing it. They want you to promise them everything and tell them you love them. They want you to make them pretend they don't want it. They want you not to love them, they want to hate you.

She pulled her dress up; she didn't have anything on under it. This shocked me and I must have pulled away. She thought I was really funny, she was laughing and choking and sputtering. I told her to stop it. She was laughing so hard she had to sit down on the ground. Now what was I going to do? I got down beside her and tried to talk to her sweetly. "I know you want to do it," I said. "Let's go inside the shack."

She grinned big so that her big gringa teeth all shone white in the street light, and she said to me, "You smell like sour beans. All you chavos stink."

The board was right beside my hand. I didn't even think before I picked it up. Before I knew what I was doing I had whacked her across the face with it. She never made a sound. I hit her again as hard as I could, and then I went into her purse and took everything out: some money, her passport. She had a little empty bag where she had had her dope. I'd heard somewhere you could sell a gringo passport. But I never knew where to take it. I never knew what to do with it and I didn't throw it away. I would have, later, but I was waiting, I think, until I could look at it. I wanted to take a good look at her picture before I threw it away.

The real joke in this is that nobody would ever have found out if it hadn't been for the movement. I lived in a slum and killed myself getting to school on time and work on time and staying awake day and night, and all the time these fucking students are getting my classes shut down so that I won't get my semester's credits. I didn't even know what they wanted. I figured I had enough to do and they didn't.

One of the big-shot students lived in the same slum as me. Everybody called him Figaro because he could sing. Some nice mornings he'd get out of his bed and go down on the street and just sing, like that. So everybody knew Figaro.

They were looking for him when they came to our apartment.

They thought I knew him. They went through my stuff looking for movement literature. They sure had the wrong man for that shit. They tore the place apart completely, and when this one gra-nadero finds the passport, he lets out a shout: "Well, fuck your mother." He was grinning ear to ear. "Didn't we find ourselves a smart thief?" He made me take all my clothes off in front of my mother so he could search me. He let me get dressed to go, though. I've met prisoners who came to jail stark naked.

They didn't find Figaro so they took his little brother. Twelve, thirteen maybe. They threw us in the same paddy wagon. This kid was scared to death but cocky. They had grabbed him by the hair and chopped it off at the top. He looked like a sick cock.

Now I'll never be anything, all because of that American puta. My life is over, because she couldn't keep her mouth shut. They shouldn't let American women into Mexico alone. They don't belong here. They ought to keep them out.

"What a sad story this turns out to be," Daniel said. "I feel sorrier for him than her."

Adele watched Abilene read the transcript. It made Abilene's stomach turn over.

"Now *I'm* dreaming about her," Adele said. "Last night. I thought I heard her say, 'What should I do?' I thought I heard her weeping. I went looking for her in my dream. It was dark. I was going to take her in my arms. I was going to save her. I looked and looked for her in my dream, until I woke up. In my dream, I never remembered that she was dead."

Abilene didn't think Adele heard herself talking. "What should I do?" Abilene had asked, and Adele didn't have time to talk about it. Now she wanted to save a dead woman in her dreams.

"I just couldn't remember she was dead," Adele said again.

"She is," Abilene said. "Tell Pola I'll be by some time."

That night, Abilene went to the cantina where she had been with Angel, but the doorman wouldn't let her in alone. When she turned to leave, young men yelled after her, and one followed her onto the street. "You come in with me?" he said. He had a scar on his cheek. He was ugly, and she was tired.

"When the Revolution is finally made," she said. It cheered her up, that she'd thought of that.

12.

ABILENE MET the famous Gato one afternoon. She was coming out of the university library with Hallie and Refugio. She had heard his name dozens of times; he was what they called an *acelerado*. An agitator. He was too old to be a student.

If she had passed him on the street she wouldn't have given him a second look. He was dark and thin, his chest sagged in, his hair was too frizzy to hang right. A real *pachuco*. And smug.

Refugio introduced them. Refugio, son of a baker, who still kissed Hallie with his mouth closed tight. Gato said, "Another *gringa*?" Abilene said, "Another *chavo*?"

He had a smirky smile. Abilene knew immediately that Hallie had been wrong; that he would know just what to do in bed. Sarcasm, subtlety, a sense of superiority and a taste for conflict—she saw it all in his smirky smile.

She saw that trouble lay around him, waiting for a nudge to get it tumbling. He was the kind of danger Tonio had warned her about. And he despised her on first glance. It showed in his eyes: *Gringa*. What could be so low?

She knew something else, something she had learned from some of the best teachers. A man who wants to put you in your place wants you on your back. He never knows you want it too. You never tell.

Still, she went to hear him speak when she had a chance. The sloganeering and rhetoric were everywhere. The whole city was like something on fire. It had started with a clash between two groups of kids, some nonsense, probably an insult or a dare. It was just what the *granaderos* had been waiting for; they had been tethered only by lack of incident. How could the anti-riot squad work if no one rioted? They saw to it that a minor street fight qualified. Students, passersby, janitors all fell beneath the blows of billy clubs. A woman with a bag of fruit from the market ended up in a paddy wagon on her way to Women's Detention. Another, shaking a dirty mop out a window, ended up in Military Camp.

Sure, there was a lot of talk now. Mostly it was wild and unreasonable: kids were going to change the world. They demanded open dialogue with the government, when the authorities wanted nothing so much as to paddle them on their collective butts.

The students listened to Gato; rumor had it he had been in Colombia when thirty thousand students struck. Now he talked about rights.

"Peasants were promised redistribution of their lands, and what do they get? Land without water, rocks, the bleaching sun."

The students said, "The fat cats get all the rewards." They called them that—fat cats—in English.

"They invest, their risk absorbed by the government, and they take the profits. Is that economic development?"

They liked to cry out. "The Revolution was a lie!"

The speeches were like favorite poems; everyone knew the verses and followed along. Gato cautioned them. "A strike is effective only if there is an immediate cause, an incident; only if there is a broad base of support. You can't mobilize a city, let alone a nation, on a base of rabble-rousing." They listened, but they knew something was going on. Mobs appeared at every public meeting. He kept a grim view. "You have to read more." He wanted them to talk ideology and strategy. He said they had too short a vision.

He advised a long look.

Hallie arrived one day with two men in tow. One was Gato; the other, disheveled and tired, was an older man named Alfonso. They were looking for a place to spend the night.

"I haven't the bedding," Abilene said. She knew bedding

wasn't the issue. They stared at her until she said, "Is it so urgent?"

"It's better if you don't know, *señorita*," the older man said. He looked ready to drop. "The floor, please?" It was so little to ask.

Some days later Gato came again with a duffel bag. "For a few days," he announced, no interrogative in his voice. Abilene pointed to a corner of the living room. "Down here," she said. "This is not by invitation. It's only because I'm friends with Hallie." *And she has a damned crush on all of you!* she thought.

He gave her that same smile.

She thought: The last thing I need is another lover.

Hallie started bringing her other friends. They needed a place to meet. Whole groups of kids came, arguing and yelling at one another, talking all at once, terribly young and sincere and excited. They drank cheap wine and touched one another, arms across one another's shoulders, hands clasped as they talked. Young men got up on chairs to speak, a position that became riskier as the evening progressed.

One night someone suggested a stroll. The rain hadn't been heavy in the afternoon, and it was warm. They went down the avenue toward the Zócalo, five across, dipping their heads and calling out greetings to tourists and gawking boys, to scowly scratchy-faced men, and a saucy girl with beehive hair. They piled into two booths in Denny's and spent a long time reading the menu before they ordered three cheeseburgers, to divide ten ways.

Gato stayed behind.

Later he said, "They're naive. Babies, all of them."

"They know what they want," Abilene countered. "A just world."

"Political prisoners freed. Indemnities. Electricity in shanty houses. New paint for their classrooms. Real jeans. They don't know what matters and what does not. They're too young."

"I can sympathize," Abilene said, to provoke him. She was warming up to this. She had felt so bad for so long. She had even thought of looking up Angel again.

"They wouldn't know a good life if they had it."

"Why don't you like them?" Why are you here? that was the question. She knew why he could make trouble. He made your skin prickle. He dared you.

"If they turned out of the prison all those who are not criminals, if they abolished the rightist groups on campus, what would be different? It would take a week to see that everything is exactly the same. What the students ask for is impossible to achieve under this government, and it wouldn't help anyway. They might as well ask for dialogue with the devil. They're like peasants in a jungle; they believe in witches, magic. Bah! The university is the wrong place to start a revolution."

Abilene remembered Hallie's talk. "What about Paris? The students nearly shut it down." She regretted what she said as soon as she said it. She had no idea what was going on in Paris now! Gato didn't care, though.

"The students are bait," he said. "They make incipient repression more visible. It's a good thing for the *federales* to yank bankers' children. They're little seeds. The real roots are in the country." He stared at her coldly. "It's all nothing to you. American. Not your matter."

"I'm curious, though." Her remark, oddly enough, seemed to please him. He leaned forward, his hands on the floor in front of his knees. He was like any other man, zealot or not; he needed release. Let him think it was all his idea.

She thought him least attractive when he was most didactic. Why did all men like to lecture! She thought she would divert him with sex, but he had a schedule for it, just before he slept. Once she succumbed, she relished the way he took her attention. Adele was all caught up in a new role she had made for herself as social historian. Pola was starting back to school. Hallie and Ceci and their friends were always going at full speed, as if every day had to *mean something*. There was so much to accomplish. Abilene liked thinking about Gato. He was fine and lean, his belly inconspicuous, and he was nimble, not so much like a dancer as a burglar. He moved with intention, but it couldn't be apprised until it was accomplished. His very gait was full of secrets, he defied scrutiny. His ordinary Mexican-ness made him almost invisible on the streets, good

for rabble-rousing. Abilene had an idea that beneath his sheen-
less hair his ears were blocked off, and so he had a way of
looking around jerkily, a way of bringing his nose up sharply at
some sudden scent. His eyes were narrow and slanted, the
bones under his eyes took too much room; he had an altogether
sly look.

She tried to think of what Tonio would say. (She didn't know
why she hadn't heard from him. She had thought he would
send someone for her: Constanzia, Bruni, Felix, maybe even
Tacho. To tell her to get to the ranch or else. What she wanted to
know was *or else what?*)

She thought of Tonio and her skin was cold. She was afraid.
She was lying in bed beside Gato, who stared at the ceiling and
thought great thoughts.

"If you had a lot of money what would you do?" she asked.

"Such a stupid question!" he said. "I'd buy guns, of course."

Though he hadn't asked, she said, "I'd go to the south of
France and try to learn French." She had read somewhere that
the beaches of France were pebbles, but she didn't care.

"You're a dumb bitch," he said. She caught her breath, afraid
he would get up and get dressed and leave, when what she
needed from him was something to do.

He turned on her with gruff insolence and made love
harshly, short of pain or insult, but pushing past detachment
for the first time, straight to the quick, where the body is
carried away; and in one moment, one evasive, tricky, deceiv-
ing, compromising moment, she felt free.

She forgot Tonio. At least there was that.

He took her out to Netzahualcoyotl. She could not believe the
insects! Half a million people lived in seventy square kilo-
meters. One-room dwellings of metal sheeting, beaten from
cans and drums, of cardboard and wood scraps. They walked
across a street in which garbage glided along on a film of putrid
water. There was an elderly woman on a pallet in a dark smelly
room. Gato squatted by the woman, speaking rapidly, and he
gave her something from his pocket—money, Abilene decided.
Outside the shack he said to Abilene, "She is from my village in
Guerrero. She's not much older than you. Her children are
away, in the streets, stealing." Abilene was gagged by the

smells and sounds and colors. Gato took her arm, steered her back to the avenue and the bus. On the way she began to call out, wildly, the names of things she saw: the paint of buildings, an old woman with a basket of clothes on her head, little girls in white socks swinging on a metal bar. Gato's face grew dark, full of contempt. "Damn you!" she shouted. "What do you want me to say?"

"I don't want you to say anything. I want you to look."

He took her out again, on a long jostling smelly series of rides on the cheapest buses. He took her to a municipal garbage dump, and before she knew where she was, she smelled its incredible stench. It was a lake of odor more than a quarter mile across, and as they approached it, coming up among low-lying bushes at its crest, she was met by the spectacle of acres of rubbish. In and among piles of refuse, she saw pigs, goats, dogs, chickens and children scrabbling and grunting. Adults with boxes and bags stooped into piles of trash.

"They're looking for salvage to buy a bowl of beans for their day's food," Gato said. His voice was cold, unmoved. Abilene was clutched by nausea. She despised Gato for bringing her. She walked quickly away from the dump.

"They're not so bad off," Gato droned behind her. "They have a water ration, better than hundreds of thousands in shanty towns. Every day they find a little salvage, enough for a *peso* or two. Not so bad, when you think of it."

"Oh stop!" she said, as if he had been teasing her.

Stubbornly she made a beautiful soup for dinner, with a whole plump chicken and yellow squash, red tomatoes and rice. He ate with satisfaction. She watched him bitterly. *Is it for them you eat my soup?* she wanted to say. She banged dishes and pots, putting things away.

When she went into the room where he was sitting in the near dark, he made an ambiguous gesture to her, an invitation, she thought. She sat down beside him. Then he revealed to her how ignorant he was, how dismal was his knowledge of her country. He was a believer of myths. He said he wanted her to remember what she had seen, and to tell all her friends when they make their plans to grow brown on Mexican beaches. "You can make them a little less ignorant. Maybe it will mean something when they hear that poor people seek liberation in Latin America."

He thought she was like all Americans, rich and vacuous.

"I don't have any friends," she said icily.

He sighed. "Then what are you good for?" he said.

One night the students stayed late, folding their pamphlets and eating pots of rice. They set their bowls aside and found places and positions to relax. A girl lay with her head in another girl's lap; a boy leaned against the wall. Someone had brought down Abilene's pillows from off her bed.

"Talk to us, Gato," they said.

"In the mountains, they are weary of waiting. They move against thievery and repression." He went on, telling a long story about his father. Abilene sensed that the story was familiar to the students; their heads nodded expectantly, they sighed and murmered. There had been a fiesta. The governor's party paid for *pulque* and *mariachis*, for paper to hang on poles around the square. It was the time when the president-to-be was "campaigning" to gain popular support for his already certain election. The governor wanted to be "in touch" with his people as well. He wanted to hear his people's needs, he told them. The townspeople made a kind of throne for him under an awning. In the afternoon after the drunken dance, the people came from their huts, many walking miles into the village. They wanted to hear what the governor would do for them. First a bold boy of sixteen stepped forward. He played the guitar, but he couldn't afford new strings. "Music is in our soul!" cried the governor. He would buy the strings; he would buy more instruments to make more mariachi bands for the village. Then a shy nun came forward. She said she tried to teach the people to read, but she had no books. The governor said he would buy slates for her. Then she could teach them to write stories of the Revolution, and to read them. (This was the students' cue. 'The Revolution!' they mocked.)

Next Gato's father, a communal landowner, came forward. He wasn't afraid to look the official in the eye. He was a brawny man, short but strong, like a brave bull. He said he and his

211

fellow landowners had been given the wrong lands by mistake. "What mistake?" the governor said, biting the hook. "We've been given all the dry land," said Gato's father. "There is only one area with water to irrigate for crops. It belongs to one man alone, and he lives most of the year in Acapulco." Gato's father said he had submitted claims against this man's land; he had asked for wrong to be righted, according to the laws of Mexico. But in the city he learned that there were thousands of such claims, that they lay about in large rooms until they grew brittle, and cracked and fell to dust. A hush like hot cotton lay over the gathering. The governor glared. "I have no authority over these things!" he shouted. "You must follow the letter of the law and wait for wheels to turn. Are you more important than the man who waits before you?" Gato's father was bitter beyond caution. "Wait?" he cried. "In silence? Forever?"

The governor's men pushed him back and the crowd parted as if for a man on a stretcher. That night men came to Gato's hut and took his father out. Gato's mother held him, her hand over his mouth, and he bit her until he gagged on her blood, but she would not let go. They found his father in a ditch with his throat cut. Soon after that Gato went to Mexico City.

The students were mesmerized. Gato's voice was now full of passion; Abilene was amazed at the power of it. "The authorities will learn what is right! The people of the country will teach them. You will hear them, and then you must decide what to do. The peasants will lead you. I promise you this."

The students went home. Gato and Abilene lay in bed in silence, as if a gorge lay between them. For Abilene, it was too risky to reach across.

She felt small, and foolish, and sad. She wasn't surprised when, in the morning, Gato was gone.

ABILENE SAW MICKEY again at Tonio's office, where she had gone to see if Tonio had left money for her. If he cut her off, she would have to go back to the ranch, unless she wanted to spend her little savings, now in a Mexico bank. She realized that her summer in Mexico was nothing more than the sojourn in Zihuatenejo had been—a little time away. She had been excited by the students, by the enthusiasm of Hallie and her friends, even by Adele's company, dead woman and all. But she was going in circles. She had not written Sage again, nor he her, and the thought of him had grown less real or possible. What she wanted was something new from Tonio, something more than waiting for what he would give. She wanted to be more to him than a cat or a monkey. She wanted to know if he could understand what that meant; if he could, maybe she could love him again, or better. She had felt her spirit push up against his insistent memory, but now she thought it was adolescent of her, the same as Pola wanting to go to L.A., or just to a market without her mother's okay. Recently she had seen a very simple truth: that she belonged to Tonio, or with Tonio, in a way she had never belonged with anyone. He was not her first lover, but he was her first attachment. In his way, he had looked after her for nearly five years. She didn't want to go with Sage until she knew who she was with Tonio. Sage had been right, he and Abilene were alike, but Abilene added one important additional factor: Tonio was something else altogether.

Señor Muñoz said that *Señor* Velez was out of the country, but he had left instructions to give the *señorita* what she needed. "He expects you at the Tecoluca after the rains," Muñoz said. Abilene was surprised; already she had won this concession, when Tonio had seemed so adamant that she return immediately. Of course he wasn't there! He had never cared much what she did when he was gone, and if he had minded, or even known, how she spent her time, he had never said. She didn't think that Tonio spent much time thinking about other people, certainly not her. He thought of her when he wanted her. All in all, that hadn't been so bad.

Mickey came out from the inner office, his face flushed, and when he saw Abilene, engulfed her in his greeting. She thought, maybe I can talk to Mickey about it, but the idea was silly. Mickey had such a distorted perspective.

"Oh good, you remembered our lunch date!" he said now, with a huge, false cheer that could have fooled no one. Muñoz had the face of a statue.

"Sure, let's go," Abilene said.

Constanzia called out. "Oh *Señorita*, you left a package here the other day. See, I've saved it for you." She handed Abilene the bright yellow bag from the shoe store. Abilene was stunned. Constanzia shook the bag in her hand. *"Señorita!"*

Abilene took the bag. "Who brought it in?" she asked in a voice scarcely above a whisper.

"No one, *señorita*. You left it here, don't you remember? You must have been preoccupied to forget your shoes!"

In the elevator she told Mickey she had lost the shoes. "In a cafe near the museum, or maybe on the bus. But not in the office, I'm sure of that!"

Mickey cut her short. "You ought to have thrown those old *huaraches* away anyway, Abby. Your new ones are much better. When he saw her impatient frown, he added, "Everything doesn't have to make sense."

"Well of course it does!"

"Don't you know Tonio knows everything?" This he said merrily, like a joke. Though she was incredulous, she argued it no more.

Mickey said he had to run an errand for his father in the elegant Lomas de Chapultapec *colonia*. He was carrying a package.

"Well then, I'll see you later. We didn't really have the date you said we did in the office. That much I do know."

"But don't go now. I was going to come see you next." He whistled for a taxi. When they had settled into the seat he leaned over her and thrust his hand up on her thigh. "I need you," he said fiercely.

"Oh, do stop it!" she said. So Mickey was in a mood. She relaxed as he sat back. They pulled onto a street of old elegant buildings. They stood outside the fence of a large house; over the top she could see the heavy amber panes of windows. He rang for admittance. The door swung open, and he was ushered inside. She wondered what was in the package he carried, and she wondered about her shoes.

Mickey came out and said, "I know a good place not far from Chapultepec, they do grilled beef Argentine style." As they walked, she asked him about his errand. Mickey sighed importantly. "A friend of my father's lives there. He did some work for Tonio and Tonio didn't pay him. My father intervened. I was returning some property, I'm not sure what it was." Abilene accepted this explanation; she had been in Mexico long enough to appreciate that everyday things were often cloaked in intrigue.

They ate on the outdoor terrace of a quiet restaurant in an old converted house. Fawning trees bordered the terrace. The waiters moved slowly, without the self-importance of those in Niza restaurants. She offered to buy a bottle of wine, and Mickey chose a red one, surprisingly dry. They spent a long time eating and drinking. They talked about the students—Mickey said they were looking for trouble, it was the first inkling of his new self-importance—and he said her skin was pink and pretty. She thought of telling him about the abortion, but he would want to know whose baby it was, and she couldn't have said.

"Tell me about your new job," she said. Mickey now worked in the same bank as his father. He described his co-workers. He had a talent for description and mimicry. She wanted to tell him that he was most charming when he imitated himself. His clerkship wasn't so bad, he said. It was slow work and there would be no reward for hurrying; they had twice as many clerks as they needed. "It's part of the function of government to provide employment," he said. She found she was amused by his seriousness. "Of course," she answered. "It stirs loyalty and devotion." She also noted that he had been able to get away for a very long lunch, to which he made no reply.

"I was talking to Tonio recently," he said instead. Her chest began at once to ache. She ordered more wine. "He is having horses brought from Portugal this year; there is a possibility I might go over there and accompany them back."

She could not help smiling broadly. "Will you travel in their stable?"

"He's gone to Switzerland, you know," Mickey went on. He was swollen with this information. Abilene realized he had been saving it to tell.

"Why Switzerland?" she asked in a lazy way.

"He's gone to a music festival with his mother."

"Odd. I didn't think he was so devoted to her, nor to music."

215

Mickey smirked. "Anne Lise is in Europe. I have a friend at the American Embassy who knows I like to hear what's going on. Of course it is all circumstantial—" He shrugged, amused. She was perturbed to be caught ignorant. She didn't think she cared, other than that. She found Tonio a remote concept, harder and harder to retrieve from her store of memories.

Mickey leaned over and touched her hand on the table. "You know I would love you if you let me, Abelita." She had to suppress a laugh. Behind his glasses, the lenses terribly smudged, Mickey's eyes were round dark moons. She half-expected him to weep. They were both drunk.

"Go ahead," she teased. He broke off a piece of roll and wiped up the grease from his plate. "If you want, I'll go back to Texas with you," he said. He ate a huge bite of soggy roll. With his mouth full he said, "I've never divorced Janice, and our kid is American. I could get a permanent visa. Or you and I could get married." He licked his lips and wiped his face on the back of his sleeve.

"How can we, if you are still married to Janice?"

"Maybe she's gotten a divorce. What do I know? She's a hippie now."

"What brings this on?" Mickey was so often serious about impossible things, about bullfighting apprenticeships and Pemex jobs, falling in love with attaché's daughters. This most recent idea was the dregs in a bottle of wine.

"You can't stay here forever," he said.

"I have a visa. I'm not leaving." The joke was it was a student visa, renewable every year.

"Where can it lead?" His words had a sharp edge. He was always a little angry when they talked seriously. He had never really forgiven her for using him. "Texas would be better. I could bring my son up there. What will he ever have here?"

"What would he have in Texas?"

"Opportunity! A life that depends on no one's favors."

Abilene laughed. "Like I had? The opportunity to grow up and get a shitty job and live in debt and envy? You think that's different? Better?"

Mickey's face turned bright red.

"Mickey," she said gently. "Do you want me because Tonio—" There was no good way to say it. "Because Tonio has me?"

Mickey exploded. "He treats you like a second-rate horse, Abby, and you go for it. You like it! It's sick. He orders you around, sends you off to have your face shaved, abandons you for months at a time, *passes you around*—" Abilene stood up. "He knows what you're like! He knows what you're doing here! He'll make you sorry, make you wish you hadn't. He beats you, doesn't he? *Doesn't he?*"

"Of course he doesn't!" Mickey lunged for her arm as she said this; he grasped it and used it to pull himself up. As he stood, the table tipped and dishes clattered onto the terrace floor. The table wobbled and Mickey, seeing it, made a growling noise and gave it a vicious kick. A man at a nearby table stood up and screamed at them. Waiters ran out, followed by the maitre d'. Abilene held onto the back of a chair. Mickey shouted in every direction that it was all an accident. He held onto Abilene so tight he was cutting off circulation. The other diners yelled that they saw him do it, that he was a clod, a drunk, not civilized enough for restaurants. "Eat your tacos on the street!" they yelled. Mickey reached into his pocket and pulled out his money, squashed in his pocket like balled-up hankies. He let go of Abilene, and she rubbed her arm. He threw money onto the chair and onto the toppled table on the terrace. He stuffed bills into the maitre d's hands. The maitre d' was a figure of calm, but he said he would call the police if he ever saw either of them again. He said that they were pests and clods. A waiter on his hands and knees was picking up pieces of dishes.

"Jesus, Mickey," Abilene said, shaking, halfway down the block. Her arm was burning. "You're crazy. You've gone daffy." Mickey pushed her against a light post. She could feel his hot breath on her throat. So close to her, he looked wild and ugly and threatening. "I've seen pictures," he said. "Tonio has pictures—"

Tonio had so many pictures, Swedish girls with their labia held apart, their sex turned to winking eyes. "So what?" she said. Then she realized that Mickey meant pictures of her. Her mind raced—what pictures were there? Tonio had a Polaroid. There had been pictures, long ago. But Tonio wouldn't show them. Not to anyone, not to Mickey. He wouldn't.

"What pictures?"

Over his shoulder she saw a girl had stopped a few yards away. She was a child, maybe fourteen. She was country girl, dressed in a long skirt and *reboza;* her feet were bare. She had no expression whatsoever; the blankness of her stare was alarming. *I won't come closer,* her stare seemed to say, *but I want to see.* As if seeing were everything. Abilene stared back, and the girl dropped her eyes. She looked like one of the maids at the ranch, called in for scolding—humble, resigned, unrepentant.

Mickey was talking on and on. He had seen pictures. He described them, pictures of Abilene with her hair down over her breasts in tangles, her chest glistening with sweat, pictures with her mouth open, her tongue wetting her lips. "Oh God," Abilene said. *Pictures of the two of us.* It made her sick to think of him mooning over them. He was a weasel, a snake! She wouldn't let him make her care. What was it to her if he fed his lust? "So what?" she said coldly.

Her eyes darted back and forth from Mickey and the girl. The girl had something in her *reboza,* a package; she backed up a few steps and looked down into the shawl. A baby. The child had a baby. Abilene grabbed Mickey's arm. "Look!" she said, pointing to the slowly retreating figure. "What's she doing in Lomas, *and with a baby?*"

Mickey looked at Abilene as if she had said something very stupid. He whistled to the girl, who stopped at the sound. "Come here," he said roughly. Her face was thrust forward, almost as if she were off balance, too far out over her feet. Her hair was tied back with string. "Come," he said again. The girl approached slowly, tentatively, glancing over her shoulder to check her escape route. Mickey dug into his pocket for change and gave it to her. She took the coins and trotted away.

"She's like you," Mickey said. Except for the sweat on his face, he now looked nothing like he looked two minutes ago, in the midst of his feverish monologue. "She has heard there's life in the city. Maybe she had a cousin come here, someone who was lost in the maw and didn't come back. She decided to follow. Anything is better than the village. She walked to Mexico, to find her cousin. Now she sees how it is, and she's waiting for someone to notice that she needs a place to live. She'll go with some young man, if she is lucky, maybe to one of the caves below Lomas; or she will go with bad men and do whatever they say, for tortillas. Her baby will die of diarrhea. But now, knowing none of this, without an ounce of perception, this stupid stupid girl is walking around. At night she sleeps in the street."

"When did you see the pictures?" Abilene asked softly. "Did Tonio show them to you?"

Mickey, now embarrassed, or ashamed, answered quietly. "They were on his dresser. It was a long time ago. Years ago."

"And now you tell me?"

"Can't we go back to your apartment? Please?" His whole posture had changed. She remembered a story Tonio had told her, about Mickey showing up, passport in hand, begging to go with Tonio to Spain. He wanted to get novice fights, but if he could not do that, he would place the beribboned barbs for Tonio, like Tacho, as crazy and brave as Tacho, he would place himself in the path of death, to humble and provoke the bull, to make Tonio look good. On his knees he had said these things! Of course Tonio had told him he was a fool. Chilling, Tonio could be, in his disinterest. Mickey on his knees had hardened his heart. Only a woman should kneel, he would have said.

"Please? Please?" Mickey was moaning now. Something had tipped him right over the edge.

"I have plans."

"Change them." He put his hands on her shoulders.

"You leave me alone. You stay away from me!" She turned and ran, the bag with the box with the shoes inside bouncing off her thigh. She didn't look back until she came to a busy street where she could get a taxi. Mickey was nowhere in sight. In the taxi she opened the bag and the box, and changed from her expensive sandals back into her comfortable old ones.

In the apartment she went to the bathroom and stood looking

219

into the mirror for a long time.

She thought she looked like the Indian girl, her face like a statue's. Wandering around in a state of stupid faith.

Knowing that Tonio was away, Abilene threw herself into the life of the city, with unusual energy. She spent her time with the girls' brigades. Ceci and her friends were very high-spirited. They went to the Merced market to make street theatre, and to La Lagunilla; they went to parks and cafes. They rode trolleys and buses and talked to everyone! Hallie had not gone back to school at all; she had moved in with the family of a student in Tlatelolco.

Felix came by one day and took Abilene to lunch. He said he was worried about her. Tonio had returned, and he wanted Abilene to come home. "The city is no place to be, anyway," Felix said. He was a big engineer for the government; it was his job to keep certain buildings from sinking into the ground. He heard things.

"Oh, but it's all exciting," Abilene said airily. She had seen plenty of Mexican girls sitting in little groups in the expensive cafes through the long afternoons, with nothing to do but gossip. She liked what she was doing: belonging to no one, running around as she liked with a bunch of girls. She thought this must be what college would have been like, if she had been luckier, if she had made friends, had money. Of course, in college there would have been classes!

"Is it exciting to see a shark in the water?" Felix asked.

"Tonio is a real chump," Abilene said. "He had to come right through the city, and he didn't try to see me. Now he wants to snap his fingers and have everything back in place."

Felix replied, not unkindly, "Remember it's his hand that feeds you. He can write you off altogether. That will be the end of your little vacation in the city. He can cut you dead. In a matter of speaking."

Petulantly, Abilene said, "That goes two ways."

Felix snapped his fingers. "Wake up, little *gringa*. Tonio can't help you if you're shot dead. They've set up hospitals all over the city. And jails. I hear they've picked up one of the leaders, and he has told them about plans for an insurrection. Do you know what that means? M-1s and tanks if the Army wants. In the streets of Mexico.

"Let me tell you something else. I think Tonio didn't like Europe all that much. I think he gets very bored with nice girls and music. I think he has been a very tough guy to be who he is, and he has never had to be tough with you. You're the only girl to come along who never seemed to want something from him."

"Now I do."

"What?"

"Something." Abilene knew she sounded stupid. "Fuck it, Felix. I've gotten used to being amused."

"He wants you to settle down and stop playing around with risky ventures that have nothing to do with you."

"What would I do at the Tecoluca?"

"Stay alive."

Her stomach did a flip-flop. "You exaggerate."

"Five years in Mexico, *chica*, and you don't know where you are," Felix said. They drank half a bottle of wine without speaking. Felix called for the check, disgusted, or perhaps merely bored with her.

"Felix?"

"Yes?"

"Do you really think he wants me there? Not just to make me, but because he really wants me there?"

"I do."

She had an idea. "Then let him get hungry, Felix. Let him wait a while. I'm in the middle of something here."

Felix put her in a cab. He gave the driver money and bent to say goodbye. "Don't make too much of yourself, Abby," he said. "Remember there are more women than men in the world."

She stopped at Tonio's office to see if there was money for her. There wasn't. Muñoz said he had a ticket for her to San Marta. Abilene was embarrassed.

Later, she told Isabel, and laughed at herself. "I was embarrassed because the money wasn't there, but I've never been embarrassed when it was."

Isabel was worse than Felix. She laid a wad of bills down on the chair beside Abilene. "Go get your hair cut and go home," she said. "I expected you to have some common sense. Demonstrations are not sport."

"You're being a stuffed shirt."

"I'm worried about my sister."

"I thought you were going to let her hang herself with her own noose. You know a lot of English, Isabel."

"My mother is sick about it. I've got a business to run. I went out to Lecumberri to see my cousin's son Jaime. He says the cells are full of students and professors, even lawyers."

"Ceci isn't doing anything dangerous. We're going to distribute pamphlets this afternoon at the chocolate factory."

"My mother worked there once. It made her vomit." Isabel tapped her fingernails on her purse. "Don't kid yourself that you're doing this for fun. You know you're going to get in trouble, and you think it will be something new."

"What's wrong with that!" Isabel had touched a tender and true spot; Abilene felt her pulse in her temples. If she left now, what an anticlimax! As if she had not, for once, been where something was going on!

"You'll have to find out."

"They want to catch the workers at four when they change shifts. Park on the street in front and wait. I'll tell Ceci you'll pick her up. You can take her home for dinner with your mother. Relax. Everybody's so full of threats. You thought Tonio would cut off Sage's balls, and all he's done is cut off his lease."

"A little past four," Isabel said, disgusted. "You make sure she's there. And Abilene, about Sage. Maybe he was lucky. Maybe he didn't have any balls in the first place."

AIDEE HAD AN ORANGE VW bug. She parked it on the avenue near the factory exit. They went into the cafeteria and gave flyers to the few people there. One of the men wadded up a paper and threw it back at Aidee. "You fucking kids are showing your dirty linen at the wrong time!" A woman whispered to Abilene, "He's management. He thinks the kids are unpatriotic. He feels very strongly about it." The woman saw the manager look at her and she fled the room.

The girls huddled to discuss strategy. They decided to station themselves by the outside of the exits. Aidee and Abilene stood at one near the car, Ceci and Estrella stationed themselves at another door on that same side, and Hallie went around the corner. They would meet at the car when the shifts changed.

The flyers repeated the demands of the strike committee for the release of political prisoners, the disbandment of police units, the repeal of the "dissolution" provision in the penal code, under which hundreds had been detained without charges, and other statements that had to do with university life. The flyers also listed groups that had publicly declared their affiliation with the strike, including unions, artists and writers congresses, university professors, and many others.

Men coming on the next shift took the papers from the girls and began reading as they went inside the building. Several stopped to express their admiration for what the students were doing. One said his daughter was at UNAM, too. Some of them said, "We're on your side!" Two men got out of an American car parked close to Aidee's VW and came over to ask what the girls were doing. They were nice-looking men in casual clothes and they were very friendly and curious.

"We're just admiring the view," Ceci said flirtatiously. She was being friendly, but guarded.

"Weren't you in the Zócalo the other night?" the other man asked. He was wearing white chinos and an Hawaiian shirt. "That was really something, wasn't it?"

Ceci relaxed. "Yeah, it was. It's beautiful when you see the people out."

"Surprising that there are so many citizens with you," the first man said. "When you think it just started out with some disgruntled students." He wore jeans, a lightweight khaki jacket and a polo shirt. He walked over to Aidee. "What's that you're handing out?"

Aidee didn't seem to know how to answer. She had an aunt in Lecumberri serving seven years on trumped-up charges. She was naturally nervous.

Ceci called out from her spot, "It's just a bunch of flyers about the strike. To let people know what it's about. Nothing, really."

The man in the jacket said, "We'd like to read those."

His companion said, "We could take some—say a dozen? We've got friends."

They were all uneasy now, suspended in their doubt. Nobody did anything. Abilene saw Isabel's yellow Fiat roaring down the street towards them. Maybe Aidee didn't know Isabel's car. For whatever reason, the approach of the car threw her into a panic. "Give them the papers!" she shouted. "Ceci, give them yours!"

One of the men took out his identification.

The other said, "Guess who?"

"Police! Oh shit!" Ceci yelled, and headed for Aidee's car, with Aidee and Estrella right behind. Hallie was around the corner and had had the sense not to show herself. Abilene looked at Isabel, sitting in her car at the curb. Then she ran and jumped into Aidee's car just as Aidee pulled away.

Ceci mumbled, "Those sonsofbitches. Those fuckers." Aidee was driving fast and not saying anything.

The men chased them in their car. Their car was bigger and it began to close the gap. Abilene caught a glimpse of Hallie racing around the corner of the building. Then Aidee shot across two lanes of traffic to get away from their pursuers.

They had raced a mile or so when a little red sports car came alongside. The driver, a nice-looking fellow, smiled and waved at them, and Ceci shouted out her window, "Police! Police!" pointing at the car behind. The sports car began to weave in and out of the traffic very expertly. The driver gave the girls a "V" sign. He had managed to cut off the policemen's car so that when Aidee made a sudden turn onto an off street, they had lost them. Her hands were trembling. The sports car came up behind and parked. Estrella had made the sign of the cross and was saying a Hail Mary for thanks. The man got out of his car, waving to them. He was handsome and young, some rich family's darling. The girls got out to go and thank him. "Say, he's cute," Ceci said under her breath.

The man's smile broadened as they approached. He took out a revolver.

He was a plain clothesman too! Just then the other car caught up with them.

The girls stood like stunned animals and watched as the men

pulled out knives and slit the tires of Aidee's car. They were kidding and joking among themselves, enjoying the girls' fright. They used the ignition key to open the trunk, and took out a tire iron, and broke all the windows. Then they started calling the girls names and punching them on the arms. They laughed and swished knives in the air. Aidee was wearing a dress with a cinched waist, and one of the men reached over and slit the belt—swish!—and the dress bloused out. Aidee burst into tears. The others were white-faced.

The men shoved the girls into the back seat of the big American car. They blindfolded them with black scarves, and when Aidee would not stop crying, they gagged her. The man in the rider's seat in front said, "Now you babies can find out what you're into. You didn't think anybody would mind, pretty little girls like you? You thought you could do what you wanted because you're so snotty and rich and lazy?" He went on and on reviling them. Abilene tried to listen to another sound in her head, a kind of low buzzing like when Tonio's plane got close to the ranch.

At the police station someone shoved the girls into a very small room. There was nothing—no table, no chair, no window. There wasn't even an electrical plug. It was dark, but the light that crept through the edges around the door kept them from total blackness. Ceci and Estrella bundled Aidee between them and tried to soothe her. "You okay?" Ceci said to Abilene.

All Abilene could manage was a nod. She was so numb. She guessed she was as scared as Aidee but too stunned to show it. She kept thinking about how flip she had been with Felix, and with Isabel. Isabel! Where was she?

At least they hadn't picked up Hallie.

Two women in uniform came and took their names. They told the girls to lay their purses down and to take off their shoes and their underwear.

"But why that?" Estrella asked. Her face was turning a deep hot red.

One of the policewomen snarled and then laughed. "It's to let the air in, to cool you off. You hot pants ladies. It's to air you out so you won't stink!" She snickered as she picked up the shoes and purses, the panty hose from Aidee, and panties from all four. She made Estrella give up the crucifix on a chain around her neck, and she took Abilene's gold bracelet. Then she said to Estrella, "Bend over."

"What?" Estrella looked desperate. The matron gave her a shove that made her fall. When she got back up, the matron said again, "Now bend over, girlie." Estrella turned and leaned against a wall. The woman pulled one hand down and forced her to bend, to keep her balance. She flipped Estrella's dress up in the back; Estrella's buttocks shone bare. She shoved a finger right up Estrella's backside and then waved it in the air, shouting "phew! phew!" Then the matrons left.

"Oh my God, my God," Estrella wept.

"This is more awful than I ever imagined," Aidee said.

"Oh stop it!" Abilene said. "Nothing has happened yet. They've had a good time at our expense. They're making fun of us, they want to frighten us. What can they really do? What have we done? We stood outside a building and handed out pieces of paper. Get yourself together, all of you. You've cried and now you must stop. We have to wait until someone comes and tells us what is going to happen. There's no sense in guessing. And we do have one another."

"You can call the American Embassy," Ceci said. They turned to Abilene as though she knew something they didn't. "Yes," they said in chorus. "Call the Americans to come and get you."

"Sure," she said. "Hand me that phone!"

They all shut up. She thought about what the girls had said. She didn't think for a moment that anyone would care what happened to her, Abilene Painter, in some police precinct in Mexico City. What a fool she was! She had asked for this, just like she had got in line for every other fool thing.

Felix had her number!

They sat on the floor for a long time. They all needed to go to the bathroom. In a while men in uniforms came to get them. Aiblene got her courage up to ask about the bathroom. The men—these were new ones, they hadn't seen them before— kidded them and told them they could pee in the street like tough boys. Aidee began to cry again. In the end the men let them take turns going into a toilet, but they had to leave the door wide ajar. "Tinkle tinkle!" the men would call out. "Pssshhh!"

They took the girls out to a police van and told them to climb in. There were three other women in the back already. The doors swung shut. The women looked at one another.

An attractive black-haired girl spoke first. "I heard them say they were taking us to Lecumberri. The precincts are too full, and the women's detention center." She had blood on her cheek.

"You're hurt!" Estrella said.

The girl dabbed at her cheek. "It's not much. A scuffle. I wasn't too meek. I was so mad! Someone scratched me. I don't think he really even meant to." She shrugged and looked away.

They were in the cafeteria at the prison, two dozen or more women.

"Look at this, we're all political prisoners," Ceci said. She sounded better, almost excited. The sight of the other women had cheered her.

Ceci began going around the room talking to the women. Most of them knew someone she knew; one had been in a class with her the year before. Every once in a while she came back to report on what she had learned. "That girl in the red pants? She won't be here long. Her father is head of the department that issues drivers' licenses. He has to know somebody!"

Abilene, Estrella, and Aidee couldn't catch Ceci's good spirits. They sat on one of the concrete tables, their bare bottoms very cold. There was a pregnant Dutch girl on the table with them for a while. Her husband was working on a dig two hundred miles away. She had come into the city to do some shopping and to get Olympic tickets. She had been standing near some students outside a department store, her bad luck when the police van came up and took them all away. She said they had all been in the prison cafeteria since mid-morning and so far nobody had questioned them or told them of any charges. She wanted to call the embassy, or an archeologist she knew in the city, but there wasn't anyone to ask for permission. They hadn't been fed, either.

There were other girls dressed in dance clothes. They had

been coming out of a rehearsal!

Girls were there who had been picked up the night before with their boyfriends as they left cafes or dance halls. They were worried about their boyfriends, that they were being tortured.

"It's not so bad," one of them said. "Except for being hungry." In truth some of the girls seemed very gay. They were the real student radicals, Abilene thought. They knew why they were there. They were talking about meetings and provocations that had taken place. They talked over every detail with relish. Abilene wanted to ask them, don't you think someone might be listening? But what difference would it make. At least they were happy, talking about the meeting in Tlatelolco, where they had been tear-gassed, and some boys had been shot. And just the other day the army had attacked the Santo Tomas campus and occupied the medical school. They had already invaded University City. Abilene knew these things; now she remembered hearing about them. She hadn't paid attention. One meeting, another meeting. A big scuffle, a small one. She hadn't been paying attention.

A glum woman in prison garb rolled in a wagon with kettles of lukewarm soup. There weren't enough bowls. As soon as the women saw that this was so they began talking among themselves, to decide how they would share, who would eat first and then pass the bowls. They gave soup to all the skinny ones first, including Abilene. Everyone got about a cup of soup, a watery broth with tomatoes and corn in it. Abilene felt the soup go to her stomach. She felt her toes again. She felt the hair on her neck. She felt the awful vulnerability of her bare thighs, her uncovered genitals. She thought of how the woman had treated Estrella at the precinct. She hoped that being overcrowded meant they wouldn't be harrassed, that there wouldn't be the time for it. That they wouldn't all be kept, for lack of room.

The pregnant girl began to vomit. Some of the women pounded on the locked doors of the cafeteria until matrons came and took the sick girl away. She never came back.

It was night when a matron brought in tins of canned sweet milk, and pork and beans. The cans had been opened and the lids taken off, but there were no spoons. The women passed the cans from hand to hand, dipping their fingers in for a lick.

Someone began singing a lovely song, a country song, that most of them knew. Once they had sung that song, the singing went on softly for a long, long time into the night. They sang about love and disappointment. Sometimes there was only one voice that wouldn't give up to the night. Sometimes many voices joined in. They tried to make themselves places to sit. The concrete floor was terribly cold, and there were no blankets. There were half a dozen mattresses that had been tossed in, and the women arranged them as though for a giant slumber party, and crowded onto them. There wasn't room for everyone. Some of the girls said they didn't need to be comfortable, didn't need to sleep. They didn't need anything except to be free to fight. They tossed their hair like horses' manes.

Abilene wondered if that made them feel better.

She wondered if Hallie was sorry to have missed this. The idea almost made her smile.

One by one, in the very early morning hours, the prison guards began to call the women out, some by name, some by description. The girl in the red pants! The girl in the green skirt! The fat girl on the end of the mattress!

Abilene was wearing a blue cotton skirt and a white blouse with a scooped neck. She thought it was a good outfit to be wearing, if only she had her panties and her shoes (her expensive Italian shoes!). She heard someone say, The American! The *gringa!* Quick! She had been dozing. She came out of her sleep startled, like someone from underwater. She clutched at her companions. They were still there, Ceci and Aidee and Estrella. They were all so tired. Outside the high windows the courtyard was lit by floodlights.

A young man shoved Abilene ahead of him down a long hall to a room where several men were standing around. They told her to sit on a chair. A paunchy older man in khakis pulled up a chair across from her. Their knees barely touched. He had a stack of photographs on his lap. He needed a shave, and he smelled of garlic. Abilene thought: This is a put-on. It's a movie!

She thought maybe Tonio was doing it, to teach her a lesson. Well, she would do what he wanted, or she would leave Mexico altogether, she knew that. She thought of Michael Sage. My

God, what would she have to say to him, after this? Could he ever understand?

The man asked her her name. He asked why she was in Mexico. She said she was a tourist. They asked her where she stayed. She gave them the address of Claude's apartment. "I met the owner in the country," she said. The questions were easy to answer. She wasn't going to die of fright. It wasn't horrible.

She hadn't brought this on herself.

The man spoke gently. He didn't seem to be enjoying himself. Probably he would rather be at home in bed with his wife.

The man began slapping down photographs, right side up, on her lap. "Tell me their names," he said, more curtly than anything he had said so far. "This one. This. And this. Who are these students? Are they really students? Who are these agitators and spies? Tell me their names." His fingers were round and fat and smooth.

He showed her dozens of pictures. She saw that one of them was the girl she had seen that first day on campus, with Hallie. What was her name? Carmen, Carlita, something like that. There were maybe half a dozen others whose faces she recognized from meetings or gatherings at the apartment. They were Refugio's friends, for the most part. The rest were strangers. What would this man say if she told him what was true, that Mexicans mostly looked alike to her. She shook her head over and over. "I don't know him. I don't know her." Her Spanish had gone flat and Texas in her ear. She hoped that was to her advantage.

"Now we will do it all again," the man said sternly. This time you will tell me." He laid each picture in her lap and waited for long minutes. His knees pressed against hers. He caught her looking at them and moved his legs so abruptly, she fell forward against his thighs. She sat back up, her face aflame. He was smiling.

"I tell you, I don't know them," she said. "I don't know Mexicans." If it got worse, she would tell them she knew Tonio. Felix. She would see if that would help.

The man laid the photos on his chair and they left her alone in the room. She tried not to look at the pictures. She tried to think of Hallie. Hallie must be frantic. Why didn't she go home? Maybe she would now. Maybe her parents would make her come home.

Twice she fell asleep and woke as her head slumped forward. She had no idea what time it was.

She felt a sudden warm stickiness high on her thighs. Had she gone to the bathroom while she was asleep and not known it? Such an indignity would be terrible to bear. The stickiness trickled toward one knee. She put her hand up under her skirt to feel it. When she drew her hand out she realized what it was. It was her period. She was bleeding, here, in a prison room, with no underwear.

It was too bizarre. It made her laugh.

"So it is a joke?" the interrogator said as he came back into the room. An assistant picked up the pictures. The interrogator was wiping his hands on a towel, which he let drop to the floor. Abilene couldn't take her eyes off it. She wanted to wipe her thighs. The blood was warm, thick, dark. It was her first period since the abortion. She had not even worried about it.

"Now tell me what you know, please."

He wasn't wearing a watch. Abilene looked into his face and saw that he did believe that she knew something. She saw that he would never go away unless she gave him something. He would wait and wait for the names. After that he would do what he would do.

The assistant handed the questioner the photographs again, and rubbed the knuckles of one fist with his other hand. She thought: Will he hit me? Will they hurt me?

She closed her eyes. It was so unfair! To be punished for things she had not done. To pay for sins she had not committed. She was no more a radical than a sheepdog.

There were other reasons to punish her. She probably had it coming. She was so tired.

The man slapped her arm. He hit her quite hard. "Wake, up, señorita," he said.

She couldn't open her eyes.

He hit her again, harder.

He began to lay the photographs in her lap.

She shook her head at each one and said, "I don't know."

Then she saw Gato's face staring up at her. His insolence was there like the set of his chin. She couldn't believe he had ever touched her. He had a cold ugly face and she didn't care what she said about him.

"I've seen this one," she said. "I've seen him on campus."

"What is his name?" The interrogator's face had the same sullen defiance as Gato. Why would she help him?

"But you must know, everyone does," she said. She hated this man. "They tell me everyone knows him as the Cat."

"His name. His real name."

"I don't know. Black-cat. Tom-cat."

"We will see," the man said of Gato, and he set the picture on the floor. He showed her others. She began to say, "I saw this one at a meeting on campus," and she said a name. "I saw this one once in the Museum, in the room with the sun dial. I don't know her name."

They went through the stack over and over. It went on for such a long time. She pretended Adele was watching her—now would Adele take her story?!—and Daniel, and Arturo. Pola was watching and Pola thought she was brave.

She wouldn't tell, and they would all be proud of her.

The interrogator stood up and left the room. His assistant stayed behind.

Abilene began to cry with relief.

The assistant was a young man, maybe twenty years old. He looked at her with the insolence of a street *chavo*. It would have been different in a dance hall. He would have worn a nylon shirt and she would have danced with him.

He was repulsive, too young to be genuinely frightening, but hateful. He didn't have any weapon that she could see. She stood when he said to do so, and went out of the room with him behind her. She went to the right. "No, stupid!" he barked. "The other way, back to the cafeteria."

She trudged the other way.

Suddenly he grabbed her from behind, by her hair. "Stop, *gringa*," he said. He sounded as though he was trying to be very authoritative. Maybe they let him practice on the unimportant ones. They were standing by what looked like a closet. He opened the door and shoved her in and reached up to turn on a bare dim light above them. Along one wall stacks of paper in reams filled two shelves. On other shelves there were small boxes, maybe paper clips, or staples.

He jerked her around. There wasn't quite enough room for both of them, and one of his legs was stuck out in the hall through the partly open door. This calmed her. She didn't think he would do anything too terrible with his leg out like that. He probably wanted a quick feel; if she knew anything, that was all it would take for him. He was a boy.

He pinched her breasts through the blouse. She was so tired, she reached out to rest one arm against the shelves.

He yanked her away from the wall. He put his hand in her hair and pulled her to him to kiss. She had known it was coming, and she didn't fight it, but it made her gag. She could imagine any horrible thing coming out of his foul-smelling, foul-tasting mouth: snakes and beetles, poison mushrooms, moldy cheese. He thrust his tongue deep into her mouth.

"You *gringas* like the fuck, huh?" he said in English. When she reached up involuntarily to wipe her mouth with her hand, he stuck his huge tongue out and licked her face like a dog. He stepped back a bit and jerked her skirt up toward her waist.

"Aiee!" he cried, and dropped the skirt. "What's that blood?"

She thought: How funny that a little blood makes me strong. He doesn't want me because I have my period. Good for me.

She shoved past him and out the door. She was thinking of the mattresses in the cafeteria, the arms of Estrella and Ceci.

He punched her in the back with his fist. It took her breath away, and she stopped short, almost stumbling.

"Turn around!"

She complied.

"I asked you, what's that blood?"

"It's my period." She wasn't certain of the word in Spanish. My monthly blood."

"I don't like it. I don't fuck girls with blood."

She shrugged. He was pathetic. She turned again. His fist caught her high on the cheekbone, in front of the ear. The blow sent her to the floor. The lights went out. The lights went on. She was on her hands and knees.

He had undone his pants. He stood, in the middle of the

hallway, with his erect penis sticking out at her. He was grinning. *"Pues,* you sucky me."

She put her hands to her face. His cock nudged at her fingers.

Felix was waiting for her in the morning; he had arranged her release. He took her to a hotel to bathe and sleep. Later on he brought her clothes. He had things she needed from the pharmacy in a white bag. He said his sister had helped him. It was her lovely soft violet dress Abilene put on. Her shoes were a little too large. They slid on Abilene's heels.

Felix had food sent to the room, and they ate on the bed. He said he had a ticket for her to go to San Marta the next day. "And Claude's apartment has been ransacked. I've paid the concierge to get it back in order. The police were there in the night. I called Girard, too. He wasn't happy."

She moaned, but she couldn't really think of those things.

"What did they do to you, you look awful." Felix said.

"It was nothing. It all seems so bad because it was my period and I had nothing I needed."

"I wish I believed you," Felix said. "I'm so sorry. I told you I was afraid for you, but I don't think I really believed this would happen."

"How did you know?"

"Isabel."

"And Ceci?"

"She's still there." He washed his hands and said he would go. He would be back for her in the morning.

She put her hand on Felix's chest. "Don't go away and leave me by myself."

"I'll pick you up in the morning, eight o'clock."

"I want you to stay, Felix. Please stay. I don't want to be by myself."

"I've always wanted to," he said.

"It's my period." Men were like that.

"It's because I feel sorry for you. First you made a fool of yourself, and now you're hurt when you don't really deserve it. I wish I knew how to make it better. But not as a man and woman. This pity, it kills the desire. You must go back to the Tecoluca with your head up; Tonio won't like it, either, seeing you so down. It's funny. I always thought Tonio would get tired of you and I would come along behind and save you. I've done it before, you know that, with other women. Now here you are, and it isn't what I want at all. I just feel sorry for you."

He might as well have slapped her. He must have understood her expression, because before he left he added, "This is much better, really, the feeling between friends. You'll never have to worry about me coming on to you, and I'll still like you."

She was alone in a hotel room. She thought of the women back in the prison. They were all innocent, but there was a reason for them to be there. It was for something they believed in. They were part of something bigger than themselves.

But me, she thought. I've finally gotten what I came for, everyone was right.

> You think you know better, and you don't know anything at all. You go around like a bird on the ground, pecking and squawking and forgetting all about the sky. You surprise yourself with your stupidity.
> What that awful boy did—it was nothing more than what I've done to myself a hundred times over.
> Tonio will see. He will smell it on me, not fear, but humiliation, shame. He won't want me. He won't want to put his mouth on mine.

Her throat constricted with pain. To start over would take such courage, and she had none. It was like that day in Texas, when she said, in the back of someone's car, "There's no one I could tell."

Then she remembered that Adele had dreamed of Sylvia Britton. Barton. Had dreamed of reaching out to her.

"I'm alive!" she would tell Adele. "You've got to help me."

When she got to the apartment on Obregon, she had to make the taxi wait, and go up and ask Adele for the taxi money. When Adele opened the door, she threw her arms around Abilene. "We've been so worried!" she said.

235

Hallie had been there, too. She had left money for Abilene to take to the family in Tlatelolco. She had left her address.

"Her father came for her," Adele said. They smiled. They understood that Hallie had always been safe.

Daniel said, "You can stay as long as you want."

Adele said, "I'm sorry I've been so preoccupied. I want you to stay."

Pola called her name from the door across the room. Abilene crossed to her quickly and hugged her.

"Did they do things to you?" Pola whispered. "Did they touch you there?"

PART VI

13.

October 2, 1968

Four green flares shot off at six-ten p.m. were the signal for troops attached to the Olimpia Battalion, dressed in civilian clothes, to open fire on the students and workers demonstrating in Tlatelolco that afternoon.

-the press secretary of the Autonomous National University of Mexico, quoted in *Massacre in Mexico*

From Adele's transcripts:

Abilene:

We had been talking about going to L.A. Pola was looking forward to being fourteen. She saw it as a real crossroads. She was angry with her mother because she was no longer the center of the universe for Adele, because of Daniel. Sometimes I said, "Oh Pola, you can't mean it," or "Oh Pola, you can't think that," but my objections were weak. I don't know anything at all about relationships, about how people work out problems, how they show love. Besides, the idea of going to California appealed to me. I managed to convince myself it was possible. Pola wanted to go to Yannis. Yannis travels, is very busy, wouldn't be able to be with her enough. I would go along to look after Pola. Pola had already written Yannis to ask about it. I felt worse and worse, I knew I had to talk to Adele, but I couldn't seem to get the energy, and she was busy. She was kind, but she was very busy. To go to L.A. Imagine, that was how I was going to work out my life. I hadn't thought of anything else.

We should never have gone out to Tlatelolco that day. Adele had been very firm about it; she wanted Pola off the streets. Adele was going out to the meeting that had been called in the Plaza of

Three Cultures, to take pictures. She was excited, because she had heard that Oriana Fallaci was in town for the Olympics, and Fallaci had already sniffed out the trouble with the students and was sure to be there, too. She said she might be late. It was a Tuesday night, and Pola would need to go to bed at a reasonable hour. Adele said if I was still up when she got home, she would tell me about it.

We felt cooped up, Pola and I. We didn't like being told to stay home like children, though I no longer cared about the strike. Pola reminded me that I hadn't taken the money left by Hallie out to the family in Tlatelolco, and that was enough to make me "give in," as though we had something to take care of, and it didn't have anything to do with the meeting.

The meeting was supposed to be held to call off the strikes until after the Olympics. I don't remember if I knew that before the meeting, or if it's something I heard right after. Because it was so ironic, they were going to call it off so they wouldn't be an embarrassment to the government, and before they could even say that, the army moved in.

The crowd was incredible. We came into the square from one of the narrow alleyways and saw people were hanging out of windows and over balconies. Kids had climbed onto the fountains and onto one another's shoulders. There were students going around handing out flyers about the suspension of the strike. They said the government was going to have an open dialogue with them after the foreigners all went home. A compromise, but it would keep the army out of it, someone said. It would keep them out of jail, too.

People were streaming through the cramped corridors off the avenue, into the plaza. There were old people getting off work and going home, and there were bureaucrats coming out of the office buildings to get a look. There were old ladies with black scarves on their heads, and everywhere you looked, little kids were racing around playing tag and hide-and-seek. There were people all the way from the edge of the ruins to the church. People were moving around but not really going anywhere, like they were in jelly.

I knew we shouldn't have come, but I thought if we just went about our business, if we got into the apartment building, we would be okay. I put my arm around Pola's waist. "You stick close to me," I said, trying to sound really stern. She pointed to the other side of the plaza. "We've got to get over there!" she said. It was going to take some doing.

We worked our way through the crowd, and we were more than halfway there when someone started yelling through a mega-

phone. Pola wanted to stop and listen. I kept pushing her on, closer to the building. Pola just stopped, like a balky animal. For the first time, really, I looked around me. We were in the middle of thousands of people. I looked up toward the speaker on the balcony. There were photographers leaning out of windows snapping pictures of the crowd.

"I wonder where Mommy is," Pola said.

There was a man standing on the other side of Pola, with binoculars. I heard Pola ask him what he could see. He wasn't especially friendly, but he said, "Just a bunch of crazy kids." I leaned around to take a look at him, and I saw the funniest thing. He was holding the binoculars in his right hand, and he had his left hand, by Pola, stuck in his jacket pocket. I could tell that he was wearing a white glove—just on that one hand, in the pocket. The edge of it showed above the top of the cloth. I almost said something about it to him, and then I thought, oh it must be something awful. Maybe his hand is deformed, I thought.

Pola asked, "Can I use your binoculars for just a moment, to look for my mother? She's on one of those balconies over there. She's a photographer."

He hesitated, holding the binoculars up to his own eyes for another moment, and then he said, "Okay, for a little look."

Pola loved the binoculars. Maybe she had never looked through binoculars before. She was so excited. "It's amazing!" she said. "I can see the mouth of the speaker moving. His shirt gaps open at the top, like he needs another button." She moved her head a couple of inches, and swept a look across the balconies. "Mommy could be anywhere!" she said.

I had a tight grip on Pola's arm. I was starting to get nervous. I didn't like the way people were hanging out of windows. Somebody could throw a rock and hit a head sticking out too far, I thought. I didn't like being in the middle of so many bodies.

The man took his binoculars back and used them to look straight up into the sky. It had begun to sprinkle just a little bit. It would rain harder in a while. It was that time of day.

"We're going to get wet, come on, we've got to get to the apartment in Chihuahua," I told Pola. I held her hand and almost dragged her, winding our way through the crowd. We had almost reached the steps of the building when a light gashed across the gray sky. "What is it!" Pola yelled. There was a terrible racket, a droning, and then a whack! whack! whack! People started screaming. Lights flashed across the sky again. All I could think to do was grab Pola up against my body and hold on tight. Then I realized I was hearing shots, and screams.

241

Pola was trying to wiggle away from me. "Where's my mother?!" she screamed over and over.

"You've got to come on," I said. She was so strong, I couldn't pull her the last few yards.

It was so quick, Pola's change of heart. It only took those seconds, the sounds of helicopters and the screams in the plaza, and she knew she wouldn't leave her mother. She looked at me and said, "I'm sorry, Abby." I didn't know what she meant yet. POLA! I screamed. This was for real, this wasn't a movie, or a story about something happening someplace else. "I can't go with you," Pola yelled. "I can't go to L.A."

"IT DOESN'T MATTER!" I screamed. "COME ON!"

I was facing her when I yelled. Over her shoulder I saw that man, the one with the glove and the binoculars. Pola must have seen the funny look on my face, because she swung around and saw him too.

"Please!" she cried to him. "Let me use your binoculars to look for my mother. Please."

Then we could both see he wasn't the man with the binoculars. He was another man with a white-gloved hand, and it was in the air, above his head. In his other hand he held a gun. All of a sudden I saw that there were many men like him, all with their white hands in the air, and guns.

People were falling to the ground. Someone's shoe flew into the air beside us and landed right in front of Pola. It was a backsling sandal like Adele sometimes wore. Pola grabbed at it, and came up, holding onto the shoe. I started screaming and crying and pulling at her all at once.

She never cried out. She must have seen it, the black heart of the gun. It was like a great hole into which she fell and fell. Open-mouthed with astonishment, holding onto the sandal, she fell. The blood from her shattered cheek oozed into a puddle and was trampled underfoot by children racing past. The rain began to pour hard. When it stopped, the Plaza of Three Cultures was stained crimson. White gloves lay about with shoes and purses and sodden pamphlets. Like the wounded. Like the dead.

Daniel:

When I write in my ledgers I feel nothing. Names, numbers, places. The killing has stopped, but the arrests go on. Everything in me that has feeling is dead. I am a machine. When I wake in the night and stare at the dark, the names come back to me, as if they are being spoken aloud. I see them lying at the police stations, the Red Cross headquarters, on the lawn. I was looking for Pola. When I found her, they said I would have to

sign a paper that said she was an agitator against the government. I had to sign it to get her body. There were so many
others. Elisa Avendano, fourteen, a Prep student. Señora
Paula Lopez, a housewife. Juan Duran, teacher of mathematics.
Who were they? Who loved them?

What would they be doing now? What would they have become? They were mostly young people, full of mystery. They
hadn't had time to develop their complexity. They had not yet
become themselves.

Ceci:

I've been sentenced to an indefinite period, and moved into the
section with women who had been tried for crimes. When I was
first arrested I was very frightened. I waited all night to be
questioned, and then they blindfolded me and beat my shoulders.
They told me about the terrible things they could do to me. They
kept me from the toilet so that I soiled myself. I told them nothing
at all, and they lost interest. There were so many new ones coming
in. We tried to keep one another's spirits up. Now they try to
separate us, but there are too many of us. They would have to fling
us, like a chain, the length of the country. I'm not scared anymore.
It's not so bad, day to day. It's terribly noisy, and boring, of
course. I'm sorry that I missed so much—the last battles, even
Tlatelolco. And I don't know when it will be over, that's the worst
of it. How long? What will I look like in a year? Two years? Ten?
That's what tortures me, not knowing. That, and being as ignorant today as I was yesterday. I realize now that I loved my
studies. Some of the women mock us students, but others ask us:
What did you learn in school? Is it too late for me to learn, too?
I'm teaching a prostitute to read. She's a year older than I am, and
she has been on the streets since she was eleven or twelve. "Next
time I can read my charges," she says, and laughs about it. I never
laugh, never. But I don't cry, either.

Adele:

When I met the Italian journalist, she said, "This is the real
news in Mexico. The Olympics are nothing beside this." She was
so excited, a small peppery woman. Later I saw her on the balcony
next to mine.

By 5:30 five thousand people had gathered to listen to the
speakers from the National Strike Committee. I was thinking:
Have I taped their voices? Do I know what they want? It had
become so important to me to hear them. There was a mosaic I was
constructing, and I had to have all the pieces: young girls in mini-

243

skirts, and mothers in shawls and sturdy shoes. Professors and anthropologists, nuns, businessmen, factory workers, railway workers, artists. My list had grown. Each tape took a space in the picture I was making of Mexico in a time of change. I knew that what was happening would affect Mexico for a generation to come. For the first time I felt the thrill of the journalist, the documenter. I thought I understood Fallaci.

So many of the victims were bystanders. They had not come with malice in their hearts. Whatever they say, whatever the papers say, I was there. The malice was brought in like cannon.

The flares. The terrible sounds. Down in the crowd I could see there were white hands cutting the air, and then there was the panic.

What kind of government murders pregnant women, children, and students, randomly? What did they fear so much?

And my love! My child! She was one of so many. She didn't even have the privilege of her own death.

I heard Fallaci crying out in English, "I'm shot! The sons of bitches have shot me! I'm going to tell the whole world!"

I ran down the stairs, it seemed I ran for hours. There was blood everywhere, and already hundreds shoved against walls waiting to be hauled away. Hundreds had gathered by the ancient church; its doors were never opened that whole terrible night.

They were piling bodies in the rain.

I could not speak to Abilene, I was mute. I looked at her and all I could think was that she had seen it happen. She had been there, and not me.

I remember thinking a long time ago, when we were in Zi that winter, that she had a funny schoolgirl's thought, that when a man fucked you, there must be a reason. That it ought to be for something. Now I should have said to her, it's true of death. Death must be for something, when it cuts lives so cruelly short. I was so numb. Tears kept pouring out of Abby's eyes, but she didn't make a sound. She was crying like that the morning she left, and still she hadn't cried aloud. I just watched her leave. I couldn't say anything. She was all the way downstairs, and out on the street, when I knew what I had to tell her. I ran to the window and threw it open, I leaned out perilously above the walk, and I screamed after her, "Let it make you live! Dig down inside and bring up the anger, and you'll live!"

Let it be for something.

I don't think she heard me.

On All Soul's Day the hotelkeeper's wife, Nando Piñeda's mother, came to the apartment for me. We took flowers and candles to the Plaza. Women hid in the shadows. Then one of them went out and laid a photograph on the ground and beside it, a votive candle. She made the sign of the cross and knelt.

The rest of us came out of our shadows with our flowers and candles. Into our half-lives.

I looked at the mothers, and I thought: We've counted your dead, Daniel and I. We've saved their stories. Some day I will be able to tell them.

For the mothers.

Sister Rita:

I remember the day Adele told me she was taking the stories from the students and supporters. She came out to see me. I was in a courtyard bathing a wretched baby whose legs and face were covered with sores. Adele offered to buy me lunch. Before I could even think, I laughed. We were miles from anything other than a place to buy pulque, and maybe a taco with meat from a goat's head.

We went back to my little place and ate bread and cheese. Adele couldn't believe I hadn't heard about the demonstrations. I told her the shouts I heard were angry men beating their wives or children. Neighbors screaming at neighbors. That upset her, she said, "But you've always said that they were so good." She didn't understand how desperate they are, the poor. How they worry about the most basic elements of staying alive. They don't have time for politics. They'll be dead and nothing will have changed, whatever gets written up as policy and law. All I can do is patch up tiny holes in the fabric of their lives. Little holes.

I realize now that Adele had come to me for some kind of approval. She thought what she was doing was important, and it probably was, but I was tired and distracted and busy and I couldn't be very thrilled about her playing at Man on the Street.

I was a spoiled surburban California girl who grew up and looked around and couldn't see a single reason to get up in the morning. I was halfway through college, so bored I thought about killing myself. But I was Catholic. I went to talk to a young priest on campus. He had just spent two years in Bolivia. He said I ought to stop worrying about myself and worry about people who have real troubles. One thing led to another. Now my superiors decide who will have my help. I am such a tiny drop in the universe. But I'm not bored, I'm not unhappy for myself anymore. I just try to be my small bit of good displacing bad. I've never had any interest in the rhetoric of revolution, although plenty of my fellow sisters have. I guess I have too small a vision. I can't see ahead. Or maybe I haven't the courage. But when someone finally comes along and shows me how to do it, I'll probably join in. Listening to the Gospel for the first time. Listening to what people are saying about Him. Letting Christ take on a new face, one the angry students would like. Christ the fighter. God help us, He's coming.

Abilene:

The archeologist Martin once talked about how the Huasteca was changing, the old ways being lost. When he first started to dig in the Huasteca, the Indians who helped him would recognize pieces of pottery as they took them out of the ground. They didn't seem to understand that the objects were old.

Now young workers say, "What's this old thing?"

During his last visit, the winter of 1966, Martin, lover of old things, hiked with Antonio to the place they call Golindrinas, the Pit of Swallows. They went to the end of the road above Valles and hiked past little plots of coffee and bananas, into the forest. The rim of the pit was thick with bushes and vines. They arrived at dusk and stayed away from the edge. They chose a flat place for their tents, careful to see that there would be no chance of stumbling, in a dream state, into the abyss. In the morning they woke to see clouds of swifts ascending from the pit, and behind the swifts, bright swaths of parakeets. They looked down into the pit and saw how the light picked up the color and the striation of the limestone, and then vanished into the depths. A rock tossed out toward the middle plunged and then wobbled out of sight like something made of paper or cloth. I guess that's when Tonio got it in his head that he had to climb down. Martin said he didn't have time—it would be a big venture—and then news came within a year that he was dead of some fever he had had many times—left over, probably, from one of his trips to Indonesia.

Martin had seen right away that I had a taste for the exotic. He said he hadn't wanted to live in Switzerland since he was old enough to decide. He told me about a favorite Indonesian island. He loved its seacoast and bay, the river and stream, forest and beach, the coco palm and spices. He told me a legend. There was a woman who lived in a garden and went down the shore at night to watch for a proa to come and carry her away. Some said she was young, some old.

He said, "Once I heard the indios across the river saying that sometimes they saw a woman along the river bank here, on your side, but only at night. They didn't know anything about her. Then I met you, and I wondered if you sometimes walked down to the river at night."

Of course I didn't. The bank is too steep and tangled. In the *dark you would be caught in the brush, or you might slide into the water.*

Martin said it was my red hair that fascinated the indios. *Then he said, "There are so many places where the souls of women have been trapped by circumstances and their own nature. I think of them as women with longings too great to be lost in death."*

I said I don't believe in ghosts.

He said he believed in an after life. He said it might be a mirage, a mere vapor, but does it matter? When you die, he said, disappointment goes with you.

Unless you cannot die, unless you wander.

I asked if he had ever seen a woman like he described, the island wanderer.

He said, "Only in the eyes of living women."

The night after Pola was killed, I dreamed of the pit. I was on the bottom, where the earth was soft with rich rotted vines and mosses. I had landed easily, like a child in hay or snow or sand. Tonio had said: Don't lose the rope.

I saw it dangling above me, almost invisible. To look up the side of the pit was to look up a cliff.

I heard my name. It was Pola, half-hidden in the ground cover. She was naked, and her body was as white as talc. She kept whispering my name. She opened her arms to me.

I scrambled to my knees. I didn't know what I wanted to do. Pola began to roll away. Like a ballet dancer in a turn, she looked at me as her head came around each time. She rolled and rolled, into the caves.

I looked for the end of the rope. I couldn't see it, and I began to wave my arms in an arc, to catch it with my hand. The sky was a hole of light above me. I knew I'd never find the rope again.

Abby! Pola cried from the blackness.

Pola! I cried back, but she was gone. Somewhere in the caves she waited.

I will go to Tonio, and I will wait for him to tell me how things will be. I will wait for him to say what he knows about me. I will wait for him to say what will happen to me, or if this is my life and it will go on and on.

247

PART VII

14.

"SO," TONIO SAID. "Look who's back." He seemed glad.

He was just coming out of the stables. He was wearing tight jeans, boots, and a blue shirt like Abilene's father used to wear to work in the oilfields. Abilene wondered if Tonio knew that shirts like his were worn by men who worked hard and got very dirty. Probably there were people wearing them now who didn't ever get dirty. Probably they were in style in the states, and that was why Tonio was wearing one of them. Abilene had ironed her father's work shirts once—she was eleven or twelve then—and he had been embarrassed. There had been sweat stains under each arm. "You don't have to do that, honey," he'd said. "Shoot, don't."

It was the middle of the afternoon. Abilene said, "I thought you would be at siesta." She had seen herself going in the house quietly, lying down in a room with pulled drapes, getting used to the idea of the country again.

"Too much going on," he said. He didn't kiss her, or touch her, either.

Together they walked to the guardhouse. "I want Sapo to put in a call to Mexico," Tonio said. He went in, and Abilene waited outside. The way the light hit the screens, she couldn't see inside. She wondered why Sapo would put in a call instead of Sofia, unless Sofia was sick. Sofia never missed work. If Tonio wanted her to, she would come in on Sundays. She felt important doing Velez business. She liked it especially when Tonio sent her to give someone an order for him. "The *señor* says to hose down the plane and get it ready to go to San Luis Potosi."

"The *señor* says to bring beer and a plate of caviar and crackers to his office for his guests." Before Abilene came, there had been some times when Tonio asked Sofia to work late, to stay over, a different sort of business. It didn't bother Abilene that Sofia didn't like Abilene; it bothered Abilene that she minded.

The little jaguarundi was pacing on the ground in front of the guardhouse. Back and forth it went, in a pattern of double arcs, and you could see the path it had worn in the dirt. It went as far as it could in one direction, twisted its head against the tug of the chain, and then went the other way.

When Tonio came out of the guardhouse, he reached down to scratch the cat's head. The cat stretched, extending its front legs and pushing up against Tonio's hand, then pulled back, arching and tucking the head. Tonio grabbed the fur on the top of the cat's neck and tugged on it hard. The cat's head dipped down toward its neck, and its eyes closed to slits.

They went through the gate into the grounds of the house. Abilene had been nervous as she climbed the bank up from the ferry. She had not known how Tonio would act, if he would be angry or contemptuous, or if he would be indifferent. She had not asked him before she came. Then Tonio had disarmed her with the casual affection of his greeting. Now the familiarity of the ranch rushed around her like water. From the climbing vines above their heads, the heavy scent of flowers fell on them.

On the right of the covered walk was the building that housed Tonio's sleek, well-appointed office. The other half of the building was his saloon, ornate Victorian, with a brass footrail and a matching backbar of Honduran mahogany. Framing the back of the bar was an array of mounted trophies from the northern Rockies. A pair of massive bighorn rams were heavy-necked, with ridged, coiled horns and jaundiced eyes. Two mule deer heads hung frozen in taxidermy, their antlers locked as if in mortal combat. At both upper corners of the mirror, whole carcasses of mountain lions hung by their front paws as if they had just been killed.

Tonio wanted Abilene to see the new pinball machine he had acquired during the summer. It was a gift from a friend in

Houston who was going to go with Tonio to hunt cats in Campeche. Tonio plugged in the pinball machine. Lights flashed zanily, and he assumed a pose suitable for his purpose, one leg bent behind, leaning into the other. Of course he was an expert player.

He insisted that Abilene try her hand. Everything about the game seemed random. There was no way she could make the balls go anywhere. There was no way to control her game.

"Here, you want a beer?" Tonio was down behind the bar, where he had a half-sized refrigerator, actually a much better one than the big one in the house. That one was in a closet with cases of beverages. It had to be defrosted. Abilene had done it for something to do, in the middle of the night, four or five times in the years she had been here. In between, ice had built up, inches thick in the freezer, until it was like a cave. When it was like that, the refrigerator wasn't very cold.

"Is there a Coke?" she asked.

Tonio held up a Fanta orange. Abilene shook her head and said she'd take the beer. She reached down and unplugged the pinball machine. She sat down at the bar. Tonio gave her the cold bottle, and she smiled at him. She never forgot how beautiful he was, but it was different, actually looking at him.

"You Americans fall into two categories," he began pleasantly.

Abilene felt her scalp prickle. She tried to hold the smile. Tonio was going to lecture her, but if he was including all her countrymen, maybe his criticism wouldn't be as bad as it could be.

"One kind is the suspicious guy, always guarding things against the thieving Mexicans: his wallet, his car, his daughter. He doesn't mind paying a lot, but he doesn't want to feel he was *taken*.

"Then there are *gringos* like you, down here for the ride. Sure of yourself because you've got so little to lose."

Abilene's face began to burn. She could feel the sting start all along the edges of the surgery, like someone drawing a mask on her face with a hot pen.

"You never figure you're going to be taken here, in a foreign and *backwards* country, the way you are taken in your own.

You're not a fool, whatever the natives think. When things go wrong, you can say it was the language, the climate, the food. You don't plan things, so it's no surprise when they don't turn out. You can dismiss anything as misunderstanding." He leaned over the bar, putting his elbows on the smooth dark wood, eye to eye with her. "It's what the experts call cultural dissonance. You use it for self-forgiveness. You think it's to your advantage.

"The problem, Abilene, is that you badly underestimate the scope of the trouble you can get into when it turns out you were wrong."

It took her a moment to collect herself. Tonio's speech was not a warning, it was condescension. She had already proven his case. She licked the tip of one finger and, very carefully, she slid it in a short stroke across the top of the bar between them. "Your score, Tonio," she said.

Tonio put his hand over hers so quickly she jumped. She could feel the pressure of his body on hers, at the site of their two hands.

"It's my game, Abby," he said. Then he kissed her.

They ate at half-past seven, in the breakfast room at the kitchen. The light of the chandelier, set on a dimmer, was low. The small room was dark and crowded with heavy furniture.

Tonio always ate the same supper: a small piece of thick steak, and a tortilla warmed and folded with hot salsa and crumbled cheese over it.

Abilene wasn't hungry, but she tried to eat. She had not eaten steak in months, not since the one she ate with Constanzia the night before she went into the hospital. She realized that she didn't like steak anymore. She could hardly chew it.

The maid had left a pitcher of orangeade. Abilene drank it, a little at a time in her glass, keeping busy with the pitcher and the pouring.

Tonio told her about the call. He said, "I had auditors in this past month. They went over the books at the hotel, the ranch, and the packing plant. I had them arrive one morning without warning."

He seemed to be waiting for Abilene to say something. To

oblige, she said, "Is that what you do, in business? Make sure your books are in order?" She couldn't imagine anyone having the nerve to cheat Antonio Velez, though she had heard that the hotel manager before Claude Girard had robbed Tonio's father blind.

"Claude Girard gave me his notice. November 1 he's going to move to Aruba. I thought, you fat old fag, you should have just walked out. Immediately I decided to find all the ways he had cheated me."

"He seems so scrupulous," Abilene said. "The type of person who worries about his honor."

Tonio lifted his lip in a brief sneer. "He has suffocated me for years in blankets of figures. Why does he do this? I asked myself, if not to hide?"

"He picks at things like the bones of fish." Abilene meant to insist that Claude was honest. She had despised him for his moral superiority. She remembered him, every morning, in his glassed-in office, going over the market receipts with whoever had gone in to shop, shouting and screaming numbers, accusing.

"I've had enough of him," Tonio said.

Abilene was certain it must have galled Tonio to have Claude quit. He would much rather have fired him, but the truth was Claude was a good manager. The hotel made money, or so Claude had told her. He had run a tab for her bar bill, and for her room. She was a drain on his profit. "He speaks five languages," she said. It was the best thing she could say about Claude.

"He's not the only one."

Abilene shrugged.

"And your Spanish? Did it improve over the summer, with all your practice?"

"I suppose it did. It didn't seem hard."

"You must have confused the authorities! Is the *gringa* a bright girl who has bothered to learn our language? Or is she a spy?"

"A spy!" Abilene sputtered.

"A troublemaker." Tonio was smiling now. Abilene assumed he knew everything.

She wasn't ready to talk about the city. She didn't want Tonio to decide what had mattered and what had not. She didn't want to hear him say anything about Pola, ever.

So she said, "Did he?"

"What?"

"Did Claude Girard cheat you?"

Tonio laughed. "He was exact, to the very *peso*. The auditors say a blind man could have read his books, they are in such perfect order."

"So it was for nothing." There was no side to be on in this matter. Either way, she could have enjoyed the outcome.

"On the contrary. I'll let you wait. You will see what I learned."

Abilene shoved her plate toward the center of the table and folded her hands in front of her. "I want to know about Anne Lise," she said. "Are you going to marry her?"

Tonio smoothed his hair. In the past five years his hairline had been slowly moving back. That could push a man to make decisions.

"You lack a sense of proportion," he said. "You misjudge the importance of things. I have my mind on bulls. On a first-class *ganaderia* for the brave bulls. I've fought nearly nine hundred fights. I've been gored seven times, and lost two horses. I'm going to move the rest of my bulls to the Palmita. I'm going to give up fighting."

He rose and walked briskly from the room and toward his bedroom. Abilene half-ran to keep up, and when she touched him on the shoulder, he stopped and turned around to face her.

"Sage is gone now," he said.

She thought they might as well get that out of the way. It was a different order of anxiety from the terrible things that had happened in Mexico City.

"He grew very careless. He was having accidents. He lost an outbuilding, and a cowboy. He wrecked his plane taking off—"

Startled, Abilene drew breath in puffs, as though she were asthmatic.

"It was not so serious," Tonio said smoothly, "but it was a warning. He had his plane repaired and flew away for good."

"Because you wouldn't renew his lease?" She was scared, asking him that, and there was no real reason to ask, except that she wanted him to know she knew. It was a very small thing she wanted to do, for Sage.

"Why no," Tonio said. "We had never been able to sit down to negotiate the lease, for all his troubles with the ranch. You Americans have the expression. He was losing it."

"So, like Girard, he left without being run off?" This was a surprise to Abilene, that Tonio had preferred it that way. There was no doubt in her mind that he had manipulated everything. Nothing was outside his jurisdiction.

If he had not wanted her at the ranch, they would not have brought her across on the ferry.

"I am going to redecorate the ranch house," Tonio said. "You could help me with that. Colors, furniture, all that sort of thing. You could give me a woman's view." He seemed sincere, as if, half a moment before, they had not been speaking about the American, Michael Sage.

"I have never chosen so much as a curtain in my life," Abilene said.

"All you have to know is what you like."

Abilene felt exhausted from the long day, the trip from Mexico. The tension of seeing Tonio again seemed to strike her from behind, like someone with a board. She almost lost her balance.

"Go to bed, *chiquita*," Tonio said gently. "I missed my siesta, myself." He kissed her forehead and patted her arm. "I knew you'd come back," he said.

That was when she realized he had never been sure at all.

It was afternoon. She went down by the river bank and stood near the ferry, looking up and down the bank, to see where you could walk if you were out at night. She thought it could be done, like so many things, if you knew your way in the dark.

She was down by the river when a jeep came, and a car. There were men in uniforms, carrying guns. Workers appeared out of nowhere to line the central yard and watch. Abilene walked up to the guardhouse to ask Sapo what was going on.

Two of the young groundskeepers were teasing the cat with sticks, poking at it and jumping back as its paws clawed air in front of them.

Sapo said it was the *federales* come to take Sofia away.

Sofia!

The audit had caught her thievery. Hers, not Claude's.

Her little red Volkswagen sat parked near the overgrown tennis courts.

"And look," Tonio said of it, later on that evening. "Look what we found in her things. You didn't say you had lost it."

He handed Abilene her gold bracelet.

He took her for a ride in the jeep. She had been home for days, but they had not been together. She had been going to her room early to lie and wait for sleep that came hours and hours later. Tonio had not pressed her. He had called her once a day, to go with him when he went down to the practice ring. When they brought the horses out for him to ride, the *javelina* came out of the brush too.

The lowering sun illuminated the land. Tonio was sweaty from the horses. He said, "I've been wondering if you are anemic, something left over from the surgery, maybe, or you didn't eat right in the city."

She said nothing.

Somewhere far out he stopped the jeep and climbed down. They walked around for a few moments. She was standing by the jeep. He came behind her and pushed against her through her clothes. She could not help herself; she drew away from him, against the metal of the jeep.

"So it isn't buggery that turns you on?" he said harshly. "What do I have to do? If I talk revolution, will you be horny? Will you come back to life? If I lock you in a room and take away your shoes, will you be excited then, Abilene? Will you?"

He jumped into the jeep and drove away, leaving her behind. Over a little knoll he disappeared. It was raining now. In a quarter of an hour it would be dark. This far out, there would be cats. She didn't know where they went in the rain.

She sat down to let the dark and wet pour over her. The smell of woman would attract animals. That would settle things. This was what she had expected. It was so like Tonio to find a perfect way.

Tonio had made a great arc with the jeep. From another direction, he came back to her.

"I missed you," he said at supper. She said quietly, "I missed you too."

"I'm bringing over the young secretary from the packing house. Remember I told you she is learning English? You can practice with her."

"All right."

"And you're going to learn to ride, too. We talked about that."

"Maybe." She was afraid of horses. Of course they would put her on an old horse, a gentle animal. They would not expect much of her. She thought the cowboy assigned to teach her would resent her. It would shame him to spend his time that way.

Still, it was better than doing nothing.

"Where's Tacho?" she asked. If Tacho came around, he could take her over to the hotel to swim. Maybe after Claude was gone.

"He's gone. For good. He's gone to Torreon, to work in his brother's shop, selling clothes."

"Gone?"

"I tell you, I am retiring. It was time for Tacho to settle down. You see, now he'll get a wife, have babies."

"But not me? It's not time for me to go away and have babies and settle down?"

"You wouldn't want that." He knew her.

"Everyone else seems to be going."

"Oh yes. Mickey too."

"Where has Mickey gone?"

"Back to Austin. He's going to work on an advanced degree in geology. He thinks he can work it out to stay in Texas, because of his son."

"How can he do that? I mean, how can he afford it?"

"It seemed a reasonable plan to me, not like his fantasies about fighting bulls."

"You gave him money?" She knew Tonio had only contempt

for Mickey. There had been a reason for this generosity. Something had been settled between them in this way.

"He did some things for me. Earned his out."

"But here I am."

"With me."

Tonio had a packet of psylocibin. The tablets were small and pink. A friend had bought them in Amsterdam, where such things are carefully made. Tonio showed them to Abilene in the palm of his hand.

She looked at the pills, tiny compressed pods of memory and sensation. The helicopters, the flares, the bodies in the rain. Pola's hand slipping from her own.

The tablet left a taste of lipstick in her mouth. There was something in the binder that tasted of lipstick. She sat propped against pillows on Tonio's bed, greedy for the first wave of sensation.

Tonio, benign, brought a stack of photographs, some large manila envelopes, and a letter opener to bed. Most of the pictures were for publicity releases for the new season, shots of Tonio on horseback in his fine regalia, his three-corner hat, his arm arched over the bull with the long barb headed for its neck. "In my last season," he said, "I will fight only four times. And I will give all the money away, to charity."

He used the steel knife to slit an envelope along one long side.

The washes came over Abilene like a thousand hands massaging her. They were suspension and forgetting. Tonio showed her a photograph of a house he was thinking of buying in San Miguel de Allende. The house floated up, and through its open door Abilene saw Pola sitting on a chair, her needlepoint in her lap.

Tonio took the photographs away. Across the room from her, he sat in a wicker chair with a high winged back, and he watched her for a long time. "You're very high?" he said in his faraway pleased voice. "You don't really need me, do you?"

Later in the night he came to her and helped her take off her clothes. She felt sweet cream flowing from her. She felt him beside her, but she could not tell what he was doing; she could not tell where they came together, and where they separated.

Once she looked at his face and saw his eyes, tiny reduced eyes, like in his photographs. He cared for no one. She saw his eyes as he looked at the bull, and the eyes said, *the bull has lived for this moment with me.* He looked at her like that. His eyes were windows onto what was real, in his past, and in the future. She saw how the bull wavered, looking for an escape route, dreaming wildly of pasture, even as it was caught in Tonio's gaze, trapped in the path of the horse, hapless, hapless bull.

She woke and watched Tonio dress. It was morning. She was surprised to be in his bed. It was the first time she had ever spent the whole night in his bed.

"I don't want to do that anymore," she said. "I was scared. I didn't like it."

He took something from one of his drawers. She saw that the stacks of photographs, and the envelopes, lay on the dresser. He poured a glass of water from the thermos on the table by the bed, and he came and sat down beside her.

"This is Valium. Take it and sleep it off. You're right, you've gotten too spacy for drugs now." He smiled at her. "But you were very sexy, Abby. You were very wet and open for me."

He knew what he was doing. He had known she was in bad shape from the city, that it would not be so simple a thing to be herself again. He had given her the drug to help her break a barrier in herself. Tlatelolco had covered her like a membrane, until last night.

He was always in charge. He always knew everything, and that was a way of protecting her.

"Thank you," she said.

It wasn't until she woke for the second time in Tonio's room that she saw how he had transformed his spare African room into something lush: carpet on the floor, embossed shades on the windows, a mink bedspread folded and laid on a lacquered trunk at the foot of the bed.

She had not noticed the changes before.

She went to her room and bathed in a deep bath of tepid

murky water. She dressed in a white blouse she had bought in the city, and a yellow skirt, with an old pair of sandals she had not taken to the city. She put her bracelet on her arm, wondering where it had been, and what was true and what was not.

She went into the library and looked at the spines of the books there: books on the *corrida*, books on Hitler, all kinds of books on nature and wild animals, and shelves of old novels, mostly romances, that must have once belonged to Tonio's mother.

She went to each bedroom and tried the door, but all were locked except hers and Tonio's. She went into the kitchen. The lunch had been cleared away, and all the pots were washed, hanging from hooks above the warming table. A plate of cold tortillas sat to the side, on the stove. She ate them with a piece of cheese from the refrigerator, and then ate an orange, peeling it slowly.

Everyone was at siesta.

She went back to Tonio's room. It was still unlocked, the bed unmade. He wasn't there.

She took the things from his dresser to the bed, and began looking at them. First she looked at the bullfight pictures again. She had never felt the thrill of the fight when she watched Tonio, not like other bullfighters. She had never considered the possibility that he might be hurt, though she knew he had been in the past. He was aloof and mighty, above the bull, until he dismounted for the kill. The crowds went wild for him when he killed. He made clean and deep and swift kills, not like other matadors who sometimes struck bone or a pad of flesh too far off mark, so that bulls bled from their noses and fell on their knees to die slow ugly deaths.

Out of the slit envelope she pulled more pictures. The first one was of her.

She is coming out of a store with a package under her arm. Her shoes!

Another. *She stands in front of the library mural on the university campus, with Hallie and Refugio.*

She walks on a broad avenue with Adele.

She is getting out of Isabel's car.

She stared at the images. She felt dirty and afraid.

"You're very photogenic," Tonio said, from behind her. "And utterly naive."

"How could you?" She was still staring at the pictures.

"Mickey wanted some old pictures of you, and I wanted new ones," Tonio said playfully. "We made a trade."

Now she looked at him. "Old pictures!" she remembered Mickey that day at lunch when he was so crazy. Pictures—"Tonio," she said. Just his name.

"I only gave him two. You look very pretty in them."

"It's nasty, Mickey having anything like that. I was with you. You took those pictures."

"I'm not sentimental." He had thousands of photographs of himself, in fights, on hunts, with beautiful women.

"But why? Why these?" She swept her arm across the pictures, brushing them off the bed. There were more, part of the way out of the envelope. She drew them out.

She stands on the step in front of her apartment—Claude's apartment—and on the walk in front of her stands Gato.

"Why, Tonio?"

He was changing his boots, getting ready to ride. "You were very stupid, all summer," he said calmly. "I tried to warn you."

She pulled her head up, stretching her neck, and heard it crack. Her heart was beating very fast. All right, she thought. He was looking out for me.

Knowing everything is a kind of protection.

Felix would have talked to Tonio before he got her out of the prison. Maybe, even, it was Tonio who called Felix. Maybe Isabel called Tonio. Maybe the officials—

She got off the bed, onto her hands and knees, to pick up the spilled pictures. When she reached for the envelope on the bed to put them away, she saw that there was one more.

She is with Pola, turning into an alley at Tlatelolco.

That day. It had to have been that day.

"Mickey," she said. "That miserable—"

"Now Mickey is in Austin." Tonio sounded neutral, neither smug nor annoyed.

Abilene looked at him. She was kneeling by his bed with

photographs in her hands. "You were—" Her voice was small. Her throat had constricted, and the sound would not come out clearly. "You were looking out for me?"

Tonio gave the smallest nod of his head. Maybe.

She picked up the photograph of herself with Pola.

"But you know. You would have known." It had been planned so precisely—flares and white gloves and hidden revolvers. Army trucks on the avenue, ready to move in on signal.

She stared at Tonio, daring him to deny it. Sadly, she said, "You could have stopped us."

"It's too bad, your little friend—" He hadn't run out of words when he stopped. He had simply said all that he thought was worth saying. *Too bad.* Not meaning it.

It was true, he could have stopped them.

She said it again, shrieking her grief and anger. She grabbed for Tonio's letter opener and stood, holding it up near her head, point out, toward Tonio. Anger was a clean white light bleaching everything around her.

Tonio took the knife from her in one swift motion and slapped her face hard. "I have no interest in this kind of melodrama, Abby. This is your life. I didn't make it, you did. You took that girl out to the plaza. You came back here."

Anger filled her and swept around her and held her in place. If she could find its center, she would know what to do.

"I do want you here, you know," Tonio said, and walked from the room.

She realized that Pola would have been dead by the time Tonio saw the photograph, but she still thought he was to blame.

She washed her face and steadied herself, and she walked down through the gate into the yard. The stable boy was bringing the white Arabian out. Tonio was standing near the guardhouse, waiting. Sapo stood at the door, saying something to him and laughing, rubbing his belly, and once patting his pistol like a pet.

Abilene saw the little *javelina* with its high stickery back, trotting out of its hiding place, ready for Tonio's ride. Down toward the ferry, before the ground sloped, a big truck was parked and workers were climbing in the back for the ride to San Marta. The foreman's pickup was parked in front of the bunkhouse.

She heard birds and the shriek of the monkey leaping down onto the guardhouse roof to watch Tonio. She heard the chatter of men down by the trucks.

She stood away from Tonio, but he saw her and smiled.

Tonio knelt beside the cat where it lay sprawled in the sun. He reached to stroke it, and the cat turned onto its back to have its belly scratched. This was all the cat had—sleep, the dreams of prey, and Tonio.

She saw Tonio looking at her, and then she saw the cat's head surge upward, and its teeth close on Tonio's hand. As Tonio jerked away, he pulled the cat forward till its chin rammed into his knee. At the impact, the cat sprang back to the end of its chain as the man stepped back and up, holding his torn and bleeding hand out from his body.

Tonio's face filled with amazement and rage. Without a sound he turned to Sapo and, with his left hand, reached toward the pistol on Sapo's belt. Sapo withdrew the automatic, chambered a round, and passed the pistol to Tonio. Tonio fixed the pistol in his good hand and stepped back to the cat. At his movement, the cat pulled back against its chain and crouched facing Tonio, its ears flattened against its skull. Tonio stopped two feet short of the cat, and without a pause, extended the pistol and fired, all in one continuous motion. The cat sprang upward slightly, and then fell limply on its side, its feet churning in slow convulsive spasms. The bullet had entered between its eyes, slightly above center. Tonio turned back toward Sapo and held the pistol out to him, careful to keep his injured hand from dripping blood onto his trousers. Still not speaking, he turned and walked back toward the house.

She spent only a few moments in her room, and then she slipped out of the house. She waited near the ferry for a long time. The truck with the men went across. A taxi came and got the new girl from the packing plant who had taken Sofia's place. The sun was setting.

When the foreman's truck stopped at the river, she sprang up and waited by it for the ferry. On the other side, she got in.

The foreman didn't like it, but he didn't say anything. "Just to San Marta," Abilene told him. "By the cafe."

At that the foreman grinned a little. The cafe was nothing more than a taco stand, with beer stacked in cases and seldom cooled.

She walked around the dirty little square and then went and bought a bus ticket to Mexico. The bus pulled in a little after eight, but she watched a few people load and when it pulled out again she was still standing. There would be another bus at midnight anyway.

She decided to spend the hours of waiting by walking the length of the village and around its side paths. She walked past houses of patched-together palm, and others of sheet metal and scraps. There were real houses, though, like houses in a cheap development in Texas, better than the houses Abilene had grown up in. Abilene knew the people in those houses owed their good fortune to the packing plant, to their union, and to Tonio.

It was a little after nine when she found herself standing across the road from the packing plant. Three trucks were lined up, their motors running.

She ran up to the first truck and shouted to the driver. "*Señor* Velez said I could ride with you to Mexico." The driver waved his arms. "No!" he said, but she had already managed to open the door, and she climbed up inside.

The driver motioned to the space behind the seat, where she could stow her things. Later, if she wanted, there was room there for her to sleep.

The driver pulled out onto the highway with Abilene sitting high above the road on the seat beside him. They had not gone very far, and had not spoken again, when the night suddenly turned black and cold. They climbed into the mountains and left the village far below.

"Tomorrow you could take a plane," the driver said. He was used to driving alone, and not to making conversation.

"Tomorrow I will already be there," Abilene said. The driver nodded, because she was right.

They rode for another hour or so, Abilene dozing and waking fitfully, neither of them speaking. Once she fell soundly asleep and was wakened suddenly when the driver's hand slid along her leg.

She pinched his skin very hard across the knuckles. "I am *Señor* Velez' *novia*, you fool!" she said.

The truck driver laughed, showing his gold teeth. "And *I* am the cousin of El Cordobes!" he said back to her. She was lucky. The driver was a genuinely friendly man, and he had come that same afternoon from his wife and their bed. He had heard things about *gringas*, but he didn't think they were true of this one. He took his pleasure from the rhythm of the road, and the clear air.

"You might as well sleep," he said to Abilene pleasantly, and she crawled behind the seats into the little bunk there. He sang Abilene to sleep, just before they reached the crest of the Sierras and started down the other side, toward the city and the rest of the world.